Cat Walker was born and raised in Minnesota, USA, where she first developed her love of creative writing. In 2006, she visited Ireland and fell in love, literally. She moved to Ireland in January 2007, and now lives in County Meath with her Ireland-born husband, and spends her time expanding her imagination and enjoying the beautiful Irish countryside.

To my loving husband, whose belief in my talent has been unwavering.

Cat Walker

IRISH FIREWORKS

Karan,
Believe in Dreams

Cat Walker

AUSTIN MACAULEY PUBLISHERS™

LONDON • CAMBRIDGE • NEW YORK • SHARJAH

A CIP catalogue record for this title is available from the British Library.

ISBN 9781035836352 (Paperback)
ISBN 9781035836376 (ePub e-book)
ISBN 9781035836369 (Audiobook)

www.austinmacauley.co.uk

First Published 2024
Austin Macauley Publishers Ltd®
1 Canada Square
Canary Wharf
London
E14 5AA

Table of Contents

The First Spark

Chicago, IL

Dr Henry Wilson heard the door to the outer office open. He held up his hand, indicating that he would be back in a moment, and then left his private office, closing the door behind him.

Sarah stood and walked to the window. The doctor had opened it slightly to let in the summer air. Despite it being after ten in the evening, the night air was still very muggy and she opened the window further to let in the light breeze. They had been in the middle of her session and she had been about to tell him about the latest in the saga of her pathetic love life when he had stepped out of the room.

From the outer office, she could hear the sounds of Dr Wilson and another man speaking, and their voices were beginning to rise in anger. Frowning, she suddenly felt anxious. Grabbing her bag, she was about to leave the office via the second door, feeling that her presence would not be welcomed when she heard something break in the other office.

Now she was frightened. Spying her case file on his desk, she quickly grabbed it and stuffed it in her bag, then she heard what sounded like a loud pop, followed by two more and she instinctively knew that her psychiatrist had just been shot, and quite possibly killed. Then she heard the man say, "Make sure that there's no one else here, and then torch the place."

Realising that she was now in danger, she ran to the window and crawled out on the ledge. Thankfully, it was wide enough for her to sidestep her way around the corner to the back part of the building. There she found a tall tree that had grown alongside the building, and she was able to reach out and grab one of the large branches and pull herself onto the tree.

Her first instinct was to crawl down the tree and run to safety, but she was afraid that the men who had killed the doctor would be watching the place, so she crawled higher in the tree. The explosion that followed had her holding on

9

to the tree for dear life. Suddenly she saw that the flames were making their way towards the back of the building and that her position was precarious at best. Making her way down the tree, she was relieved to find that she could reach the adjacent lot and was able to jump down in between two parked cars. She saw several people beginning to gather to watch the flames and in the distance she could her the sirens telling her that the fire trucks were in route.

Standing, she walked up to the growing crowd and tried to act as if she was just a passer-by. "What happened?" She asked a woman who was staring up at the blaze.

"Must have been a gas leak," the woman surmised. Sarah stared up at the flames, but kept quiet. She had no idea if she could trust any of these people, not knowing who had all been in the office, so she would wait until the police arrived to come forward.

An hour later, Sarah was still there with a handful of other stragglers watching the firefighters battle the blaze. The explosion had blown out all of the windows on the north side of the building and had caused serious structural damage to the rest of the building. Several fire departments had been called in to assist and it was only now that they were allowed to go into the building to do a quick search for bodies.

Sarah held her breath, waiting for them to find Dr Wilson's body. Praying beyond hope that she had been wrong and that he had somehow escaped the tragedy. But when the firemen carried out a stretcher with a body, covered in a sheet, she knew that her suspicions had been true. Dr Wilson had been a very tall man, and the body that was brought out was clearly that of her psychiatrist. Brushing away the tears that began to fall, she headed towards the man who seemed to be in charge.

"Miss, I'm sorry, but I'll have to ask you to stand behind the yellow line." One of the police officers stopped her.

Sarah glanced over at the man who had spoken. "I believe I have some information about the fire," she said briefly, hoping that he would allow her to pass.

"I can take your statement in a minute, but I have to ask you to please step behind the yellow line." When she started to protest, he added, "It's for your own safety, miss."

Sarah nodded and stepped behind the line he had indicated. Ten minutes later, she saw him walk up to the man who appeared to be in charge and point her way. The man nodded his understanding, and then the officer approached her again. "Miss, if you can step this way," he invited her to follow him.

When the officer had approached him and told him that there may be some information about the fire, Detective Jake Summers had turned to see the woman that he had indicated and from the look on her face, he knew he would need to speak with her directly. There was something about her that told him that she would need to be handled delicately.

Walking to the back of one of the ambulances, he asked the attending crew to give them a few minutes, and then he waited for the officer to bring the woman to him.

"Sir, this the woman who said she has some information about the fire." Jake thanked the man and then turned his attention to the young woman standing before him. She looked ready to collapse. "Hello, I'm Detective Summers, would you like to sit down?"

Sarah nodded and sat on the bottom step of the ambulance. Jake gave her a minute and then asked her name. She paused a moment and tried to rein in her emotions before saying, "Sorry, I should have said. Is this a safe place to talk?" Jake frowned. "Yes, I believe it is. But if you'd prefer to have this interview at the station, that's fine too."

Sarah considered what he said for a moment and then decided that she would let the detective determine which he felt was best. Leaning towards him, she whispered, "I'm Sarah Coffey. I…I was in Dr Wilson's office when he was murdered." Jake stood back and studied the woman for a moment. She didn't look like a nut job, but Dr Wilson was a renowned psychiatrist, and it was suspected that it was his body that had been found burned beyond recognition. They would have to confirm his identity via his dental records, but as the man was well over 6'5" feet tall in life, he suspected that it was indeed the good doctor that was on his way to the morgue.

"I'd like to ask you to accompany me down to the police station where we can record your testimony." Sarah looked up at the man who had spoken and nodded her agreement. Jake helped her to her feet and then walked her to his car. After helping her into his front seat, he stopped briefly to talk to the officer and to tell him that if asked, no one had come forward. The officer nodded his understanding and then joined his fellow officers who were dispersing the crowd.

Fifteen minutes later, Jake was handing the woman a cup of coffee and sitting down at the interview table with the woman seated across from him. There was a knock on the door and another man walking in.

"This is my partner, Detective Allen Caffrey. He's going to listen in if you don't mind." She shook her head no, and then waited for the man to sit down.

Jake turned on the recorder, he began by stating his name and the intent of the interview. "Why don't you start from the beginning, Miss Coffey."

Sarah nodded and then concentrated on what she should start with. "I had a last-minute meeting scheduled with Dr Wilson."

"When was that?" Jake interjected.

"I arrived at 9:00pm," she confirmed.

"Go on," he prompted her.

"I've been seeing Dr Wilson for about a year. He was very kind and told me that I could meet him in the evenings as it is easier to get away."

Jake wanted to ask her what she meant, but let it slide for the moment.

"We were talking when he heard the door to his outer office open, so he went to see who it was. When he left, he closed the door to his office."

Jake made a note on his notepad and then looked up for her to continue. "I heard raised voices and then I heard a scuffle. It sounded like someone was pushed up against the filing cabinet. I decided I didn't want to be around if there was a fight, and was about to leave by the second door when I heard a pop. Then I heard two or three more pops and somehow, I knew that he had been shot. Then I heard the man say something to the effect that they should check to see if there was anyone else in the office and to torch the place. Dr Wilson had left his office window open to let in some air, so I grabbed my case file and crawled out the window. I got around the corner of the building and found a tree that was near the building. It was close enough so I was able to crawl onto it and then I was afraid that they would see me climb down, so I climbed further up the tree."

She paused a moment.

"Why did you grab your file?"

Sarah looked up at the man, realising now that she had been looking down at her hands as she spoke. "I was afraid they would realise that he had a patient and then they'd be able to find me," she answered him.

Jake nodded his understanding. "Then what did you do?"

Sarah thought a moment. "It was about then that there was an explosion. I guess the fire had blown out the windows, and I realised that the blaze was coming towards the tree and so I climbed down. Luckily, the tree straddled the next lot and I crawled down and ducked down between a couple of parked cars until I saw a crowd gathering. I guess I felt that it was now safe to join them and then wait for you to get to the scene."

Jake looked down at his notes. "You mentioned that you heard the men talking. Do you remember what was being said?"

Sarah closed her eyes and tried to concentrate on the conversation she had heard. "Most of it was muffled. To be honest, I hadn't really been paying attention until I heard the scuffle." Looking down at her hands, she came clean, "I went to see Dr Wilson after I ended an abusive relationship. I know the sound of aggression and violence and that's what drew my attention. I think the man had said something about being betrayed. I'm sorry I can't be of more help."

Jake shook his head. "You've been very helpful." He reassured her.

Turning to Caffrey, he asked if there were any other details he needed. Caffrey shook his head no, and then he leaned over and whispered, "I've got to get down to the lab," he said by way of apology and then stepped out of the interrogation room. Jake turned back to the young lady. Looking back down at his notes, he went back to the first question he had written down. "Earlier, you had said that Dr Wilson agreed to meet you in the evenings as it was easier to get away? What did you mean by that?"

Sarah blushed. "I'm going to college and I work a couple of jobs. I usually have Tuesday nights free, but I usually study until 8:30 or 9:00 in the evening."

Jake studied her a moment. "Can you tell me about the abusive relationship you were in?"

"There isn't a correlation, if that's what you are wondering," she was quick to say. But then as if she realised how silly that would have sounded, she added, "Sorry, what I meant was that I know it wasn't John or one of his friends. This was an older man. He had a gruff voice like he had throat cancer or something; and he had a slight accent of some kind. I'm not very good at accents, so I couldn't tell you for sure what it was."

Jake leaned forward. "What is John's full name?"

Sarah swallowed back the fear she felt building. "John Grimm," she whispered. "But please, don't contact him. He, he doesn't know that I live in Chicago."

Jake frowned. "What do you mean?"

13

Sarah knew that she was opening herself up to all manners of problems but she was learning not to step away from a fight and she knew that she would have to own up to what she did in the past. "I…I ran away from him. As far as I know, he believes I'm dead."

"Dead?" Jake frowned.

"I left a suicide note and drove my car into Lake Superior."

"When was this?" Jake started to make additional notes.

"A year and a half ago," she answered him honestly.

"Where was this?" Jake needed to confirm her story.

"Wisconsin. We were living in Duluth. I left him a message to say that I couldn't take it anymore and then I drove to the Wisconsin side of the lake and drove my car in." Looking down at her hands, she told him the rest of the story. "I had meant to end it all. But when the ice started to crack under my car, I suddenly realised that I wanted to live, and even though I was scared to death that John would find out that I had lived, I decided that I would try to make one more attempt at getting away from him."

"One more attempt?" Jake pushed.

"I had tried to leave him twice before. Only I hadn't been smart enough to cover my tracks. The first time I had just told him I was breaking things off. I…" she swallowed back her tears. "I learned a hard lesson that time. The second time I ran away, he found me at my friend's house. He knew that I didn't have much money and that I would have to stay with friends. He beat up my friend, breaking his arm and spent 6 months in jail. But when he got out, he was determined that I would never get away again."

"How did you get away this time?"

Sarah looked up at him again, "By deciding it would be easier if I just died. John had gone to work, and I was to have a dental appointment and then join him at the office right afterwards. You see, we worked together too, so he always knew where I was. But instead of going to the Dentist, I had driven to the Wisconsin side of the lake and drove my car in at a place that looked pretty remote. There had been warnings all week that the ice was thin, so I thought I'd been in luck."

Shaking her head, she added, "Isn't that pathetic? I thought I'd be in luck to fall into the ice and die."

"Anyway," she shook her head. "When I pulled myself up onto the beach, I realised that I wanted to live, so I hitched a ride to Michigan and then down to

Alabama. I had taken all my money out of my saving account; it wasn't much, but I was determined that he wouldn't have a penny of it, so I had some money to live on. Over the next year, I got the odd job here and there, working on a cash basis, to save up more money and then I applied for a college grant and headed to Chicago."

Frowning, she admitted her final sin. "I've been living under my mother's maiden name. Mom died seven years ago, right before I met John. My real name is Jennifer Murphy. I know that I've broken all kinds of rules, but please, let me continue to be Sarah Coffey?"

Jake understood her position. A good friend of his had also been in an abusive relationship that had gone sour and Jake knew the dangers that involved.

"Miss Coffey, thank you for your honesty," he said, telling her that her secret would be safe with him. "I would like to help you make it all official, but we can discuss that later."

He could see Sarah visibly relaxing. Whoever this John was, he would need to be dealt with; but right now, he had a murder investigation to conduct.

"I'd like you to sit with a language therapist. They may be able to help us lock down the accent you heard. Is that ok?"

Sarah nodded. She had a question for the detective, but she wasn't sure how to broach it without sounding paranoid.

"Detective, is there any way to keep my name out of all of this? Not just because of John, but…"

Jake understood where she was going. "I'll be speaking with my Captain about offering you some protection," he answered her.

"Thank you," she whispered.

~

Jake called Kevin O'Brien, who was working with the lead fire investigator, to see if he could give him any information about the fire, and to see if they could get an early break in the case.

Kevin was studying to take his final exams to transition from Fire Fighter to Fire Investigator. The present Fire Investigator, Thomas Grady, was getting ready to retire, and he had set his sights on Kevin to replace him.

The phone was picked up on the second ring. "O'Brien."

It was Kevin's older brother David O'Brien. Jake frowned. "David, where's Kevin?"

"He's in the lab. I just stopped by to see if he wanted to go to lunch and saw it was you. I'll get him."

David was the eldest O'Brien, a family of four siblings who had all followed their father's footsteps and had become fire fighters.

"Hey Jake, how can I help you?" Kevin had picked up the phone from where his brother had left it on his desk.

"Hi. I was hoping you could tell me you got a lead already on the latest fire," Jake told him.

"Maybe," Kevin confirmed. "We found a partial print on a fire extinguisher that had been chucked outside one of the windows. I've sent it up to your guys to see if they can make a match."

"Good," was Jake's reply.

Kevin could hear something in his voice. "What's up?"

"We have a witness. Of sorts. Seems she heard the shots that killed the Doc and then heard the order that the place should be torched. Seems like a professional job, which is worrying," he answered him.

"You thinking mob?" Kevin asked.

"The witness said the leader had a strange accent. So yeah. I'm leaning that way. Hopefully the print will confirm my suspicions," Jake confirmed.

"You have her under lock and key?" Kevin asked. It was Kevin's sister that had been in the abusive relationship, and the situation had gotten complicated. Jake had helped to get her to a safe place, but Kevin knew that where the mob was concerned, they couldn't be too careful.

"I'm working on it," Was Jake's answer. What Jake hadn't told him was that he had already contacted his Captain who had informed him that due to budgetary cuts, they just didn't have the resources to place Miss Coffey in protective custody. Jake was still trying to figure out how to keep her safe.

In the background, Jake could hear David asking Kevin something. He didn't have long to wait to find out what it was. "Hey, David wants to know if you are up for a game of golf on the weekend."

Jake smiled. He could use some time off. "Sure. I think I can manage a game," he added.

"Perfect." Kevin said before covering the phone and speaking to his brother again.

"Hey Jake." It was David. "You still got my rescue club?"

Jake laughed, "You mean my rescue club?" It was a running joke between the two men. David had borrowed Jake's rescue golf club for an outing with his department and had played beautifully with it. Since then, he had hinted that he wanted the club, saying that Jake never played that well with it anyway.

"Don't worry, it'll be in my bag," Jake confirmed and then he rang off.

Glancing down at the paper work on his desk, he wondered about his next step. Picking up his phone, he called the finger print lab to get an update on the prints Kevin had told him about.

The lab tech confirmed that they had a clear print and that the computer was chewing on it. They hoped to have a match shortly. "Let me know as soon as you get the results," Jake told the man and then hung up.

Walking into the interview room where he had left the witness, he found her sitting with the language therapist. They were laughing at something as Jake walked in. "No, I definitely don't think he sounded like Donald Duck." Sarah was laughing. Mathew Travers was one of the best linguists the department had. He had a special knack for relaxing witnesses and then getting them to remember the nuances that a particular accent had and then Mathew could work out what region the accent was from.

"He's blaming it on the duck again, isn't he?" Jake laughed with her.

Sarah smiled back at the detective. "He was even trying to blame Foghorn Leghorn." She laughed. "You are really good at those accents."

Mathew leaned towards her as if sharing a secret. "Hey, your Miss Piggy was spot on," he smiled.

Sarah laughed. Jake didn't want to bring a stop to the fun they were having, but he did need some answers. But Sarah was the one who brought the conversation back to the real reason they were there. Smiling at Jake, she said, "He's good. I think we have the accent I heard ironed out."

Jake looked over to Mathew. "That's right. Miss Coffey and I have identified that the accent is German. From the Bavarian region."

Jake was surprised. "How?"

But Mathew shook his head. "Never ask a chef for the recipe for their signature dish."

Standing, he reached out and shook Sarah's hand. "It was a pleasure meeting you, Sarah."

"Thank you for all your help." She took his hand in both of hers, and then released him. After Mathew had left the room, Sarah turned to the detective. "So now what?"

"I've a few more things I have to take care of," Jake said, stalling. He didn't have the heart to tell her that he couldn't offer her 24-hour protection. Not yet anyway. Not until he knew who they were dealing with. "Do you mind waiting a bit longer?"

Sarah shook her head no. "I have to do some studying. Is it ok if I study here?"

"Of course," Jake relaxed. "Can I get you some coffee or tea?"

"Coffee would be nice," she confirmed. "Two sugars and a dash of milk would be great if you have it."

"Coming right up," Jake confirmed and then left her to study.

He had grabbed her coffee and was on his way back to the interview room when his mobile rang. Setting her coffee on the desk next to him, he pulled his phone out of his pocket. "Summers."

"Detective Summers, this is John down at the finger print lab. We just got confirmation on those prints you're were waiting for."

"Go on," Jake prompted him.

"The prints match those of a Scott Turner."

Jake closed his eyes briefly. Thanking the man, he left Sarah's coffee on the desk and headed back to his Captain's office. This changed everything.

Knocking on the door, he waited for permission to enter. Receiving it, he walked in and closed the door behind him. "Sir, we just got confirmation on the prints that were found near the scene of the fire where Dr Wilson was found murdered."

"Go on." Captain Weatherton already knew he wasn't going to like what his lead detective was going to tell him.

"The prints belong to Scott Turner," Jake told his Captain.

"Nemetskiy's guy?" The Captain asked.

"That's right sir," Jake confirmed. Victor Nemetskiy was a well-known crime boss running his operations throughout Chicago and the neighbouring communities. Then Jake pushed forward. "Sir, I believe this changes the importance of ensuring Ms Coffey's safety. Don't you?"

The Captain sat back in his chair and looked up to the ceiling. It was a common habit of his when he was weighing out the options. But Jake knew that there were no other options. The girl needed to be put in protective custody, especially if they wanted to keep her alive.

The Captain focused his attention back onto the man in front of him. He had known Jake Summers for the majority of his career in the police force and he had never known the man to be wrong. His instincts were always dead on. "Ok, you have a point. But the fact is, resources are tight. I'll put a call through to the FBI, but you and I both know that after the last time we dealt with them, it got a bit messy, and I think they are still a bit sore about it."

"Surely this changes things? I mean…" Jake began, but his Captain interrupted him. "I'm banking on it, but until I get confirmation, I'd rather go on the assumption that we'll be flying solo on this one."

Jake didn't like it. He hated all this political bullshit.

"Do you have a secondary plan in place?" His Captain suddenly asked him. Jake knew what his boss was asking, but so far, he hadn't come up with a plan. He couldn't exactly invite the girl to his house. That would be the first place they would look.

"I'm still working that out," was his reply.

"Let me call the Feds and we'll see if they want to cooperate. Since its Turner, maybe they'll be hungry enough to let bygones be bygones." The Captain picked up his phone and started to dial the number he knew by heart. Turner was known to be Nemetskiy's right hand man. It could be that if they caught him, they would catch Nemetskiy as well. At least, he hoped that would be the direction the FBI would be going.

Jake left his Captain's office, knowing that he would need to use diplomacy to get the security detail and he didn't want to distract him.

Walking back towards the interview room, he picked up the coffee he had poured and found that it had gone cold. Turning around, he headed back to the canteen to make Sarah a fresh cup of coffee.

Five minutes later he knocked on the interview door and after hearing a faint, "Come in," he opened the door to find her with her nose in a book. The table had been transformed into a student's paradise with her papers spread out across the table, and several books open to the pages he presumed she was using as references.

"Your coffee, madame." He placed the cup on a clean spot on the table not too far from her right hand.

Sarah glanced up from her book and thanked him.

"What are you studying?" Jake asked as he took a sip from the cup of coffee, he had brought for himself.

"Law," she said briefly as she took a sip of the hot coffee. "This isn't too bad," she smiled at him. "Thank you."

Jake simply nodded. "What kind of law?"

"Family practice. Actually, I'm studying for the bar exam. I was in law school when I met John, but he put a stop to my finishing my degree. When I applied at the university, I transferred my college credits and was able to convince the admissions board to allow me to just retake my senior year."

"Tough test. Best of luck," Jake acknowledged.

"Thanks, I'm going to need all the luck I can get. I used to be a straight A student, but it's been three years since I did any serious studying, and I have to admit that it's not as easy as I thought it would be. I had hoped it would be like getting back on a bike, but no such luck. I have the test in four months' time, so I have a lot of studying to get through."

"Then I won't keep you," Jake said as he started for the door. "Any luck on the security?" He heard her quietly ask. Jake turned and told her the truth. "My Captain is calling the FBI as we speak."

"The FBI?" She frowned. "It's that bad, huh?"

She was smart, he decided. "We've been able to identify a print from a fire extinguisher that was thrown out the window. The man is known to the police and he has some serious connections," was Jake's reply.

"I'm guessing that he's associated with the mob?"

Jake studied her for a moment. She could see it in his eyes that he was about to ask her how she knew that when she blushed. "I'm studying law, Detective. I've studied how the FBI are called in for specific types of cases. Federal cases against the mob are one of those that usually prompt the FBI to offer witness protection services. I'm just making a logical assumption. But feel free to correct me if I've got it wrong."

Jake sat down in the chair across from hers. "I wish I could. Unfortunately, you're dead right. The print belongs to a known associate of the Chicago South cartel that is run by a man by the name of Nemetskiy. He's the leader of a Russian backed mob who are trying to make a name for themselves as quality suppliers of crystal meth and other illegal drugs."

"Wonderful," Sarah said sarcastically. "I really was in the wrong place at the wrong time."

There was a knock on the door and Jake excused himself. It was the Captain. "The FBI said they're interested in joining us on this one and are sending over a couple of seasoned agents. They should be here within the hour."

Jake breathed a sigh of relief. Knocking on the door again, he and the Captain walked back into the interview room.

Sarah had resumed her studies, but put a flag on the part she had been reading, and closed the book. "You have some news for me?" She asked. While her voice sounded confident, Jake could see the worry on her face.

"Sarah, this is Captain Weatherton."

Sarah would have stood to greet the man, but she wasn't sure her legs could hold her. As soon as she had heard the mob were involved, she had been fighting a losing battle against her fears.

The Captain shook her hand and then sat down across from her. "Miss Coffey. First of all, I'd like to thank you for coming forward. A lot of people would have simply left."

Sarah shook her head. "Dr Wilson was a kind man." She offered by way of explanation for her actions.

The Captain nodded. "So, I've heard." Glancing over at Jake, he continued, "As Detective Summer has probably already explained, we have contacted the FBI about this case and they have agreed to offer their assistance. They are sending two agents down now and should be here within the hour."

"Then what?" Sarah asked. She wanted to know all the details as it would help her plan. It was one of the techniques Dr Wilson had taught her. With John, it was the uncertainty that had caused her anxiety. She had never known when or what would set him off. She had been left a broken woman. Afraid of everything, including her own shadow. But with Dr Wilson's help, they had worked hard to get her to overcome some of her neurotics. By planning mentally for possible outcomes, she was better prepared for the unexpected.

"Well, once they arrive, then they will take you to a safe house. There, you will be watched 24/7 until we apprehend the men who killed the good doctor."

Sounded simple enough, but Sarah knew that simply locking her away someplace wouldn't solve all her problems. "Any idea how long this could take? As I was telling Detective Summers, I am taking the bar exam in a few months, and I have gotten an exception but it's contingent that I take the test before the end of the year."

The Captain nodded his understanding. "I understand, and I promise you, we'll do everything in our power get you to the test on time, but as you can imagine, we can't guarantee that the danger will be over by that time. It can take time to build the case and bring it to court."

"Will I be required to testify? As I told the detective, I'd like to keep my name and identify out of all of this?" A mob trial would undoubtedly attract the press and she couldn't afford to be discovered.

Again, the Captain tried to reassure her. "We will speak with the DA and see if we can use your sworn testimony as evidence. The fact that Nemetskiy is well known for his intimidation methods, I'm sure the DA will agree that it will be in their best interest to keep your identity safe."

Sarah considered this and nodded her agreement.

An hour later, the FBI agents were in with the Captain and Jake was going over the details with Sarah when his phone rang. Glancing down at the number he saw it was Kevin O'Brien. Excusing himself, he stepped out of the room and took the call.

"Hi Kevin, what's up?"

"Hi Jake. I got the results back from the blast analysis. There's something here that I thought you might want to take a look at. Do you have time to come down to the lab?"

Kevin wasn't usually secretive unless he had a reason to be, and Jake didn't like it. "I have to finish something up, but I can be there in a half hour. Does that work?"

Kevin agreed and Jake glanced back at the closed door to the interview room. Whatever Kevin had found was bound to be bad news and he wondered if it would involve his witness. He hoped not. The woman was already strung tighter than a drum. He didn't want to send her over the edge.

Hearing voices coming his way, he looked down the hall and saw the Captain approaching with the two FBI agents. The sooner Sarah was in protective custody, the better.

~

The fire investigator's lab was fifteen minutes' drive from the precinct and Jake made record time getting there. It was twenty minutes to one in the morning.

22

Both men tended to work late hours, but they only stretched themselves when the case dictated it.

On his way, he stopped at the McDonalds drive through and picked up a couple of coffees and some burgers. If he knew Kevin, he would have worked right through lunch and dinner.

Knocking on the lab door, he pushed the double doors open and walked in. Kevin had his face to a microscope and Jake waited for him to complete the task he was working on before speaking. Without raising his head, Kevin acknowledged his presence. "Give me another minute. And thanks for the food. I forgot to eat, and I'm starving."

Jake chuckled. The man was thirty-one years old and 6'3" tall; how could he 'forget to eat'? Setting the bag down on Kevin's desk, he pulled out the burger he had bought for himself and after carefully opening it and arranging the paper around the burger to prevent anything from spilling out of it, he took a bite. The flavour hit his tongue and his stomach instantly growled, reminding him that he too had missed his dinner.

Kevin picked up the other burger and the men ate in silence. Once they had filled their stomachs, Jake took the last drink of his coffee and put their trash in the bin. "So, what's up?"

Kevin picked up the report on his desk and handed it to him. "I found an unusual substance at the scene of the fire."

Jake frowned as he opened the report. "Unusual how?"

"Unusual as in it wasn't something I would expect to find at a respectable psychiatrist's office."

Jake looked up at him, and then looked back down at the report before him. "Crystal Meth?"

"And a large quantity of it. My guess is, that was what caused the explosion."

Jake continued to read the report while Kevin explained his findings. "Unless I'm sadly mistaken, the good doctor was providing more than the usual over the counter meds to his patients. If I'm reading the evidence correctly, it looks like he was cooking the shit on the premises."

"Maybe that's why he was killed? Looks like Nemetskiy is involved. Those were Turner's prints you recovered. Maybe the good doctor stepped on Nemetskiy's toes, or was siphoning off some of the profits to fund his own habit?"

Kevin shook his head. "I've checked the coroner's report, and there's no evidence that he was a user."

"Well then maybe he was starting his own operations? Either way, it would explain why Nemetskiy killed him."

"But would he torch the place if he knew there was a lab on the premises?" Kevin asked.

Jake shook his head. He doubted it. Nemetskiy was a business man. There was no way he'd willingly throw away that amount of cash. The street value of the amount of rock that was indicated in Kevin's report would have accounted for nearly two hundred thousand dollars.

"If he didn't kill the Doc because of the Meth, then why?" Jake asked out loud.

"That's your line of inquiry, Jake, not mine. I can only tell you that there was a lab on the premise and that it was a very active lab."

Jake thought about Sarah. Could she have been mixed up in it as well? She didn't come off like a junky, but then again, she could be a supplier and not a user. He'd have to dig into her background a bit more.

"Thanks for the report, but let's keep this under wraps for now. I'll tell the Captain and we'll decide how to proceed from there."

Kevin nodded his head.

~

Sarah was tired. They had been driving for over an hour and it was nearly three in the morning when they finally pulled up to the safe house.

The three men in the car with her had been introduced to her as Agent Thomas, Agent Smith and Agent Jones. She had nearly wanted to ask if the first agent's real name was Alias but had decided that they may not appreciate the joke, so she had kept it to herself.

She knew that they were still in Illinois, just as she knew that they had been driving around to ensure that they weren't being followed. Now, she guessed, that they were convinced that no one had followed them and they finally stopped at the safe house.

A man stepped out of the house and waved at them, which must have been their signal that the cost was clear. Stopping the car, they quickly escorted her into the house and then they locked the door.

"Miss Coffey, this is Agent Hanson." Agent Jones introduced her to the man who had opened the door to them. "And this is Agent Cane." He introduced her to a woman who had just entered the room from what appeared to be the kitchen. "Hello Miss Coffey. Just call me Ann."

"It's Sarah." Sarah shook her hand and then waited for them to tell her what to do next.

"I'm sure you're very tired." Ann was saying, "So I'll just show you to your room. We'll cover the rest of the details in the morning," she added as she led her upstairs to a room at the back of the house, "it's not much, but the bed is comfortable and you have your own bathroom." Ann sat a bag down on the bed. "We took the liberty of getting you a few things to tide you over."

Sarah thanked her, wondering what things she was referring to, but waited to look in the bag until Ann had left the room.

Walking over to the bed, she opened the paper bag and found a toothbrush, toothpaste, pyjamas, some fresh underwear and other items of clothing.

"Thank you," she said to no one, and then she turned and locked her bedroom door.

Stepping into the bathroom she turned on the shower, then stripping out of her clothing, she took a quick shower. She wanted to wash away the memories of the day and hopefully relax herself enough so she could get some sleep. Drying off, she changed into the pyjamas, and put the rest of the things in a drawer she found in the bathroom. After brushing her teeth, she turned off the bathroom light and crawled into the bed. She was asleep in minutes.

~

Incipient

"My Daughter! Please, someone help me!"

The house was going up in flames, fast.

Tara ran up to the woman. "Where is your daughter?"

"In there! My Lizzy is in there!" The woman pointed towards the house. "On the second floor." She cried.

"Tell the firemen when they get here," Tara replied as she pulled her tank top off over sports bra and dumped her water bottle over it. Then she ran into the burning building.

The heat knocked her back a step, but she scanned the area and located the stairway. Running up, she called out the girl's name. She finally located the young girl huddling in the back bedroom. "Come on honey, let's get out of here." Taking the wet top, she tied it around the girls face and said, "This will help, hold on!" Picking her up, she started out of the building.

They were nearly out when Tara's leg broke through the floor. The pain was instant and it took her breath away. Setting Lizzy down, she yelled, "Run! Out the door!" She pointed towards the front door. "GO!" She added as she pushed her forward. Pulling at her leg she watched the girl ran out of the house, then she concentrated on the floor. 'Damn' she thought as she saw that she was really wedged in. Looking around, she tried to find something to help break the timber.

The smoke was burning her eyes and her lungs as she fought to stay alert. Using her other foot, she began kicking at the wood, praying that both feet wouldn't end up stuck. Coughing, she felt her lungs burning and she knew that if she didn't get out soon, smoke inhalation would get her before the flames did. 'Damn it' she thought as she kicked. Feeling the lumber give way, she collapsed forward and started to crawl out of hole. She felt herself starting to pass out but she told herself that she won't give up. She didn't plan on dying in a damn fire on her vacation. But the blackness was winning.

Feeling strong hands grabbing her arms and pulling her into a sitting position, Tara tried to swim out of the darkness. Flung over a shoulder she knew that she was going to be ok…assuming they got out of the building before it collapsed around them.

The bright light told her when they had finally emerged from the house, and as she was lowered onto a stretcher, she grabbed for the fireman's arm. Opening her eyes, she found herself staring at the darkest eyes she had ever seen. "Thank you," she whispered as an oxygen mask was slipped over her face. Then she allowed herself to drift back into the blackness.

"Captain!"

Shane looked up at one of his men and nodded. Then turning to the ambulance attendant, he said, "Get going."

≈

When they had come upon the scene, the mother had been frantic, claiming that a young woman had ran in the burning house after her little girl. As they headed in, the little girl had suddenly emerged, wearing a wet shirt over her nose and mouth, crying that the lady had fallen in.

He had found the woman dragging herself out of the hole. He had picked her up and carried her out. He hadn't gotten much of a look at her, until she had grabbed his arm. The green eyes had arrested his breath.

Two hours later, the fire was contained and the clean-up had begun. The press had been there, drinking up the drama of the brave woman who had saved the little Hispanic girl.

As Shane walked through the emergency room, he was once again accosted for information about the woman. Declining comment, he went in search of the mystery woman.

"Hello Captain. How can I help you?" Shane smiled at Martha Johnston, the woman who ran the emergency room.

"Just looking for our little hero," he smiled at her. "Well, good luck."

Frowning, Shane asked for an explanation. "She checked herself out."

"What? No way. Not with the amount of smoke she swallowed."

"Sprained ankle and all," Martha nodded. "And stubborn! If she hadn't saved that little girl's life, I would have guessed she was a fugitive from justice.

Wouldn't tell us her name, nothing. She just took some O2 and a couple of stitches and hobbled out of here."

~

That had been two weeks ago, and he still couldn't get her eyes out of his mind. Damn. *How the hell could he be so hung up on a gorgeous pair of eyes? Maybe he just needed to get laid?* He thought. Maybe then, those misty green eyes would stop haunting him.

Walking into the station, Shane looked around and found that his crew had their noses pushed up to the bulletin board. "What's so interesting?" He asked as he filled a cup of coffee.

"The new guy's stats," James Thompson piped up. "Chief's in with him now."

Shane studied the brief resume and photo that had been posted. T. O'Brien. The photo showed a short firefight in full gear. Mask down, holding the active end of a hose. The resume looked impressive. Seven years as a firefighter out of Chicago, and a forest fire fighter for the four years he went to college. Earned an undergraduate degree in Biology. Passed all the department tests with flying colours. Short, only 5'6" and weighed in at only 140 pounds. But there was power behind the small frame, it was noted that the fireman had carried a 170 lb man out of a burning building. 170 lbs dead weight. Sounded like the kind of man he would want on his team.

"So, why'd he leave Chicago?" Sam Beckman asked from behind him.

"You'll have to ask her that question?" Came the answer from behind them.

"Her?" Came a chorus of voices.

Tara was standing next to the chief taking in the casual banter about her resume; the gender assumption hadn't surprised her. She had expected it. But as the men turned and saw her, it was the Captain that had her cursing.

Shane felt locked into those green eyes.

Chief McCaffery looked from his Captain and back to the new 'man'. "You two know each other?"

Tara pulled her eyes from the handsome Captain and addressed the chief. "We met briefly."

Shane had recovered from his shock and now his anger warmed up. "Very briefly. You left the hospital."

Tara really didn't want to get into all of this right here, and as she started to suggest that they go somewhere more private to discuss it, the alarms went off.

'Saved by the bell' she thought as she waited for her instructions. "O'Brien, you go with Captain Cavanaugh. He'll take care of you."

Tara nodded and headed towards the engine room. Dropping her bag, she quickly took out her helmet, jacket and stepped into her pants and boots. Dressed in a matter of seconds, she ran up to the engine and got in as the other men joined her. Slamming the door behind her, she started to button up her coat as the men introduced themselves.

The squad was made up six fire fighters—James Thompson, Sam Beckman, Terry Judd, Hecter Ramirez and Rocko Ginnelli. Tara would be the sixth man on the team. Captain Shane Cavanaugh was sitting in the front seat with Clyde Jackson, the engine man, who was concentrating on driving the rig.

As she shook each of their hands, she caught the Captain's eyes as he stared back at her. Nodding at him, she turned her head and looked out the window and said her usual prayer for safety.

Shane studied her for a moment and wondered if she would be nervous now that she had had a close call. He expected that she would.

As they pulled up to the apartment fire, she was out the door and grabbing the hoses before he got out of the vehicle. "O'Brien, you're with me."

Nodding, she handed over the task to Hector and walked over to where the Captain was getting the details. Calling out some orders, Shane had his men briefed and in the building minutes after they had arrived.

"Sir," Tara spoke up, "where would you like me?"

Shane looked down at her, "You'll be observing on this one."

Tara had expected as much, so she wasn't too upset by it. She knew that as the new-be there would be a probation period. She also knew that as a woman, she was going to have to prove herself—despite her experience. Nodding, she accepted the fate and studied how the men worked together. Good teamwork was vital in a fire and she would have to know how each of these men worked together.

Half an hour later, the fire was contained, and the Captain allowed her to assist with the clean-up. The clean-up was just as important as the fire fighting. If a spark was left to fester, the blaze could start again and the danger of the fire spreading to the other buildings would be great.

Now, two hours later, Tara was dirty and tired, and loving every minute of it. Climbing back into the rig, she smiled as she heard the men speculating whose turn it would be to cook dinner. All eyes turned to her, and she laughed. "Any allergies or special dietary conditions I need to be aware of?"

As the men headed off for the showers, Tara headed for the kitchen. She had been prepared for this and turning on the oven, she took out the beef and spinach lasagna she had brought to work that morning. Cutting up some garlic to make some garlic bread and throwing a salad together would complete the meal.

As the men started to file into the dining room, Tara brought out the bread and the salad, and then carted out the lasagna. She didn't have to worry if the guys would like it; she knew that it was always a hit at her last station.

"Hey, O'Brien. You got a delivery."

Tara looked up from the lasagna she was slicing as Beckman walked in carrying a large bouquet of roses. Smiling, she shook her head and said, "You can put that on the table if you'd like."

"Want me to read the card, or will it be too personal?" He asked.

Tara shook her head, "Go ahead. I probably already know what it says."

Reading the card, he laughed and then he read it out loud, "Don't burn the toast. Love Danny."

Beckman smiled, "Your husband?"

"God no," Tara laughed. "My brother. One mistake when I was four years old and he's still holding it over me."

The phone rang, and Terry got up to answer it. "O'Brien. You got a phone call," he said, holding the phone out for her.

"And that will be Kevin."

Shane watched as she took the phone.

"Hi, honey. Yes, of course I knew it would be you."

Frowning, he stabbed another mouthful of lasagna and tried to squash the hot jealousy he felt rise up in him.

"How's the new job going little sister?" Kevin listened closely to what wasn't being said.

"Fine," she replied.

"I heard you already had your first fire," he added.

"Checking up on me?" Tara laughed. "Yes, we had a two alarm this afternoon."

"And…"

30

"And, it was a good learning experience," she replied.

"The boys aren't letting you see any action." Kevin knew how hard it was for a rookie to be accepted into a new station, and being a woman would add a new level of challenges, but Tara was no apprentice. She had worked hard and had earned her stripes.

"Kevin, I'm the new kid on the block," she explained.

"Huh, huh?" was his reply.

Shaking her head, she decided that this conversation was going nowhere fast. "Listen, I had kitchen detail and if I don't get back in there, I won't get any of my lasagna."

"You made your lasagna?" Kevin was suddenly interesting in another line of questioning. He loved her cooking.

Laughing, "Yes, so I really should go," she replied. "Say hello to Mom for me and please tell Danny that I got the roses. I'll see you all in a few weeks," she said as she hung up.

Glancing down at her watch she made a note of the time and decided she had just enough time to grab the second loaf of garlic bread. Walking back into the dining room, she sat the bread down and walked over to the phone just as it started to ring.

"Station 18, how may I help you?"

"Darn it, Tara! Do they have you answering the damn phone?"

Tara laughed, and said, "It's worse than that David, they made me cook!"

David laughed, "Hey, how did you know it would be me?"

Smiling, she said, "Who else would it have been?"

"True," he smiled into the phone.

As her eldest brother he had always been the one who looked out for her, so it didn't surprise her when she heard his next question. "So, I heard the actions been a little slow."

Tara laughed. "Well, you know."

Frowning into the phone, David countered, "No, I don't. They have your resume, and I assume they have all seen your credentials. Do you need me to make a few phone calls?"

"No!" Tara ducked around the corner out of earshot of her co-workers. "The last thing I need is for my big brother to make some calls…but you know how it is." Taking a deep breath, she added, "It's just a little complicated."

"Go on." David could sense that there was something else on her mind.

"Remember that little incident a few weeks ago?"

"You mean the little fire and the incredible brown eyes?" David teased her.

"Bingo," she said and then added, "as in 'Captain' Bingo?" Tara stressed the 'Captain' part.

"Oh!" David got the picture. Tara had told the family about the fire and about the handsome firefighter who had saved her life. David had encouraged her to make inquires and she had declined, stating that it was still a little early for her to start dating.

Smiling, she nodded, "Exactly. It's OK though." Looking around the corner, she saw Shane sitting with his back towards her, "We just haven't had our little 'come to Jesus' talk about it all yet, but I'm sure everything's going to be ok." Then she turned away again and added, "I just have to do a little personal adjusting if you know what I mean."

"Still attracted to him?" David smiled into the phone.

"Not for long," was her answer, and David nodded. "I know."

"But hey, thanks for the call. I do appreciate it, but I better get going before they start thinking I always take personal calls on the job…" walking back into the dining room, she glanced at the now empty plate of lasagna, "and my lasagna is gone, so I better go. See you in a few days. Love you!"

"Love you, Tara."

Hanging up she laughed as Sam's eyes dropped down at the last slice of pasta sitting on his plate.

"My brothers always seem to call during dinner time," she laughed as she headed back into the kitchen and reached into the oven to take out the plate she had prepared earlier. Taking the plate into the dining room, she slid into the empty seat. "Thank God I was prepared." She winked at Sam.

"That was another brother?" She nodded yes to Terry's question. "How many brothers do you have?"

Holding up three fingers, she took a drink of water before saying, "That was all of them. They tend to be a little over protective."

"What do they do?"

Finishing another bite, she answered his question. "Same as us. They're firemen."

"Which one did you carry out of that building?"

Tara looked over and found the chief leaning against the door jam. "That was Kevin."

"What happened?" Terry inquired.

"Chemical fire."

"You worked together?" Shane was watching her.

"No, we all worked at different stations. It was something we promised Mom. No, it was a pretty large fire and a couple of units had been called in. There was an explosion. Kevin ended up doing a summersault from the blast. It knocked him out cold. James, that's Kevin's partner, grabbed the hose and I grabbed Kevin."

"You're telling me you carried your brother, out of that building?" Rocko questioned her.

Tara nodded at the sceptic. "I guess the adrenalin was working." She tried to make light of it. Standing up she took her plate and said, "Well, gentlemen, I hope my little meal passed mustard, but now I'm going to go get cleaned up and you guys get KP duty," she said as she left the room.

"O'Brien."

Tara turned and found the Captain standing in the doorway. "I'd like to talk to you when you're finished."

Tara nodded, "Give me 20 minutes."

Shane watched her head for the showers. Turning back into the dining room, he studied his men, now deep in discussion.

"I tell you, no way did she carry 170lbs of dead weight." Rocko was saying.

"You're right. She didn't." Shane spoke up. Rocko nodded in agreement. "It was more like 210 lbs. Her brother would have been carrying a full tank of O2."

≀

Tara had expected this talk and hurried through her shower. Now dressed in a clean uniform, she headed for the Captain's office.

Knocking, she waited for the Captain to invite her in.

"Close the door and sit down, O'Brien."

Doing as requested. Tara placed an envelope down on his desk before she sat down.

"What's this?" He looked up at her.

"That would be my medical release. I went and saw my personal doctor after the incident and I figured you would want a copy."

Shane frowned down at the envelope. "You are required to see our doctors for this kind of thing."

Nodding, she said, "If I had been working at the time I would have, but since I was on vacation and between jobs, I took care of it on my own."

Sitting back, Shane studied her. "There are a lot of people who have been wondering who you were."

Tara kept her face blank. "So, I've read."

"Well, now their curiosity can be satisfied. But why you didn't just come forward before…"

Tara interrupted, "They're going to have to keep wondering sir. I'm still not going public about that and I would appreciate if you would keep it between the two of us."

"Why?"

"It's personal. Suffice to say that I don't want the press to know my name."

Shane frowned, "Tara…" Overhead, the alarms were going off again.

Standing, she headed for the door as Shane grabbed his bag, "Tara, we aren't done with this."

"Yes, we are," she said as she left the room.

.~.

"O'Brien, you're with me."

Tara bit back a retort, as once again she was told to sit on the sidelines.

It had been over a week and she had yet to see the wet end of a hose. While she agreed that the clean-up was just as vital to correctly extinguish a fire, she had worked far too hard to just play the clean-up man. She wasn't a rookie.

As the men started to file back to the engine, she picked up her bag and sat it on the seat.

"Hey O'Brien." Sam winked at her. "You ever going to fight a real fire?"

"Very funny Beckman," she said dryly. Glancing over at the Captain, she decided that she needed to cool off. Throwing her helmet into her bag, she stripped out of her gear and slipping into the running shoes she always carried with her. Nodded to Sam, she said, "I'll meet you all back at the station. I need to get some air." Turning, she jogged off down the street.

"Hey, where the hell is O'Brien going?" Shane saw Tara jogging around the corner.

34

Sam chuckled, "Lady said she needed some air. I believe she was going to run back to the station."

"Damn," Shane said under his breath.

By the time Tara ran the three miles back to the station, the crew were already in the showers, but her temper hadn't abated. Stepping into the workout room, she slipped on the boxing gloves and worked some of her frustrations out on the bag. Twenty minutes later she felt tired and sore but a little satisfied that she had managed to work out some of her tension.

Shane was standing outside his door when she came up from the basement workout room. "O'Brien, in my office. Now!"

Tara sighed, "Come on Cap, I just spent the last hour trying to get you out of my system. Now I just want to clean up and go home."

"Now." He pressed and walked into his office. She let her anger boil over. "Fine!"

Slamming the door behind her she decided that she had had enough. "If you're going to crawl up my butt because I decided to work off some off some steam, fine. But listen here buddy. This is about trust. Those men out there need to be able to trust my abilities and if you keep me on the sidelines much longer, I'm never going to gain their trust, or their respect to be able to do my job."

Shane leaned back against his desk and folded his arms in front of his chest. "You're absolutely right. It is about trust." She frowned at him, "I need to know whom I'm working with O'Brien. Up until now you haven't been completely forthcoming about some things."

Tara closed her eyes in disbelief. "If all of this is because of the incident..."

Shane nodded, "I just don't understand why you won't let us notify the press. It would be good for the department."

"Not won't, can't!" She retorted.

"What does that mean?" Shane stood up.

"Captain, please. Just trust me when I tell you that it's for the best..." she tried to reason with him.

"No, I don't think it is..."

"Damn it, Cavanaugh." She rubbed her hands over her face. "Fine!" She threw her hands down to her sides, her fists balled in anger, "Go to the damn press. But when you do, I'll be gone." Turning, she reached for the door. "Tara, what the hell is this about? It can't be that bad..."

Turning back towards him she shook her head. "It's worse. You tell the press; you tell my ex-husband—and that would be very bad."

She ignored him as he called her back. Walking from the station, she got into her car and drove off.

~

"I'll get it!" Martha O'Brien yelled over her shoulder as she headed for the door. "Thanks Mom," Tara yelled after her from the kitchen where she and her brother David were grabbing the last of the dishes for their Sunday afternoon dinner.

Opening the door, she knew at once that this was the man who had first interested her daughter and who now was frustrating the hell out of her. "Captain Cavanaugh, to what do we owe for this pleasant surprise."

Shane was taken back from the greeting. He wasn't sure whom the woman in front of him was, but he was pretty sure they had never met before.

"I'm sorry, where are my manners? I'm Martha O'Brien, Tara's mother," she said as she held out her hand. "I've heard so much about you that I feel like I already know you. Won't you please come in. We're just sitting down for dinner. You're welcome to join us of course. We always have plenty." Shane found himself following the woman as she rambled on and he couldn't help but smile at her obvious Irish accent.

"You wish you could cook as well as me!" Tara laughed at her brother David as she carried her seafood salad out onto the porch. Her next words died in her throat when she found herself staring at Shane. "Captain, what are you doing here?"

"Tara, where are your manners?" Martha took the salad from Tara's hands. "I have just invited the good Captain to join us for dinner."

"You did what?" Tara frowned at her mother. David's chuckle behind her got him a jab in the ribs. "I'm sorry, Captain. Of course, you're welcome to join us, but I'm sure you have other plans."

"I'd be delighted to join you." Shane smiled at her.

David cleared his throat, telling Tara that her mouth was still open in surprise. "I'm sorry, allow me to introduce my family. My mother, whom you have already met, is Martha O'Brien. The man behind me, with the frog in his throat," She turned and glared at her oldest brother. "Is my brother David." Then

36

she turned back and nodded, "The guy behind the grill is my brother Kevin, and the one about to offer you a beer is Danny. Please, have a seat. I'll just get another place setting."

David shook Shane's hand. "Cavanaugh, I've heard a lot about you."

Tara reappeared with another plate and silverware, "No interrogating the guest before he eats. It's bad for the digestion."

Laughing, David nodded in agreement and they sat down to eat.

"You want to tell me why you haven't put my little sister to work yet?" Danny piped up. Tara groaned. "Danny, no shop talk at the dinner table."

Martha stepped in, "Are you originally from Minnesota Captain Cavanaugh?" Tara smiled at her mother and relaxed.

"Please call me Shane. Yes, born and raised," he smiled back at Martha. "Do I detect an Irish accent?" He inquired.

While Martha explained that she had come over from Ireland when she was just a child and had been raised in Illinois, Shane glanced over at Tara. He wondered what she had been telling the family about him. Focusing back onto what Martha was saying, he decided that he would have to learn a little more about his new fireman.

Thanks to her mother, the rest of the dinner went off without any more inquiries from her brothers. When a game of volleyball was suggested, Tara begged off and suggested Shane take her place. Picking up the rest of the dishes, Martha joined her daughter in the kitchen. "Seems like a very nice man."

Tara smiled. "I'm sure he is, Mother. But he's also my boss and…"

"And you don't think you're ready yet." Martha laid her hand over her daughter's hand. "You will be."

Tara looked into her mother's eyes and they seemed to understand each other. "Someday," She conceded.

Sitting back outside, watching the game in action, Tara let her eyes drift to study each of her brothers. David, the oldest, was eight years older than she was and very protective. She had always had a strong bond with him, always being able to tell him just about anything. Danny, who was only two years older than her, was teamed up with David. Danny was the sensitive one of the group. Thoughtful. That was why he had sent the flowers her first day. He had a good sense of humour and a romantic side as well.

Kevin had been paired up with Shane and as usual was keeping the conversation to a minimum. Four years her senior, Kevin was the intellectual one of the siblings. Quiet, but very loving. He was working to become an investigator and would be taking his last test at the end of the month. He loved his job just like his brothers and his sister, but the mystery behind the fire was what really called to him.

Tara let her eyes drift over to Shane. He had taken his shirt off and she couldn't help but appreciate the build. It was obvious that he spent time at the gym. Scanning up his torso, she felt her breath catch as their eyes locked.

Swallowing, she looked down and leaning towards her mom, said that she would be right back.

Ok, that was a mistake. She scolded herself as the grabbed a couple of more beers from the fridge. 'What the hell was she thinking?' Oh, she knew exactly what she had been thinking, and they weren't thoughts that should have been crossing her mind. He was her boss for God's sake. 'OK, no harm, no foul'. She would just act casually and hopefully Shane hadn't felt the same jolt she had when their eyes had locked. But no more beer for her, she told herself. God knew she didn't need any more encouragement to make a fool of herself.

Walking back outside, she set the beers down and began picking up the empty ones.

"Hey, Tara, you up for a game now?" Danny called out to her.

"I can sit this one out." Shane said as he reached for a fresh beer.

"You go play," Martha said to Tara as she patted the chair next to her for Shane to sit in. "Show your brothers the correct way to play the game."

Tara laughed and took up the challenge.

Shane sat down next to Martha and took a slow sip of his beer as he watched Tara get in position and set up for the first serve. Martha glanced over at him. "What do you want to know?" She asked quietly.

Shane turned and studied the older woman next to him. "Who says I want to know anything."

Martha chuckled. "I do. Now spill it. You didn't come over here tonight for nothing." Shane looked over and watched Tara dive and miss a ball. Laughing, she popped up and shrug her shoulders.

"Why does she want to be secretive about the fire?" He finally asked.

"It's for her protection," Martha replied. The sadness in her voice had him turning back to look at her. "Her protection? From her ex-husband?" Martha looked at her daughter before turning to focus on Shane's face. "The man hurt her and he got away with it. He'll try again. That was why she moved out here."

"How did he hurt her?" Shane asked feeling his gut tighten in response.

"That's for her to tell, if she wants. Suffice to say that things started to get out of hand and she decided that it would be safest to leave."

Then Martha turned and watched her family play. "So, why haven't you put her to work yet?"

Shane smiled. He wondered when one of the clan would ask him that again. "Some things take time," he said simply.

"Not if you trust her," Martha said and then excusing herself got up and walked back into the house.

Shane turned and watched Tara serve the ball. Trust. Wasn't that what she had said? Perhaps it was time. He knew that he had been over protective of her because of the fire he had dragged her from.

Looking around at her family, he thought, *They all know what she had gone through and they trusted her to be back in the field.* Then watching her again, he thought that maybe it was time for him to trust her abilities.

"Mom! Did you see that?" Kevin glanced over and saw that Shane was watching his sister.

"Hey, where did Mom go?"

Shane nodded towards the house. "I believe she said something about dessert."

"I'll help her," Tara said and jogged into the house.

Kevin walked up, grabbed another beer and sat down in the chair his mother had vacated. Glancing over at Shane, he tried to figure out how he felt about him. He knew that the man was interested in his sister. He seemed like a good man, but then again Scott had seemed like a good man at one time and look what a bastard he turned out to be.

Tara wasn't ready for a relationship. She had told him that. So, he knew he had time to suspend his judgment. But living six hours drive away wasn't what he would call a comfort.

Shane turned and looked at the man who was studying him. "Something on your mind?" He asked.

Kevin took another swig of his beer. "Just wondering if I'd like you next to me in a fire."

Shane knew there was more there—nodding, he said, "You could count on me."

As Tara and Martha came out with pie and coffee, Kevin smiled, "That's what I was thinking."

Tara couldn't help but wonder what the two men had been discussing. But knowing her brother, she knew that the conversation had been short.

~

The following Monday, when Tara got to work, she found the Captain in a pleasant mood. Holding an impromptu meeting, Shane informed the group that they had been asked to help out at a local charity event the coming Saturday. "Habitat for Humanity needs some volunteers to help build a garage, and I thought that instead of tearing down a building, you might enjoy erecting one instead. Besides, station number four has challenged us to a contest. It seems that they have been asked to help out about a block away and their Captain thinks that they can do it better than we can. Can I count you all in?" The hoots and howlers that followed told Shane that he would have a full team. "Tara, can I assume that you will also be available to help out."

Laughing, she said, "Of course. I'll even bring my own tools."

"Her own tools." Hector winked, "Gentlemen, I believe we have a ringer in our mist."

Later that day, when they were sent off on their first fire for the week, she was happy to hear the Captain pair her up with Rocko. Finally, it seemed, Shane would let her do what she was trained to do.

A one-story structure had caught fire after someone had carelessly thrown a cigarette into a garbage bin. The garbage bin had caught fire and the fire had quickly spread to the neighbouring building. The danger was that the building was next to a paint supply store. If the fire spread, an explosion would be eminent, and then they would really have a fight on their hands.

Rocko and herself were in charge of the lead hose. While Hector and Sam covered the flames from the outside, James would work his way up to the roof to ventilate the smoke. Meanwhile, Rocko and Tara would make their way into the building, extinguishing the flames and looking for anyone who may still be trapped in the building.

Luckily, the fire was quickly contained, but Tara felt that a page had been turned, and that finally, Shane was beginning to trust her.

Over the next few days, Shane paired her up with each member of the team to determine which firefighter would work best with her. They were all seasoned firefighters and it was simply finding the best partners to work together. At the end of the week, it looked like he had found his teams. James had indicated a desire to work the ladder, so that left Hector and Rocko to form one team, while Sam and Tara would make up the other team. As the new man on the team, ordinarily Shane would have been paired up with Tara, but he didn't quite trust himself where she was concerned. He knew that his feelings for her went beyond professional admiration, and he wasn't sure that he would be able to remain objective in a crisis situation. Teaming her up with Sam seemed a wiser choice.

That left Clyde, the veteran of the crew, to man the hoses from the rig, and to provide back up support if need be. It was Shane's hope that eventually, two more firefighters would be hired, and then he would have a full team for the big jobs. As it was, if they had a large structure fire, he would have to call in another department for backup, and worst-case scenario, he'd have to call the men on the other shifts for assistance. With an eight-man crew, he would be able to rotate his men in without much difficulty.

For Tara, the time went by fast and by the end of the week, she felt that her teammates trusted her abilities and she was glad that Shane had finally let go of his misgivings and had teamed her up with Sam. Sam and she worked well together, and while she felt that she could have worked easily with any of the other firemen, she and Sam seemed to click. Finally, she felt that she was once again back on track with her career.

She had wondered why she hadn't been teamed up with Shane, as was the usual course of action, but a part of her was glad of it. She still had a serious crush on her new boss and she didn't want to risk complicating things between the two of them.

It was finally the weekend of the charity event and on Saturday morning, despite an exhausting week, Tara woke early. The crew was expected at the Habitat for Humanity job site by 8:00 am but she intended to get there early. She knew the address by heart and she wanted to make sure she got there in time to talk with the tenants.

Arriving at 7:30 am, Marie Hernandez was surprised to see Tara standing at her door with a box of donuts. "Tara, what a pleasant surprise. I wasn't expecting to see you today."

"Good morning, Marie, do you mind if I come in? I need to talk with you before the rest of the crew arrive."

"Of course," Marie said as she opened the screen door.

~

41

As the group pulled up to the designated address, Shane saw that Tara had already arrived and was grabbing her gear out of her car. "Hey Tara!" James called out and got a wave in return.

Walking up to the gang, Tara finished fastening her tool belt around her waist and nodded towards a table that was sitting in the porch. "I brought some coffee and donuts if anyone's hungry."

Rocko smiled and headed towards the table without a word of greeting, and Hector gave her a quick hug. "A woman after my own heart," he replied as he also headed towards the porch.

"Yeah, tell that to your wife." Tara laughed.

Shane turned to greet the man in charge of the Habitat for Humanity project and was shocked when he was introduced to the homeowner. Standing before him was the young mother who had lost her home to a fire a month earlier. The fire that he had dragged Tara from. Turning, he glanced at Tara, curious to see her reaction. But instead of being shocked, Tara just nodded and then smiled at the young Hispanic mother. It was obvious that they knew each other.

Shane wanted to talk to Tara, but they had a job to do. It would have to wait.

The day passed quickly. The teamwork the group had been building upon during the previous weeks paid off and they had the framing up well before noon. By dinner, the garage was completed. The electrical work was scheduled to be completed on Sunday by another company who had volunteered their services for the charity.

At five o'clock, Shane disappeared and soon returned with the Captain from Station 4, who agreed that Station 18 was the winner. The celebration would begin later that evening at O'Gara's Pub, with Station 4 picking up the tab.

Everyone agreed to meet up at 8:00pm, which would give everyone time to go home and get cleaned up before hooking up again at the Pub.

Picking up the last of her tools, Tara turned to find Shane standing close behind her.

"We need to talk," he said as he walked her to her car.

"I suppose we do. I need to get cleaned up first. I have a roast that's been cooking all day if you're hungry. And you are welcome to a shower if you have a change of clothes with you."

Shane nodded, "I'll follow you to your house, if that's OK with you."

Letting him in the front door, Tara pointed him towards the spare bathroom and handed him a towel. "Help yourself to a soda or a beer when you're finished. I'll be back down in 20 minutes."

Showered and changed, she joined him in the kitchen and as she fixed him a plate she says, "OK, let's get this out of the way so we don't spoil our meal. I've been in contact with the family since the fire. Mrs Hernandez had a similar relationship problem and could relate to the position I'm in, so she agreed to keep quiet about my involvement."

"She said that you helped them get the house." Nodding, Tara said, "I work with an organisation called Simpson Shelter. I presented their case and the board agreed that they were definitely in need of shelter. Now, I visit them and help out when I can because I like the family. Does that answer all of your questions?"

"For now," Shane replied honestly.

They fell into silence as they ate their meal. "This is delicious, Tara." Shane complimented her as he helped himself to a second helping. "Thanks. I enjoy cooking, and try to do as much of it when I can on the weekends that I'm not working."

Finishing his last bite, and noting that Tara was also done with her meal, Shane looked up and caught her eye. "Tara, tell me about your husband."

Tara studied his face for a moment before nodding in agreement.

"I met my ex-husband shortly after my father passed away. Scott seemed charming, caring. The kind of man my father might have liked. But it all had been just an act." Tara took a sip of her water before continuing. "We had a short courtship. Scott said that he knew that I was 'the one' and we got married nine months after we met. Nothing big, just went to the Justice of Peace. In hindsight, it should have been the first sign. But my family was still recovering from the loss of my father. He was a fireman too. I guess you could say, we all followed in his footsteps."

"How did your father die?" Shane gently asked.

"Heart attack. He had been on medication, but…the doctors told us that he had 95% blockage. It had only been a matter of time."

Shane nodded, then he quietly asked, "What did you mean by the first sign?"

"Scott insisted that we should keep our wedding low key, that the stress of a big wedding would be too much for the family. Oh, and he never failed to mention that now that my father couldn't walk me down the aisle that a big wedding would be a disappointment."

"Jerk!" Shane winced. "Sorry, that kind of slipped."

"That's alright. Scott is a jerk."

"Your Mother mentioned that he hurt you. Is that what she meant?"

Tara shook her head. "No. Scott isn't a good person. It just took me too long to see that." Tara picked up their plates and put them in the sink. Turning, she studied Shane for a moment and then she decided that she would tell him everything.

"The abuse started shortly after we were married," she said matter-of-factly. "It was subtle at first, comments that stung. But after a while it seemed that I couldn't say or do anything right. I was brought up to believe that once you said, 'I do'—it meant forever. I tried to make adjustments. Tried to be the kind of wife I thought he wanted me to be. But nothing seemed to make him happy; and just like every other abused spouse I hid it from my family." She shook her head, "That was my biggest mistake," she added with conviction.

"When I couldn't make things right, I started to work more shifts. I thought that maybe if we spent less time together that he would appreciate me more for the time we could spend together. Instead, he started to accuse me of having affairs, and then he started to get…physical." Tara swallowed back the bitter taste the memory brought.

"Scott is a big guy. He's a construction foreman. At first, he would just use his physical strength to pin me down so he could yell at me. But when that didn't seem to satisfy him, he started to make more serious threats. The last night I was at the house he held me down and put his hand around my throat. A couple of times, he squeezed just enough so I couldn't breathe. It did the trick. It scared the hell out of me. I apologised for my behaviour, although I didn't even know what I had done to get him so angry. He left to have a beer with his buddies and I packed a bag and left."

Taking another drink of her water, she continued. "I went to the hospital and reported the incident. But he had been careful and there wasn't any physical evidence. I checked into a shelter and started the divorce proceedings."

Tara looked out the window, "The day the papers were served I had gone over to my mother's house. She had gone to visit my aunt in South Carolina and I had stopped over to check her mail." Looking back at Shane, she hurried to finish her story. "I saw Scott drive up and I knew he had gotten the papers. I called the police. He didn't even bother to knock on the door, he just kicked it in and then he started swinging. By the time the cops go there, he had me on the ground and he was kicking me. He was arrested and charged with assault and battery. The judge ordered a restraining order and for a while it looked like he would comply with it. When the divorce was final, I thought that he would finally be out of my life. I didn't ask for anything from him. My attorney said I was throwing away a lot of money. But I didn't want to have to keep in contact with him for any reason. I got my personal belongings and that was all I wanted."

Looking down she admitted, "But I was wrong. Over the next year and a half, he broke the order three times. The last time being the breaking point. That was when I decided that I had to move. To go where he would never be able to find me."

She hadn't realised that Shane was standing next to her until he gently lifted her chin with his hand, and looked into her eyes. "Tell me what happened Tara?"

Tara took a deep breath. "I had rented a small cottage not too far from my work. I had installed a security system so I felt safe. Scott knew about it. The second time he broke the restraining order he had triggered it. This time he wasn't going to give me any warning. It was two o'clock in the morning when he pulled up to the house. He had brought one of the cranes from work. He didn't wait long before he started to demolish the house. He knew where the bedroom was, so he began there."

"Shit," Shane reached out and covered her hand with his. Tara smiled at him. "I wasn't there. I had fallen asleep in the living room. I woke up as he took a second swipe at the house. My bedroom was gone and he was working his way towards me. I think he thought I was already dead. The first sweep had completely destroyed my bedroom," she shuddered.

"I ran. Well, crawled really. I was terrified. All I could think was that I had to sneak out but my legs didn't want to cooperate. If he had seen me, I knew he would get me. I managed to get out the back door. The police were there by then. One of the neighbours had called 911. They arrested him. He thought he had killed me. The look on his face. God. He seemed elated. That was until one of the officers found me." Tara walked over to the fridge and grabbed them each a beer. "He got a year in jail."

"What?"

"Yeah, that's what I said," she smiled thinly at him. "Scott isn't stupid. He had drawn up a demolition contract for the property. He claimed that he had orders and that he had been following them. The fact that his ex-wife had lived there made him happy. But he claimed that he thought I had been evicted."

45

Shrugging, she added, "Long and the short of it, he had a good attorney. That was when I decided to disappear. I moved here, laid low for about six months, and then I started my job search. I guess you know the rest. That was why I can't come forward about the fire. Do you understand?"

Shane nodded. "I do now. I'm sorry that I've ridden you so hard about it."

"I know," she smiled back at him. "I guess I just wasn't ready to tell my story."

"Why now?" Shane asked.

Tara decided that she couldn't come completely clean with that right now. She couldn't tell him that she was attracted to him. Instead, she simply said, "I guess it was just time."

Feeling a little uncomfortable about all that she had just revealed about herself, Tara, glanced at the clock on the wall, and seeing that it was nearly 8:00 pm. "I think we should think about going to that party. We did earn it after all," she smiled back at Shane.

Shane nodded in agreement. He wanted nothing more than to give her a hug, and to tell her that he was sorry about all that she had gone through, but he could tell that right now she needed some time. "I'd be happy to give you a lift to O'Gara's if you'd like," he offered.

Tara considered the offer. "Thanks, I was planning on taking a taxi, but since you've offered. But I will be taking a taxi home, so you won't have to worry about that."

"That's a good idea. I know a place I can leave my car about a block from O'Gara's, if you don't mind the walk."

"Of course not," she replied as she picked up her purse.

Locking the door behind them, Shane ushered her to his truck. O'Gara's was only a few miles from her house and they were there with in minutes. Parking the car, Shane turned towards her. "Tara, I just want to say that I'm sorry that you went through all of that. If you ever need to talk, or anything, I hope that you will consider me a friend that you can confide in."

Tara studied his face and then leaned over and kissed him gently on the cheek. "Thank you, Shane. I appreciate that." Then she turned and got out of the truck.

The topic was not raised again, and the rest of the evening was filled with nothing but laughter and good times. The crew, it seemed, were in the mood for a good party. Pitchers of beer, shots of tequila and various other alcoholic beverages were consumed in large quantities. No one would be driving home, and so everyone let their guards down and enjoyed the free drinks. Somewhere around midnight, Hector persuaded the owner to start up the karaoke machine, and soon the two stations were locked in a fierce karaoke competition.

Tara laughed when her coworkers tried to persuade her to get up and sing; and she only agreed after she was promised that their Captain would also get up to sing. Shane agreed, reluctantly, but only with the group. Tara insisted that they all sing 'King of the Road', which they all did good naturedly. When it was Tara's turn, she scanned the play list and found a song that she knew well. Keeping the title a secret, she climbed the stage and sang a hardy rendition of Somethin' Stupid.

At the end of the song, she was greeted by a standing ovation from both stations. Laughing, Tara bowed, and accepted Shane's offer for help off the stage.

Clinking beers with her fellow teammates, she accepted their congratulations and then slipped away to the ladies' room. She knew that she was beginning to feel the effects of all the alcohol she had consumed. She also knew that despite her best efforts, while she had been singing, she had focused her attention on one man in particular. Shaking her head, she scolded her image in the mirror.

"You're playing a dangerous game, deary," she whispered to herself. Washing her hands, and applying a fresh coat of lipstick, she straightened her shoulders and told herself that she would not slip again. Then she rejoined her comrades and spent the rest of the night trying not to watch the man whom she was still dangerously attracted to.

～

Two weeks had passed since she had told Shane about her past, and it seemed like a page had turned in their relationship. Since he was her boss, she made sure that no lines were crossed when they talked. Always keeping things on a professional level, but it did feel like they had formed a friendship, which she was glad for. She knew that she would probably always have a crush on him, but she had decided that she wouldn't mess up their friendship with trying to bring romance into the equation.

She had flown to Chicago on the Friday to visit her family and she was back again Sunday night. It had been a great weekend seeing her mother and her brothers. As it had been Mother's Day, she had spent the day on Saturday treating her mom to a spa treatment and a shopping trip. It had felt like old times, and Tara felt like her life was finally back on track. Saturday night, her brother David had invited the family over to his house for a barbeque and they had talked through the night, regaling stories of the past and making plans for a trip to the family cabin in a few weeks' time.

On Monday morning, Tara opened her morning paper and found her image splashed across the front page. "Mystery Woman Found!" The caption read, "After weeks of searching, the woman who risked her life to save young Lizzy Hernandez has finally been found, once again helping the little girl she saved." The article went on to state her name and the fact that she was working as a fire fighter for Station 18, who had volunteer to help the Habitat for Humanity, who had built a garage for the Hernandez family.

Sitting down, Tara pushed away her uneaten breakfast and buried her head in her arms. 'What the hell was she going to do now?'. Her next thought was, who the hell had talked to the press? Shane? He wouldn't have. Would he? Her blood started to boil. Grabbing her bag, she stormed out of her house. Intent on getting some answers.

"Damn it Shane!" Tara stormed into his office and threw the paper down on his desk. "I thought you understood."

Shane glanced down at the paper. He had seen the article himself that morning. "I didn't leak it, Tara." She stared at him and then collapsed into the chair. Her hands on her face. "I know. I know. I'm sorry." Looking back up at him. "Damn it."

"Maybe nothing will come of it." He tried to offer her some hope. "Maybe." She nodded. She could hope. Standing up she started to leave, "Umm. Tara, if you have another minute…."

Tara turned back around and waited. Standing up from his desk, he threw the paper in the wastebasket and then shoved his hands in his pockets. "I realise that this is really short notice, but I've got a dinner with the chief tonight. It's a benefit dinner for the new children's wing at the hospital."

Seeing that he seemed uncertain, perhaps even nervous, Tara couldn't help the smile that slipped on to her lips. "And…" She prompted him.

Shane looked up and wanted kick himself. Why the hell was this so hard? "And, I was wondering if you would like to join me." Looking back down at his feet, he continued, "I realise that it's pretty short notice."

"What time is the dinner?"

"That's the thing, it's at 7:00 pm."

"OK."

"I realise that it really doesn't give you much time, what with work and all. I'd have to pick you up at 6:30pm, and it's a damn black-tie event…"

Shane looked up, "What?"

Tara smiled at him, "OK. I'll see you at 6:30 pm." Turning, she walked from the room.

Shane stared after her. Had he just asked her out on a date, and had she just accepted?

~

Slipping into her black halter dress, Tara asked herself again what the hell she was doing? This was not a date. She told herself again. Shane had asked her, last minute, to attend a benefit with him, and the chief. His date had probably cancelled on him and she had just been handy.

So why had she taken extra care in fixing her hair, and why the hell had she picked this dress to wear tonight? It wasn't very glitzy. Just a plain jersey material…unless you counted the rhinestone broach, she had pinned into the front vee of the dress. Add the rhinestone earrings and bracelet, and it looked pretty good. Pretty damn good she told herself. *Hell, the man would have to be dead if he didn't notice her in this outfit.* Frowning. She didn't want him to notice her. Right? This was her boss. What the hell was she doing? She asked herself again as the doorbell rang.

Picking up the second earring, she was putting it in her ear as she opened the door. "Hi! Come on in. I'll be just a minute," she said as she tried not to stare at him. God the man could fill out a suit! She started to work the clasp of her bracelet but having troubles, she looked up at him for help. "Would you mind?"

Shane tried to catch his breath. She was beautiful. "Not at all," he replied and taking the delicate piece of jewellery from her, he stood close to her and slipped it around her wrist. Then he tried to concentrate on working the clasp.

Tara took a deep breath and told herself to relax. Focusing on what he was doing, she tried to ignore the soft touch of his hands. Tried to tell herself not to think about how those hands would feel on her body. 'Stop it' she scolded herself and shifted her eyes up to his face. His head was bend down, concentrating on the task, and she looked at his mouth. What would those lips feel like? What would he taste like if they kissed? Breathing in, she could smell the cologne he had chosen. Pure male.

"There." He finally had the clasp done and he looked up into her eyes. If he thought that he had been having trouble concentrating, now he had trouble thinking at all. Taking a deep breath, he stepped back, "You look beautiful," he whispered.

"Thank you," she whispered back.

Smiling, she turned to pick up her handbag and he was awarded with the sight of her bare back, as the dress draped low in the back. Shaking his head, he tried to remind himself that he had to get through dinner with the chief, and not let on that all he wanted to do was to get his hands on this lovely lady. "Ready?" He heard himself ask.

"Yes," she smiled back at him and turning her head she studied him. She thought she could read something in his eyes. A look that she hadn't seen in a man's eyes in a long time. But she had to be sure. "Shane?" She whispered. "Is this a date?"

Shane looked into her eyes. Smiling, he decided to take a chance. "If I kiss you, it's definitely a date. And lady, right now I definitely want to kiss you."

Tara smiled and took a step forward. Looking into his eyes she whispered, "Good," before reaching her hand up to bring his head down to hers. It was a gentle kiss. But the passion was definitely there, smouldering behind it. Lifting his head, he smiled, "That was nice." Laughing, she nodded and stepped back.

"Shall we go?" He asked as he held out his hand.

"I think that would be best," she said as she took his hand.

~

They located the chief and his wife and after a brief introduction, they were seated and offered drinks. Tara decided that tonight she would go easy on the alcoholic beverages and opted for a single glass of white wine. She needed to keep her wits about her. They may have shared a kiss, but she wasn't about to make any assumptions about their relationship.

The dinner conversation was pleasant and Shane did his best not to act differently towards Tara. When the band started to play, the chief suggested that Shane take Tara out dancing. It was a fast song and she laughed as he led her in several spins. "You're good, Cavanaugh," she smiled at him and he winked. "Bet you didn't think I knew how to dance."

Laughing, she said, "You are full of surprises."

As the music slowed, he brought her closer and started to guide her in a waltz. With his face close to her ear, he whispered, "This feels good."

Tara allowed her eyes to drift closed as she melted into his embrace. "Yes, it does," she murmured. Then tilting her head back, she looked into his eyes. "This could get dangerous, Cavanaugh."

"It already has," he smiled at her.

"Mind if I cut in?" Chief McCaffery tapped Shane on the shoulder. "Of course not, sir." Stepping back, he gave Tara's hand to the chief.

"I'm not one to dance the fast ones, but the slow stuff I can do." Tara smiled at him as he guided her into the box step.

The chief had been watching the two dancing. He liked this girl. He had been surprised when Shane had said she would be accompanying him. What bothered him was where this dance seemed to be taking them. He knew about the girl's previous problems and he felt himself wanting to act as a father for her. He liked Shane, but he knew that she would be vulnerable right now. And as for being her Captain, while it wasn't strictly against regulations, the chief wasn't sure a romance between the two would be a wise decision.

When the dance ended, he escorted Tara back to the table, where Mrs McCaffery was starting to stand. "I think that's about all the fun I can handle for one evening."

Saying their goodbyes, Shane took Tara's arm and led her to his car. Opening the door for her, Shane took her hand into his, and kissed the back of her hand as he handed her into her seat. After he got into the driver's seat, he took her hand in his and held it as he drove her home.

Parking in her driveway, he got out and opened her door for her. Linking fingers, he walked her up to her door. Tara felt a little lightheaded—not from the wine, but from the anticipation of the kiss she felt sure Shane would be giving her. Reaching for her keys, she started to put them in the lock when something caught her eye. "How did that fall down?" She said as she started to bend to pick up a ceramic sign she had hung above the doorway.

Shane had been looking into the house and he thought he saw smoke hanging by the light. He was about to say something when she froze. "Oh my God," she whispered as she saw smoke suck in under her door. "Backdraft" she yelled. He grabbed her arm and started running with her when the house blew up behind them, sending them flying onto the front lawn. Rolling over, Shane reached for her.

"Are you alright?" Sitting up, she stared in horror at the fiery remains of her house. "Damn you, Scott," she said and then buried her face in her hands and choked back a cry. Taking her in his arms, he held her as she let go of her emotions.

≈

Shane had given her his coat, but she was still shaking when the fire department and the police arrived. They both knew that nothing could be done to save her house, and as they answered the questions the police asked, Shane kept an eye on her. She seemed to be shaking herself out of her shock.

Turning to him, she reached for his hand and held it. "I need to call my family." She told him.

"I can." He offered.

Shaking her head, she said, "No, I need to do it. If you call, they'll think the worse." He sat her in his truck, letting her have her privacy.

Tara decided that the first call she should make would be to her brother David. He lived the closes to their mother, and Tara would need him to be there when she heard the news. While Martha O'Brien was a strong woman, she was in her late seventies and news like this would not be easy for her to handle.

David answered his phone by the third ring. "Hello," he seemed distracted. It was Monday night, and she guessed that he would be watching the Bears game. "Hi David, it's Tara."

"Hey! How's it going? Damn it! What kind of play do call that?" Despite her situation, Tara couldn't help but smile at her brother yelling at the television. "You tell them, big Bro."

"Sorry about that, Tara."

"Listen David, I hate to bother you, but…" Tara wasn't exactly sure how she was going to tell her brother that her house had just been blown up.

David noted Tara's hesitation and promptly turned off his television. "Tara, what's wrong?"

Taking a deep breath, she plunged into her explanation. David, for his part, kept quiet until Tara was finished, and then he asked, "Are you alright? Any injuries?" When he got a negative from her, he asked her to hold on a second, then setting the phone down, he letting go of a string of curses that would make a trucker blush. Picking up the phone again, he apologised and then said, "Have you called Mom yet?"

Shaking her head, "No, not yet. I kind of thought you should be there when I do. If that's ok with you."

"Why don't you let me tell her and the other fellas as well. I'm sure they will want to talk to you, but at least you won't have to go over it four times. I'm sure you've already told the story more times than you cared to. I'm assuming the police are there, and that they have gotten your statement."

"Yes. The fire investigator is already working the case as well. Hopefully Scott got careless and left a fingerprint or something else that will help us nail him for this."

"He will, Tara," David tried to give her hope. "Where are you staying tonight?"

"I'm not sure just yet. But I'll text you when I know."

"OK, get some rest, honey. Don't worry about Mom, I'll tell her. She'll probably want to fly you home, but I'll try and keep her maternal instincts unwraps."

Tara smiled at the comment, "Thanks, David."

When Shane saw her put her phone on the dash, he knew that she was done. Getting into his truck he looked over at her before starting the engine and pulling away from the curb.

They didn't talk as he drove her to his house, nor when he led her into the house. His golden retriever, Flame, met them at the door and after a brief introduction, Shane let him out of the house to do his business. While he was gone, she texted David, stating briefly that she would be at the Captain's house.

When he returned, he found her standing in front of his fireplace, looking at his photos. She had removed his coat and her shoes. He pushed down the desire he felt rising within him. Turning, she looked at him. "I like your dog," she said quietly.

"He likes you too," he replied.

Studying her for a moment he said, "Tara, I have a guest room. I want you to know that you'll be safe here."

She tilted her head and waited for him to continue. "I won't touch you tonight. I just wanted you to know that you don't have to worry about that."

Tara closed her eyes briefly and then walked slowly up to him. Looking into his eyes, she reached up and played with his shirt buttons. "That's too bad. Because I really wanted you to touch me tonight."

Shane closed his eyes and took a deep breath trying to remember why he had to be a gentleman tonight. "Shane?" She waited for him to open his eyes again. "We both know where we were heading tonight." She touched his face, "Please don't let him take that away from me too." And as she drew her thumb over his lips she said, "I want to forget everything but you tonight. Is that alright?"

With a soft moan, he took her into his arms and took her lips with his.

Tara melted into his kiss. She wanted to leave the last few hours behind her and only think about the passion that had been evident earlier in the evening.

Leaving her mouth, Shane drew a trail of kisses along her delicate jaw bone and then down her slender neck. He could feel her pulse jump in response when he kissed the hollow of her neck.

Reaching down and he lifted her into his arms, and carried her up to his bedroom. Setting her down next to the bed, he caught her gaze as he slowly untied the fabric of her halter dress, leaving her naked from the waist up. Holding her gaze, he slipped his hand down her back and released the zipper that held the gown around her waist. Only now did he step back and allow his eyes to travel down her lovely body. "You're beautiful," he whispered.

Tara could easily read the desire in his eyes, and she felt herself warming to thoughts of what was to come.

"My turn," she whispered in return and then she reached up and slowly unbuttoned his shirt. She allowed her fingers to linger on his broad chest before she slipped the shirt from his shoulders and hung it on the corner of the bed. Then she reached down to loosen his trousers. Unable to help herself, she leaned towards him to capture his mouth with hers as his pants dropped from his hips.

Stepping out of the rest of his clothes, Shane guided her down onto his bed, covering her with his body. Kissing her soundly on the lips, Shane rolled off of her and propping his head up with his hand, he gazed down into her lovely face. "Lady, you sure do know how to kiss."

Tara couldn't help but laugh. She didn't know whether she could kiss well or not, but she did know that the man next to her was sending her emotions into overdrive. Reaching up, she gently touched his lips. "Mister, you have no idea what your kisses do to me," she admitted honestly.

Smiling slyly, he winked at her and then leaned over and captured her lips with his before kissing a trail down her neck. Her breath caught in her throat, as she laced her fingers in his hair, urging him on. Her body felt on fire, and she knew that the sweet pull of his lips was gently teasing her to surrender completely to him. Pulling his head up, she kissed him deeply. Wrapping her slender legs around his waist, she guided him into her.

Their passion ignited.

Content, they laid wrapped in each other's arms. Neither spoke a word, and soon they drifted off to sleep.

～

Tara felt something warm and wet bump into her hand and then that something nudged her hand up over its head. Opening her eyes, she smiled at Flame. "Good morning, sweetheart."

"Good morning," she heard a muffled voice behind her as Shane pulled her closer. Laughing she said, "I was saying hello to Flame." Who, upon hearing his name promptly set his front paws up on the bed and licked her face.

"Hey Buddy!" Shane rolled her over onto her back and told Flame 'Down'. "You know the rules. I get to kiss the pretty lady first." Then he looked down into her eyes and as he lowered his head said, "Good morning" again.

It was another 'knock your socks off' kind of kiss that left her feeling warm and bubbly inside. When he lifted his mouth from hers, he kissed the tip of her nose, then her closed eyelids and finally her forehead before taking her into his arms and hugging her.

Tara smiled into his chest. She felt the words bubble to the surface before she had time to check them. "I love you."

His arms tightened around her. Oh God, what had had she just said? "I mean, I love that."

Shane pulled back and smiled down at her. "Yah? I love that too." Tara breathed a sigh of relief. *She hadn't blown it after all.*

Shane kissed her again and then caught her eyes with his. "I'm falling in love you with you too Tara," he said before he swallowed her shocked reply with another passionate kiss.

Opening her eyes, Tara looking up at Shane, unable and unwilling to hide the love she felt for him. Shane smiled, "Happy?" He asked.

Tara smiled and nodded. "Very," she whispered.

"Then it's ok?" Nodding again, she felt her heart swell.

"More than ok." Rolling over, he pulled her next to him. "I'm glad," he said.

Flame jumped up on the bed and looked down at them. "OK, you can kiss the lady now."

Shane laughed as he got a thorough face wash. "The girl, the girl. I said you could kiss the girl!"

Laughing, Tara sat up and grabbed his shirt, which was hanging from the corner of the bed. "I'll let you out Flame," she said as she stood up and headed for the door. Flame bounded after her and Shane smiled. He knew that this would probably complicate things between them at work, but he really didn't care. He had known he was falling in love with her for weeks and it felt good to be able to finally tell her.

Sitting up he grabbed his boxers and slipped them on and then reached down and picked up her dress. The burn marks on the side of the dress brought back the reality of the night before.

"Damn," she said from the doorway. He saw that she was looking down at the dress he held in his hands. Looking up she held his gaze. "We're going to get him Tara."

Throwing the dress down, he stood up, and he walked to her. Taking her into his arms. "I promise you; he's not going to hurt you ever again."

~

Despite Tara's arguments, Shane encouraged her to tell the rest of the crew about what she was up against. "That way," he argued, "all of us can be on the lookout for this lunatic."

Calling everyone into the dining room, Shane nodded to Tara and then he began. "I'm sure most of you have heard about the explosion that levelled Tara's house last night." Holding his hand up to quiet his men, he continued. "What you should know is that it was not caused by a gas leak as the press has indicated."

Looking back over at Tara, he waited for her nod of approval. "You all should know that Tara's life was targeted."

"What?" Every man in the room shouted in astonishment. Once again holding his hand up to quiet the group Shane continued. "We believe that Tara's ex-husband set up a backdraft explosion."

Tara knew that it was her turn to speak up. "I'm sorry about this. I moved here from Chicago in the hope that Scott wouldn't find me. Unfortunately, Monday's headlines seem to have tipped him off on my location."

"God, I'm so sorry, Tara," Rocko spoke up. "I had no idea that reporter would cause you any trouble."

Tara shook her head, "How could you? Don't worry about it. Maybe I should have told you about Scott before any of this happened, but…anyway, the police have an APB out on him and with luck they will catch him before he can try anything else."

"And that's why we are telling you all about it." Shane took the lead again. "Until this lunatic is caught, we all have to be on our guard in case he tries something again. This guy obviously knows something about starting a fire, and we can't put it past him that he won't try and set something up to get to Tara while she's on the job. Tara has volunteered to take a leave of absence, but the chief and the police agree that the quickest way to flush this guy out is to keep her in the open. Unless you guys have some reservations, they'd like to keep her in the field."

Standing up, Clyde looked around and receiving a nod from his fellow fire fighters he said, "Cap, I believe I speak for everyone here when I say that we are definitively on board." Then turning towards Tara, he added, "You're one of us Tara, and we watch out for our own. We'll watch your back."

Tara swallowed back the tears she felt building and she quietly said, "Thank you."

"So, what do we watch for?" Rocco spoke up.

While Shane handed out the copies of the report, the police had given him that morning, Tara took her cue and left the room.

She felt exhausted. She wanted all of this to be over. When she had moved to Minnesota, she had hoped that the horrors of the past were behind her.

Stepping out the side door, she leaned back against the building. Turning her face up to the warmth of the sun, she closed her eyes and wished herself away from her current circumstances. A soft sand beach, waves lapping on the shore. It sounded heavenly to her. But as a cloud passed over head, blocking the suns warmth, she couldn't help but think that until they caught Scott, not even her island fantasy would be peaceful. If Scott had found her in Minnesota, then there was always the possibility that he would find her anywhere she went to get away.

She realised that until they caught Scott red handed that the threat would always be there, haunting her.

"Tara?" Turning her head, she found Shane standing in the doorway. "Are you alright?"

Tara looked down briefly, considering his question. "I will be. I'm just realising that until we catch Scott, my life won't really be mine."

Holding her hand up to his advance, she smiled. "As much as I'd love a hug right now, I think I need to try and hold on to what little backbone I still have left."

Shane halted his movement, but reached out to grab her hand and gave it a squeeze. "Lady, you have more backbone than most men I know. We'll get through this. Together," he added with conviction. "That bastard will make a mistake soon and then you can get on with your life."

"Captain, you've got a phone call," James called from the office.

"I'll be right there," he replied before turning back to Tara. "In the meantime, I think it might be a good idea that you keep close by. I don't want that asshole getting in a cheap shot, and the side of this building isn't exactly what I would call the most secure of places for you to hang out alone."

Tara nodded in agreement and followed Shane back into the building.

Stepping into his office, Shane picked up the phone, and then motioned for Tara to have a seat.

"I'm sorry Lieutenant, can you repeat that?" Tara leaned forward in her seat, now realising that Shane was speaking with the police Lieutenant in charge of her case.

"Huh huh." Shane nodded into the phone. Then he looked at Tara, "Ok Lieutenant, I'll see to that. Thanks for the call. Goodbye, Lieutenant."

Tara couldn't help herself. "What will you see to?"

Smiling Shane winked, "Keeping you in my sights."

Tara raised her eyes at him. "Really. Ok Cavanaugh, spill the beans. What else did the Lieutenant have to say?"

"It seems that your ex has finally made a mistake." Pulling a chair up next to hers he sat down. "They found Scott Chamberlain's fingerprints on the welcome sign and…"

Tara interrupted him, "Scott will have an excuse for that."

Shane took her hands into his, "Honey, let me finish. They also found Chamberlain's fingerprints on your bell box."

"What?" She couldn't believe it.

"It seems that the bastard took a ladder up to your outside alarm box and tampered with it. That was how he got into your house without your alarm going off. Somehow, he must have figured out how to disable your alarm." He frowned.

"Not somehow, he would have known exactly how to do it." she explained, "Before Scott got into construction, he worked for a security company installing house alarms. This was years ago, and I thought I had bought a system that he wouldn't have any knowledge of. Obviously, he did his homework."

Shane rubbed his hand against the back of her hand to reassure her, "Well, the Lieutenant says we have him. They've already got a warrant for his arrest, and from what the DA has said, the case they have against your ex should put him away for a very long time."

"OK, what's the catch?" Tara asked, not daring to hope that her nightmare was nearly over.

"The catch, is that they still have to find him. His photograph has been given to all areas of law enforcement, and they will be making a public announcement shortly. By tonight, everyone in the country will know what he looks like and what he did."

"In the meantime, we need to make sure that you are safe, so the Lieutenant is sending over a couple of officers to guard you. They are going to take you to a safe house to wait it out."

Tara sat back. She felt numb. She wanted to believe that her nightmare was nearly over, but part of her wouldn't allow it. She had gotten this close before only to have Scott beat the system, finding a loop hole to slither through.

Shane studied her for a moment. He could see that something wasn't quite right with her. He had thought that his news would make her happy. Instead, she seemed withdrawn. "Tara? We'll get him honey. You have to believe that."

Tara looked up and shook her head. "I haven't given up hope Shane. Not yet anyway. But it's not over yet, and I'm not going to celebrate until Scott is behind bars for good."

"I understand." Standing up, Shane took her hand and helped her to her feet. "Tara, I'm not going to let anything happen to you. I promise you that." Then taking her into his arms he added, "I love you, and now that I've got you in my life, I'm not going to let anything get in the way of that."

Tara closed her eyes and allowed herself to melt into his embrace.

Hearing a knock on the door, Tara slowly stepped from his embrace. "Come in." Shane replied.

"Cap, there are some cops here for you."

Nodding, he turned back to Tara. "Looks like the Calvary has arrived." He tried to make light of it. Nodding, Tara straightened her shoulders, took a deep breath and replied, "Then we better go meet them."

Oxygen

Chicago, IL

Detective Jake Summers had just finished eating what was left of his burger when his phone rang.

The burger, which had been delivered to his desk over an hour ago, had gone cold, but he was too hungry to care. He had gotten pulled into an interrogation with his partner Allen Caffrey and he was only now able to finish the sandwich.

He had been researching a possible extortion attempt that had mob implications and he felt sure he was getting closer to making a break through. The interrogation had been of a known associate of Nemetskiy. Unfortunately, they hadn't come up with any concrete evidence, but Jake was confident that they were on the right track. The sooner they caught the guy, the sooner they could bring their witness out of hiding. Sarah had been in protective custody for over a month, and Jake was starting to worry that her safety would become jeopardised. The longer a witness was in custody, the more likely they would be found.

Reaching for his phone, he swallowed the last of the burger before answering. "Chicago PD—homicide."

"Detective Summers?"

"This is he," he replied as he gathered the wrappers from his desk and threw them in his trash can.

"This is Lieutenant Jim White of the Minneapolis Police Department. We have a situation here that we need your assistance with."

Jake flipped open his notepad and started jotting down the information the Lieutenant was giving. "Go on."

"I believe you are familiar with a Scott Chamberlain?"

Jake frowned. "Yes, I believe he's currently serving a stretch for destruction of private property."

"He was. He got out early for good behaviour." The Lieutenant informed him.

"Shit," Jake swore. He had told the parole board that it was his opinion that Scott was still a risk to society, but he supposed that some bleeding-heart liberal had over ruled his recommendation. "Go on," He prompted the Lieutenant.

"It appears that Scott Chamberlain tried to murder his ex-wife."

"Is she ok?" Jake had known Tara most of her life and he had helped her move to Minneapolis in the hope that her bastard of an ex would never find her.

"Yes, she is," the Lieutenant was telling him. "We were able to lift several prints from the scene and the evidence is looking pretty good for a conviction."

"That's a relief," Jake muttered. He had tried hard to convince the judge that Scott had intentionally tried to kill Tara when he used the crane to destroy the house she had been living in, but he had been unsuccessful. A finger print however, was evidence that would be harder to ignored or rationalised.

"Yes," the Lieutenant said. "We currently have an APB out for his arrest, but we aren't sure how he got to Minneapolis, so he could be driving. That's why I'm calling you. I've already sent the rest of the case details over to you, but we'd like to ask your assistance to gather any additional information you can find that will help us put the nail in this guy's coffin."

Jake asked what the Lieutenant wanted him to do, and he wrote it down in his note pad. He had felt like he had let Tara down before, and he was determined not to let that happen again.

"Has her family been informed?" Jake asked next.

"We believe that Miss O'Brien notified her family after the explosion, but they have not been updated with the latest developments."

"Leave that to me," Jake replied. He had known the O'Brien's for the better part of fifteen years and he had become very close to the family.

"One other thing." The Lieutenant was saying. "We aren't sure if Chamberlain knows that she survived, so on the off chance that he tries something against the family…"

Jake understood where the Lieutenant was going with his conversation. "I'll contact the family and assign the necessary protection."

"Thanks," the Lieutenant replied.

After getting a few additional details about the evidence, Jake hung up the phone.

"What's up?" Allen Caffrey, his partner of seven years asked. "Scott Chamberlain."

"What about him?" Caffrey asked.

"He tried to kill Tara."

"What? But he's in prison," Caffrey began, but Jake shook his head.

"That's what I thought, but I guess he's out. I've got to go tell the family. In the meantime, we need to get an ABP out," Jake said as he stood from his desk.

"I've got it," Caffrey said.

Jake nodded and grabbing his keys, he left the office. On his way out of the station, he told the sergeant on duty that he would be out of the office and then he headed for his truck. He decided that this was the type of conversation that needed to take place in person and he headed for the O'Brien's ancestral home, knowing beyond a shadow of a doubt that the clan would be gathered there to comfort their mother.

While Jake drove to the O'Brien's family home, he couldn't help but wonder how Scott had gotten so much information about where Tara was living. He knew that the paper had ran the article about her rescuing the little girl from the fire, but it wasn't like it was national news. The Minneapolis Star newspaper may be a fairly large paper for the Twin Cities, but it wasn't the New York Times, and Tara's address would not have been easily found. How did Scott see the article and gotten her address? And more importantly, who had helped him find his ex-wife?

Jake felt in his bones that there was more here than just a possessive ex-husband stocking his ex-wife.

As he pulled into the drive, he decided he would look closer into Scott's background when he got back to the office. Right now, he had a more delicate situation on his hands; convincing the O'Brien's to accept police protection would be like wrestling a den of bears, but he knew he had to try.

~

Minneapolis, MN

It didn't take long for the Minneapolis police to find Chamberlain. He had been so sure that his bobby trap would work that he hadn't even thought about covering his tracks. They found him waiting at the airport for a flight back to Chicago.

At the arraignment, the police had argued that they considered him a flight risk and the judge set a one hundred-thousand-dollar bond, knowing full well that there would be no way for Chamberlain to post that kind of bail. The DA had an airtight case, and the defence knew it.

Tara went back to work. Now that Scott was behind bars, at least temporarily, she felt safe to go about her business.

Walking into the dining room, Tara was about to join the others for lunch when the phone rang. "Station 18."

The voice on the other end stopped her in her tracks. "You bitch!"

Shane saw the colour drain from her face and switched on the speaker phone.

"I'm going to get you, Tara. You're going to be sorry you ever crossed me. When I'm finished with you, that boyfriend of yours won't even recognise you."

"Stop it!" She tried to sound calm, despite the fear rising up inside her. But he continued. "You won't even know when I'll get you. It could be at a fire, at your house. Who knows, maybe I'll get your family first." Something in her snapped, "NO!" She screamed into the phone. She was shaking, and her knees buckled. Sliding down onto the floor she began to hit the phone on the wall, breaking it. Throwing it down, she crumbled.

Shane gathered her up into her arms and held her while she sobbed uncontrollably. Lifting her, he took her into his office and laid her on the sofa.

Clyde stuck his head in the door and told them that he had called the police and that a copy of the conversion was being sent to the DA. He added that the police had already contacted the detective in Chicago and that Tara's family have already been put under guard just in case Scott had ways to take out his frustration on the them.

Shane nodded and looked back down at Tara. "That was his final mistake honey," he whispered as he drew her up tighter into his arms.

Tara's nerves were shattered and it took a while for her to calm down. When Shane suggested they call a doctor and get her a sedative, she declined, but she did agree to take a rest, and after being covered with a blanket, she fell asleep under Shane's watchful eye.

~

When Jake had gotten the call from the MPD telling them about Scott's recent threats, he had immediately contacted David and explained the gravity of the situation.

Since he had first learned that Scott had tried to kill Tara, he had been doing some research into Scott's past, and it didn't like what he saw.

It appeared that Scott, in the past, had some dealings with one Victor Nemetskiy, the very man he had been looking into on the extortion and murder charges. He wondered if perhaps Scott had asked Nemetskiy for a favour. But asking a favour of Nemetskiy would mean only one thing. Scott was on his payroll.

Over the next couple of days, Jake and his team conducted several searches of Chamberlain's home and his work place. They found the supplies and equipment for making bombs. Three completed bombs were also discovered, which prompted a thorough search of each of the O'Brien's homes, cars and places of business.

Two bombs were found, both set to detonate within days of each other. The bombs were defused and then dusted for fingerprints. Once again, they found that Chamberlain had been careless. His fingerprints were found on the tailpipe of David car next to a bomb that was set to detonate when the car was in motion. Luckily, David had been using his motorcycle the last few days and it was determined that Chamberlain had placed the bomb sometime during the past week.

The other bomb was found at Danny's fire station under the extra hoses. Once again, Chamberlain had been careless. A review of the station's security cameras showed a hooded man placing the bomb when the crew was out at a three-alarm fire. A second camera showed the hooded man exiting the building and entering a dark blue Chevy truck. The licence plate number was easily read, and the vehicle was registered to Scott Chamberlain.

A traffic meter camera caught a clear view of Scott driving a block away from the station. The shot showed that he was wearing a dark hooded sweatshirt, this time with the hood removed from his head. The timing proved that it had to be Scott who had planted the bomb.

Further investigation revealed that the fire call had been arson, and the FBI believed that Scott was responsible for this as well. The fire had been set in an abandoned warehouse close to Scott's current job site. It had already been determined that a bomb had caused the fire. The bomb fragments were compared to those found in Chamberlain's home, as well as the bombs found attached to David's car and the bomb found at the fire station. The materials were identical, as was the basic design of the bomb.

Jake called Lieutenant White at the MPD and told him their findings.

"This should get the trial moved forward," The Lieutenant told him. "Let me contact the DA and I'll let you know."

An hour later Jake got a call from the Minneapolis DA requesting his presence at the trial to present evidence. Jake agreed and was then told that the trial had been moved forward and it was now set for the following Monday. Despite strong objections from Scott's defence attorney, the judge had decided that due to the nature of the crimes, and the list of previous convictions, including the fact that Scott had continuously breeched the restraining orders that were in place, the judge had insisted on the trial date taking place as soon as possible.

Jake hung up with the Lieutenant and then he called David, who was at his mother's house. "We have him this time, David."

David interrupted him. "Wait a minute, I want to put this on the speaker so the rest of the family can hear it."

Jake waited as he heard David tell his mother and his brothers that it was Jake on the phone and that he had some news. "Hello Jake." He heard Martha O'Brien greeting him. "Hello Mrs O'Brien. I have some news. We've been able to confirm that Scott planted the bombs we found at David's and at Danny's station. The trial date has also been moved forward and will be on Monday. The DA has confirmed that the charge of committing arson to commit another felony carries a mandatory 10-year term of imprisonment, to run consecutive to any other sentence, and a $250,000 fine. Add to the fact that at least one of the bombs were placed in a government facility, and the DA has enough evidence to put Scott away for at least 20 years." He could almost hear the sigh of relief coming from the entire family.

On Monday, the courtroom was crowded with fire fighters from Minneapolis and Chicago alike. Tara sat in the front row, but as far from Scott as was possible. She was flanked by her mother, her bothers and Shane. Jake and Caffrey had also made the journey to support their friends. Standing nearby, two burly guards stood at attention, ready to act should Scott try anything stupid.

When the charges were read, Scott scoffed at the DA. "You'll never prove it," he boasted. But as the evidence was laid out before the court, it was obvious to everyone, even to Scott, that he would be convicted. When he tried to make a move towards Tara, the judge ordered him shackled.

Leaning over to his attorney, Scott said something that had his lawyer frowning.

"Permission to approach the bench," the lawyer requested.

Tara looked back at Jake, who was seated directly behind her. Jake nodded to her for encouragement, but he didn't like it.

Even though he hadn't been able to prove the connection, he knew that Scott was involved with Nemetskiy. If Scott was now seeking a plea, then there was a chance the judge would give him a reduced sentence. Bagging the known crime boss would be a big feather in the judge's cap and would set him up nicely for re-election.

As the defence attorney returned to his seat, the judge began speaking. "We will have a short recess while I consider my verdict. We will readjourn at two o'clock."

Jake looked down at his watch and saw that it as eleven o'clock. He didn't like it, but he put on a strong front for Tara. Until they knew for sure what the verdict would be, he didn't want to worry her unnecessarily.

Scott was taken back to his cell and Tara and her family exited the courtroom via the side entrance to avoid the press.

Walking up to Lieutenant White, Jake introduced himself. He hadn't had the opportunity before the hearing to meet with the man. Shaking his hand, Jake cut to the chase. "Any idea what's that all about?"

But White shook his head. "Not a clue, but I don't like it." The Lieutenant echoed Jake's thoughts. "But I can tell you one thing, Judge Taylor is a hard noser and doesn't tolerate any messing in his court. Chamberlain's lawyer must have handed him a carrot that he couldn't refuse. At least, not immediately."

"Is he the type of judge who would ignore the safety of a victim to advance his own political agenda?" Jake asked him.

The Lieutenant frowned. "What do you know?"

"Nothing concrete. Well, nothing I can prove right now," was Jake's answer.

The Lieutenant looked like he was considering Jake's question. "Ordinarily, no. But I guess we'll have to wait and see." He finally answered him.

Jake nodded his understanding and then left to be with Tara and her family.

At ten minutes before two o'clock, the O'Brien's returned to the court room. They had managed to get a bite to eat sent in, and thus had managed to avoid any of the press that were hanging around to ask them questions.

Jake got a call from the Lieutenant asking him to meet him in the corridor.

Excusing himself, he went in search of the Lieutenant.

"We've a problem," Lieutenant White began. "Scott Chamberlain was just found in his cell. He hung himself."

"What?" Jake couldn't believe what he was saying. "Suicide?"

But the Lieutenant shook his head. "It was definitely made to look that way. But it's obvious that his throat was cut, and unless Mr Chamberlain was ambidextrous, and somehow managed to smuggle a knife into the court room past the metal detector, then I'd say it was murder."

Jake shook his head. "Any CCTV?"

The Lieutenant shook his head. "I just got done reviewing the footage. There is a gap of five minutes in the footage."

"Shit."

Lieutenant nodded, "You can say that again. We better get back in the court room. The judge is going to make the announcement. Then I need to meet with you to discuss your theories."

Jake nodded his consent and went to join the O'Brien family. Knowing that this would be a new shock that they would need to absorb.

Jake slid in to the row next to his partner. "What's up?" Caffrey asked him as the judge walked into the court room. "You'll find out soon enough," Jake told him.

Calling the room to order, the judge sat a moment considering what he was going to say. Then he looked up and focused on Tara.

"Ms O'Brien. I am very sorry to have to tell you that your ex-husband has been found in his cell. It appears that he has killed himself."

Tara gasped and David took her arm to steady her. "There will be an inquest, but first there is the matter of this court proceedings."

Then he paused before delivering his verdict. Looking down at the paper before him he read, "It is the finding of this court that the defendant, Scott Chamberlain, is guilty on the three charges of attempted murder in the first degree. On the charge of committing arson to commit another felony, Mr Chamberlain is guilty as charged. On the charge of committing an act of terrorism against the state, Mr Chamberlain is guilty as charged." Then the judge looked up at Tara again. "Ms O'Brien, in reading the history of abuse that you sustained at the hand of this man, I can only say that I am very sorry that it took this long to bring this man to justice."

Tara thanked him, and then she finally accepted her family's hugs and words of congratulations.

Shane had stood aside, allowing her family to comfort her. At one point, she had looked up and had offered him a tearful smile as she whispered, "Thank you."

As Jake approached his friends, he made a mental note to check in on his witness. If the Nemetskiy had gotten to a Scott, then he could get to Sarah.

~

Somewhere in IL

The sunlight was streaming in the window and Sarah rolled over on her side, hoping to block out the light. Glancing at her watch, she saw that it was eight thirty. Still too early to get up, she told herself. She had stayed up late the night before studying, still hopeful that she would be able to take the bar exam as scheduled. But as the days dragged on, she became more and more worried that it wouldn't happen.

With only four hours sleep, she knew she needed at least another hour before she would be able to function.

Closing her eyes again, she willed her mind to be blank and then told herself to go back to sleep.

Hearing a knock on the door, she glanced at her watch and saw that it was nearly ten in the morning. 'Shit'. "One moment," she said and then pulled on the sweatshirt she had worn the day before.

Unlocking the door, she opened it to find FBI Agent Ann Cane standing there with a mug of coffee in her hand. "Sorry to wake you, but we've a few things we need to get done today." The woman agent said as she handed her the mug. "Go ahead and get showered and dressed, and meet us in the kitchen."

Sarah thanked her and after closing and locking her door, she rushed to get showered and dressed.

She had been in hiding for over a month, and while she kept mostly to herself, she had tried to get to know the FBI agents who were there to protect her. She suspected that they were getting tired of babysitting her, but they were kind and didn't often show their boredom. After the first week, two of the agents who had brought her to the house had been pull off the detail and now it was just the four of them. Agent Jones was a quiet man who liked to read cookbooks. Both Agents Hanson and Ann Cane would tease him about it, but it was all in good fun.

Sarah had learned that Hanson and Ann had been working together for the last four years, and had only worked with Jones on one other assignment. But the three seemed to enjoy each other's company, despite the task given to them.

She and Ann had gotten a little friendlier, but she still couldn't say that she knew that much about the woman who was protecting her. But something told her that Ann wasn't telling her everything, so she hurried through her morning routine.

Packing up the last of her law books, she decided that she was ready to go should the need arise. She had packed the rest of her things the night before. It was something she had done each day since she had moved in. She didn't have much to pack. While Ann had provided her with a few items of clothing, Sarah had decided to keep her options few, that way she could pack everything up in her backpack and be ready to go at a moment's notice.

When she got to the kitchen, she saw that the team had gathered and were going over some kind of plan.

Looking up from her computer, Ann gave her a warm smile. "We've decided that a change of scenery is in order," she said light heartedly.

What she didn't tell Sarah was that they had received word that a known associate of Nemetskiy had been murdered while locked in a cell at a federal court house. This moved Sarah's security level up a notch.

Sarah couldn't help the frown that appeared on her face. But she tried to sound positive. "Good thing that I'm already packed then," she said and forced a smile on her lips.

Closing her laptop, Ann stood and put her arm around Sarah's. "Don't worry. This is common practice." She lied.

"We better get going," Agent Hanson said from the door.

It had been over a month, and Sarah still didn't know any of the guy's first names, as they always referred to each other by their last names.

"Let me grab my bag," Sarah offered, but as she turned, she saw that Agent Jones had already grabbed her bag. "Thank you," she said as she took her bag from him.

Ushered out to the car, she got in the back seat with Ann and Hanson on either side of her and then they headed off.

Four hours later, they pulled up to a house that looked suspiciously like the one they had just left, with the exception that this one had a large fence around the property.

"Home sweet home," Ann said with a smile as she helped Sarah out of the car.

"Let's get you settled in, and then we'll have some lunch. After that, you and I are going to get some shopping done as well. I'm sure you're getting tired of wearing the same clothes all the time," she added and then turned and walked down the hall.

After Sarah was shown to her room, she put her backpack on her bed and then she followed Ann into the kitchen and found Agent Hanson standing at the stove.

"Good afternoon, Sarah. I'm making toasted sandwiches. What would you like on yours? I've got eggs, ham, and cheese."

Sarah smiled at the man with the apron on. "A ham and cheese sandwich would be great. But I don't want to be any trouble."

Agent Ann laughed. "Oh no you don't. You can't let him off the hook that easy. He lost the coin toss fair and square."

Sarah laughed and sat down at the table next to her. "Would you like another cup of coffee?" Agent Hanson asked as he cracked an egg into the pan.

"Thanks, but I can get it," Sarah said as she started to stand. But Ann put her hand out to stop her. "He's got it," she chuckled.

Sarah remained where she was and let the man serve her. Looking over at Ann, she asked, "Why is he on KP duty?"

Ann looked around at her partner and winked. "He lost the coin toss," she said simply. Then she added, "And he made some strange comment about there being two women in the house to do the housework, so he's paying for the comment."

Sarah smiled. "Serves him right then," she laughed.

As Hanson served a toasted ham and cheese sandwich to her, and a fried egg sandwich to Ann, Ann opened her laptop and typed in a web address. "Unfortunately, we can't take you out to Bloomingdales to get you a decent wardrobe, but we can order some things and collect them," she explained. Pulling up the Macy's website, she pushed her laptop over towards Sarah.

"After you've eaten your lunch, feel free to buy a few outfits. Get the under garments and shoes as well. You'll be here another few weeks at the least, so let's have some fun," she added.

Sarah looked at the website and smiled. She could tell that the young agent was trying to keep her nerves at bay, and she had to admit she was doing a good job at it.

Finishing her sandwich, she pushed the plate to the side and pulled the laptop in front of her. "So, what are you buying?" She asked.

Agent Ann laughed. "I wish," she said and Sarah winked, "who will know?" Ann laughed, and scooted her chair closer to her. "Mmm…let's do some shopping then."

Despite the situation, Sarah found herself relaxing. Ann was easy to talk to and she was making the shopping experience a fun one. Together they had chosen four interchangeable outfits for Sarah and one top for Ann. Ann had convinced Sarah to step out of her comfort level with regard to the styles, but she liked the outfits they had chosen. Sarah usually dressed very conservatively. Sticking to plain clothes that wouldn't draw any attention to herself. But Ann said that she could definitely use a fashion upgrade and had pointed out several trendy, yet edgy outfits. Sarah had agreed to try the outfits, but had insisted on getting one outfit that was more to her usual way of dressing. That way she could slip back to her conservative self if she needed to. Ann reluctantly agreed.

The clothing would be ready later that day, and in the meantime, Ann said that it was time for Sarah to do something different with her hair. "A new fashion deserves a new hair style," Ann said with conviction.

Sarah studied her a moment. "Ann, are you trying to make me look different? I mean, is this part of the plan?" She asked.

Ann smiled. "We just want to make sure you're always safe," was her reply. Then Sarah understood. New clothes, a new hair style, they would be the start of a whole new Sarah. Or would she still be Sarah?

One step at a time she told herself, and nodded her head in agreement.

Two hours later, there was a knock on the bedroom door and Agent Jones informed the ladies that he had collected the clothing they had ordered.

Opening the door a few inches, Ann grabbed the bags from the man and then promptly closed the door again and locked it. Giggling, she set the bags on the bed and waited for Sarah to emerge from the bathroom.

After cutting her hair into a blunt bob with angled bangs, Ann had talked Sarah into dying her blond hair into a dark cherry colour.

Sarah was currently washing the rest of the dye out of her hair.

Stepping from the bathroom, she had a towel wrapped around her head and another around her body.

Ann smiled. "Your new clothes arrived. I took the liberty of throwing in some make up as well. Why don't you pick out one of your new outfits and get dressed, and then come down for the big reveal?"

Sarah laughed. "OK. But on one condition," she added.

Ann looked suspiciously at her. "And that would be?"

"You have to change into the new top you bought and get dolled up as well. Otherwise, I'm going to feel like a kid playing dress up."

Ann laughed but agreed. "See you in thirty minutes?"

Sarah nodded and then gave the woman a quick hug. "Thank you for all your help."

Ann smiled. "It's been my pleasure." Then she walked out of the room, shutting the door behind her.

Locking the door, Sarah opened the bags and started to hang the clothing in the closet, leaving one outfit on the bed.

As promised, Sarah also found a combination of makeup. Grabbing the items, she walked back into the bathroom to dry her hair.

Thirty minutes later, Sarah looked at the image that stared back at her. The changes Ann had suggested had definitely changed how she looked. Once a mousy looking blond, she now had stunning dark cherry hair that complimented her skin tone and looked fun. She had added dark eye makeup and dark purple lipstick that gave her a mysterious look.

One of the outfits Ann had picked, was black jeans and biker boots with a grey studded tee shirt and Sarah had decided to wear it for the reveal, and then she added a raspberry-coloured zip up that she had chosen. The sweater gave the outfit a bit of colour, without having her stick out like a sore thumb, and toned down the rough biker image a bit.

Putting on her own hoop earrings, she looked at her image in the bathroom mirror and smiled. She liked her new look. It gave her a sense of confidence.

Hearing a knock on the door, she asked who it was. "It's me," Ann said. Squaring her shoulders, Sarah unlocked the door and opened it.

Ann had purchased a beautiful pink form fitting blouse that had black strips running through the body of the shirt. It looked amazing on her. She had pulled her hair up into a messy bun and had also added some make up.

Smiling she stepped into Sarah's room and gave her a hug. "You look amazing, Sarah!"

Sarah couldn't help but smile. "Thank you, Ann. I feel amazing. You have a great eye for this kind of thing."

"Let's go down and surprise the boys," she said and then she linked arms with Sarah and they went down to the living room.

The whistles that greeted them told Sarah that they too like the change in her appearance. Blushing, she thanked them. "Thank you everyone. I know that this is all part of the protection package, but I do appreciate your kindness."

Agent Hanson nodded. He was glad she understood why the change was necessary. Or at least understood part of why she needed to change her appearance. He knew that she hadn't been told the whole story. Not just yet. Ann was in charge of her transformation and would be telling her the next stage of the plan in the next day or so. For now, they would allow Sarah to believe that this transformation was just for the time she was to stay at the safe house.

"This calls for a really good meal." Ann winked. "Jones, I believe it's your turn to cook," she said, "and I think Steaks are definitely in order."

Agent Jones laughed. "As I would have expected," he said. "How do you like your steak, Sarah?"

Sarah smiled. "Medium well if you don't mind."

"Not at all. I'm the BBQ king." He boasted and then went out to the kitchen to start planning their meal.

"In the meantime, since you seem to have a whole biker thing going, how would you like to learn to drive a motorcycle?" Agent Hanson asked her.

Sarah gave him a puzzled look. "How did you know that I've always wanted to learn to ride a motorcycle?"

Smith smiled. "I'm physic." Then he laughed. "Actually, you said it to Ann when you were shopping. I just happened to over hear you."

Over the next hour, Agent Hanson walked Sarah thought the physics of riding a motorcycle, and put her through an extensive training program. By the end of the session, Sarah was able to drive the motorcycle around the enclosed driveway with some efficiency. She still had trouble picking up the bike from the fallen position, but Agent Hanson told her that she would eventually be able to pick it up. He told her that it would just take some time to master the technique.

It was nearly five thirty by the time they called it quits and Agent Hanson told her that they could continue the lesson tomorrow if she'd like and she readily agreed.

Agent Jones stepped out of the kitchen with an apron wrapped around his waist. "The baked potatoes will be ready in a half hour if you want to get cleaned up."

Sarah nodded and headed to her room to wash her hands and get cleaned up after her lesson.

Dinner was delicious and Sarah couldn't help but wonder if this was how they always celebrated a transformation, or if they were preparing her for something. Despite her curiosity, she was too nervous to ask. She suspected that she would be told things when the time was right, and if she was honest with herself, in this case, she preferred not to be forewarned. Dr Wilson had been training her to accept changes without the fear she used to experience, and she felt that with his guidance, she was finally able to roll with the punches. Metaphorically speaking.

After dinner, Sarah excused herself and headed to bed. It had been a long day but she knew she needed to get some studying done.

Three hours later, Sarah was lying in bed, thinking about the course her life had taken. After she had left John, she had lived in constant fear that he would find her. She had read her obituary in the paper, but she was afraid that he wouldn't be convinced. Lake Superior was known not to give up it's dead, so it was reasonable that her body wouldn't be found, but John was often a sceptic and he would undoubtedly hire divers to search the wreck of her car. She had left plenty of evidence that she had taken her life.

Along with the suicide note she had left John; she had sent another note to her boss. She had wanted it clear that John was the reason she had killed herself. She wanted other women to be aware of the abuse she had endured, in the hope that no one else would ever experience the same treatment she had endured for over three years. She had carefully planned her suicide, and when she had backed out, she had left everything in the car. If they found her car, they would find a backpack filled with heavy rocks. She had planned to strap two of them to herself to ensure that her body was never found.

A search of the house would show a receipt for the two backpacks. She had stuffed the money she had taken out of the bank into the second backpack and she had planned to fill it too with rocks. It was her hope that the authorities would believe that she had filled the bag with heavy rocks like the other bag, and that it was now weighing down her body on the bottom of the deep lake.

She had left her mobile phone in the car, along with her shoes. More clues that she hoped would lead them to the believe that she had indeed killed herself.

Once her boss informed the police about the second suicide note, she hoped they would arrest John. Unfortunately, she never read any subsequent articles about that, so she wasn't sure if he had been prosecuted or not. Sarah knew that John would claim that she made it all up, but there were those who could collaborate her claim. She had suffered broken ribs and more than one black eye at the hands of John, and her doctor would have her complete medical record, collaborating her claim of abuse.

She wished she could have been braver to just walk away and go to the police, but she knew that he would find some way to punish her. Suicide, she had believed, had been her only solution.

She thought about the mess she now found herself in. She wouldn't consider herself a brave woman, although she supposed some would think she was because she came forward. But she wasn't. In truth, she would have run away already if she thought she would be safer on her own. But escaping the mob was a lot more serious than running away from an abusive boyfriend. Right now, the mob didn't even know that she had been a witness, and both Detective Summers and his boss, Captain Weatherton had ensured her that this would remain the case. But she knew that things could change, and somehow, they could learn her identity. So, she would stay put and wait to see what was going to happen. Tomorrow, she decided, tomorrow she would grab some courage and ask the FBI what the plan was.

Rolling over on her side, she told herself to get some rest. Tomorrow she would get the answers she needed. She hoped.

～

Shane planned on getting to the office early but he was running late. Today was the day Tara would be returning to work.

It had been two weeks since the trial. Tara had taken an immediate leave of absence, needing to spend some time with her family. Since two of her brothers had also been targeted by Scott, the family had decided to take an extended vacation to Ireland. Martha O'Brien still had close relatives who lived near Ennis, Ireland and they had invited the family to spend time with them.

Shane had spoken with Tara nearly every day that she had been abroad, and he had missed her terribly. While their time together had been brief, Shane knew that he had fallen in love with her. What he didn't know, was whether Tara's feelings for him had cooled during her absence.

Tara had flown back to Minnesota on Friday and had spent the weekend looking for a new apartment. She had lost nearly all her belongings when her house was destroyed by the fire that followed the blast, and she said that she needed to shop for everything she would need to start over as well. Shane had volunteered to help her, but she had said that she needed time to herself. He had respected her decision and had let her be.

But he couldn't help but wonder if she was taking the first steps to break it off with him. Hell, since Scott wasn't a threat any longer, Shane couldn't help but wonder if she wouldn't just pack up and move back to Chicago. For all he knew, she could show up at the station and simply hand in her resignation.

But instead of waking up early, as he had intended, he had forgotten to set his alarm or had turned it off in his sleep. All he knew was that it was already 9:00 am and he was still in the shower. Hearing the doorbell, he cursed, "I don't have time for this," he said to himself, before stepping out of the shower. Grabbing a towel, he wrapped it around his waist and headed for the door, calling out as the bell rang again. "I'm coming, I'm coming!"

Flame was barking at the door; the bell obviously having woken him from his morning nap. "Flame! Quiet!" Shane commanded, and the retriever obeyed immediately.

Shane unlocked and opened door, "What can I help you with?" He said before he even saw who was at the door.

"Do you always answer your door wearing nothing but a towel?" Tara smiled up at him.

Shane reached for Tara, pulled her into the house, closed the door behind her and engulfed her in his arms. "God, I missed you!" He whispered before devouring her mouth with a passionate kiss.

Tara hugged him close to her, and returned his passionate kiss. If she had had any doubts about her life, they were gone now.

Lifting his head, Shane gazed into her beautiful eyes. "Before you say anything, Tara, I need you to know that I love you more than ever and I am not going to let you get away from me ever again."

"That isn't a creepy threat or anything." He hurried to clarify, "I love you, and plan on spending the rest of my life showing you just how special you are to me."

Tara smiled, "The rest of your life huh? I don't know." She began to tease him. "Life seems like a pretty short sentence."

Shane smiled back and reached up and touched her cheek. "You're right. It isn't long enough." Then he took her hand and knelt down on one knee. "Tara, will you be my wife? I promise to spend the rest of eternity loving you and showing you how much you mean to me."

Tara knelt down next to him and with tears of joy, smiled, "Yes, Shane. I love you so much. And it's going to take an eternity to show you how much."

Shane pulled her close, only then fully realising that he had proposed to her in nothing but a towel. Not exactly the romantic jester he had hoped for. Smiling against her hair he knew that despite the unconventional method of his proposal, that she wouldn't hold it against him.

～

Fuel

Oak Park, IL

Noise. And lots of it. It seemed to be screaming in her head. And then silence.

She wanted to turn over and fall back to sleep. But she felt like something was pressing her into her bed; And God, her head was pounding. Everything seemed to hurt. *Must be the flu,* she thought as she drifted off to sleep.

Sirens. She said a quick prayer that whoever needed help would be ok and that the rescuers would be fine too. *Keep them safe.* She thought as she drifted off again. Then she could hear someone talking near her. "Female, approximately thirty years of age."

Nice voice, she thought. She wanted to open her eyes and see what was playing on the TV, but her head was killing her and she really didn't want to give her stomach anything else to rebel against. She was fighting nausea, and she couldn't stop shaking.

Someone touched her shoulder. Then her neck. Feeling for a pulse. Ignoring the pain, she opened her eyes, and gazed into the most beautiful blue eyes she had ever seen. "Oh my," she whispered. The blue eyes blinked in surprise. Then they disappeared. "We need a kit over here. Now! She's still alive."

The blue eyes were back. "Miss? Can you hear me?" Shawnee smiled. "Loud and clear handsome." Trying to ignore the pain, she blinked a couple of times trying to focus more on his face. Did she just call him handsome? That was an understatement. Surrounding those great eyes was a strong face, and curly dark brown hair. *Wow,* she thought. As her vision cleared, she started to take in more of her surroundings. Blue eyes was wearing a helmet and a coat with reflective tape. *He's a fireman,* she thought, and then closing her eyes she started to remember.

"Oh my God," she whispered. Opening her eyes again she frowned, "Is everyone else ok?"

He smiled at her, "Yes, everyone else is ok, Miss."

"I tried to stop. I saw the truck starting to turn in front of me." She closed her eyes to the memory. "But my brakes didn't seem to be working. I pumped them and nothing." Shaking her head, "I even tried the damn emergency brake but it felt loose. I couldn't stop."

He touched her shoulder again and she opened her eyes. The tears were streaming down her cheeks. "It's going to be alright," he tried to reassure her. Shawnee gave him a weak smile. "What's your name?" He asked quietly.

"Shawnee. Shawnee Keegan."

"Can you tell me how you feel?"

Shawnee closed her eyes and swallowed back her tears. "Let's see, my head feels like it going to split open at any moment. My back is sore, and so is my left leg. My right wrist hurts a little. Basically, I feel like I got hit by a Mack truck," she said with a smile. She heard him chuckle and she opened her eyes again. "What's your name?" She asked.

"Danny."

"Are you married?" She asked him. That had him blinking in surprise again. "No. No I'm not." She could hear the question in his voice. "Good," she said, "because I plan on seriously kissing you once you get me out of this tin can," he smiled again.

As the truck above her shifted, she closed her eyes and waited for things to settle down again. "Hey, but don't let that deter you from getting me out of here. Ok?"

Danny leaned closer to her and said, "Lady, I'm looking forward it." She looked at him and smiled.

"Keep it up handsome and you may get a little more than just a kiss."

"O'Brien," they heard from behind him.

Danny winked at her and said, "I'll be right back."

"I'm not going anywhere," she replied.

Shawnee closed her eyes, trying not to think about where she was. She couldn't make out what they were saying, but she figured they were determining a plan of action.

"Shawnee," Danny was back. Opening her eyes again she focused on what he was saying. "I need to figure out if you are pinned anywhere, so I need to feel around and check things out. Ok?" Shawnee nodded and closed her eyes again.

She felt him lean in over her and then she felt his hands moving around her body. Touching her hip, her thigh, and her legs.

"Nice legs," he said when he had finished.

"Nice hands," she smiled at him. "I'll be right back." Shawnee kept her eyes closed until he returned.

"How are you doing?" He asked. Shawnee looked at him and smiled weakly, "Did I happen to mention that I'm slightly claustrophobic?"

He shook his head, "Then, I'll try not to do that again."

In spite of herself, she smiled, "Oh, I didn't mind you snuggling in, it's this tin can that I'm not really digging."

"We're working on that right now," he reassured her.

"I trust you. But I don't mind telling you that I'm more than a little frightened right now," she replied honestly.

Danny smiled at her, "You're hiding it well."

Shawnee really didn't want to think about where she was, so she decided to focus on getting out. "So, what's the game plan?"

Danny looked up and said, "Well, first we're going to lift the Mack truck off of your car and then I'm going to slide you out."

"Piece of cake," she said shaker than she wanted.

Danny laid his hand on her shoulder, "I'm going to get you out of this Shawnee."

She looked deep in his eyes and tried to put on a brave face. "Don't get all serious on me O'Brien." Then smiling, she added; "Unless you're serious about the kissing part," she winked.

Danny smiled back. He could see that she was trying to be brave, and damn if she wasn't doing a good job at it. But he also noted that she was also having trouble keeping her eyes open. Checking her pulse again he found it to be still strong. "Get some rest," he said, "we have some stuff to do before we get started." She nodded and let her eyes shut.

She didn't know how long she had slept, but when she felt Danny's hand on her shoulder again, she opened her eyes. "Shawnee, I need to put this blanket over you. It's going to protect you from any broken glass and debris that may fall down when we are lifting the truck."

"Ok," she said quietly.

"Danny," she spoke suddenly.

"Yeah?" He answered her. Her throat was dry and she licked her lips. "I want you to promise me something."

"If I can," he said hesitantly.

Nodding her understanding, she looked him directly in the eyes and continued, "I want you to promise that if anything starts getting too dangerous, that you'll get out of the way."

He started to reply but she pushed on. "I know, it's your job, but I'm the one stuck in this tin can. It's probably my own fault anyway and I'll be damned if I let anyone else get hurt because of me."

Danny didn't know what to say. He knew that he would do whatever was necessary to protect them both. But damn it, he was going to get her out of there. She knew the danger, that was evident. Putting on his sexiest smile he said, "Having second thoughts about giving me that kiss?"

Shawnee smiled. "Not a chance."

"Good, then we have an understanding," he said as he placed the protective blanket around her.

"Shawnee, can you hear me, ok?" Nodding, she tried to control the panic that was starting to overwhelm her.

"Just concentrate on my voice honey. I'm going to grab you under your arms. When the time comes, I'm going to pull you out. We have to do it quickly, so I apologise if you feel any pain because of it."

"That's ok. It'll just cost you another kiss." Her reply was muffled by the blanket. Danny couldn't help but smile at her.

"Get ready."

Danny listened to the men around him, waiting for his signal. When it came, he pulled her out of the car, and several other men joined in to carry her to safety. The blanket was removed, and the paramedics started to work on her just as a portion of the truck fell from the wench and crushed her car. Shawnee stared at the wreck and then turned and asked for Danny. "I'm right here," he said, leaning over her.

She searched his handsome face. "That was a close one, huh?"

Danny smiled. "Plenty of time."

Shawnee reached up and grabbed him by his collar, pulling his head down to hers.

The kiss held all the passion and promise that had been pent up inside her.

Clearing his throat, the paramedic smiled, "Excuse me, but I think we need to get this little lady to the hospital."

Danny pulled away, still a little dazed by the kiss. "Sorry," he murmured to the man.

Shawnee caught the look in his eyes before she was being lifted onto the gurney. "Hey, I warned the man," she said, pleased with the feeling the kiss had left her with.

The paramedic glanced back at the fireman, "Yeah? Well, by the looks of things he's still trying to find his legs after that kiss. Maybe you should have given him more of a warning."

Shawnee laughed quietly as she was lifted into the ambulance.

Danny nodded to the paramedic who let him step into the vehicle. Brushing her hair from her face, he smiled down at her. "Hi. I have to get some stuff done here, but then I'll come see you at the hospital. OK?"

Shawnee smiled back at him and nodded. Then he leaned over and whispered in her ear, "And then we'll talk about that kiss." Shawnee's smile widened and she felt her heart turn over in anticipation. "Looking forward to it," she whispered back.

Jumping down from the ambulance, he helped them close the doors and watched as it sped away.

Turning back to the scene of the accident, he saw that the investigator was already surveying the scene. Walking up to him, he nodded towards the wreckage. "What does it look like to you?"

"A mess." Kevin O'Brien looked over at his younger brother. "And that looked like quite the kiss."

Danny continued to look at the wreckage for a moment before turning his head, "It was." Then nodding back towards the accident, he added, "She said she couldn't stop. Tried the brakes. Nothing. She said even the hand brake didn't work."

Kevin frowned and looked over his shoulder at the direction she had been travelling. No skid marks could be seen. "Looks like I have my work cut out for me."

Danny nodded and added, "I'd like to be kept in the loop on this one."

Kevin looked at his brother and saw the warning in his eyes. Nodding, he said, "I'll see what I can do."

Patting him on the back, Danny smiled, and said, "I know you will." Then he walked over to start helping with the clean-up.

~

It was over two hours later before Danny could stop back at the hospital. He had received word that Shawnee had suffered from a laceration on her head, a concussion, a sprained wrist and a gash on her ankle; that and her back was going to be sore for a while. The doctors had reassured him that they had found no evidence of internal injuries. A small miracle in itself considering the severity of the accident.

Kevin had said that he would need to talk with her about the accident, and had given Danny specific orders not to ask her any questions about what had happened. Danny knew that the preliminary evidence didn't look good.

Shawnee was sleeping when he walked into her room. She would be staying a couple of days for observations, and had been offered a sedative to help her sleep.

Walking up next to her bed, Danny looked at her. Her arm was wrapped up and her head had a large bandage on it to cover the cut she had gotten in the accident. There were dark circles forming under her eyes—further evidence of the trauma she had sustained.

Pulling up a chair, Danny settled himself down to wait out the night. He wanted to be there when she woke up. It seemed important, although he really couldn't explain why.

Half an hour later, he heard movement at the door, and turned to see Kevin standing there. "How is she?" He inquired, walking up to the foot of the bed.

Danny stood up and stretched. "Concussion, sprains...by all accounts she got off pretty damn lucky."

Kevin heard the frustration in his brother's voice and wondered about it. "Has she woken up yet?" He was curious if Danny had 'followed orders' and not spoken to her about the accident.

Shaking his head, Danny said, "No. Not yet. They offered her a sedative. She may sleep through to the morning."

Shawnee heard the voices and smiled, "Or, she may not," she said groggily. Opening her eyes, she was awarded with the sight of two very handsome men. "Now that is what I call a great sight to wake up to, two handsome men standing

84

over my bed." Smiling, she shook her head, "Sorry, whatever they gave me has certainly loosened my tongue. My apologies."

Danny stepped up to the bed and took her hand into his, "I seem to remember I liked that tongue," he winked at her. Blushing, she smiled up at him.

"How are you feeling?" He asked.

"I'm alright. It's nice of you to stop by." Then looking past him, she added, "And it looks like you brought some company." Tilting her head, she studied the other man briefly. "Do I detect a family resemblance?"

Kevin smiled. "Captain Kevin O'Brien, Miss Keegan. Danny's brother."

Like his brother he had dark curly hair, although his was cut shorter, with hazy green eyes. Both men were over six feet tall and built. *Linebackers,* she thought. Unlike Danny, who was still in his uniform, this man wore jeans and a sweater.

Danny shifted to stand at the head of her bed as Kevin continued. "If you are feeling up to it, I'd like to ask you a couple of questions about the accident." Danny frowned at his brother, and laid his hand on her shoulder. "But if you aren't feeling up to it, it can wait until the morning."

Shawnee looked up at Danny and saw the frown on his face. Then she focused on Kevin. "Captain," she acknowledged his title. "Can I assume that you are with the fire department as well?"

Kevin nodded. "Yes, Miss. I am the investigator assigned to the case."

There was something about the look in his eyes that gave her a warning that his questions were not going to be easy ones. Pushing herself up to a sitting position, she tried to ignore the pounding in her head and concentrate on his questions. "Ask away."

Reaching in his coat pocket, he took out a small tape recorder and a notebook. "Do you mind if I tape this conversation?"

"Not at all." She looked directly into his eyes. Kevin like her directness.

"What can you tell me about the accident."

"I was driving down the expressway, on my way to go grocery shopping. I'm not sure what exactly happened up ahead, but I saw the semi swerve and then it started to topple over. I slammed on my brakes. Or I should say, I tried to slam on my brakes. They didn't work."

"How do you mean?"

She looked down, considering her answer—trying to remember it all accurately. "They felt loose." She shook her head, "Not loose. Just not there. My foot went all the way down to the floor. There wasn't any resistance at all." She looked back at him, "I tried to pump them a few times…but once I hit them, they never came back up from the floor. I guess I panicked, because I tried to pull the emergency brake as well, but that didn't help either."

Closing her eyes, she took a deep breath before continuing. "I must have closed my eyes when I hit the semi. I think I tried to turn to miss it. I tried to get my seat down too. I don't know if I did or not. The next thing I remember is the noise." She rubbed her hand on her arm as she opened her eyes again. "Then it was quiet. I must have passed out. I don't know. I remember hearing the sirens and thinking that I wanted the noise to stop."

Smiling, she chuckled, "I was kind of out of it. I thought I had the flu and needed some sleep." Then she looked up at Danny and winked. "Then I heard your voice and I wanted to know who had the great voice. I thought you were on the television."

Danny smiled down at her.

Kevin studied her for a moment before asking, "Miss Keegan, when was the last time you had your car serviced?"

Shawnee looked back at him. The question obviously had surprised her. "I don't remember." Then frowning, she admitted, "I'm not very good about that kind of thing. I think it was about a year ago? Last fall? I took it in to have the oil changed before the snow started to fly."

Kevin looked down at his notepad. "And you haven't had anyone else work on your car since?"

Shawnee frowned. "No…Captain O'Brien, can you tell me what this is all about? What does not having my oil changed have to do with my accident?"

Kevin looked up at his brother with an unmistakable look of concern on his face. "What?" She asked.

Danny put his hand on her shoulder again before Kevin continued. "Is there anyone that you know who would want to scare you or harm you in any way?"

Shawnee's eyes widened at the implication, then she looked up at Danny. "What the hell is he talking about?"

Danny looked in her eyes and repeated his brother's question. "Shawnee, is there anyone?"

Shawnee shook her head, "No! I don't understand. Why are you asking me that?"

She reached up and put her hand to her head. It was really starting to pound and she was having troubles concentrating. She had to have misunderstood what they were asking.

Danny saw the confusion in her eyes, and he looked over at Kevin who was watching her as well.

Kevin looked at his brother, then addressing Shawnee, "I'm sorry," he said, "but it appears that someone cut your brake lines."

"Cut them?" Shawnee really couldn't believe what she was hearing. "You mean they broke. Right?" Shrugging off Danny's hand. She needed to focus on what was happening and not be distracted by his presence. Rubbing her temples, she tried to gather her thoughts. "It's my fault, right? I should have taken better care of my car." Then looking up into Danny's eyes she looked for some reassurance that she was on the right track. "That's what he meant right?"

Danny sat down on the side of her bed and took her hands in his. The look on his face spoke volumes. "No!" She whispered in disbelief.

Kevin had come around the bed and pulling his mobile phone out of his pocket, he scrolled down the list of contacts and hit the number he wanted. It was answered on the second ring.

"Jake, it's Kevin O'Brien. I need to you come down to Mercy Hospital as soon as possible." Nodding into the phone, he said, "Yes, that's right. I've just confirmed that with Miss Keegan." He listened for a moment and then ended the call.

"They will be here in a few minutes."

"Who? Who will be here?" Shawnee was having difficulty taking it all in. Sneezing her hands, Danny drew her attention back to him. "The police. Shawnee, everything is going to be alright."

But Shawnee just shook her head. "No, it isn't," she whispered. "Not if what you're implying is true." Closing her eyes, she allowed him to pull her into his arms. Her head rested on his shoulder as she felt her control slipping.

Danny looked up at his brother and Kevin could see the concern on his face. Laying his hand on her back, he gently rubbed her back, trying to calm her.

"Why?" She whispered; her voice clogged with unshed tears. Danny shook his head, unable to speak. His throat was raw with emotion.

But she knew that they had no answers for her. Not yet anyway.

Taking a deep breath, she pulled back from Danny's embraced and looked into his troubled eyes.

A knock at the door drew their attention, and the nurse requested a moment of her time for some tests.

As both men waited outside the door, Danny turned towards Kevin. "Does Jake have anything yet?" Kevin shook his head. "Not that he told me. But we'll know soon enough."

～

Jake Summers walked into Mercy Hospital where he was met by one of the patrol officers from his precinct. "John." He nodded to the man as they both entered the elevator for the fourth floor. "How's Milly?"

"She's doing good. Ready to burst." Jake smiled. Milly was expecting the couple's third child and it was due any time. The office pool had her going full term, but Jake had her pegged to go early. He had ten dollars ridding on it. He had worked with John Doyle for the better part of a decade and he had been there for the births of his first two sons.

He found Danny and Kevin standing outside the room. One look at the two brothers and he knew there was going to be more to the story then he would have liked.

After shaking hands, Danny spoke first. "What do you have?"

Jake studied him a moment. "Rumour has it you and the young lady locked lips. Anything I should know about that?"

"Not a damn thing," Danny replied hotly.

Kevin shook his head and turning towards his brother, he reasoned with him. "I would have asked the same question, Danny."

Running his hand through his hair he nodded. "Sorry Jake. No, I do not have a prior relationship with her. She kissed me to thank me for saving her life."

Jake smiled, "From what I heard it was quite the kiss."

Danny smiled, "It was. And if you're going to ask what I think you are going to ask, yes, I'm interested in her. But right now, I just want to get to the bottom of this mess."

Nodding, Jake motioned to the closed door. "Is she ready to talk to me?"

Danny's smile faded. "I guess you'll have to ask her that." Then he added, "Go easy on her. She's had quite the shock." Jake nodded in agreement.

～

After the nurse had left, Shawnee was left alone with her thoughts. 'Who could have tampered with her car, and who would want to hurt her?' It had to be a case of mistaken identity she decided. Some idiot had simply messed with the wrong car. All they had to do was lift some fingerprints, run a make on them and they'd have their guy. Isn't that how it worked in the movies? Her life would be back to normal in no time.

Closing her eyes, she tried to ignore the nagging feeling that it wasn't going to be quite that easy.

Hearing a knock on the door, she opened her eyes to see Danny coming back into the room, and looking past him, she saw his brother Kevin and another man walking in behind him.

"I see you brought the Calvary with you," she swallowed back the lump of fear she felt rising in her throat.

"Shawnee, this is Detective Jake Summers with the Chicago Police Department. He'd like to ask you a couple of questions."

"Detective." She nodded to the man. He looked to be just less than six feet tall with dark hair that was salt and peppered at his temples. A handsome man who, she estimated to be in his thirties. But by the tired look on his face, he looked closer to forty.

"Miss Keegan, Captain O'Brien has filled me in on your statement. I will have to ask you to make a formal statement downtown when you are up to it…but right now I just have a few more questions. If you don't mind."

Shawnee nodded. "If you're going to ask me who would want to hurt me, I can tell you that I have absolutely no idea. I really believe that it's going to come down to a case of mistaken identity." She rushed on, wanting to put this matter to rest. "I was parked at the North Oak Shopping Centre before I drove on the highway, and someone must have mistaken my car for someone else's."

Jake studied her for a moment, and decided that he believe her. She really didn't have any idea of what this was all about.

Walking up to her, he looked over at Danny before addressing her. "Miss Keegan. We've already checked that angle. Unfortunately, it isn't looking quite that cut and dry."

Shawnee frowned. Then taking a deep breath she said, "I was afraid you would say that." Looking up at Danny, she shook her head, "Maybe you should have opted out of that kiss. It looks like my life is going to get a little more complicated." Danny tilted her chin up and said, "No way, lady. I like complicated."

Clearing his throat, Jake frowned, "This is more than just a little complicated. Miss Keegan."

Shawnee turned back with a loud sigh. "Please call me Shawnee."

Nodding in agreement, Jake continued, "Shawnee, do you know a man by the name of James Prizrak?"

Shawnee shook her head no. "I didn't expect that you would have." Jake replied. " He doesn't usually work in these parts, and unless I miss my mark, he doesn't usually mingle in your crowd."

Kevin had come up to join them, "The Rack?" He whispered with a frown. Jake looked back at him and nodded.

"The Rack? What the hell kind of name is that?" Danny questioned his brother, but he was met with a stern look.

Shawnee frowned as she studied their sombre faces. "I take it he's not one of the good guys."

Jake shook his head. "No, he isn't. Prizrak is usually hired to encourage witnesses into not testifying. He specialises in creating 'accidents', setting fires…anything to scare the victim into not working with us."

Danny now understood why they called him the Rack.

Shawnee was shaking her head. "No. You have to be wrong about this. I'm not testifying against anyone."

Jake looked grimly at her. "It's definitely Prizrak."

Pushing herself up out of the bed, she reached for the robe at the foot of her bed and slipped it on. She was feeling her control starting to slip and she wanted to take some control over what was happening.

"Well, that may be, but I'm telling you, Detective, you've got the wrong girl. I haven't been asked to testify against anyone, and I'm not planning on testifying against anyone."

Standing now by the window, she folded her arms in front of her, and tried to control the shaking that was threatening to buckle her knees, as she faced off in front of the three men.

All three men saw the same thing. A frightened woman who was trying desperately not to be.

Shawnee saw Danny start to move towards her, but she held up her hand. She didn't want to crumble in front of them.

"I'd like you all to leave now if you don't mind." Biting her lip, she tried to control the shaking in her voice. "I'm a little tired and I'd like to get some sleep now."

Danny nodded his understanding, and turned towards the other two gentlemen. "You heard the lady. Let's go."

Jake wanted to press for more answers, but he too could see that she was about ready to break.

At the door, Danny led the other two out before turning back to look at her. "I'll be right outside if you need anything Shawnee."

Shawnee nodded as the tears began to fall.

Turning, he was about to leave when he heard her whisper, "Please hold me."

Closing the door, he was by her side in three strides and held her close as she gave into to her tears.

Reaching down, he picked her up and carried her to the bed and gently laid her down. "I'm sorry," she whispered.

"Stop it," he said quietly. "You have nothing to be sorry for."

Taking a deep breath, she laughed shakingly. "Yes, I do. I'm sure this was the last thing you wanted in your life right not." Shaking her head, she tried to take control of her emotions. "I'm all right. Really. I think I just need some sleep."

Danny saw that she did look exhausted and kissed the top of her head before standing up. "Ok. You get some rest. Jake has an officer staying outside your door so you'll be safe, and I can stay if you'd like. Or is there anyone I can call…"

"No, that's ok, Danny. You're probably exhausted too. Thank you though. It means a lot to me." Danny nodded and started for the door.

"Danny," he turned back to look at her.

"Thank you for saving my life," she said quietly.

Smiling at her, he said, "It was my pleasure, Shawnee. More than you know. Now get some rest."

Sliding down under the sheets she said, "The pleasure was all mine, Danny. Good night."

Danny quietly closed the door behind him and found Kevin and Jake waiting for him. Kevin nodded towards the closed door, "Is she alright?"

"No, but she will be," Danny said, turning to Officer Doyle. "I'd appreciate a call if she needs anything."

John looked to Jake for confirmation. Getting it, he nodded and said, "She'll be fine. Get some rest, Danny."

Danny nodded. Looking back at the closed door, he turned and said, "Let's go get a beer first. I think I need one."

Kevin grabbed Danny around the shoulders. "You're buying."

"And then you're going to tell me everything you can about this Prizrak character," Danny told them.

~

It had been a hell-la-va couple of days.

Every few hours a nurse would come in to check her vitals. She seemed to time her visits just as Shawnee was starting to fall back to sleep. When the nurse finally decided that Shawnee was going to live through the night and that her vital signs had not drastically changed over the last few hours, she was finally told to 'get some sleep' and then mercifully left to do just that.

Danny hadn't stopped by, or at least not that she had known about. She had slept most of the time. She had heard that there had been a large warehouse fire and had wondered if he had been called in to work it. She had said several prayers for his safety.

Now it was morning, and despite her fitful sleep, her internal clock was telling her that it was time to wake up.

Rolling out of the bed, she padded to the bathroom. After using the facilities, she was happy to find a comb, a toothbrush and tooth paste at her disposal. While brushing her teeth, she took a hesitant look at her face. The dark circles under her eyes did little to add colour to her pale cheeks. Shaking her head, she realised that it could be worse.

Walking back to the bed, she sat down and began to comb out her hair, as there was a knock at her door. "Are you decent?" She heard Danny say as he slid open the door. His handsome face appeared around the corner of the door, and he faked a frown. "Darn, you are."

Shawn shook her head and smiled. "Good morning."

"Good morning to you." He sat down next to her and kissed her soundly on the lips. "Mmmm, minty fresh."

Shawnee gigged, and pushed him away. "Look what I've created." She joked.

"I'm sorry I didn't get a chance to see you yesterday." He looked seriously sorry.

Shawnee smiled at him, "That's alright. I heard there was a fire." Surprised that she had heard, he studied her for a moment, "Yeah." He confirmed. She couldn't help but ask, "Everyone make it out alright?" Kissing the top of her head he said yes.

Seeing that he held something in his hand she looked around him in interest. As he hid it further behind his back, she tilted her head seductively and looking out of the corner of her eye said, "What do you have there?"

Looking back over his shoulder, he said, "Oh, just a little something I picked up." Then looking at her, he pulled a bouquet of daisies from behind his back. "They reminded me of sunshine. And of you," he said sweetly.

Shawnee blushed at the compliment, but looked from the flowers to his eyes and thanked him with a kiss. "Thank you, Danny."

"I'll put them in some water," he offered. As he filled her water pitcher with more water, he said, "I also brought you a little bag of something."

Putting the impromptu vase of flowers on her table, he reached down and pulled up a shopping bag. "I, ummm…" he cleared his voice, "took the liberty of picking up some of your clothing from your townhouse. Rumour has it they are going to spring you today and since your clothes were a little worse for wear…" he smiled at her shocked face and handed her the bag.

Looking up at him she shook her head, "Mister, you are definitely full of pleasant surprises."

Taking the bag from him, she excused herself and went into the bathroom to change.

As she slipped in the bathroom, Danny walked over to the window and looked out at the brightening skies. What he hadn't told her was that he had talked Jake into letting him accompany him to her townhouse to look for some clue about who was trying to scare her. They hadn't found much. From what Jake had hold him, Prizrak wasn't known to leave clues behind. Danny had asked him how he was so sure it was Prizrak, and he had stated that it was certain patterns that had been established, which he could not discussed. "Suffice to day, the 'accident' has all the classic Prizrak trademarks."

In the bathroom, Shawnee opened the bag and found a short sleeve shirt, a pair of shorts, sandals and one of her skimpiest bra and panty sets. She blushed at the thought of him going through her lingerie drawer and finding them.

Stripping off her hospital gown, she was glad she had taken a shower the night before, and quickly got dressed.

Folding up the gown, she put it in the clothesbasket. Taking a glance at herself in the mirror and feeling relatively sure she looked 80% alright, she opened the door.

Danny was standing by the window and turned to look at her. He saw the blush on her cheeks and remembered the pretty under garments he had picked out for her. He had liked what he had seen in her drawer and had taken his time picking out the right one.

"Hi."

He smiled at the husky sound of her voice. "Hi to you," he replied walking up to her. Running his finger up her arm, he laced it around her collar. Smiling down at her he whispered, "I liked your pretty things."

She blushed, and smiled up at him. "Ahh huh. You must have. I'm pretty sure this particular set was in the very back of that drawer." She saw his eyes cloud over with desire as he brought his head down to hers.

There was fire behind the kiss and she heard herself sigh as she melted into it. Danny pulled her into his embrace and felt her body mould into his. God, she felt good. Perfect. And he knew that a kiss would not be enough to put out the flames he felt building within him.

Lifting his head from hers, he watched her eyes slowly open and look into his, and he saw her desire as well. "I want you," he said simply.

Shawnee blinked, clearing her vision and looked at him clearly. Smiling, she nodded. "But damn if our timing doesn't suck."

Danny tipped his head back and laughed. Kissing her soundly on the lips he smiled down at her. "Lady, you do have a way of telling it like it is."

"Ah um…Am I interrupting anything?" Kevin was standing at the door smiling.

Putting his arm around her, Danny, smiled at his brother and said, "Not yet."

Kevin smiled at Shawnee. "How do you feel this morning?"

"Good thank you." Then she frowned slightly. "What do I owe you for this visit?"

Danny nodded over at his brother. "Don't worry. He's with me." Shawnee looked up at him for an explanation as she stepped out of his embrace.

Danny smiled at her. He had a mischievous look in his eyes and she looked at him suspiciously. "What have you got up your sleeve, Mr O'Brien?"

Kevin laughed, "Can't put much passed her, can you, Danny?"

Danny winked. "Now darlin' you know you can trust me." Shawnee folded her arms in front of her and smiled. "Uh huh…"

Danny smiled, "It's Saturday. And since we're going to spring you from this place, we thought you'd like to join us for a little fun." Her eyebrow moved up a notch.

Kevin shook his head and intervened. "What my little brother is trying say is that we would like to invite you to join us for the annual Fireman/Policeman's softball game. It's usually a pretty good time. Lots to eat and drink and all the proceeds go to the children's hospital." Putting on the charm, he smiled adding, "And I would be honoured if you accompanied me."

Danny put a possessive arm around Shawnee and added, "Back off, Bro."

Then he smiled down at her, "What do you say honey? Is it a date?" He added with a wink.

Shawnee laughed, "Now, how can I possible turn down two charming gentlemen? Thank you. I'd be happy to join you."

Danny gave her a kiss on the cheek. "Great! Now let's spring you from this joint."

~

An hour later, and after much argument with the nurse on duty, Shawnee was sitting in a camp chair, with a beer in her hand, watching the two teams square off.

Danny had taken great care in establishing that she was his guest, and she couldn't help but laugh at him. Everyone had heard about 'the kiss' and he had been teased since they had shown up at the field. She felt a little embarrassed by it all. But as she watched him take the field, she felt her heart thump. He was an attractive man, and there was something that really pulled her to him. He turned and smiled at her, and her heart did another summersault. The man liked her and that sure made her feel good.

"Mind if we join you?"

Shawnee looked up and saw Officer Doyle with a little boy in his arms and another hanging on his leg. "Of course not," she smiled.

"This," nodding towards the boy in his arms, "is Tony, and the monkey on my leg would be John Jr."

"Hi!" She smiled at the boys. Then she saw a very pregnant woman standing behind him.

"This is my wife, Milly." Shawnee smiled at her. "Hello." She looked down at the woman's oversized belly and couldn't help but ask, "Due anytime soon?"

Milly smiled, she like this lady already. "A little less than a month," she replied.

"Two weeks." came an answer from behind her, and Shawnee looked around and saw Detective Summers wave, as he joined his teammates.

"He has a couple of bucks riding on the pool at work," John smiled. "Thinks that just 'cuz he's been right twice before that he'll win again this time around."

Shawnee smiled and studied the woman who was now sitting beside her, cheering the police team on. "Less than that. I'd say any day now," she said, and Milly turned to look at her. Yes, she definitely liked her.

"Put her down for less than a week John," then she winked at her, "my money's on her."

Shawnee laughed and turned back towards the game. The firemen were in the field, having won the coin toss. She saw that Kevin was pitching while Danny was playing shortstop. She watched Danny chatting with the second baseman, and when she caught his eye, the look took her breath away. *Man, oh man,* she thought. That man was going to be dangerous. Then he shifted his eyes to the plate. Settling back, Shawnee took a sip of her beer and concentrated on the game.

꒛

"Hey Ump! Whose payroll are you on?"

Shawnee laughed and handed Milly another cold water. "He's going to eject you if you keep that up," she smiled at her. Milly flushed. "He won't dare. I know his wife." She let out another curse and groaned.

"Up!"

Shawnee looked down and saw little Tony standing next to her chair. Picking him up, she sat him on her lap.

"Honey," Milly reached for her son.

"He's alright." Shawnee smiled down at him. He smiled up at her and snuggled up to her. Milly smiled as she saw his lids begin to drift shut. Shawnee smiled back at her and then focused on the game again.

The game was a close one, going into extra innings; and while the competition was fierce, the men also razed each other good-naturedly. It was the top of the eleventh inning and the game was once again tied. The firemen were up to bat, bases were loaded and Danny was up to bat. He had played well, but had failed to hit his legendary grand slam.

Milly had told her that every year he had managed to sneak at least one grand slam into the game, and she was surprised that he hadn't hit one today. Shawnee looked over at him and hoped that she wasn't somehow the cause of it. He had chatted with her between every inning, and she had seen him looking over at her several times throughout the game and she didn't want to be the reason for any lack of concentration.

The first ball was high and away. Danny stepped back and looked over at Shawnee. Tony had fallen asleep on her lap and she had her cheek resting on the top of his head. Their eyes met. "Hit it out of here, handsome," she whispered. Danny smiled and turned back towards the pitcher.

It was a beautiful sight. Milly was out of her seat screaming, despite the fact that her husband's team had just lost the game. Shawnee smiled and kissed the sleeping Tony on the head as she watched Danny take the bases in a slow jog, receiving high fives from both team members. When they heard a car alarm sound, they knew that the ball had finally fallen out of the sky and she chuckled. She had a suspicion that he had waited for that moment to pull out all the stops, but she couldn't be sure, so she decided to enjoy the feeling that he had done it for her. Silly she knew, but she liked the idea all the same.

Shawnee watched Danny stride up towards her. He had a twinkle in his eyes that had her smiling.

"Here, I can take him." Milly reached down and picked up her sleeping son, who wiggled briefly in his mother's arms before settling back into his nap. "I think another boy is going to want your arms for a moment," she winked.

Shawnee smiled up at Danny as he pulled her to her feet, "I missed you," he whispered as he lowered his lips down to hers. The kiss was gentle, but held the promise of more. Tipping her head back, she smiled, "Nice hit."

Looking over his shoulder to where the ball had disappeared, he said, "Yeah? Not too bad." Shawnee stepped back and laughed.

"Hey O'Brien?" One of Danny's teammates called over to him, "You and your girl coming over to Sweeney's?"

Danny looked back down at Shawnee, "You still feeling up to it?"

Nodding, she said, "Sure."

Danny turned and called back, "We'll see you over there."

Shawnee turned and started to help Milly gather up her children's toys. "Will you and the boys be going?"

"For a little while. It's fun. Did you bring your suit?"

"Suit?"

Milly laughed, "Swim suit."

Looking back up at Danny, Shawnee asked, "Did I?"

Danny smiled and said, "I'll go get my gear."

Milly laughed. "That boy is going to get himself into some serious trouble one of these days." Shawnee smiled and shook her head. "If he hasn't already."

Danny was putting his gear bag in the back of the truck when Kevin joined him. "'Your girl' huh?"

Danny looked over to where Shawnee was helping Milly with the kids. "Sounds pretty good."

"Danny." He heard the warning in Kevin's voice. Turning back to his gear bag, Danny frowned. "I know." Then he looked over at his brother. "Let's just find the son of a bitch, ok?"

Kevin studied his brother for a moment and saw something in his eyes that he knew meant business. "We'll get him."

"Are you boys finished discussing my life, or do I have to remind you that this is supposed to be when you guys take my mind off my troubles?"

The look of guilt that flashed over their faces was priceless, and Shawnee bend over in a fit of laughter. "Oh, that was good." Milly laughed with her.

"Women!" The bothers agreed, and helped Shawnee with the cooler.

～

Sweeney, it turned out, was a former fireman from Danny's station. He owned a large house on five acres of land just outside of Palos Park, Illinois. And he liked to entertain. As tradition would have it, he always invited the players and their families out to his place for a post-game celebration. Tents were pitched, the grill was lit and the pool was filled with bodies.

Shawnee felt a little overwhelmed as she was introduced to a number of people, all who had already heard about the kissing episode. Danny had indeed brought one of her bathing suits. The bikini, of course, and Shawnee was 'encouraged' to slip into it. Danny led her to the upstairs bathroom, and slipped into the adjacent bedroom to change into his swim trunks.

Shawnee pulled on her suit and stood scrutinising her appearance. While, the bandage on her head had been downgraded to a smaller one, she still had one wrapped around her strained wrist. There was a bruise on the calf of her left leg that was turning a dark purple, and she had bruises on her right thigh and across her lower back.

Reaching for her shorts, she was about to change back into her regular clothes when she heard a knock. "Shawnee? Is everything alright?"

Closing her eyes, she said, "No. I have to change back into my shorts."

Danny started to open the door, "Can I come in?"

She gave up. "If you want."

Danny caught her eyes in the reflection. "Hi," he said. His voice was husky and she felt her heart turn. As his eyes started to follow her reflection, Shawnee watched his face for some reaction. "You're beautiful," he said, his voice was thick with desire. It wasn't until he reached out to touch her shoulder that he noticed the bruising on her back. "Oh baby," he said. Feeling self-conscious, she wrapped her arms around her stomach.

"I need to put my clothes back on."

The look of confusion was instant. "Why?"

Turning around, she faced him. "Danny, I can't go out like this."

He could see the sadness that had crept into her eyes. Putting his finger under her chin he lifted her head to look at him. "Shawnee, you're beautiful. Those are nothing but bruises and believe me honey, they don't take anything away from that."

Shawnee shook her head. "Shawnee, we're talking about a bunch of firefighters and policemen. They've seen their share of injuries in the past; and honey, they all know what you've just been through."

Smiling, he added, "Trust me. One look at you in that suit and I'll be beating them back with a stick!"

Shawnee laughed and put her arms around his neck. "Why are you so nice to me?"

"Oh honey, if you haven't guessed that one yet, then I'm going to have to work a little harder at showing you why." He drew her up against him and took her lips in a scorching kiss. Shawnee groaned as she felt his hard body pressed up against hers.

"Danny" she breathed his name as his kisses left her mouth and blazed a path down to her neck. His hands were sending quivers of pleasure down her back and she arched to press herself closer to him. She buried her hands into his hair and drew his mouth back up to hers, needing to lose herself again in his kiss.

A sound outside the bathroom door had him groaning in frustration. Shawnee giggled, and he lifted his head to look into her eyes. "Lady, you don't know what you do to me."

Shawnee smiled and kissed him lightly on the lips again. "Handsome, I know exactly what you do to me and, whew…" she shook her head. Stepping back, she smiled at him and said, "Maybe we should join the others before we get too carried away."

"You are far too practical," he complained as he picked up her bag and opened the door. Grabbing the sarong that he had also brought for her, she wrapped it around her waist, smiling, she added, "I don't know about that."

She looked shyly into his eyes. "I just don't want to be interrupted when the time is right."

Danny tilted his head back and groaned. "You're going to kill me."

Laughing, she took his arm and led him down to the party.

She was glad that the party was in full swing when they got down to the pool. Danny's easy-going nature helped her to forget her self-consciousness and she found herself relaxing and enjoying herself. When Danny was grabbed from behind, she turned and laughed as Sweeney said, "It looks to me like Danny Boy could use a little cooling off." And with the help of a couple of other firemen, he was thrown into the pool. Laughing, Shawnee saluted the man and took a sip of the beer that had been handed her.

She yelped in surprise when she was suddenly grabbed from behind. Kevin winked at his brother and said, "This little lady looks like she could use a swim as well."

"Oh no you don't," she warned as Kevin dangled her over the pool.

"She's just a little thing," he said to his brother. Sliding her in the water, she laughed up at him. He winked and whispered to her, "I know you shouldn't get those bandages wet. I was just foolin' with you."

Shawnee smiled up at him and laughed when he too was suddenly pushed into the water.

Danny swam up to her and draping his arm around her shoulder, he held her eyes as he took a sip of her beer. "Hey, get your own," she elbowed him in the side and took her beer back from him. Danny flashed her a quick smile, "I'll be right back," he promised and pulled himself out of the pool.

Shawnee leaned back against the side and taking another sip of her beer watched as several other guys were tossed into the pool.

Feeling Danny next to her, she looked up at him as he sat down on the side of the pool next to her. She laughed as another man fell victim to the pool patrol.

A whistle sounded and Kevin swam over to retrieve Danny for a game of water volleyball. Asked if she would want to play, Shawnee frowned and held up her bandaged wrist. "Sorry, but I'll have to sit this one out. Go ahead though. I'll watch."

Offering her a hand out of the water, Danny lifted her gently onto the side of the pool. "Are you ok?" She nodded and smiled up at him. Kissing her, he winked and said, "This shouldn't take too long."

Kevin shook his head and laughed.

Three sets later, Danny joined her with fresh beers for the both of them. "Having fun?" Smiling she nodded and asked, "How long have you been with this group?" Danny looked around for a moment and said, "My whole life." Tilting her head, she looked questioning at him.

"My father was a fireman. So was my granddad. I guess you could say it's in the blood." Danny flashed her a quick smile.

Shawnee held up her beer and clinked it to his. "To firemen." Clinking his bottle with hers, he looked deep in her eyes, and at that moment, Danny knew. This lady was special. Shawnee felt drawn into his gaze. Her heart did another summersault.

"Anyone hungry?"

Shawnee smiled up at Milly who was holding a plate full of brats and potato salad.

Standing up, Shawnee thanked her and took the plate from her. Then she saw a look pass over Milly's face and she handed the plate to Danny and grabbed Milly by the arm. "Sit down," she ordered as Milly suddenly grabbed her stomach.

Danny took one look at Milly's face and looked around for John. Grabbing his wrist, Shawnee put one hand on Milly's belly and watched the second hand on his watch.

Milly was breathing through the contraction, and as it passed, Shawnee smiled at her. "Well, it looks like I may win that bet after all. Danny?"

Danny had taken his watch off and had given it to her. "You need to find John now. And you better call an ambulance as well."

"What?"

Danny looked from Milly back to Shawnee. "It's time Danny," she said matter-of-factly. Then as another contraction came, she said, "Go!"

Danny didn't need to be told twice. Turning, he located John, and grabbing his cell phone from his bag, he started to dial 911 as he hurried towards him.

࿚

"They said it would be about half an hour before the ambulance gets here," he informed them. Shawnee, looked up at Danny and he could read the urgency in her eyes. "I think we need to move her someplace with a little more privacy," she said calmly.

Gently lifted by a number of the men, Milly was put in the guest bedroom. Shawnee turned to Danny and said, "Have you ever helped deliver a baby before?"

Danny frowned at her. "The ambulance…" Shawnee put her hand on his shoulder and looking in his eyes said. "The ambulance is not going to be here on time."

"How do you know that?"

Shawnee smiled. "This is what I do, Danny. I'm a midwife. I help deliver babies. Now, is there anyone here who has delivered a baby before?"

"I don't know, but I'll find out."

Shawnee reached up and kissed him. "She's going to be fine, Danny. She is just going to have her baby here and now."

Danny found one officer who had delivered a baby in the back of his car and dragged him to the bedroom.

Milly was swearing as another contraction took her. "You're doing fine Milly." Shawnee looked over at John who looked a little whiter than she would have liked. "John, I need you to sit behind Milly, and hold her up. OK?"

Doing as he was told, John sat behind his wife and held on to her hands. Turning to Danny, Shawnee asked him to keep an eye on Milly's pulse, and to let her know if he felt any significant changes. Turning to the officer who was there to help, she asked him to be ready should she need him. Receiving a nod from the officer, Shawnee lifted the sheet and examined Milly again.

"Ok, Milly, it's time to push now. Just one good push ok?" Milly nodded, took a deep breath and pushed.

"Good." Looked over at Danny, she received a nodded, she said, "One more push Milly, you can do it." Milly pushed again.

Shawnee looked up and smiled at Milly and John, "Congratulations," she said as she produced a crying baby, "you have a beautiful baby girl."

Handing the baby to the officer who wrapped the crying baby in a blanket, he then handed her to her parents, Shawnee looked over at Danny, and after he confirmed that her vitals were stable, she then she concentrated again on the task at hand.

When the ambulance came, Danny stepped out of the room and was handed a beer. "The lady's full of surprises, isn't she?" Kevin nodded towards her. Danny took a long drink and nodded.

Stepping into the bathroom, Shawnee stripped out of her bathing suit and set it in the sink to soak while she took a quick shower.

Ten minutes later she was clean and dressed in her shorts and tee again. The bandage on her wrist was tossed, and she decided that she would forgo another one. Opening the door, she found Danny waiting for her. He seemed quiet.

"Kevin drove John and the boys to the hospital to see Milly and the baby," Shawnee nodded, watching his eyes.

"Care if we take off too?" He added.

She took the hand that was offered her. "That's fine."

After saying their goodbyes, Danny helped Shawnee into the truck and they drove off in silence. Half an hour later, Danny pulled off onto a dirt road and stopped the truck. Turning to her, he pulled her into his arms and kissed her. Shawnee was instantly lost in the kiss, caught up in the passion.

Lifting his head, Danny tried to catch his breath. Shawnee opened her eyes and looked deep into his eyes. She would read the desire in his eyes and knew that she wanted to drown in it. Unbuckling her seatbelt, Shawnee reached over and unbuckled his seatbelt as well, then she opened her door and tugged on his hand in an invitation to join her.

Around them dusk was starting to settle on the valley. He walked up behind her and drew his arms around her. "It's beautiful out here," she said softly, enjoying the feel of his arms around her. Kissing the top of her head, he murmured in agreement and then buried his lips in her neck. With the simple kiss, Shawnee felt desire warm through her. Turning in his arms she looked up at him.

"I don't move fast," she said.

"Neither do I," he replied as his lips took hers. Desire slammed through her and she knew that this time would be an exception. Stepping back, she locked his gaze in hers as she started to unbutton his shirt and smiled, "Today however, I don't think 'slow' is going to be an option."

She drew his head down to her lips. "I want to touch you," she whispered as she took his lips with a kiss that left his knees weak. Her light touch brought a moan to his lips and he pulled her once again into his arms and captured her lips in his. They were caught up in the passion instantly.

Stepping back, Shawnee looked at him as she pulled her tee shirt over her head and as she started to unbuckle her shorts she was awarded with another moan. "Let me," he pleaded, as his fingers softly ran down her stomach. Shawnee's breath caught in her throat as her eyes began to cloud over with desire and she felt herself sway towards him.

Reaching for his shirt, she pulled it off his arms, needing to feel the touch of his skin. When he pulled her shorts down past her hips, she had to hold on to his shoulders for support as her knees started to buckle from desire. And when he kissed the triangle of material she gave into the desire and allowed him to gently guide her down to the grass.

Fumbling with his belt, she heard him mutter a curse and he sat up and quickly disposed of the barrier. Shawnee moaned with delight when her eyes were finally permitted to feast on his beautiful body. "Danny," she breathed his name as his hand brushed her bra aside to kiss her soft mounds. His hands sending tantalising quivers down her body as he explored her body. His mouth leaving a trail of heat in its wake.

"God, you're beautiful," he said as he gazed into her eyes again.

Shawnee felt her belly tighten with anticipation and she reached up and drew his head down to her lips, and she was lost in his kiss. She could feel his body tighten in response. "Shawnee," he lifted his mouth from hers and looked deep into her eyes. "I want you."

Shawnee held his eyes as she reached for him, and guided him into her. His eyes clouded over when she wrapped her legs around him and they moved together to nature's beat.

Drawing her up in his arms, he murmured her name as he felt her tighten around him and watched as her passion took her over the edge, and carried him with her.

~

Kissing her shoulder, he wasn't sure he could move, but feeling the chill of the night air, he reached for his shirt, he draped it around them. Shawnee turned her head and looked into his eyes and smiled. "Ok, wow!" She whispered.

Danny chuckled. "Lady, you do have a way with words."

Kissing her deeply, he drew back and studied her face. "You ok?"

Shawnee nodded and reached up to bring his mouth back down to hers. Danny moaned. "Lady, we better move this indoors or we're going to end up with a brush fire."

Sitting up, he pulled her into a sitting position and put his shirt on her before handing her shorts to her.

After sliding into his jeans, he picked up her 'pretty things' and slid them into his pocket winking at her. Taking her hand, he led her back to the truck and helped her into her seat.

When he got in behind the wheel, she slid over and leaned her head on his shoulder. Buckling them both in, he drove carefully back to his house.

He had barely parked his truck when her hands began a slow exploration of his torso. She had been itching to touch him the entire ride back but she hadn't wanted to distract his driving. Unbuckling her seat belt, she looked up and caught his gaze as she drew a line down his chest and flicked open the button of his jeans. Smiling, she leaned over and kissed him. "I may need a little help with this," she glanced down, indicating his jeans.

With a groan, he took her face into his hands and kissed her deeply. "Lady, I may need a little help just walking right now. But if you can wait just a couple of minutes, I'd be very happy to oblige."

Opening his door, he reached for her and with their hands linked together he led her into his house. Closing the door behind them, he reached for her and together they began peeling off their clothes. Naked, he lifted her into his arms and carried her to his bed.

~

Danny heard someone pounding on his door and he decided that nothing in this world was going to drag him out of Shawnee's embrace.

They had come together again in the middle of the night and they had taken a slower pace. Kissing her shoulder, he smiled at the thought of waking with her snuggled close. "Danny!" He heard his brother's voice, this time in the house. "Shit," he cursed as Shawnee giggled.

"Danny! Get the hell up! Shawnee's missing." Kevin's stormed into the room. Upon seeing the two tangled up in the sheets, he cursed. "Shit. Sorry. Shit," he said again as he turned and left the room. Shawnee giggled again as Danny dragged himself out of the bed and pulled his shorts on.

"I'm glad you find this funny," he grumbled as he left the room. Shawnee laughed again and stretched. She felt damn good she decided. Sitting up she tried to remember what had happened to her clothing. Hearing the boy's voices starting to rise, she decided to grab whatever was handy and get in to the kitchen before tempers really started to flare.

Wearing Danny's boxers and a button up shirt, she made her way to the kitchen and leaning up against the door jam, took in the scene. "Didn't Mom teach you to knock?" Danny was saying, standing toe to toe with his older brother. "Well, if you had the sense…."

"Good morning." Shawnee said to the two men. Kevin took in her appearance and glanced over at Danny, who was also appreciating the view. "Umm…Good morning," he finally replied. Shawnee laughed, and straightening from the door, she started towards the refrigerator. "Would you like some coffee and maybe something for breakfast?"

Kevin smiled and looked at his brother. "Boy, if you don't marry her, I will."

Shawnee shook her head and laughed. "Have a seat."

Opening the refrigerator, she started to take out some items when Danny walked up behind her. Wrapping his arms around her, he kissed her neck. "Good morning," he whispered.

Shawnee turned her head and looked seductively at him. "Good morning," she whispered back.

"You look good," he added.

Smiling, she said, "So do you. I hope you have some coffee, or I'm going to look pretty silly."

Reaching past her, he grabbed a brown bag. "Now you just look pretty."

"Sit," she ordered and took the coffee beans from him.

Coffee was soon brewed and poured as Kevin explained that he and Jake had stopped by her place to ask a few more questions, and when she wasn't there, they had started making the rounds. Kevin's first stop had been Danny's place. He had tried to call. 'Several times' he added but no one picked up, so he had headed on over. Shawnee was about to ask what questions they were going ask her when Kevin's phone rang. "O'Brien." He frowned and stood up and nodded to Danny. Shawnee knew that look, and pulled the eggs off the stove.

Pulling two paper towels off the roll, she made two eggs sandwiches with the toast she had just buttered and wrapped them up in the towels, just as Kevin was hanging up the phone. Handing them to the men, she said, "Here, at least you can eat these on your way."

Kevin smiled and said, "Will you marry me?" which got him a shove from his brother.

"She's spoken for," he grunted and then he turned towards her.

She continued to surprise him with things like this and he asked, "How did you know?"

Shawnee caught the questioning look in his eyes, "My family is in the business," she said briefly. "Go! Be safe!" She nodded towards the door. Danny wanted to press the issue but knew that he didn't have the time.

Grabbing her to him, he kissed her, and then in a soft voice said, "I won't be too long. Take a nap. But whatever you do, don't change out of that outfit. I'd like to do that for you."

Shawnee laughed and kissed him soundly on the lips. "Maybe."

As he was closing the door, he heard her say, "Please keep them safe."

He caught Kevin's glance. "I know," was all he said as they headed for the fire.

~

Shawnee finished saying a quick prayer for their safety and then took a look around the room. It could use a woman's touch she decided and rolling up her sleeves went to work cleaning up the kitchen.

Half an hour later, she stepped into a hot shower. She needed this she told herself and relaxed under the warmth. She allowed herself to take a long shower, and half an hour later, as she was stepping out of the shower, she heard her cell phone ringing. Grabbing a robe that was hanging next to the shower, she stepped into the bedroom and answered it on the third ring. "Hello?" She was happy that she had beat her answering service.

"Shawnee?" She heard a man's voice on the other end. "Yes?"

"You won't be so lucky next time." Her heart seemed to stop, then he hung up.

Shawnee stared at the phone for a moment, and then she reached for her purse. Grabbing a pen and paper, she wrote down the number she still saw displayed on her cell phone. Then she pulled out the card that had been given to her three days earlier and using Danny's landline, called the number on the card.

"Detective Summers," Jake was busy writing up a report when he answered the phone, but the voice drew his full attention.

"He just called me," he heard Shawnee's voice shaking on the other end. "Slow down, Shawnee, and tell me what happened."

"I just got a call on my cell phone. It was him. The number was 307-1404. At least, that's the number on my display."

"Where are you?" He could hear her voice cracking.

"I'm at Danny's house."

"Stay where you are, I'll be right there."

Hanging up, he handed the phone number to his partner and said, "Get this guy," as he dialled Kevin's cell number.

"O'Brien."

"Where's Danny?" Jake demanded.

Kevin frowned into the phone, "He's right here."

"Get him home. Now! Prizrak just called Shawnee."

~

After she had hung up, Shawnee started to shake. Sliding down to the floor, she pulled her knees up to her chest and buried her face in her arms trying to control the shaking.

It seemed like forever before she heard the front door slam open and her name being called out. "Shawnee?" Danny rushed from the kitchen through the living room and into the bedroom. He found her sitting on the floor.

Shawnee looked up, and he saw the fear in her eyes. Kneeling down in front of her, he fought the urge to pull her to him. He didn't know how she was going to react and he thought it might be best to take it slow. "I can't stop shaking," she whispered. Putting his hands on her arms, he gently caressed her with his thumbs. She was shaking like a leaf.

Jake arrived a moment later. When he walked in the room, Shawnee turned to him and nodded towards the bed. "My cell phone is right there."

Jake picked it up and knelt down next to her. "You did good, Shawnee." Shawnee blinked back the tears that now threatened to spill over. "I need you to tell me exactly what he said to you."

Taking a shaky breath, she closed her eyes and relayed the phone conversation to him. "But I don't know him." She swallowed back her tears. "I don't have any new clients right now. I don't even have any potential clients right now." Then she looked up at Danny. "Why is this happening? I don't understand."

"I know, honey." He pulled her close and rocked her as she finally gave in to her tears. Looking over at Jake, Danny wanted some answers too. Jake saw the look and nodded. Standing up, he handed Shawnee's cell phone to the officer that had accompanied him, with instructions to find out whatever they could. Then looking back, he asked Shawnee. "Who all has access to this phone number?"

Catching her breath, she pulled back from Danny's embrace, and looked up at Jake. "Friends, family, a few clients." She took a deep breath. "I have an answering service for my business, and they forward calls to my cell number. Otherwise, it's an unlisted number."

"I'm going to need a list of those people."

Shawnee nodded in agreement. Then she closed her eyes and said, "I suppose I'll have to notify my family now too." Shaking her head, "Damn, I hate to worry them."

Jake had been looking down at his notebook, flipping back a few pages, when he heard her last statement, looking back at her he frowned. "You haven't contacted your father yet?"

He had been surprised that he hadn't gotten that particular call yet. Shawnee looked up at him and could see by the look on his face that he already knew whom her father was.

Danny saw the look in Jake's eyes, "Who's your father, Shawnee?"

Shawnee closed her eyes briefly. Then looked directly into Danny's eyes. "Robert Keegan."

"The Commissioner?" Kevin asked from the doorway.

Shawnee kept her eyes on Danny and tried to smile, "I told you my family is in the business."

Danny and Kevin exchanged glances. "Shit," was all he said as he gathered her close again.

~

She had barely gotten dressed when she heard the commotion in the living room. Word sure travelled fast.

"Where the hell is my daughter?" Commissioner Keegan was fuming. "I want an explanation damn it!"

Shaking her head, she opened the bedroom door and stood looking at her father. Danny and Kevin were both standing at attention, receiving a thorough dressing down. "I don't think it's very polite to yell at the men who saved your daughter's life."

Robert Keegan turned and stared at his daughter, taking in the bandage on her head, the black and blue circles under her eyes…Then he walked up to her. "Why didn't you call me sooner? Scratch that, why didn't you call me at all?" He demanded.

Shawnee tilted her head and smiled up at her father. "Because I didn't want to worry you."

"Damn it girl, I'm your father. I'm supposed to worry about you," he said as he took her into his arms. "How are you doing?"

Shawnee sighed and said, "I'm fine, Daddy. Just scared," she said honestly.

Kissing the top of her head, he turned and sat her down on the sofa, and then turned to the two men who were standing at attention. "At ease," he said without thinking, and Shawnee smiled. Her father may be a fireman, but he still ran his team like the military man he once was.

Jake chuckled from where he stood in the corner, until Commissioner Keegan turned his attention to him. "And you, I want a full report. Now!"

While Jake didn't fall under the Commissioner's jurisdiction, he felt it was right to give him a full briefing.

After he had heard the update, Commissioner Keegan addressed his daughter. On his way over to Danny O'Brien's house, he had made several phone calls and had learned some of what had happened. "Any idea what this guy wants Shawnee?" Shawnee shook her head, "Not a clue."

Nodding, he then turned his attention to Danny O'Brien. He had heard about the kiss, and the fact that his daughter was now at Danny's house concerned him. While he had heard good things about the man, he was still weary of anyone dating his daughter. "Where do you fit into all of this?" He asked him directly.

Shawnee sighed; she should have seen that one coming. "Dad, Danny's the man who saved my life."

"Yes, I heard about that." Then he turned back to his daughter. "I also heard something about you kissing the man while he was still on duty."

Shawnee laughed then, and said, "I had to thank the man, Dad!"

"Huh huh," was her father's reply.

Standing, Commissioner Keegan turned back to face Danny and extended him his hand. "I do want to thank you for saving my daughter's life, O'Brien."

Danny took his hand and felt the grip tighten. "She means the world to me and I don't want to see her hurt." The Commissioner added. Danny looked him in the eye and read his meaning. Nodding, he met his look. "Neither do I, sir," he replied and applied equal pressure to the handshake.

Keegan studied the man and nodded.

"Shawnee, why don't you get your things. You can stay with me until this mess is cleared up."

Shawnee had taken in the little exchange between the two men and had felt somehow comforted by it. Standing up, she folded her arms in front of her, as she regarded her father's suggestion. "I really don't think so Dad. But thanks."

"Ms Keegan," Jake saw that it was clear he would need to explain the severity of the situation.

Shawnee shook her head and stopped him. "Detective, I may be frightened, but I'm not going to let some lunatic drive me out of my home; and I'm certainly not going to endanger my father trying to hide at his place."

Looking around the room she saw that she was going to get the same argument from every man there. "Don't even start with me." She warned them.

Turning back into the bedroom, she grabbed her purse and then kissed her father on the cheek. "If you talk to my mother," which she suspected he was planning on doing, "please tell her I'll call her later," she said as she ushered him towards to door. Her parents had divorced she when she was three and she had gone to live with her mother in Racine, Wisconsin. When she had graduated from the University of Wisconsin—Stout, Shawnee had decided to move to Illinois in the hope of building her career.

"Shawnee,"

She cut him off. "No Dad. This is precisely why I didn't call you. I need to take care of this on my own."

Then she turned to the detective. "I'll get you that list you requested. In the meantime, I'll keep in touch."

Ignoring the frown he received from the Commissioner, Danny walked up to her and took her by the shoulders. "Shawnee, I think it would be a good idea if you reconsidered your father's offer," he said diplomatically.

Shawnee smiled at him, and touched her hand to his cheek. "I know. There are a lot of things I'd like to do, but I can't," she said simply, as she stepped closer to him and kissed him softly on the lips. "Keep safe, Danny." Stepping from his embrace, she nodded to Kevin and stepped past her father and out of the house.

Danny and Keegan's eyes locked and Keegan read something in the man's eyes that he had to respect. "Whatever you need to do, son," he said as he stepped out of his way.

Danny nodded and said, "I'll keep her safe sir."

Catching up to her, he twirled her around and picked her up into a fireman's carry.

"Danny, put me down."

"I will," he said and then he put her in his truck and scooted her over to the passenger seat. Getting in the driver's seat, he quickly switched the automatic door locks on.

"Very funny," she said, trying not to get upset about his over-zealous behaviour. As he pulled away from the kerb, he nodded at the three men now standing in the doorway of his house. Shawnee turned and said, "I hope you are planning on dropping me off at my townhouse. Because if you aren't, this could be considered kidnapping."

Danny flashed her a quick smile but failed to make a comment. Settling back in her seat she decided that she shouldn't panic just yet. But when he turned on to the highway, she felt her temper rising. "Danny," she said in a warning voice. Danny glanced over at her.

"Fasten your seat belt, Shawnee," he ordered and then he reached over and turned the volume up on his radio. He knew better than to listen to what she had to say. He might break down and change his mind if she started to use any of those techniques that women were so good at using to get what they wanted.

Shawnee stared at him as he passed another car. Fastening her seatbelt, she sat back and let her anger build. He would have to stop sometime and by then she just might be ready to kill him.

～

They had been on the road for over two hours when her eyes began to droop down. God, she was tired. She wanted to curl up and go to sleep, but she fought the urge to close her eyes. It really was a dirty trick she decided. She always did have trouble staying awake on long drives. Today was no exception. Several times she had felt herself nod off, only to be woken when her head nodded down to her chest.

Flashing him an angry look, she wanted to scream for him to stop. But he hadn't said another word to her since they had started off. She had no idea where he was taking her. She knew that they had headed south, and then east, but she had lost track of what state they were in.

Her eyes burned and her head was beginning to pound again. Closing her eyes, she told herself that she would just rest her eyes for a moment.

～

Two hours later, Danny pulled down the dirt road that led to his family's hunting shack. It was a well-guarded secret that he felt sure would give them a safe place to stay until this mess was cleared up. Glancing over at Shawnee, he noted that she was still deep in her sleep. She looked so tired. But he knew that when she woke, she would be fuming mad. The woman had a stubborn streak in her that put others to shame. Shaking his head, he concentrated on the road again, careful not to miss the turn off.

Sitting up, Shawnee tried to get her bearings. She was still in the truck, but it had stopped. Blinking away the sleep from her eyes, she jumped when Danny got back in the truck and started it moving again. Looking around she saw that they were in a dense forest. Ahead of them was a small dirt road, or what had once been a road. It was covered over with vegetation, and they bumped along, barely keeping on the covered track.

Turning a corner, Danny slowed down and then Shawnee saw a small log cabin. "Where have you taken me?" She whispered. The view was spectacular.

Behind the cabin, she could see a large mountain range rising up, and below it, a pristine mountain lake. It looked like something out of a national geographic magazine.

Stopping the truck, Danny braced himself for the fight, but one look at Shawnee and he knew he would have to wait. She was caught up in the beauty, and he had no intention of spoiling the moment for her. Slowly turning down the music, he switched off his ignition and let the sounds of the forest close in around them. Reaching for her seatbelt, Shawnee unbuckled herself and opened her door. She walked past the cabin and stood at the top of the hill, which overlooked the lake. She was mesmerised by the beauty and all she could think about was taking it all in.

She felt him move behind her and she closed her eyes. "Damn it, Danny," she whispered. Opening her eyes again, she blinked back the tears that she felt building behind her lashes. Danny put his arm around her shoulder and stood looking at the beauty with her.

"I shouldn't be here," she finally said. "I can't risk getting you hurt."

Danny turned her to face him, and tilted her chin up to look at him. "You belong here, Shawnee." She started to pull her head back but he held her face in his hands.

"And you are a risk I'm willing to take," he whispered as he took her lips with a gentle kiss.

Shawnee breathed him in. He did make her feel safe. He had since she had first opened her eyes and looked into the blue depth of his eyes. Despite her uncertainties, she trusted him.

Opening her eyes, she looked deep into his eyes again. "Trust me, Shawnee," he whispered, not wanting to break the connection he felt so sure they were building.

Smiling she leaned her forehead on his and said, "I do, Danny. I can't explain it, but I trust you."

Turning her head, she looked again at the beauty. "What is this place?"

Danny looked out at the valley and smiled. "Beautiful isn't it. We're in Kentucky, believe it or not. My family owns this land, and the hunting shack behind us." Then he pulled her back and looked into her eyes. "But no one but my family knows about it." He chuckled. "Not even Jake knows about it."

"I do," she smiled up at him.

Kissing the top of her head, he said, "Well, you're practically family."

When she stiffened, he laughed, "Hell, Kevin practically asked you to marry him when you made us breakfast, remember?"

Shawnee looked up at him and felt her heart do a summersault in her chest. She knew she was falling for him. Correction, had fallen for him. She couldn't deny it no matter how impossible it seemed. What to do about it was another thing all together. *Enjoy the moment,* she thought, and smiled that the solution seemed so clear.

"What?" Danny asked when he saw her smile.

Shawnee shook her head, "I'm just…" she looked up into his eyes. "Happy."

Danny took her in his arms and hugged her. "You know what?" Shawnee smiled into his chest, "What?"

"Me too."

Taking a deep breath, she stepped out of his embrace and looked over at the cabin. "So, what now?" Danny winked and received a light slap on the chest. "Ok, we'll get to that later. Would you like a tour of the shack?"

The 'shack' was pretty much just that. One large room held a well-furnished kitchen with a centre isle with two stools, a large dining room table with six chairs around it and a large living room/bedroom area that had a fireplace, two pull out sofas and a coffee table. There was also a small bathroom that thankfully had a shower installed. Despite its sparse appearance, it looked warm and comfortable.

Danny waited for her response. He had taken a chance that she wouldn't be the kind of woman who required the four-star hotel treatment, but he couldn't be sure. Her smile told him that he hadn't been mistaken. "I like it," she finally said. "Lady, I may just have to ask you to marry me," she laughed, "I also like the five-star hotel treatment," she warned, obviously aware of his thoughts.

Danny laughed and walked up to the refrigerator. "Hungry?"

"Starving. Are you offering to cook dinner?" She asked as she sat down at the counter. "Yep. Assuming we have something to fix. Kevin was just up here last weekend, so there should be some provisions." Danny took a quick perusal of the contents in both the refrigerator and the freezer and proclaimed. "We are in luck. How does Pasta Punteneska sound?"

"Dangerous." When he started to defend himself, she smiled and added, "Dangerously good?"

He laughed and got started with their meal. "There's some wine if you'd like some."

While Danny threw together the meal, Shawnee opened a bottle of Shiraz and poured them each a glass. Sipping the wine, she slowly walked around the cabin, taking in the various photos and artwork. Occasionally she'd ask a question about a photo. When it was taken, or where. She found a photo of what appeared to be his family and she asked him about it.

Wiping his hands on a towel, he glanced at the photo she had indicated. "Yep, that's the bunch of us. The tall one on the left is the eldest, David. Then it's Kevin and between us is our sister, Tara."

"Are your parents still alive?"

Danny reached past her and pointed at another photo as he answered. "Mom is. We lost Dad a few of years ago."

"I'm sorry, Danny."

Danny continued to look at the photo of his parents at their last wedding anniversary. The kids had pulled out all the stops and had sent their parents to Ireland to celebrate. "Thanks," he replied. "This was taken at their last wedding anniversary. We sent them to Ireland so that they could spend time with family."

"Are they immigrants?"

"Mom is, but Dad was born in Chicago. Grandma and Grandpa were both from Donegal but moved to Ennis just before Mom was born. Then they moved to Chicago when she was still a baby."

Shawnee squeezed his hand and then he said he had to check the sauce, so she continued with her exploration. When she found an old fashion record player, she plopped herself down and found an album and put it on the turntable. It was an old Nat King Cole album and she turned to look at Danny, who was testing the sauce. Smiling, she got up and walked over to him, setting her glass down on the counter, she reached for him. "Dance with me," she whispered.

Danny took her hand and led her to the centre of the room and started to dance a slow waltz as 'Unforgettable' started to play. It felt good to be in his arms and she enjoyed the gentle sway of his hips as he guided her around the room. When the song ended, Danny kissed her gently on the lips. "Thank you," she whispered, still caught up in the magic of the song.

"Any time, honey," he said, then twirled her towards the kitchen. "Dinner will be ready in another minute or two if you want to sit down."

Taking their glasses to the table, she was pleased to see that he had set the table and had even lit a candle.

The dinner was spectacular. Shawnee couldn't help but moan with pleasure with nearly every bite. By the time the dinner was over, Danny was taking her hand and leading her to the sofa. "Lady, you don't know what you do to me," he said as he lowered her down and devoured her mouth.

Passion and need slammed through him as he took her mouth, and she rose up to meet his demands. Clothes were shed and they came together quickly. Each needing to satisfy their hunger with an urgency that left them both breathless.

Laying in his arms in the aftermath of their lovemaking, Shawnee kissed his shoulder. "I liked the desert," she smiled at him as he ran his finger down her hip. "Mmm. Me too," he took her hand and kissed her fingertips. Her heart somersaulted again.

"Danny?" Propping herself up on one elbow, she looked into his eyes. "I have to warn you about something." He studied her face and brushed her hair from her forehead. Brushing his thumb over the frown that had formed on her brow, he said, "What's wrong, honey?"

Shawnee swallowed back her apprehension. "I think I'm falling for you," she said and held her breath waiting for his response. She was taking a gamble, but she knew it would best to throw the dice now and lose, then to wait until she fell too hard for him.

Danny felt his heart swell and smiled. "You make that sound like a bad thing," he whispered as he kissed her lightly on the lips. Then he looked deep into her eyes, "Shawnee, I have to warn you too," he waited a heartbeat, then smiled, "I'm falling for you too, and I definitely don't think that's a bad thing," he added as he drew her head down and covered her mouth with a passionate kiss. Gazing into her eyes, he could see the love and the caution in her eyes.

"I don't want anything to happen to you Danny," she closed her eyes, "I'm so frightened about what is happening."

Danny waited for her to open her eyes again, and then he said, "Shawnee, I know that a lot has happened in such a short span of time, but as sure as I am of anything, I know that I have fallen hard for you, and honey, you're just going to have to trust that I'll keep us both safe. You have my word on that."

Touching his cheek, Shawnee looked into his eyes and nodded. "I trust you Danny," and then shook her head in wonder.

Taking her in his arms, Danny drew her head back down to rest on his shoulder and smiled. They laid snuggled in each other's arms. Quietly enjoying just being with each other. Danny knew he was already falling in love with her.

There really was no question about it. It was the speed of the realisation had surprised him, but he knew in his heart that it was an honest feeling.

When her arm slipped off the edge of the sofa, he realised that she had fallen asleep and he shifted to gently lay her down on the sofa. Covering her with a blanket, he kissed her gently on the cheek before pulling on his clothes and walking into the kitchen to start cleaning up the mess he had created.

He knew that she hadn't gotten much sleep since the accident, and she was obviously exhausted.

Quietly putting the dishes in the dishwasher, he put the pot into some soapy water to soak and then left the cabin.

Reaching in his pocket, he pulled out his cell phone and called his brother. "Hey Kev. I'd like you to run a check on something for me."

"What have you got?" Kevin said on the other end of the phone.

"It's just a hunch, but I'd like to you find out what the Commissioner is currently involved in."

"You think he's the target?" Kevin could see where Danny was heading. "Maybe, or maybe someone just thinks that shaking up his little girl is going to get things rolling."

"I'll see what I can do. I'll have to call Jake on this too. He may have better luck then me." Danny nodded into the phone. "Do whatever you have to do."

"How's she doing?" Kevin asked quietly.

"She's going to be alright," Danny said more to himself than to his brother.

"Danny?" Kevin had to ask, "Are you falling for her?"

Danny chuckled, "Head over heels Bro. Head over heels."

"What does Shawnee think about that?"

Danny looked back towards the cabin and smiled. "You want to be the best man?"

Kevin smiled, "Ask me again that when this mess is over with. Keep in touch and Danny, keep you both safe."

"I will Kevin. I've made a promise to the lady that I don't intend to break."

Hanging up, Danny walked to his truck and reaching into the back seat drew out the 35 MM he kept there. Checking the clip, he slid it into his jacket and went back into the cabin.

~

Opening her eyes, Shawnee was awarded by the sight of Danny sitting in front of the fireplace. He was busy setting a fire, carefully placing each log into a teepee. "Do you have any marshmallows?" Danny turned and smiled at her. "I think we might."

Stretching, Shawnee picked up the shirt she had taken off of Danny earlier and slipping her arms through it, stood up in search of the treats.

Danny couldn't help but watch her. She was so beautiful. And his shirt never looked as good as it did on her near naked body. Warming to the thought of coming together with her again, had him hurrying with his fire preparations.

When she joined him by the fire, she handed him the marshmallows and started opening the chocolate bars. Looking up, her breath caught in her throat. "Shawnee," he barely said her name and he had her in his arms again.

Spark

Chicago, IL

"I want to know where my daughter is!" Commissioner Keegan demanded once more. Jake and Kevin stood before him in his office and continued to decline to answer. It had been over two weeks and he hadn't heard anything from his daughter, and he didn't like it.

"If you would just answer a few more questions Commissioner Keegan, I'm sure we can get to the bottom of all of this and have your daughter back home to you before too long."

Commissioner Keegan ran a hand through his hair and motioned for the two men to sit down.

Turning to his phone, he called his secretary and told her that he was not to be disturbed. Then he looked at the photo of his daughter before focusing on the detective's questions.

Jake had agreed with Kevin that there had to be a connection between the attempts on Shawnee's life and something that the Commissioner was involved in. He also agreed that Kevin may have run up against a stone wall if he were to make inquires.

Ordinarily he would have had his partner, Allen Caffrey, with him for this interview, but Caffrey had broken his leg while in pursuit of a suspect. The suspect, who had been apprehended, had jumped a fence near the railroad tracks. Caffrey had followed him over the fence, only to discover that the drop was much bigger than anticipated. The suspect had sprained his ankle in the fall, but Caffrey had landed on a piece of metal that was sticking out of the ground and had suffered a severe fracture. Now he was laid up at Chicago Medical Hospital and would be out of commission for the next month or more.

Jake had brought Kevin along on the interview in the hope that he could dispel any concerns the Commissioner would have with regard to his daughter's safety. Jake suspected that Kevin knew where Danny had taken Shawnee, but he had refrained from asking him. He knew that her safety relied on their location remaining a secret and the less people who knew where they could be, the better.

Kevin noticed the Commissioner's obvious concern for his daughter and said, "Sir, I want to assure you that your daughter has been taken someplace very safe. Danny has assured me that he will keep it that way."

Keegan turned his attention to Kevin. "I've done my research son. I know that your brother has received several medals of accommodation and valour. But there is a lunatic out there looking for my daughter. A well-paid lunatic, I might add, and I don't like the idea of not knowing where she is."

"The secrecy of the location is vital, Sir." Jake took over again. "The fewer people who know where your daughter and Danny are, the better. To be perfectly frank sir, we have reason to believe that your daughter is not the final target."

Now he had the Commissioner's attention. "You think the son of a bitch is planning to get at me through my daughter?" Jake studied the man a moment before continuing. "We have been going over your recent campaign contributions. There have been several large contributions from a company called," Jake consulted his notes again. "August Productions."

Looking back up at the Commissioner he asked, "What can you tell me about them?"

Keegan frowned at the name. "August Productions. I believe that is an organisation ran by a man by the name of Hickok. Joseph Hickok. August Productions is a vacation resort company. They have outfits throughout the Northern suburbs, offering timeshare condos and townhouse on Lake Michigan and throughout Cook County." Leaning forward, he added, "Now, you tell me what I don't know."

Jake and Kevin exchanged glances. "My research tells me that Mr Hickok also has a strong interest in the railroad. Most specifically, the land that the railroad currently owns."

Keegan sat back in his chair and drummed his fingers on the arms of his chair, "Continue."

Jake watched the commissioner's face for some change as he added, "You are currently investigating several possible alternatives for the use of that land."

Keegan stood up and leaned over his desk towards Jake. "Are you suggesting that I would take a bribe, Detective?" Jake studied the man before shaking his head.

"Not anymore sir," he said honestly. "But perhaps, Mr Hickok is about to request a favour of you?"

The Commissioner sat down again. "He can try," he said simply. Then he added, "How do we get him if he does?"

When they left the Commissioner's office, Jake and Kevin felt sure that the Commissioner would cooperate with the sting operation they were planning on setting.

On the drive back to the station, Kevin turned to Jake. "You don't exactly look like a man about ready to make a major bust."

Jake shook his head. "Two things are worrying me."

"What's that?"

"First, getting Hickok isn't the end of it," he said, then he looked over at Kevin. "Prizrak prides himself on his record. If Hickok's already paid him for the job, he won't stop until he's finished what he's started."

"What's the second?" Kevin asked.

"How did Prizrak get Shawnee's phone number, and are they really safe?"

⁖

It was 9:00 pm. Most of the offices in the building that housed the Commissioner's office were dark. The only lights were on the seventh floor where the Commissioner was waiting for his last meeting of the day. The only other occupants were Jake, his Captain John Weatherton, Officer John Doyle and FBI Agent Pete Monroe who were waiting for the signal.

Jake had spoken with his Captain, and they had agreed to keep the operation classified. Jake had expressed his concern that there was a leak somewhere, and they both agreed that this was too sensitive of an operation to risk exposure, so they had limited those involved. Agent Monroe had worked with them several times in the past, so he had been brought onboard to facilitate some of the more sensitive surveillance steps.

Commissioner Keegan's office had been wired taped, and the Commissioner himself had been fitted with the latest undetectable wire taping devices. They weren't going to risk him being caught. If Hickok brought Prizrak along as suspected, they weren't going to risk the Commissioner's life. Prizrak would be suspicious and FBI Agent Monroe had warned the Commissioner that he may ask to be searched. The Commissioner had been instructed to act indigent, but to submit to the search. He was assured that the bug would not be found.

With the basics of what they needed Hickok to agree to being laid out, they were leaving it in the Commissioner's hands not to blow it. The man was understandably upset by the attempt on his daughter's life, but being a military man, Jake and Monroe were convinced that he would play his part out as planned.

At 9:15 pm, a black Mercedes limo pulled into the underground parking lot. All units were informed and were to remain alert. The first report came back that only Mr Hickok had emerged from the vehicle. Once he was in the elevator, an undercover police officer approached the limo. Disguised as a maintenance worker, he knocked on the window and asked if the man could move the limo, explaining that they were going to resurface the parking lot. Instructed to move the vehicle to the other elevator bank, they then moved in and arrested the man. He was not Prizrak as they had hoped, but he would be held for questioning all the same.

Meanwhile up on the seventh floor, Hickok has been monitored since he entered the elevator. He had not made any calls, nor did anything indicate that he is wearing a wire or that he had any hint of suspicion. He is a shrewd man, so they aren't taking any chances. The infer-red camera they have installed in the elevator revealed no weapons.

At 9:19 pm, Hickok exited the elevator and after a brief pause to verify his directions, he turned left to approach the Commissioners offices.

Knocking briefly on the outer door, he was invited in. The officers who are in the vicinity close in.

"Good evening, Mr Hickok, if you don't mind, I just have to finish this last email and then I can devote my attention to our meeting."

Robert Keegan finished typing the letter he had composed to his daughter and hit the send button. He had wanted to keep an even keel on his emotions and had decided that it would be best if he were to send a quick email with a shared joke to his daughter. This, he hoped would put him in the right humour for the task before him.

"Thank you for waiting. Can I get you anything? Water, coffee?"

"No, I'm fine." Hickok replied and then took the seat in front of the Commissioners desk.

"I'd like to thank you for meeting me at such a late hour," the Commissioner continued, "as you can imagine with the election around the corner, I've been burning a little of the midnight oil." Keegan forced a smile on to his lips.

Hickok didn't seem to notice, and laughed, "I can imagine. I must say that I don't envy your position Commissioner. Election time must be the pits."

"You could say that." Looking down at his notes, he added, "If you don't mind, I have quite a bit more to accomplish before I can call it a night, so I would like to get down to business. I see here in my notes that you had a question regarding the zoning in area 14?"

"Yes, you could say that." Hickok replied. Keegan looked up and waited for the man to continue. He knew that he could not direct the conversation to exact a confession, the bastard would have to hang his own noose. "Go on," he simply prompted.

Leaning forward, Hickok smiled, "Commissioner, I think we both know why I'm here." Keegan blinked and looked back down at his notes. "I'm sorry Mr Hickok, but my notes aren't that clear. I have a lot of businesses and interest groups making requests and I have a hard time keeping them all straight. You are going to have to be more specific."

Hickok laughed, "Ok, Commissioner. I'll cut you a break. I have a special interest in Area 14, and considering my rather sizeable contribution to your currently election funds, I would think that you could see clear to umm, shall we say, granting me full access to the property."

"Mr Hickok, I'm sure that you can understand that such a request is highly inappropriate." The Commissioner tried to sound somewhat shocked.

Hickok then turned serious. "I mean business, Commissioner. Tell me." He paused as he sat back in his chair, "How is that daughter of yours? I heard that recently she was involved in a rather serious accident."

"What?" Keegan swallowed back his rage and tried once again to sound shocked.

"Accidents have a way of happening to our loved ones. You may want to keep that in mind when you are voting on Area 14."

"Are you threatening me Hickok?" The Commissioner allowed some of his anger to boil over.

"Threatening you would have no impact Commissioner. But, know that I do have the power to make things happen. Unpleasant things."

"What are you saying, Hickok?"

"I think you know what I am saying." Keegan shook his head in denial.

"Your daughter's little accident was just a warning Keegan, the next time I will see to it that she doesn't come out of it alive. Do I make myself clear Commissioner? If you don't vote in my favour for Area 14, I will make sure that the next accident I plan for your daughter is a fatal one."

Commission Keegan grasped the edge of his desk, holding himself back. "Are you saying that you arranged to have my daughter killed in that accident?"

"That is precisely what I am saying Commissioner. Now do we have an understanding?"

"I believe you have said everything that needs to be said." The Commissioner then stepped back from the desk as the office doors busted open and Jake and several of his officers entered the room.

"As for Area 14," Keegan growled out, "you can go hell."

The bust had been a good one. There was no way any judge would disallow the taped confession. The only problem had been that Prizrak remain elusive, and no amount of plea-bargaining could persuade Hickok to reveal Prizrak's whereabouts. In Hickok's way of thinking, it would be suicide to tell them anything. Besides, he claimed that he didn't have any idea where Prizrak was.

According to Hickok, he had contacted Prizrak through another party, whom he happily volunteered the name of, stating that he had no loyalties there. After all, Prizrak had failed to kill the girl, so as far as he was concerned the deal had been questionable from the start. Hickok stated that his only contact with Prizrak had been in the form of a hand delivered letter telling him to take the money and the instructions to a hotel in Rockford, Illinois. He left the money and the instructions at the reservations desk for a guest by the name of Mr Billy. Jake and his team followed up on what they had been told, but no leads had been found. Once again, it appeared the Prizrak had slipped by them.

～

Chicago, IL

David O'Brien's phone rang, waking him from a deep sleep. Turning over, he fumbled with his phone and was finally able to answer it on the third ring. "O'Brien," he said in a slurred voice.

"Sorry to wake you David, but I need your help." David recognised the voice as that of Jake Summers.

David was suddenly wide awake. "What's wrong? Did something happen to Danny?" If Jake was calling him, then something was wrong.

"Danny's fine. And before you ask, as far as I know, so is the entire family." Jake tried to reassure him. The last time he had called David in the middle of the night, it had been to inform him that his sister's ex-husband had planted a bomb at his brother Daniel's station, and that had set in motion an extensive investigation into all the family's residence and places of business.

David rubbed his hand over his bearded face and sat up. "Then what's the problem, and how can I help."

Jake had called David out of desperation. He ordinarily wouldn't have pulled a civilian in on a case, but something wasn't feeling right and he needed to get some help from someone that wouldn't have ties to the case.

"It's complicated," he finally said. "Can you meet me at Molly's?"

Molly's was a greasy diner near the precinct. It was open 24/7 and would be the perfect place to talk. "Give me twenty minutes," was David's reply.

"Make it thirty, and pack a bag," Jake told him. "I'll explain everything at Molly's."

David mumbled, "Okay" and hung up. Pack a bag? What the hell did that mean? Whatever was up, he realised Jake was in trouble and needed his help. Jake was like another brother to him, and he would do whatever he could to be there for him. Jumping into his shower, he quickly cleaned himself and then he grabbed his gym bag and threw a few items in the bag. He always had a bag ready in case there was a big fire, so it only took him a few minutes and he was ready to go. Grabbing his White Sox baseball hat, he threw on his coat and was out the door with time to spare.

When David arrived, Molly's was pretty quiet. There was only the service staff on duty and he easily found Jake sitting in the back booth. Asking the waitress for a pot of coffee, he slid into the seat across from Jake's. After the coffee was delivered, David added two healthy spoons of sugar and added some milk to the coffee. Taking a sip, he found it to be hot, but not boiling, and took another drink before focusing on Jake. "So, what has you calling me at three in the morning? It's not a fire. That's for sure, unless Molly's kitchen has a grease fire."

Jake studied his coffee for a moment and then leaned forward. "To be honest, I'm not even sure I should have called you. But I'm up against it and I need someone who isn't associated with the precinct."

David frowned. "That bad, huh?"

Jake nodded. "I have a witness to a fire that has mob implications and I don't trust the FBI who are supposed to be protecting her."

"Why not?" David took another sip of the coffee.

"I just found out that one of the agents is under investigation. He's under suspicion for working both sides of the law, and the very guy who I'm trying to pin the fire on is rumoured to be this guy's co-conspirator."

"Shit."

Jake nodded. "To put it delicately."

David sat back in the booth. "What do you need me to do?"

Jake shook his head. "I'm not sure. I was going to ask you to help me spring her from the detail, but now I'm not sure that's such a good idea."

"Other than the fact that I'd be kidnapping a witness from the FBI, and the chances of getting killed in the process are pretty high; what are your other reservations?"

"The fact that they'll know I tipped you off for one. And the publicity," Jake answered him honestly.

"What about the publicity?" David didn't understand. Jake leaned forward. "Right now, no one knows that she's a witness. As soon as we kidnap her, the FBI will plaster her face on every news outlet."

"But that could mean anything," David reasoned. But Jake shook his head. "It's more complicated than that. She ran away from an abusive boyfriend who thinks she's dead. As soon as her face hits the news, he'll know she faked her death."

"Shit," David said again.

"You can say that again," Jake replied. David gave him a sour look.

"So, what's the plan?" David asked after a moment.

"I was kind of hoping you could come up with a plan," Jake said. "I'm at a dead-end."

David sat back and thought about the situation. "Do you know where they have her?"

Jake nodded. "That's another thing. They moved her from one location, and took her to one of the usual places. No surprise there. They're arrogant enough to think they won't be found out. But it means that if I could find her than the perp could too."

"Just who are we talking about here?" David wanted to know exactly what he was getting involved in.

"Nemetskiy."

"Wonderful," was David's reply. "Ok. The way I see it, we need to get her out of the house and away from the FBI without them knowing who has her, but not worrying about it either. Right?"

Jake laughed dryly. "Is that all?"

"It's simple. We stage a fire, grab the girl and tell the FBI that she ran away. As soon as they think she left on her own accord, they'll just think she had a change of heart and that will be the end of it."

Jake was about to laugh off his simple solution but then he stopped. It was a simple enough plan that it just might work. "Ok. I could add that I wasn't convinced she'd testify in the long run, that just might stop them from splashing her face up on the media outlets. How do we stage the fire?"

"Leave that to me," David told him. "The less you know about the details the better."

"Ok. Once you grab the girl, what are you going to do?" Jake asked him. "I'll need her testimony to convict. Even if it's just a sworn statement, but how are we going to get that without the Feds knowing we got her?"

David nodded but said, "Let's cross that bridge when we get to it. First, we need to get the girl. If she's smart, she won't just go with us. So, we'll have to drug her. That will be simple enough. I can just give her some sleeping gas in the gas mask I put over her face. Then we can put her on a gurney and take her out in a borrowed ambulance."

"Then what?" Jake asked. He wanted to know that every detail was worked out. "They aren't going to just let you take her away in the ambulance without one of them tagging along."

"Do you suspect all of the agents as being corrupt?" Was David's answer.

"No, but with this case, it's getting harder and harder to know who we can trust. Could you knock them all out?"

"In theory, yes. The only caveat is that they all have to be in the house," David replied. "Do you have the floor plan of the house they are staying in?"

Jake nodded yes, and then he thought about the plan for a moment. "If we could do it in the middle of the night, then most of them would be asleep. The FBI usually leave only one, maybe two agents on the graveyard shift."

"Perfect," David said. Looking at his watch, he reached for his phone. "Give me a couple of minutes," he said to Jake, and Jake stood up and went to the till to pay for the coffee they had drank. Returning a couple of minutes later, he saw that David had set his phone down and was pouring himself another cup of coffee.

Sliding back into the booth, Jake waited for David to bring him up to speed. "We've talked about it, and we've agreed that knocking them all out isn't a good option. Unless we know all of their medical conditions, there would be too many risks that the knockout gas could cause issues if they have any underlying health concerns." Then he paused a moment. "We'll have to go with plan B, and take one of the agents along with us. Who do you think we should trust?"

Jake gave it some thought. "There are two women at the house. Sarah, that's our witness, and Agent Ann Cane. On the assumption that the ladies may have bonded, let's use her."

David nodded. "Are you ready to run with this now?" David asked. Jake was taken a back. "You arranged it all already?" David smiled. "We firefighters are always ready to respond to an emergency."

Jake thought about it for a moment and nodded. "Okay. They will probably be on their guard now that they've moved locations again, so let's give it a few days." Grabbing a napkin from the holder, he quickly wrote the address on the napkin. "From what we've been told, our witness should be in the back bedroom. She's about 5'4' with blond hair; although, they may have dyed her hair already." Jake answered David's unspoken question.

"There are three agents currently stationed at the house," he added, and then, when he was about to ask what the plan was when he stopped himself.

David stood up. "Remember, the less you know about the details the better." He reminded him and then he shook his hand. "I'll be in touch," he added and then walked out of the diner.

Jake understood why he was being so secretive. The less he knew about the extraction, the safer it would be for Sarah. Standing, he too left the diner and headed back to the precinct, where he was still running additional inquiries into Agent Thomas's background. He was the man who was under investigation, and one of the men who knew where Sarah was hidden.

~

Back at the cabin, Shawnee and Danny fell into a pleasant routine as they waited. Each morning they would wake tangled in each other's arms, and with much reluctance they would slowly rise out of bed. They would sit on the large glider chair and drink their coffee in silence as they watched the sun rise over the hillside. The view was always breath taking. On the mornings that it rained; they would sit on the porch swing snuggled in a blanket. There, wrapped in his tender embrace, she felt safe. It was easy to forget the reason they were there, hiding in the mountains. Danny did everything he could to make their stay there seem like a lovely vacation. One which neither one of them was in a hurry to end.

Each day they would spend hours talking about their past, slowly getting to know each other; They had fallen in love quickly, and now they spent their time learning about the person they loved, sharing moments from their past, and wishing to put it all behind them so that they could move forward without any regrets or misgivings.

They talked about their future, their hopes and their dreams. Shawnee cried bitterly when she told him that she wasn't able to bare children of her own. Her doctors had told her early in life that because of a medical condition that the likelihood of her conceiving naturally was very unlikely. The doctors had even gone as far to say that she wouldn't be a likely candidate for artificial means. Her only option, it seemed, would be adoption. But with politics being as they were, that option seemed a daunting task to undertake.

Their nights were filled with love. Late night dinners, dancing cheek-to-cheek and snuggling before the fire led to hours of tender loving. The passion they felt for each other never waned. They never questioned their feelings for each other, just accepted that what they had was special.

Time passed quickly and before they knew it, over a month had passed. Danny had limited vacation time, and while his Captain had approved a temporary leave of absence, Danny knew that he could not stay out much longer. But with Prizrak still on the loose, he was damned if he was going to leave Shawnee alone in the mountains.

Shawnee too realised that Danny was pushing the limits of his Captain's patience. While she loved her time with Danny, she was beginning to feel restless. She too needed to get back to work. Her business depended on it. But damn it, how was she supposed to get back to work with that lunatic still on the run? She knew she couldn't come out of hiding just yet, not only would she be risking her own life, but she very well could be risking the lives of her clients. Who knew what this mad man would try to do, and the last thing Shawnee wanted to do, would be to put one of her clients' lives in jeopardy.

Danny could tell that Shawnee was getting impatient, and despite reassurances from Jake, Danny wasn't convinced that they would ever find Prizrak. The man was a professional hit man for God's sake. If he wanted to disappear, then no one would be able to find him. He hadn't gotten away with countless murders before just to be caught by a bulldog of a detective, no matter how good Jake thought he was.

The FBI had offered to put Shawnee in the witness protection program, but she had declined. Danny couldn't blame her. Given the choice, he knew that he wouldn't hand his life over that easily. Not when there was still a chance that they would catch the guy. No, their only choice was to remain in hiding until Jake finally caught the guy. With luck, it wouldn't be much longer.

～

Danny heard his phone beep. Carefully extracting himself from Shawnee's embrace, he stood up from the sofa and checked his phone. It was a message from Jake telling him that he urgently needed to speak with him.

Danny glancing at the time, he saw that it was close to two in the morning. He knew Jake wouldn't contact him unless it was important. Looking down at Shawnee he saw that she was still fast asleep, and so he decided not to wake her. Slipping on his clothes, he grabbed his jacket and walked down to the dock, where he knew he wouldn't disturb her.

Dialling Jake's home phone number, he heard it ring twice before it was picked up. Jake's groggy voice told him something was wrong. "It's Danny. I just got a text from you saying it was urgent."

Jake was awake in minutes. "Where are you?"

"You know I can't say…" Danny began, but he already knew something was wrong.

"I didn't text you Danny, now tell me where the hell are you." Jake was already dressing.

"I'm at the cabin," he answered him. Looking back at the cabin he knew that Shawnee was in danger. "Get here!" He told him the address and then he pulled his gun out of his pocket.

～

Shawnee woke with a start.

131

It was pitch dark, and she could barely make out where she was. Blinking to clear her vision, she looked around and saw that she had fallen asleep on the sofa where she and Danny had laid together. Sitting up, she looked around for Danny, but he wasn't in the cabin. Slipping back into her clothing, she stood up and started for the door when something caught her eyes. Turning her head, she screamed when she saw the face of a man peering in the door.

She felt paralysed with fear as she watched him hold his finger over his mouth, telling her to be quiet. Then he opened the door and walked in. She saw he had something in his hand and when the moonlight caught it, she saw it was a gun.

Looking back up, she kept her eyes on his as she started to move backwards.

"Hello Shawnee," she recognised his voice. It was Prizrak. "I told you that the next time you wouldn't be as lucky."

"Where's Danny?" She asked, her voice hoarse with fear.

Prizrak smiled. "He's fine. He wasn't part of the deal, and I respect his work, so I'll leave him alone. I just sent him on a little errand," he laughed.

"What kind of errand?" She asked trying to stall for time. She needed to try and figure out how she was going to get out of this mess.

Prizrak reached down and picked up her bra. "Missing something?" He smiled.

Shawnee's stomach turned over and she felt like she was going to be sick.

Trying to get back on track she asked, "What deal?"

Prizrak seemed surprised by her question. "What do you mean?"

"What deal?" She repeated the question. "You said that Danny wasn't part of the deal. What did you mean?"

Sitting on the edge of the table, Prizrak considered her question. "I suppose it won't hurt to tell you. I'm actually very civilised in my profession. When Hickok hired me, he specifically stated your name. Shawnee Keegan. I did my research and located you. I don't make mistakes. I kill only those that I am hired to kill. There are never 'innocent' bystanders killed when I do a job. I pride myself on that record."

"But you didn't kill me. You weren't successful," she said, hoping that she wasn't making a mistake by doing so.

"No. You got lucky." He toyed with his gun for a moment. "I wanted to ask you about that. How did you manage to escape my little 'accident'?" He tilted his head in question, "You should have been crushed by that semi."

Shawnee couldn't help the shiver that shook her. He seemed to be honestly interested in her answer.

"Maybe I wasn't supposed to die after all?" She whispered.

Prizrak shook his head. "That won't work little lady. I don't believe in fate or God or anything like that." He stood and started to walk towards her again. "I would like to know how you managed to cheat death."

She had been slowly backing away from him and now her back was at the wall and she had nowhere else to go.

Closing her eyes briefly she said a quick prayer for courage and then opened them to look at him.

"I used my brain," she finally said.

Prizrak stopped. "I like that," he said, "tell me."

"When the brakes didn't work, I tried the hand brake."

He shook he head, "I cut that too."

"Yeah, I figured that one out, and I seriously thought that was it. But I tried one more time," she answered him.

Prizrak frowned and shook his head. "It still won't have worked."

"You're right. The brake didn't work. But my seat release did." He looked genuinely confused.

"When I pulled up on the hand brake, I also used my other hand to pull up on the seat release. I fell backwards just before impact."

Prizrak laughed. "Brilliant," he smiled. "I don't know that I would have thought of that one." He chuckled. "In fact, I'm quite sure that none of my other 'clients' have ever thought of that one before. Congratulations" he bowed towards her. "You have proved to be very worthy target."

As he raised his gun hand she said, "May I ask you a question?"

He seemed to pause and then lowered his gun, "I don't see why not."

"Have you ever considered letting one go?"

Prizrak blinked, "The target? Let it go?"

Shawnee swallowed back her fear. "If you catch a trophy Bass, you let it go, don't you? To let it grow and breed? That way you'll have another chance another day to outsmart it?"

Prizrak smiled and nodded. "I suppose I do. But lady, you may be beautiful, but you are no trophy Bass."

"No, but I am capable of breeding, and if you kill me, you will be breaking your own rule."

He frowned, and she continued. "If you kill me, you'll also be killing the baby I'm carrying."

Prizrak looked down at her belly and said, "You're lying."

Shawnee shook her head. "I'm a midwife, Prizrak. I know a hell-la-va lot about babies, and I assure you, I am definitely pregnant. I can tell you the day I conceived. I can tell you that right now, my baby has fingers and toes, and a strong heartbeat. He gets the hick ups and he sucks his thumb. He's already forming memories, and feelings and I can feel him move. He's alive Prizrak, and if you kill me, he will be an 'innocent bystander' caught in the cross fire."

Shawnee was shaking when she finished. She wasn't just scared, but now she was angry as well.

Prizrak studied her for a moment and grabbed her by the arm, "We'll just see about that," he said savagely, and started to drag her towards the door.

The blast jerked him around, and Shawnee pulled her arm out of his grasp and dove behind the sofa.

The second blast was from Prizrak's gun and Shawnee began to crawl towards the other end of the living room when she felt him grab her ankle. Turning, she kicked at him when she heard another blast and screamed when she saw him fall back dead.

Danny rushed to her side, praying that Prizrak's bullet hadn't found its mark.

She was staring at the dead man and she was screaming. He shook her, calling her name. Shawnee turned and stared at Danny, and then she collapsed.

Thirty minutes later Jake and several other police officers busted through the door and found Danny holding Shawnee in his arms. His head buried in her hair. "Danny?" Jake took a step towards him. Danny looked up; his face was streaming with tears. "She's alright. She just fainted."

~

Jake and his team had arrived via helicopter. After Danny had hung up the phone, he had called Kevin and gotten the exact location of the cabin and had alerted the FBI.

When they had arrived, Jake had been sure he was too late. It was only after Danny told him that Shawnee was all right, that Jake began to ask questions. How had Prizrak find them, and who had tipped him off?

It had taken two hours before the police had finished their forensic, Jake had gotten everything he needed, and he had told his men to clear out. Jake had turned to Danny and told him that he could leave an officer if they'd prefer, but Danny had shaken his head, explaining that he would be taking her home.

When the police had left, Danny had bundled Shawnee up and taken her out to the porch before packing up their belongings. He didn't think she would be able to stay another moment at the cabin. She hadn't said a word since she had stopped screaming. When she had woke from her faint, she had sat staring at her hands.

He had just finished packing up the truck when he turned to see Shawnee looking out over the lake.

Walking up behind her, he waited for her to acknowledge him before he touched her shoulder. She seemed to melt back against him. Wrapping his arms around her, he held her as they looked out at the beauty.

"Thank you" she whispered.

"For?" He kissed her temple.

She smiled, "For saving my life again."

"It's quite the life worth saving." He whispered before turning her to face him, he kissed her gently on the lips. "I love you, Shawnee."

"I love you too, Danny." She looked deep into his eyes and saw a question there. "Danny?"

Danny took her by the shoulders and led her to the wooden swing and sat down next to her. Taking her hands, he looked into her face. "I need to ask you something Shawnee. I wanted to do this right, but I don't want to wait another minute." then he got down on his knee. "Will you do me the honour of becoming my wife?" Shawnee smiled.

"Yes Danny. I will be your wife." He kissed her hand, and she felt her heart somersault again.

"How do you feel about children?" She asked.

Danny kissed her hand again. "I love them, and we can adopt as many as you'd like honey."

Shawnee kissed him and said, "Thank you, Danny. But maybe we can have one or two on our own first."

Danny sat back and looked searchingly into her eyes. "I thought…" Shawnee kissed him again, "So did I."

Danny gathered her up into his arms and held her. "So, what you were telling Prizrak…?" She nodded, "Unless I'm losing my edge, I'm pretty sure we're going to have a baby in about seven or eight months."

Danny pulled back and looked into her eyes. "When did you know?"

"I started to suspect something when I was late, but considering the stress I've been under, I kind of blamed that. It wasn't until I started talking to Prizrak that it really made sense." Tilting her head, she had to ask, "Is that alright with you?"

Her answer came in the form of a kiss. A very passionate kiss that left her legs weak, and her body tingling. "Maybe we should go back into the shack and make sure that I'm really having a baby or make sure that one is on the way."

Danny laughed and stood up. Taking her hand, he led her back to the shack. "I do like the way you think."

~

Chicago, IL

It was finally the day. They had decided that they wouldn't have a long engagement, but when Danny's girlfriend had needed to go into hiding, they had agreed to wait until they were safe.

Looking down at the rings in his hand, Shane smiled. Tara had found the matching wedding bands in a shop when she was back in Ennis, Ireland and had taken a photo of them on the off chance that she and Shane would eventually get married. She hadn't counted on him proposing the moment her saw her, but that had suited her just fine.

The rings had a Celtic design that matched the beautiful engagement ring that Shane had given her when he had officially proposed. He had insisted on 'doing it right', and he didn't want his proposal to be anything less than perfect.

Shane had called into the station and had taken the rest of the week off, stating personal reasons, and had taken Tara on a romantic three-day holiday to New York. He had arranged everything when she had been in Ireland, and they had spent the first day taking in the sites. That evening, he had hired a carriage and had taken her for a romantic carriage ride in Central Park. Asking the driver to stop, Shane had once again gotten down on his knee and had presented her with the three stone diamond engagement ring, asking her to be his wife. Tara had been surprised. "I wanted to do this right." He stopped her from speaking. "I love you Tara, and I want to spend the rest of my life with you. Tara, will you be my wife?"

With tears of joy, Tara has nodded and said, "Yes, Shane. I love you." Then he had slipped the ring on her ring finger and sealed the engagement with a kiss.

That had been two months ago, and now it was finally their wedding day. Hearing a knock on the door, Shane turned to find David O'Brien, Tara's oldest brother standing in the doorway.

"You ready?"

Shane handed the man the rings. He had asked Tara's oldest brother to be his best man, knowing that Tara would want her brother to be involved in some way. Her other brothers would be walking her down the aisle.

Her new sister-in-law, Shawnee, had been asked to be her maid of honour. Shawnee and Danny had opted for a quiet ceremony only the month before, when Shawnee had confirmed that she would be carrying their child to term. Because of medical issues, Shawnee had been told that she would not be able to conceive. Having proved the doctors wrong, they had agreed that it would be prudent to wait until they had passed the first trimester before telling the rest of the family, and then Danny had convinced her that they should be married before the baby was born.

Shawnee had told Danny that she didn't want a big wedding, and so they had agreed to have a quiet, family only affaire up at the cabin where their relationship had grown. It had been beautiful. Shawnee's father had walked her down the dock and onto the ponton that her mother and Danny's mother had painstakingly decorated with fairy lights and wild flowers. Danny had been there with his brother David, Jake and his future brother-in-law Shane. Shawnee had asked Kevin to stand up for her, and he had said he would be honoured. After they had said their vows, David had lit off several fireworks to complete the ceremony.

Shane now stood at the top of the church next to the priest awaiting his bride. David leaned in to whisper to him. "Nervous?" The man joked. "Only about having you lot as my brothers," was Shane's reply.

Turning, he shook David's hand, and then turned back to face the back of the church as the music began to play. As the congregation, which consisted primarily of firemen from Minneapolis and Chicago, rose to their feet. From where he was standing, Shane was afforded a clear view of the double doors Tara would be entering from, and as the doors were slowly opened, he saw his beautiful bride. Her brothers, Kevin and Danny were standing on either side of her, with their arms linked in hers. Shawnee, then appeared and started down the aisle, her belly already swollen with the baby she carried. David, walked forward to meet her and escorted her to the left of the alter before taking his place again next to Shane.

Then the three O'Brien's began to walk down the aisle. The smile on their faces told Shane that one of them had made some funny remark, and he smiled in turn. Tara caught his eyes and smiled back at him.

When it was time for the rings, Shane turned to David to get the rings, only to find his German Shephard Flame standing next to him with a pouch in his mouth. Shane smiled up at David, who winked. The priest hadn't been in favour of having the dog in the ceremony, but David must have convinced the man that the dog would not be any trouble.

Retrieving the pouch from Frames mouth, he gave the dog a rub on the head, and then turned to Tara. "Thank you, Flame," she whispered to the dog, whose tail promptly started to pat the floor behind him in happiness.

The priest shook his head but smiled as he took the rings from Shane.

With the rings blessed, and their vows said, it was time for the priest to announce them as a married couple.

Turning towards each other, Tara smiled up to Shane as she heard the priest tell him that he could kiss his bride.

As their lips met to seal their pledge, Flame joined in and jumped up landing his front paws on each of them, barking loudly. But they didn't seem to notice.

Ignition

Chicago, IL

It was going to be another long night. Kevin O'Brien rubbed his eyes and tried to concentrate on the task before him.

The building had been reduced to rubble. All that remained of the 'Rumours Night Club' was smouldering before him.

"Is it our guy again?"

Kevin glanced behind him before concentrating once again at the ruins. "Looks like it, but I won't know for sure until I run a few tests."

"Damn!" Jake Summers let his frustration boil over. "Who the hell is this guy, and how the hell are we going to catch him?"

Kevin glanced over at his friend, and counterpart. He had known Jake for the better part of fifteen years and he had never seen him so frustrated by a case. But this was a challenging one. Three fires in just over a month and they didn't have a concrete clue that would tell them who the culprit was. But they definitely had a serial arsonist on their hand, and they knew it. But they weren't going to let anyone else know it. No way were they going to let this guy get any publicity. As far as the press was concerned, this was going to be just another unfortunate accident.

As for how they were going to catch the guy, Kevin was hoping that they would get a break soon. As the lead fire investigator, it was his job to determine the cause, source and details of the fire. Once he had gathered as much forensic evidence as he could find, it would be up to Jake and his team of police investigators to do the rest. They would have the task of finding the arsonist.

"Why don't you go home and get some sleep?" Kevin suggested. "I still have a load of tests to run and I won't have anything for you until tomorrow morning at the earliest."

Jake nodded, but continued to stare at the ruins. He knew he wouldn't see any 'smoking gun', but he couldn't help but take a look all the same.

"Any official comments?"

Jake groaned before turning to answer the press' questions.

Half an hour later, he was on his way home to catch a little shut eye. He knew that Kevin would be up half the night collecting evidence, running tests and going over his findings. Furthermore, Jake knew that there wasn't a whole lot that he could help him with, so he had called it a night.

Answering his cell phone, he was surprised to hear Kevin's voice on the other end. "Sorry to bother you Jake, but I thought you'd want to know that we may have caught a break. Our guy has left us another clue. Nothing much, but it is something to add to the list."

"What is it?" Jake asked as he mentally crossed his fingers.

"Well, this time he got a little creative. Instead of just rigging the fuse box to ignite, he added a timing switch. With luck, your guys can find a lead, and trace it back to him. It's a fairly common switch, but we deserve a break, and I'm hoping that this is it."

"Let's hope so," Jake answered back.

"Well, I still have a lot of work to do, so I'm going to sign off. Get some sleep."

As Kevin hung up, Jake put a call into his office. While it was ringing, Jake couldn't help but wonder when they would get a real break in this case. His partner Allen Caffrey answered the phone. "Hi Caff, listen, I just got a preliminary report for the fire investigator and it looks like we may have caught a break. Can you call the crew and have them into the office by 7 a.m.? I want to get a fresh start on this first thing in the morning."

"Will do," was the reply.

As Jake pulled into his driveway, he grabbed his phone from its cradle, and began to set his alarm as he let himself into his house.

It was quiet, as expected, as he made his way to his bedroom. He was bone tired and glancing at his clock he noted that he would only have five and a half hours of sleep. Striping down to his boxers, he made some room on his bed and slid in beneath the mound of clothes. He was out in minutes.

~

Kevin rocked his head back and forth, trying to ease the tension from his neck and shoulders. The cracking sound told him that he would have to change his position soon, or he would be in serious trouble. Standing up, he stepped away from his microscope and headed for the coffee maker. As he waited for a fresh pot to brew, he reached up and stretched, and then he got down on all fours and went into one of his favourite yoga moves. The downward dog was a strange name, but it certainly did the trick. Five minutes later, the coffee was ready, and he felt a little more regenerated.

With his coffee cup in hand, he walked over to his project board and studied his findings. As expected, there were enough similarities in the materials and the method that the fire was set, to suggest a serial arsonist. Either that or they had an expert copycat on their hands. He hoped to God, that wasn't the case. With three identical fires being deliberately set within the last month, he doubted that it was a copycat.

Copycats usually struck only after an arsonist was made public, which they had been careful not to do. After the second fire, the two departments had agreed to keep all mention of similarities out of their public reports. These were still on-going investigations and as such, vital information was allowed to remain classified.

Stepping back in front of his microscope, Kevin adjusted the table to the standing position, and took up with where he had left off. He was studying the trigger device that the arsonist had used, hoping to find some clue that would lead them to their man. Glancing at his notes, he resumed his examination of the device.

Half an hour later, he was interrupted by the shrill of his phone. "O'Brien," he said briefly, not willing to take his eyes from his work.

"Sorry to bother you, Bro, but I couldn't reach you on your cell."

"I turned it off." Kevin replied absently, before something registered in the back of his mind. Making a quick note as to the location he had last examined, he sat back from his work. "Danny, what's wrong? Is everything ok with Shawnee?"

Danny, Kevin's younger brother, and his wife Shawnee were expecting their first child. Shawnee had been the target of an extortion attempt against her father, the Fire Commissioner, and had nearly lost her life. She had a tough spirit and the family had taken instantly to her. The pregnancy had been a surprise, and they were all worried about her.

"She's fine. She was having some unusual bleeding so we came into the hospital. Thankfully the doctor just wants to run a few tests. They're going to keep her overnight so I was wondering if you wanted to go out for a couple of beers?"

Kevin glanced down at his watch he saw that it was after midnight. He had a lot of work to do, but he suspected that Danny needed to talk. He and Shawnee had gone through a lot over the last couple of months, and he was sure Danny was worried about her. "Let's make it dinner, and you've got a deal," he said to his bother.

"Yeah, I could eat," was Danny's reply.

"Give me twenty minutes and then I'll pick you up at home."

⁓

Kevin had finally gotten back to the lab at 1:30 am.

Danny had finally opened up that he was worried about Shawnee and the pregnancy. Shawnee's doctor had told her that there was still a chance that she would not be able to carry the baby full term.

Danny had told him that when Shawnee was younger, her OB/GYN had told her that because of some female issues, that she probably couldn't ever conceive. The fact that she had gotten pregnant had been a surprise for everyone.

The fact that she had some bleeding had terrified both of them. But so far, the scan showed that the baby was doing fine. There were more invasive tests that could be run, but her doctor had advised her against them, as they could put the baby at risk.

Kevin had managed to calm his younger brother down, and after getting him a couple of beers to help him sleep, he had dropped him back to his house and had headed back to the lab.

Despite having worked through the night, Kevin felt sure that the evidence he had gathered would be helpful at least to some degree, and by ten a.m. Kevin had gathered as much evidence as his tired mind could understand, and he headed over to the station to meet with Jake and his team to go over the facts.

Greeted by a large steaming mug of coffee, Kevin thanked Officer Doyle and then he sat down and brought the team up to speed.

After half an hour of going over his findings, he reached over, and took a drink of his now cold cup of coffee. Grimacing, he continued. "That's all I've got for now guys. Sorry. I'm hoping that you will see something that I've missed."

Jake thanked Kevin for his time and then addressed his team. "Ok gentlemen, you heard the man. We have our work cut out for us. Obviously, this guy knows what he's doing and he's covering his tracks pretty carefully."

Looking around at his men, he started passing out some assignments. "Chuck and Billy, I want you two to start going over the data that Kevin has brought us and compare it to the data from the previous two fires. Caffrey and Tom, I want you to go back over the reports and see if you can see anything that is linking these fires. This guy appears to be selecting his targets randomly, but I want to be damn sure. If there is a pattern, or a method to his madness, I don't want to miss it."

"I hate to interrupt, Jake," Kevin spoke up.

"No problem, Kevin," Jake stepped back to let Kevin speak.

"Allen, you may want to start with this latest fire. Our guy used a timer, which could mean that it was one of his earlier targets, if not the actual target." Allen Caffrey nodded in agreement. "One other thing, if this last fire was his actual target, you can bet that he will strike again. He seems to be covering his tracks pretty damn good, and he's going to want to try and knock us off the scent by setting another fire. Either that, or he's just getting a taste for this, and could be looking to add another notch on his belt."

Jake nodded adding, "Gentlemen, I don't think I need to remind you that all of this information is strictly for our ears only. So far, the press hasn't made any connects and we want to keep it that way. If this guy is getting a taste for it, we can't afford to give him any publicity."

As the team broke up to dig into their assignments, Jake walked Kevin to his truck. "Thanks for the update, Kevin. I appreciate you working so closely with us on this one."

"No problem," Kevin replied. "I have to admit that I'm glad the Commissioner formed this joint department task group. It certainly makes my job a lot easier."

Jake nodded, "Thanks to that sister-in-law of yours! How is she by the way?"

"She's good. She in the hospital having some tests run. Danny and I met for a bite to eat and he told me that because of her physiology, they are going to watch her carefully."

"I'm sure she'll be fine," Jake said encouragingly.

Kathlyn Flynn had just finished putting the last of the boxes into the back of her Jeep Cherokee, when she heard the explosion.

Looking back, she saw a man running towards a dark SUV, jumping into the passenger's seat and then the van speeding off. Trying to see the licence plate, she saw that it was missing and she was about to reach for her phone to take a photo when a second explosion knocked her back. Rolling over on her side, she watched as the van disappeared around the corner.

～

While Kathlyn waited in the back of an ambulance, the EMT started to assess her injuries, and she was asked a few preliminary questions. After they had checked her out to ensure that she hadn't sustained any injuries when she had been knocked to the ground by the second blast, she had been told the verdict was that other than a few minor scrapes and bruises. The paramedic told her that she suspected that Kathlyn would be fine, and would be released after they completed a few more tests and after she completed some required paperwork. Handing Kathlyn a clipboard and a pen, the EMT continued with the tests. Kathlyn glanced down at the paperwork and then looked out at the chaos before her.

A large section of the Swan had been blown away, and the rest of the venue was on fire. Several fire engines had arrived after she had called 911, along with the ambulance and two patrol cars. The kind policeman had told her that they would get a formal statement from her later, and then he had to start some crowd control as now the commotion had attracted about a dozen people.

Kathlyn shifted her gaze towards one man who seemed interested in the fire, but was content to sit and watch the flames. He occasionally wrote something down in a small notebook he had pulled out of his pocket. She wondered if he was a reporter, but quickly dismissed the idea when one of the firemen stopped and asked him a question. Then, as if he could feel her watching her, he turned his head and their eyes met.

"Well, hello handsome."

The chuckle next to her told her instantly that she had spoken her thoughts out loud. Blushing, she turned her attention to the EMT who was taking her vitals. "I'm sorry about that," she whispered.

"It's alright. If I wasn't married, I'd think the same thing," the EMT smiled and looked at the man who had attracted Kathlyn's attention. "Hell, even being married, I can say he's a very handsome man," she smiled back at Kathlyn.

"Kathlyn!"

Looking up, Kathlyn saw her sister Kelly heading towards her. The worry was evident on her face. Turning, the EMT looked to see who had called out. "Wow! She's definitely your twin."

Kathlyn smiled. "Yep, and brace yourself. She's a handful."

Kelly ran up to the ambulance where her sister was sitting and started to assess her injuries. "Oh my god Kat, what the hell happened?" She asked.

"Well, I…" Kathlyn began and then Kelly interrupted her. "What are her vitals? Does she have a concussion? Why isn't she on her way to the hospital? Who's in charge here?"

Kathlyn put her hand on her sisters' arm, drawing her attention. "Come down Doc, I'm fine. Just some scratches."

Kelly blushed and turned back to the EMT. "Sorry about that."

The EMT smiled back at her. "No problem. As your sister said, she only sustained a few scratches."

"Then I'm ok to go?" Kathlyn asked hopefully, as she handed the clipboard back to the EMT, who quickly reviewed the paperwork.

Receiving a nod, the EMT smiled. "You are," she confirmed. "But if you start feeling any headaches or other aches and pains, I suggest you see your family doctor immediately."

"Will do," Kathlyn promised the EMT, and then she stepped down from the ambulance.

Glancing over at the fire, she couldn't help the shutter that went through her body. "Are you sure that you're, ok?" Kelly asked her sister.

"Yeah, I'm fine." She reassured her. But deep down she knew that she was still freaked out about the explosion. If she had been slower at gathering the last of their equipment. Shaking her head, she told herself to stop it. Thinking about what the 'what ifs' never got anyone anywhere.

Turning, she saw the officer she had spoken to earlier, heading their way. With him, was a man who she presumed was probably his superior. He had told her that his boss would want to speak with her, and she assumed this was the man himself.

Kelly turned to see a patrol officer heading their way, and with him she spied a rather handsome man walking their way.

"Miss Flynn, I'm Detective Jake Summers, I'll be in charge of this investigation. I'd like to thank you for the statement you gave the officer."

Kathlyn nodded.

"I'd like to ask you a few more questions if you're up to it." The detective continued.

"Of course." Kathlyn gave her consent.

"You mentioned that you were removing some supplies from the premises, can you tell me why?"

"We own a company called K&K Events. We were hired to host a party here over the weekend and I was collecting the rest of our equipment," Kathlyn explained.

"What type of event?"

"It was an engagement party," Kelly spoke up.

Jake looked over at the woman next to the witness and then did a double take. They were identical. Well, nearly identical. The witness had a scrap across her forehead and was wearing a light blue top, while this lovely lady was wearing a purple top and there weren't any marks on her face.

"And you are?" He prompted.

Kelly smiled back at the handsome man. "Kelly, Kelly Flynn," she said as she stuck out her hand.

Jake reached for her hand and as he shook it, he smiled back at her. "I take it you are one of the Ks of K&K events?"

Kelly once again flashed him a smile. "That's right. Kathlyn and Kelly Events."

Looking back at his notes, he focused his attention back to Kathlyn. "Who was your client?"

Kathlyn reached into her back pocket and withdrew her phone. "Jim Smith and Janine Bell. I have their number here if you'd like it?"

"Thank you. That would be helpful." As Jake noted down the number she had pulled up on her phone, he glanced back at her sister.

While they were obviously identical twins, he was starting to see the differences between the two.

146

Both ladies were around 5'6 feet tall and both of similar athletic builds, but Kathlyn had slightly blonder hair than her sister; and while Kathlyn had her hair pulled back into a pony tail, he could tell that her hair was slightly longer than her sister's as well. He also noticed that Kelly had her ears pierced several times and that the clothing she wore was slightly edgier than Kathlyn's. When she turned her head, he noticed that she had her nose pierced as well. The jewellery she wore was subtle, but it also spoke of a rebellious side. He found it sexy.

Focusing his attention back to his witness, he asked her one more time if she could think of anything new to tell him about the man she had seen running before the explosion.

Shaking her head, Kathlyn replied she couldn't think of anything else. "Well, if you do think of anything," Jake said as he handed her his business card, "please contact me at this number. Day or night."

"Thank you," she nodded. Jake turned then towards her sister. "You can take your sister home now. I would suggest watching for signs of shock. While she looks quite capable, an experience like this sometimes hits you later." Kelly nodded. "We share a house, so I'll be there for her."

Jake smiled.

"I can tell you will make sure she's alright. One more thing, I would like to ask you both not to talk to anyone of the explosion. Until we know all the details, we'd like to keep the facts controlled," Kathlyn and Kelly glanced at each other, but nodded their agreement.

"Ladies." He nodded towards them and then turned to walk towards the fire examinator.

Kevin looked up as Jake approached him, but his attention shifted to the lovely lady behind him. Her bright blue eyes drew him in, and he studied her a moment before shifting his eyes towards his friend.

Kathlyn had felt herself growing warm under his gaze when she realised that he had caught her staring at him. When he looked away, she thought perhaps she had been mistaken and breathed a sigh of relief that she hadn't been caught checking him out again.

"Are you alright?" Her sister enquired.

Kathlyn nodded. "I'm fine. Let's go home."

As they headed for her sister's car, Kathlyn looked back for one more glance at the handsome fireman, and their eyes caught again, bringing her to a halt. Kelly studied her sisters face. "Are you sure that you're alright?"

Kathlyn nodded, but still stared back at the fireman. Kelly followed her gaze and realised now what had caught her sister's attention. Smiling, she laid her arm around her sister's shoulders and steered her towards her car. "Let the man do his job, Kat." She laughed, bringing her sister's attention back to her. "If you insist." Kathlyn laughed and allowed her sister to lead her away.

"Pretty ladies," Jake said, as he watched the sisters leave the scene of the crime. Kevin nodded, and then focused back on the job at hand. "It's too early to call it, but I have the same suspicion as you," was all he said.

"Damn!" Jake frowned as he turned and watched the firemen work to contain the fire. Behind them, he could hear the shouts of the press, and he shifted his gaze to the ladies who were getting into a Black SUV. He hoped the press wouldn't connect them to the fire, but he wasn't going to take any chances. Reaching into his pocket, he drew out his mobile and called to arrange for police escort for the ladies.

Getting confirmation from the officer, he hung up and then patted Kevin on his shoulder. "I'll leave you to it. Same drill as before?" Kevin nodded, and continued to watch the fire.

Sidestepping the reporters, Jake got back in his car and headed back to the precinct. They had already towed Kathlyn's car and forensics was already going over it. The SUV had sustained some damage from the flying debris, and Jake wanted to make sure they didn't miss any clues.

~

It had been over a week since Kathlyn had been involved in the explosion at the Swan, but she couldn't shake the feeling that she was missing something. She had been having nightmares every night, and Kelly was worried that she could be experiencing some sort of PSTD. But Kathlyn knew it was something more.

Last night, after once again waking in a sweat from the horrible nightmare, she had decided to write down what she remembered of the dream.

Now, in the light of morning, she realised what she had been missing.

Kelly walked into the kitchen and found her sister, still in her pyjamas, staring down at her laptop.

"Kat? What's wrong?"

Kathlyn looked up at her sister. "I know what's been bothering me," she replied, as she turned her laptop towards her sister.

خ

Walking into the police station, Kathlyn didn't really know what she was going to tell them, but what else was she supposed to do? She would go with the facts. She had seen the article about the fire in the newspaper, and she realised now that she had seen the same man running from the scene.

She wasn't a conspiracy theorist, but in her gut, hell, call it her woman's intuition, she knew there was a connection.

The sergeant behind the desk finished his call and then looked up at her. "Hello, how can I help you?"

Kathlyn paused a moment. She didn't want to come off as a hysterical woman. "I'd like to report a crime. An arson," she clarified.

Officer Doyle studied the woman before him and decided he trusted her. "When was the arson?" He probed.

"It was two weeks ago," she replied. "At Rumours Night Club."

This got his attention. "One moment please," he said as he picked up the phone next to him and dialled Jake's desk, then he escorted the young lady to one of the interrogation rooms.

"Miss Flynn?" Jake was surprised to see Kathlyn standing in the interrogation room that he had told Officer Doyle to put the new witness in.

After shaking hands, Jake motioned for her to have a seat and then he took the seat across from her.

"Did you remember something else about the Swan fire?"

Kathlyn shook her head, then she reached into her handbag and pulled out the photo she had printed off of the computer that morning. Placing it on the table between them, she pushed it towards him. "I saw this article in the paper a few weeks back and it wasn't until…well, it wasn't until this morning that I made the connection."

Jake looked down at the article and the photo of the Rumours Night Club fire. He couldn't help the frown. If she had already made a connection between the fires, then the press would undoubtedly be making the same connections.

Looking back up a Kathlyn, he waited for her to continue. He didn't want to inadvertently have her drawing any conclusions by what he may or may not say.

"Do you see the man in the right-hand corner of the photo?" She asked, pointing to a man that appeared to be in his late forties, early fifties. Standing approximately 6 ft tall, with a grey hair that was curling outside of the baseball hat.

Jake again waited for her to continue. "This is the man I saw running from the fire."

Jake leaned over the photo to take a closer look. "Are you absolutely sure?"

Kathlyn nodded. "He wasn't wearing a cap, but I know this was him."

"How can you be sure?" Jake needed her to be 100% sure. "Could you be remembering what he looked like simply because this man is in a photo from another fire?"

Kathlyn felt her anger rise up, and she was about to give him a snappy retort when she sat back and took a deep breath and thought about what he had asked her. Could she have jumped to the conclusion, just as he was suggesting?

Shaking her head, she explained. "I am 100% sure this is the same man. I didn't pull up this photo until this morning. I kept having a feeling that I was forgetting something. And yes, I know, I went through a traumatic experience and it wouldn't be out of the realm of possibilities that my mind would make connections out of nothing. But," then she paused and steadied herself for the ridicule she was sure to follow, "I've been dreaming about the explosion and the fire every day since it happened. It wasn't until last night that I decided to record my dreams."

"Record them?" Jake frowned.

"Well, I write them down. I've always had a very vivid memory, and I can always tell you exactly what is in my dreams; but I wanted to write it down and sketch it, in case I forgot something later."

Again, she reached into her handbag and this time she pulled out a small notebook. Opening it to a page in the middle of the book, she handed it to Jake.

He looked down at her drawing and sure enough, the image she had drawn looked a lot like the man in the photo. But he still wasn't convinced.

"How can you be sure that you didn't just remember what this other guy looked like from reading the article, and that is what you brought into your dream?"

Again, Kathlyn shook her head no. "Detective Summers, I swear to you that this is the same man. I know it seems coincidental, but…well, let me explain. It wasn't until this morning that I started to look into why this guy looked so familiar; other than being the man I saw running from the Swan. At the time I thought there was something about the guy that seemed, I don't know, familiar? But I shrugged it off. I thought I was just that I'd never get the image out of my head; or perhaps I didn't want to, in case I'm needed to testify. But my nightmares seemed to be more than that. I'm not a flake. I promise you. Anyway, so this morning I started to do a google search for anything I could think of that could explain why he seemed so familiar."

She stopped for a moment. This next part was going to be a little tricky. She and Kelly had talked about it at great length and they both agreed that this could mean trouble for their little business; but they also knew they had to speak up. Kelly would have joined her at the station, in fact she really wanted to meet with the handsome detective again, but she had a business meeting with a perspective client and so Kathlyn had come on her own.

"Go on," Jake prompted her.

Kathlyn realised that she had drawn quiet. "Sorry about that. This is a little tricky," she said honestly, "you see, Kelly and I had a job at Rumours a couple of days before their fire. I guess that's why I remembered reading about the article. At the time, I just thought it was sad that they had the fire as the owners were so nice. But now…well, quite frankly, Kelly and I are worried that someone will make the connection between our events and these fires."

Now Jake was worried. They couldn't afford for anyone to start connecting the dots, even if they were leading in the wrong direction. Or were they?

"Miss Flynn," he began, "would your sister be able to come into the precinct and answer a few questions about the work you did at Rumours and at the Swan? I think it would be good to get both your point of views."

"It's Kathlyn, and yes, I know that Kelly would be happy to come in. She had a business appointment this morning; that was the only reason she didn't accompany me."

"When do you expect that she would be available to meet?" Jake asked, hoping that it would be soon.

"Let me give her a quick call," Kathlyn said as she pulled her mobile phone out of her bag and dialled her sister's number.

~

A half hour later, Kelly walked into the precinct. Kathlyn had only told her that the detective had wanted to speak to them both, and she had come immediately.

After being shown in to the interrogation room, Kelly sat down next to Kathlyn and waited for the detective to return. She had brought them all coffees from one of the coffee shops near their house, hoping to make a good impression with the handsome man.

"So, what did he say?" She asked her sister after handing her one of the coffees.

"Not much, other than to say that he wanted to speak to us together about what the jobs we did at Rumours and the Swan. I really hope he doesn't think we're being hysterical or anything." She admitted.

"I don't." Jake had arrived back to the room.

Closing the door behind him, he shook Kelly's hand, "Thank you for coming down."

"It's my pleasure," she smiled at him and handed him a coffee. "I wasn't sure how you took your coffee, so I made it black, but I brought cream and sugar if you need it."

"Thanks, black is perfect." Jake sat down and took a drink of the coffee. "This is delicious."

"So, is it true what they say about the coffee at a police station?" Kelly smiled at him.

"Definitely. It's horrible," he smiled back.

Kathlyn watched the conversation between her sister and the detective and decided that he was definitely interest in her. She knew that Kelly was interest in him. She had said as much. She had liked what she had seen, and she wanted to meet with him again to see if the good looks were more than skin deep.

Jake realised that Kelly was flirting with him, but he brought himself into check. He had a job to do, and he would not get distracted.

Sitting back, he opened his notebook and glanced over his notes. "I'd like to record this meeting, if that is alright with you both."

After receiving a nod from both the sisters, he turned on his recorder.

"Ms Flynn," he began.

"It's Kelly," she smiled at him.

"Kelly," he nodded in agreement, "your sister has told me that K&K had an event at Rumours Night Club a few days before their fire."

Kelly nodded, "That's right."

"I'd like both of you to think back to the days leading up to and including the day of the event. Was there anything unusual about the job? Had there been anything or anybody who seemed like they weren't doing their job, maybe they appeared to be careless? Was anyone upset with the event? Did you notice anything unusual about the place? The electronics? Anything that in retrospect seemed off."

Kathlyn and Kelly shared a glance and then they both began their silent reflection.

Kelly was the first to speak. "The job seemed like any other job. There are always a few snags leading up to the event. We expect them."

"Such as?" Jake prompted her.

"Well, the usual stuff. The owners had to reschedule our planning meetings a few times; but that always happens. People are just busy and planning a party tends to fall on the woman, who in this case, had been the hospital for a gall bladder operation and I guess there were some complications that sent her back to the hospital."

Jake took note of that.

"What else?"

"Well, once we met with them, they seemed a bit unsure about the date that would work for them. Again, this is normal. But we were able to schedule the date fairly quickly. Then there was the usual stuff on the day."

Jake again took a note, "Go on."

Kelly took a sip of her coffee. "Well, let's see. They forgot to bring extra power cords, but we had brought some. Then there was a problem with the table chart. Again, this is normal." Looking over at her sister, she silently asked if there was anything else.

Kathlyn shook her head and answered, "To be honest, it's kind of hard to know what is unusual. There is always something, some little snag that we have to deal with."

Then she looked at her sister again, "Well, there was the table." To which Kelly nodded.

"The table?" Jake asked, and Kelly answered him. "Yeah, it was kind of strange. We had agreed to a specific table arrangement for the party. The morning of the party, one of the tables had been moved."

Kathlyn continued on, "We asked the owner if he had moved it, because we had been there so late the night before, we wondered if maybe he had come in early and moved the table."

"But he said he didn't." Kelly added. "Of course, we figured he had moved the table but just didn't want to admit it."

"Where was the table located in the room?" Jake prompted.

"Near the back, by the utility closet," Kelly answered him.

Jake noted this down and seemed to be considering his next question. Kelly studied him a moment. "That's where the fire started, isn't it?"

Jake tried not to show his concern, "I'm not at liberty to discuss that at this time," he answered with his rehearsed speech. But she saw that he frowned slightly before replacing his expression to a passive one before answering her.

"I'm not an idiot you know," she answered him hotly.

Jake's head shot up. "I wasn't trying to imply..." he began, but she interrupted him.

"If this is an arson investigation, I, we," she motioned towards her sister. "wouldn't do anything to jeopardise the investigation. We know better than to say anything to anyone other than you." She saw the smile crease his lips, and she took a deep breath to calm down.

Kathlyn spoke up. "Detective, we also realise that two of the venues have met with unfortunate events directly following our events. To put it bluntly, we can't afford for one of our future clients to make the same connection and decide that we are an insurance risk."

Jake nodded. "Can I ask you to wait here a moment? I'd like to bring in one of my colleagues."

The ladies nodded their agreement. After he had left the room, Kathlyn turned to her sister. "What was that all about?"

"What?" Kelly innocently asked.

"What?" Kathlyn shook her head. "You nearly bite off the man's head for just giving the canned answer he was probably supposed to give."

Kelly frowned, "I did, didn't I? I just..."

Kathlyn laid her hand over her sister's hand. "I know. You like him and thought he was just going to treat you like Stan used to. But he didn't and he won't," she said with confidence.

"How do you know?" Kelly asked quietly.

"I can just tell. OK?" Kathlyn tried to comfort her sister. "I could see it in his eyes."

Kelly nodded. "Yeah, when I saw him smile, I kind of felt the same way."

There was a knock on the door and then in walked Jake, followed by the man Kathlyn had seen at the fire.

"Ladies, allow me to introduce you to Kevin O'Brien, he is the fire investigator assigned to this investigation."

The man nodded at them, but remained silent.

Kathlyn studied him. He was dressed in worn blue jeans and a dark green button up shirt. She noticed that he kept looking from her to her sister and she realised that he was trying to find out who was who. Smiling, she stuck out her hand, "I'm Kathlyn Flynn. I saw you at the Swan," she answered his unasked question.

He smiled at her and shook her hand. "Hello, I'm Kevin." He repeated the information that Jake had just relayed. Kathlyn smile widened. "It's a pleasure to meet you." Then remembering herself, she released his hand, adding, "This is my twin sister, Kelly."

Kevin shook Kelly's hand and then sat down in the chair across from Kathlyn. "Sorry, but boy oh boy, you two really do look alike," Kevin explained himself.

But Jake contradicted him. "Actually, they do have their differences. Like, Kelly has her nose pierced and Kathlyn doesn't. and Kelly's hair is slightly darker than Kathlyn's."

Kelly smiled at this. So, the handsome detective was taking notice of her. That had to be a good sign.

Kevin was the one to bring the conversation back to the subject at hand. "Ladies, Detective Summers was telling me that you believe you saw the same man at the scenes of both the fires." Kathlyn nodded, "Yes, that's right." Jake smiled back at her and continued. "And I believe you have also remembered something unusual at Rumours Night Club?"

Kelly spoke up, "That's right. The table next to the utility closet had been moved. We had all the tables slightly angled, but when we got there in the morning, one was square to the wall."

Kathlyn watched the handsome fireman. She could see his mind working, considering a possible explanation. "That's where the fire began, isn't it?" She asked, and then a thought occurred to her. "But the fire didn't happen for another week, so there must have been a timer or something on whatever triggered the fire."

Kevin studied the woman before him. Either she was one smart cookie, or…"Miss Flynn, what do you know about the fire at Rumours Night Club?"

"Only what I read in the paper," she confirmed, and then she realised what he was insinuating. "I'm not the arsonist, if that's what you are wondering. I just happen to know something about electronics. I'm the sound and lighting engineer for our company, so I do know something about timers and other methods to delay a result."

Kevin nodded his head. Then he looked at Jake, and receiving his nod, he continued. "Ladies, we have a dilemma on our hands. As you have surmised, both fires do appear to have been set by the same man. And," he smiled back at Kathlyn, "you are correct when you said he used a timer." Jake spoke up then. "So far we've managed to keep the press in the dark, but, well, quite frankly, if you two have made the connection, there is a chance that the press will too."

But Kelly shook her head. "Actually, I don't think so. We have the ace up our sleeve."

Jake frowned at her, "What do you mean?"

She smiled at him, "We have Kat. She's the only one who has ever seen the man. That was the only connection."

Kevin suddenly frowned. Looking again at Jake he was about to speak, but Jake knew where he was going. "Miss Flynn, I think it would be best, well safest, if we put you under protective custody."

"Protective custody?" Kathlyn frowned, "but you don't really think…"

Jake shook his head. "It would just be as a precaution. No one has been seriously hurt as of yet, but as your sister pointed out, you are the only witness who can place him at both fires."

Then Kevin spoke up, "Actually, both of you will need to be placed under protective custody."

Now it was Kelly's turn to object. "Why would he target me? I didn't see him."

Kevin raised his eyebrow. Was she really asking him that?

Kathlyn put her hand on her sister's shoulder. "Kell…" But Kelly didn't need convincing. She knew what he was saying. They were identical twins, but the arsonist may not know that, or care, and just go after her just to frighten her sister.

156

"Great," she said and sat back in her chair. "So, what does this mean, exactly? We still have a business to run, and while we don't have a job scheduled for a few weeks, we would ordinarily use this time to drum up business for our next event."

Jake leaned forward, "Miss Flynn,"

"It's Kelly, remember?" to which he smiled, "Kelly, now that you and your sister have provided a face to our arsonist, there is the hope that he'll be in our database and we'll be able to apprehend him fairly quickly. I've already got the team looking into that now. However, we will need to work on the assumption that it could take some time to find him."

"What are we talking here? Weeks? Months? What?"

Kathlyn suddenly stood up. "Gentlemen, can I have a few minutes to talk to my sister? Alone?"

Jake studied her a moment before replying, "Of course." Standing, he gathered his things and then he and Kevin left the room.

Outside the interrogation room, Kevin turned to Jake. "Do you think we just lost our witness?"

Jake glanced back at the closed door. "I hope not."

Officer John Doyle walked up to them, "Jake, do you have a minute?" Jake nodded and asked Kevin to stay there in case the ladies came out of the room.

As he followed Officer Doyle into the briefing room, he was wondering what the issue was. He had left Officer Doyle and another of his team, Officer Marc Wojach searching the databases for a possible match to their arsonist.

With the photo Kathlyn had provided, they now had a face, but they would need a name as well. With his partner, Allen Caffrey, still out on medical leave, he had begun to rely more and more on Officer John Doyle to take up the slack surrounding this case. He had known John Doyle for about as long as he had been on the police force, and he knew he could trust him.

"What's up?" He asked as he closed the door behind him. Officer Wojach turned his laptop towards his commanding officer. "I think this just got messier."

Jake stepped up to the table and read the report they had pulled up. Wojach was right. Things had just gotten a great deal messier. "I don't want this information going anywhere else. Not until I've had a chance to talk with the Captain."

"Are you going to notify the FBI as well?" Officer Doyle spoke up.

Jake nodded, "That will be the Captain's move, but I suspect they will be notified."

Then he added, "Pull up everything you can about this slim ball. I want to be able to present as much information to the Captain as I can."

Leaving the officers to complete their task, he walked back to where he had left Kevin. Just as he was approaching, he saw the door open to the interrogation room.

Kathlyn looked first at Kevin and then shifted her gaze to Jake. "Will you both come back in now?"

Seated again at the table, the ladies looked at each other again and then Kathlyn started to speak. "We've discussed our options, and we've decided that while your offer for protective custody is very kind, we'd like to decline your kind offer."

Jake started to protest, but Kathlyn held up her hand and continued, "As I was saying, we'd like to decline your kind offer and propose an alternative solution. Kelly and I would like to help you lure this guy out of the shadows." She could see Jake shaking his head no, so she hurried to continue. "We know what will be at risk, but the way we see it, the sooner you get this guy, the sooner we can get on with our lives."

Now it was Kelly's turn to speak up. "If what you think is true, then this guy will want to keep his identity a secret. So far, he's been able to attend the fires without someone noticing him. If we can say that Kathlyn saw the guy, then hopefully he'll try something stupid and you can nab him. Kathlyn and I," she paused for a moment. She didn't really want to mention this next part, but she and Kathlyn had agreed that it would be best. "Well, we've had some experience with this kind of thing and we'd prefer to take control and help get this resolved as quickly as possible."

"What do you mean by some experience?" Jake needed clarification. He saw that Kathlyn reached out and held her sister's hand as if for support. Kelly seemed to take a deep breath before continuing. "I was in a…" she paused as she searched for the right word. "…difficult relationship that got a bit messy." She concluded.

"What Kelly is trying not to say, is that her ex was a piece of shit and we had to take evasive manoeuvres to ensure that she was safe. Well, to ensure that we were both safe." Kelly smiled grimly at her sister. Kathlyn had been in the army for four years and when she was stressed, she tended to slip back into army speak to cover her fear. "Similar to what you are implying now, we had to hide out for fear that he would come after one or both of us." Kelly squeezed her sister's hand.

Jake studied the women before him. "Where is this guy now?" He wondered if perhaps he was somehow behind some of this.

"He's dead," Kelly answered him flatly.

"How?" Jake began to ask for the details when Kathlyn spoke again. "I killed him."

Kevin felt himself reaching for her. Somehow understanding that it was not a pleasant memory, and wanting to comfort her. Kathlyn smiled at him, understanding his intentions, but she needed to do this her own way, and so she gave his hand a squeeze and then released it and focused back on the detective, knowing that he would want the details. "I'd rather not rehash every detail. You can read the report in your own time. I was forced to shoot him when he came after me. He thought I was Kelly, and said he was going to kill me. He had a knife, and despite the fact that I had a gun, he wouldn't believe that I would use it. As I mentioned, he thought I was Kelly, and he thought he could control her. I shot him several times, but he kept coming at me. The final shot was in the chest and he finally stopped."

She looked over at her sister. "He died on the way to the hospital," she added.

"Why did you have a gun?" Jake asked. He really wanted to know if it was a registered fire arm or if there was more, he needed to know.

"I was in the army and I had been issued a fire arm and given training." She glanced over at Kelly. "He must have thought that Kelly wouldn't know how to use the weapon and so he just kept coming after her. Well, me." She concluded and then she waited for the detective to respond.

Jake nodded. He would need the name of the man, but he could get that later. It would be easy enough to look up.

"I'm very sorry you had to go through that," Kevin whispered. Kathlyn looked over at him. Why did she have to meet him under these circumstances?

Jake drew her attention with his next words. "While I can appreciate that you and your sister would like to help, I'm afraid that in this case it won't be an option."

Now Kelly was mad. They had just revealed their greatest kept secret for nothing? "And why the hell not?"

Jake wanted to state this in such a way as to not frighten the women worse than they already were, but to ensure their compliance as well. "We've been able to identify the man you saw running from the Swan."

"Great, then we are good?" Kathlyn said hopefully.

But Jake shook his head. "I'm afraid it's a bit more complicated."

"It would be." Kelly said sarcastically.

Kevin knew from the tone of Jake's voice that what he was about to say wouldn't be good. Once again, he reached for Kathlyn's hand, but she sat back and looked up at him, wondering why he was showing concern again, but she didn't have long to wait. "The man who you saw, goes by the name of Prizrak."

Kevin turned to him abruptly. "I thought Prizrak was dead?" Kevin asked.

"So did we," Jake replied. "Don't worry, I've already sent some officers over to the hospital," he added to console his friend and partner.

"Who is this Prizrak, and why are you worried about the hospital?" Kelly asked.

Kevin looked over at her, but Jake answered her. "Prizrak is a hit man, who is often contracted by the mob to scare witness or to ensure they never testify."

"He went after my sister-in-law. She's at the hospital." Kevin finished the sentence for him.

"Did he hurt her?" Kathlyn asked, reaching for the fire investigator, and squeezing his hand. But he shook his head. "No, but we did think he had been killed during the attack." Then Kevin turned to Jake. "Then who the hell was that at the cabin?"

"I don't know, but I'm sure as hell going to find out. In the meantime, we need to get you ladies to a safe place."

Kathlyn and Kelly looked at each other, each trying to wrap their heads around what these handsome men were saying. "Wait a minute? The mob?" Kelly asked, not really believing what they were saying. "Why would the mob be setting the fires?" Kathlyn echoed her sister's scepticism.

Again, Jake shook his head. "I've no idea. Yet. But I do know one thing. If Prizrak is involved, it's not good."

～

Jake had called his Captain in on the conversation, and while they worked out the logistics, Kevin drove to the hospital to check on Shawnee & Danny.

160

Upon arrival at her hospital room, he saw that there were two officers posted outside her room. Knocking on the door, he announced himself and then walked in. There he found Shawnee and Danny sitting together on the hospital bed.

"Hello Shawnee. How are you feeling today?" He asked.

Shawnee smiled back at her brother-in-law. "I'm good. The doctor said that all the tests came back fine, so we're relieved."

"The doctor told her that she needs to take it easy, and to cut back on her hours at work," Danny added.

"Sounds like good advice." Kevin smiled back at them.

Shawnee took her husband's hand and faced her brother-in-law. "Okay, tell us everything."

Kevin didn't want to alarm them, but he also wanted to prepare them. "The man who went after you wasn't Prizrak." He began.

"But I thought," Danny started to ask, and Kevin nodded. "So did we. But it now appears that either he was a copycat, or Prizrak had taken on an apprentice. We aren't sure of the details as of yet; Jake is looking into it, but we can tell you that Prizrak is still alive and he has been identified but an eye witness who saw him running from a fire."

Shawnee looked up at her husband and squeezed Danny's hand. "We'll be fine. If it had been Prizrak, he would have come after me weeks ago," she said with confidence. But Danny could see the fear behind her eyes. She was putting on a brave front and he squeezed her hand back. "I'm sure you're right dear. But you and I are going to do everything Kevin and Jake tell us to do. We can't afford to be stubborn this time around."

Shawnee knew what he meant and nodded her agreement. When she had faced the threat alone, she had been determined not to let the mad man dictate how she lived her life, but now she had more than herself to think of. She had Danny and the baby to consider. "What does Jake suggest?"

Kevin smiled. "Right now, we're going to keep you under 24-hour guard until we know exactly what we are dealing with. As you said, he had several months to get to you, and you weren't exactly being kept under lock and key. But until we know for sure, we aren't going to take any chances."

Danny studied his brother a moment. "The witness, I take it she will also be put in protective custody?"

"The witness is being spoken to now," was his reply. He hadn't said that the witness was a woman, but Danny must have picked up on it from the tone of his voice, but he wasn't going to acknowledge that to anyone. Right now, Kathlyn was safe and he wanted to make sure both she and her sister kept that way.

He knew that his brother and Shawnee wouldn't say anything to anyone about the situation, but he mentioned it all the same. "I'm sure I don't have to tell you that this is a highly sensitive situation." Danny and Shawnee nodded.

"Mums the word, Bro," Danny reassured him.

"Thank you," Kevin nodded.

～

Kathlyn and Kelly were sitting in Jake's office waiting for him to return with the plan of action. They had been at the precinct for over an hour and Kelly was starting to get inpatient. She had always been a woman of action, and sitting around waiting for news had never sat well with her. Looking over at her sister, she was about to say that she wasn't going to wait around any longer when she saw her sister staring down at her hands.

"Kat, what is it?"

Kathlyn continued to stare down at her hands. "I…" she began, but then thought better of it. "It's nothing."

"Bullshit. Talk to me, Kat."

Kathlyn smiled and looked over at her sister. "Such language."

"Don't try to change the subject." Kelly wasn't going to be drawn into another conversation about her colourful language.

Kathlyn's smile slipped from her mouth. She looked back at the door, ensuring that it was still closed and then whispered, "I'm guessing any chance of either one of us socialising with the detective and the fire investigator will be out of the question now that we'll be under house arrest."

Kelly frowned. "Damn, I hadn't thought about that. Shit! I really thought he was a good-looking man," she added, referring to the detective.

"Yeah, and I would have liked to get to know that fireman a bit more." Kat agreed.

Straightening her shoulders, she added, "Their probably married or engaged or something anyway."

"Or gay as Christmas," Kelly giggled. They found themselves giggling.

"Remember that one guy, what was his name? The one with the red bowtie?" Kathlyn asked her.

"Stefan. Oh yeah. He came on very strong. Really macho. Too bad he forgot that he was wearing a red bowtie and white socks with his shorts," Kelly giggled.

"Or the fact that he lived with his mother," Kathlyn snorted.

Kelly knew that they were ignoring the real problem, but it was good to take Kathlyn's mind off of the problem at hand. The fact that she had admitted to being attracted to the fireman was interesting. Kat had always kept her romantic interests to herself. She supposed that was because of what happened with Matt, her former CO.

Matt and Kat had started dating when she was still in the army but only had a few more months to serve. He had told her that he was going through a messy divorce and so asked that they keep their relationship on the quiet. Two months into their relationship, she had learned the truth. He was not going through a divorce at all. In fact, Kathlyn was only one of three woman the scumbag had been 'dating'. Kat had been devastated and had immediately broken things off and had requested a transfer. She only had three more months to serve out and the General over Matt had granted her request, reassigning her to be his personal assistant.

The General had suspected that Matt had been playing the field, and had sympathised with her. Matt had also been messing around with his daughter, and he had started proceedings to have him knocked down a few ranks. Fraternisation was not tolerated, but it would be Matt who would pay the price, not the women he had taken advantage of.

There was a brief knock on the door and Jake walked in, followed by his Captain.

"Ladies, allow me to introduce you to Captain Weatherton, he'll be leading this initiative."

Kelly stood up and shook the man's hand. "I'm Kelly, and this is Kathlyn. So, what's the plan, Captain?"

Jake couldn't help but smile at her take charge attitude. Captain Weatherton invited the ladies to sit back down, then he began to layout the plan. "Detective Summer has explained the situation and we have called the FBI in to assist."

"The FBI?" Kathlyn shared another glance with her sister.

"Yes. Prizrak is on their radar, and since he tends to be linked to organised crime, they are equally interested in this case."

Kathlyn nodded. "Do we have to wait for them to arrive before we know what the plan is?"

Jake shook his head. "We have already outlined the approach we would like to take, and they have agreed that it would be the best approach."

"And that would be?" Kelly spoke up. She was getting impatient again, and stood up to start pacing the room.

Jake smiled again and invited her to sit, hoping to settle her down a bit before he told her the plan. Once she was seated again, he noticed that Kathlyn had taken her sisters hand and had squeezed it for reassurance.

"The FBI will be taking you to a safe location and you'll be kept safe until we have apprehended Prizrak," Jake said with confidence.

Kelly frowned, "How long will that take?"

Captain Weatherton was the one to answer her question. "That's hard to say. Prizrak is a very hard man to find. But now that we have a positive identification, it should be easier. We will require that you remain in protective custody until he has been apprehended, so it could take a couple of weeks."

"If you've known that this Prizrak is a dangerous character, why haven't you apprehended him before?" Kathlyn asked.

Jake decided to come clean with the twins. "To be honest, we thought we had caught him before." Then he glanced at his Captain for permission to continue. Receiving his nod, Jake continued. "As we said before, we had thought Prizrak was recently killed. However, your testimony has now confirmed that it wasn't him, but a copycat who was shot and killed."

Kathlyn frowned. "That was the incident you told us about that involved the fire investigator's sister-in-law, right?"

Jake nodded.

Then she addressed the Captain, "When will this all begin?"

Captain Weatherton glanced at the clock and told them that the agents should be there with in the hour and that after a few formalities that they would be taking them to the safe house.

Again, Kathlyn squeezed her sister's hand. "Thank you both for your help. Is there anything you need us to do in the meantime?"

The men shook their heads. "The FBI has already confirmed that they would prefer that they take you directly to the safe house, and so you won't have an opportunity to grab any of your belongings. Additional clothing will be provided for you. If you have any medical requirements, prescriptions and the like, we will need a list of those but other than that, you won't need to do anything." The Captain explained.

The policemen then left the ladies on their own to absorb all that had been told to them.

Kelly stood up and started to pace around the room again. Kathlyn knew that her sister was a woman of action, and being told that she had to do nothing, wouldn't have set well with her. Opening her purse, she drew out her phone and pulled up the internet. "Shall we start shopping? We might as well get a list together, and since they will be footing the bill, let's have some fun."

Kelly stopped in her tracks and looked over at her sister. Then she started laughing. "I love the way you think, Sis." Then she sat down next to Kat and together they started browsing the various department stores.

~

The FBI agents who had arrived looked to be straight out of the academy. Jake glanced over at his Captain to gauge his reaction. While he showed very little on his face, Jake knew from experience that the twitch on the side of his lip meant he wasn't happy.

How the hell did the FBI think that two rookies would be enough to protect these ladies from the likes of Prizrak? A known hitman for the mob?

After introducing themselves, their next words confirmed his suspicions that the FBI were not taking the situation seriously.

"It's our understanding you have a possible witness to an arson attempt that you want babysitting?"

Jake was about to correct the man when his Captain spoke up. "No, Agent Sanders, that's not correct. We have two witnesses to a federal crime that need protection."

That seemed to take the young FBI agent down a step and he glanced nervously at his partner. "We were told it was an arson attempt."

Captain Weatherton frowned. "Obviously you weren't properly briefed." As he launched into the background of the case, Jake studied the men before him.

Agent Sanders seemed to be in his mid-twenties, and had a cocky attitude that had Jake grinding his teeth. He had been the one who had spoken and Jake decided that he must have come from money. He had a slightly posh accent and he could almost smell the old money off of him.

His partner, Agent Smith was also in his mid to late twenties and seemed quieter than Sanders. He looked familiar, but Jake couldn't remember where he had seen him before. He hadn't yet spoken, but seemed to be observing everything that they were doing. Jake hadn't decided yet if he was nervous, or was simply trying to get the lay of the land. Either way, he decided he didn't trust him. Something about him didn't feel right.

It was late, and Jake had had a long day, so perhaps his instincts were a bit off.

But Jake couldn't shake the feeling that something wasn't right and that the FBI was not taking this seriously. Perhaps it was due to the fact that they had already pronounced Prizrak dead several months previously, but even if it wasn't Prizrak, the fact that they had an eye witness and a finger print that belonged to Prizrak should have been enough to have them sit up and take notice.

Captain Weatherton excused himself and asked Jake to start the paperwork required for the witness transfer. Jake knew that his Captain would be calling the FBI lead investigator and demanding an explanation.

Fifteen minutes later, Jake was just completing the transfer papers when his Captain returned to the room.

"I've spoken to your superiors and they have informed me that you two will be taking the witnesses to the safe house and will be joined there by two other agents."

Sanders nodded. "That was my understanding as well."

Captain Weatherton continued, "Detectives Summers and Caffrey will be accompanying you to the safe house and will remain there until your reinforcements arrive."

Agent Smith finally spoke, "I'm sure that won't be necessary."

Captain Weatherton studied the man before saying. "Perhaps not, but I have your superior's agreement that it is the right course of action."

Smith nodded his understanding.

Ten minutes later, Kathlyn and Kelly were sitting in the back of FBI's SUV and Jake and Officer Doyle were in separate cars, one in the lead, and one behind the SUV. The safe house was located only a half hour away from the precinct, but it would take them approximately two hours to arrive there, as the motorcade would be taking several diversionary routes to ensure that they were not being followed.

～

As expected, they arrived at the safe house two hours later to find two other FBI agents waiting for them.

After confirming their credentials, Jake turned and smiled at Kathlyn and Kelly.

"These agents will be protecting you now. I will be in touch only after we have apprehended Prizrak. In the meantime, the FBI will keep me notified of your safety on a daily basis."

With that, he shook the ladies' hands and turned and left the safe house. Getting back in his car, he glanced back briefly and saw that the agents had already closed and locked the door. *The girls will be safe.* He consoled himself and then he and Officer Doyle took the two-hour journey back to the precinct to ensure again that they were not followed.

~

Glancing down at the report in his hand, Jake swore. Picking up his phone, he dialled his Captain's extension.

"Weatherton," the man answered his phone on the second ring.

"Sir, I have something I need to you look at." Jake said simply. He knew that the Captain would hear the urgency in his voice and would grant him an audience as soon as he could.

With the information Jake had gathered about the FBI, he now knew that even his phone may not be safe, and he decided that it was time to move Sarah. He believed that her safety now was completely in jeopardy.

Dialling his phone again, he heard the man on the other end of the phone pick up. "It's time," was all he said and then he hung up. He knew that his message would be understood.

Growth

Sarah sat up in her bed, and listened again. There was another discrete knock on the door. "Sarah, it's Ann."

Frowning, she got out of bed and walked up to her door, unlocked it and opened it to find Ann standing outside her bedroom door.

Ann slipped in and locked the door again behind her. Sarah was about the ask her what the problem was when she held her finger to her lips, telling her to keep quiet.

Ann walked to her closet and reached up to the top of the closet and withdrew her backpack. Setting it on the bed, she whispered that Sarah should start packing everything.

Sarah wanted to ask her why, but she could sense the urgency in Ann's voice. In the three months she had been in hiding, she had learned to trust Ann, and so she quickly did as she had asked.

Grabbing an outfit, she quickly changed and then packing all the clothes and toiletries, she started to reach for her books when Ann held out her hand and shook her head. Sarah's heart sank at the implications, but she realised that Ann had her best interests at heart.

Dressed now in the black jeans and a black t-shirt, Ann handed her a black leather jacket and encouraged her to put it on. Then she stepped over to the window and slowly opened it. Slipping out, she then motioned for Sarah to follow her. Pulling her backpack on, she crawled out the window and then followed Ann to the back of the house and down the back alley. There she saw that Ann had pushed the motorcycle to the bottom of the road.

Looking around, Ann finally whispered, "I'm sorry about this, but there's been a leak and I need you to take the motorcycle and just get the hell out of here." Handing her a slip of paper, she said, "Go to this address. It'll be safe. I promise. I'll follow as soon as I can. In the meantime, don't talk to anyone, and don't go anywhere but here. Do you understand?"

Sarah nodded her head. Then Ann handed her a wad of bills. "Here is two thousand dollars. It should be enough for you to live on for quite a while, or until I can get there." Ann paused. "Do you understand?"

Sarah nodded her head. Ann continued. "Take I90 and then get off at exit 53. Then you can enter the address into the sat nav from there."

Giving her a hug, she said, "Keep safe." And then she turned and ran back to the house. Sarah, started the engine and headed off down the road as Ann had instructed. She didn't want to think about what had gone wrong, or if she was in danger. She just concentrated on driving the motorcycle and said a quick prayer that her new friend Ann would be safe.

Two hours later, she had to stop at a filling station and get more gas for the motorcycle. She had also grabbed some premade sandwiches and some bottles of water which she put into her backpack before heading back on the road.

According to the sat nav, she would be travelling for another three and a half hours before she would reach her destination. She didn't have any idea what would happen once she got there, but she trusted Ann, and she would follow her instructions to the letter.

Getting back on the bike, she started the engine and again and continued on her journey.

~

Jake stepped into his Captain's office and closed the door behind him.

"What's on your mind Jake?" Captain Weatherton asked as he handed the detective a glass of bourbon.

Ordinarily he wouldn't have accepted the glass, but the evidence in front of him called for him to take the drink.

Swallowing the liquor in one swig, he sat the folder in front of his Captain and waited for him to open the document.

"I was doing some digging into our FBI friends, and I found something a bit unusual"

Captain Weatherton read the report that had been handed to him and cursed. Picking up his phone, he called his second in command. "We need a task force assembled immediately."

Jake waited for his Captain to finish his call and then he followed him into the incident room, where the task force was already being assembled.

"Gentlemen, we have potential hostage situation on our hands," Captain Weatherton began. "The FBI sent us two rookies to guard a witness, and Detective Summer has just discovered that one of the agents has connections to Agent Thomas, the man who is under investigation for possible ties with the very man we are trying to protect our witness from."

"Shit," Officer Doyle said out loud, and then the Captain nodded. "That's putting it lightly. We will need to extract the witnesses."

As the Captain began to outline the plan, Jake called Kevin to give him an update and to ascertain whether or not Kevin had found any additional information that could help nail Prizrak as the culprit.

"Sorry Jake, nothing as of yet, but I'm going back over the first two fires to see if there is anything that I can find that points directly to Prizrak. Now that we know it's him, I can look for known patterns."

"Let me know if anything turns up. We hope to get the ladies out of the house with in the next hour, but it's looking unlikely that they'll be able to testify in person. If the DA doesn't accept our request for a taped interview, then we'll need concrete evidence to convict." Jake reminded him.

Hanging up, Jake got the nod from his Captain, confirming that a plan was in place. Walking into the weapon's room, he grabbed a bullet proof vest and started to suit up for the extraction.

~

As planned, Jake knocked on the door to the safe house and waited for one of the agents to answer the door.

Seeing the blinds move, told him that they had looked out the window to see who it was.

As the door was being unlocked, he signalled his team to move, and as the door began to open, he pushed his way in, as his team busted through the back door.

Agent Smith had been opening the door and stubbled backwards as Jake pushed his way in. Agent Sanders's had been sitting at the table and suddenly drew his gun.

"Put the gun down, Sanders. The CPD is taking control of the situation."

As Sanders lowered his gun, Jake saw Smith reaching for his gun, but before he could react, he had his gun pointed at him.

"Smith, what the fuck are you doing?" Sanders asked, then as if he realised that what his partner was about to do, he reached for his gun, but he wasn't quick enough, as Smith turned his gun towards him and shot.

Officer Doyle had come in through the back and opened fire. Hitting Smith twice, killing the man.

Jake ran up to Sanders and started to apply pressure to the bullet wound. He had been shot in the chest, and Jake yelled for the paramedics, but as Sanders looked up at him, Jake saw the life leave his eyes. "No God damn it," Jake yelled, but he knew that the young agent had already passed on.

"Sir, the area is secure"

"The other FBI agents?" Jake asked.

"They aren't on the premises," was the answer.

Another man on his team suddenly appeared in the door way. "We have another problem." He had been tasked to locate the witnesses. Jake ran past him and up to the open door to the bedroom where the women were supposed to be sleeping.

He could tell that the door had been broken in, and looked back at the officer who was behind him for an explanation. "We had to bust it in. They had a blanket across the bottom of the door and a chair up against the handle. They had also locked the door from the inside." The officer explained. Jake stepped into the room and looked around. The ladies were gone. The open window told him only some of the story. It was obvious that the women had left through the window. The question now, was it of their own accord, or had Prizrak found them.

Flashover

Chicago, IL

David had used his drone to drop the smoke gas down the chimney at the safe house Jake had indicated. Within minutes, smoke was billowing through the house and he waited another 50 seconds before he and his team turned on their sirens and approached the house.

Using their axe, they gained access to the house and started putting out the small fire that had erupted as part of the smoke screen.

David made his way to the back bedroom, where the girl was supposed to be sleeping. Opening the door, he found the room empty. Frowning, he began to make his way methodically through the house to find the survivors.

He found a woman in the bathroom and lifting her, he noticed that there was blood on her shirt.

Carrying her out of the house, he laid her down on the grass and began to administer first aid. She opened her eyes and he realised that this was the agent and not the witness he was supposed to be saving. "Save her," the woman whispered.

David frowned and leaned closer. "What?"

Ann grabbed the firefighter's shirt and focused her remaining energies on him. "Save her. Cheboygan, MI. The cabin on the hill. Save her. Freedom," she whispered before she fell silent.

David felt for a pulse. Finding none, he began CPR and called to his team to get an ambulance. But he knew that his efforts would be in vain. She had been shot several times and he knew that no matter what he did, he wouldn't be able to revive her.

His team had found two other agents in the house. All were dead.

David looked up and saw Jake approaching the scene as the paramedics had taken away the young woman agent. Behind him, he saw another man approaching.

"Did she say anything?" The man asked him. David frowned and looked over at Jake. "This is FBI Agent Anderson. He's in charge of this investigation," Jake told him. David could hear the distain in his voice.

"I asked you a question. Did she say anything?" The FBI agent demanded.

"Help me. That was all she said." David replied. "Unfortunately, I wasn't able to save her."

The man nodded and turned away from them and walked into the building.

David looked over at Jake. "I'm sorry," he said to his friend.

Jake nodded then David stepped forward with an angry look on his face. "I couldn't save the agent," he whispered and then he added, "but there's still hope that the other will be saved."

Jake blinked and looked up at him. "Now punch me." David told him.

Jake blinked again, "You bastard!" He shouted and then punched him in the jaw.

David stumbled back and was about to go for him when his men caught him and held him back.

David shook them off, "You know I'm right," he said to Jake and then he turned and got in his truck and drove off.

Rubbing his jaw, he knew that Jake would have understood his message.

Picking up his phone, he dialled his boss. "Chief. I need some time off," he spoke bluntly.

News of the fight had already reached his bosses desk and his first reply had been "What the hell did you think you were doing?"

David barked at him, "With all due respect sir, this is between Summers and myself. But I do need some time off."

The chief knew that Jake had been under a lot of stress lately, and rumour had it that it had affected his relationship with the eldest O'Brien. He supposed that it had all come to a head at the fire that had claimed the lives of the three FBI agents.

"Take as much time as you need. You're a good man David. Just get your shit together and come back with as soon as you can."

David grunted into the phone and hung up.

He didn't like lying to his boss, but he knew that it couldn't be helped. He couldn't afford to let anyone know what he was about to do, not even Jake.

By the force of the punch Jake had delivered, he knew that the detective was aware of what David was saying.

Jake watched as David drove away. If he understood what David was implying, Sarah had gotten away. She was still in danger, but with luck, David would be able to get to her before Nemetskiy's men did, and then perhaps at least one of his witnesses would be safe.

Turning back towards the house, he caught sight of another body being pulled from the house. Officer John Doyle had joined him, "I want to know everything you can about this mess."

John Doyle nodded his understanding. Turning, Jake got back in his truck and headed back to the precinct.

~

Jake punched his desk in frustration. With all the evidence they had against Agent Thomas and he had been told to sit tight; and it had cost the lives of four honest federal agents and quite possibly that of their eye witnesses.

They had learned that Agent Thomas called the safe house where Kathlyn and Kelly were being held shortly after he and Officer Doyle had left. The two agents who had been at the house before their arrival had been instructed to go to another safe house, and that Agents Smith and Sanders would follow with the ladies in the morning.

Jake had also explained the extraction attempt to his Captain, and while the man had been angry that he had been kept out of the loop, he had understood the reason for the secrecy. The fact that the attempt had happened too late only added to Jake's anger. Captain Weatherton understood his frustration and ordered him to take some time off.

"You did everything you could have done, Jake."

But Jake shook his head. "But it wasn't enough was it!" He demanded.

Weatherton shook his head. "Maybe not. But we finally got Thomas, and by God, the FBI will pay for this." FBI Agent Anderson had been fully briefed with regard to the evidence they had on Agent Thomas and he had immediately taken control of the investigation.

Weatherton continued, "I've already contacted the internal bureau and they've begun an investigation of our own. They won't be able to hush this one up." He promised.

But it wasn't good enough.

"Take some time off," Weatherton told Jake. "That's an order. Go home. Go fishing or something, and straighten your shit out with O'Brien." He ordered.

"O'Brien's a dick," he said.

Weatherton shook his head. He didn't know what David O'Brien had said to Jake but it had definitely struck a nerve. But he knew that the men went back a long way and he was confident that they would eventually work things out between themselves.

"Go home Jake." He ordered his lead detective again, and then he walked back to his office.

Jake watched his commanding officer walk away and then he looked down at the stack of work on his desk. "Fuck it," he said, and then he grabbed his car keys and headed home.

Officer Doyle, saw him as he headed out. "Where you off to?"

Jake nodded towards the Captain's office. "The boss has ordered me to go home. But I want an update on the two cases. Hopefully the bastard left us some kind of clue."

Doyle nodded. "Will do. But get some rest, Jake, you look like hell."

Jake ignored his last comment and walking out of the precinct, he got in his car.

David had given him a sign that Sarah may still be alive. The young female agent must have told him something, but David had been smart enough to keep it to himself.

With luck, David would be able to find the young woman and get her to safety. Even if she never testified, at least she would be safe.

Ignoring his Captain's command, he started his car and headed back to the other safe house that had been breached.

~

Kelly and Kathlyn had been shown to the room they would be sharing and were advised to try and get some sleep. Kelly thanked the agent and after he closed the door, she locked it.

Looking over at Kathlyn, she found her sitting on one of the single sized beds that had been provided for them. "Is it comfortable?"

Kathlyn smiled, "Just like camping at Lake Winnebago." Kelly smiled. That would mean that the beds would be hard as rock and probably full of broken springs.

When they were 16 years old, they had been sent to camp at Lake Winnebago in Wisconsin. The camp beds had been so hard and lumpy that the girls had spent most of the week sleeping on the floor for comfort. It had been a common joke between them ever since.

Turning off the light, Kelly stifled a yawn and walked up to the second single bed and laid down. "Very comfy," she said sarcastically as she tried to adjust to find a spot that didn't have a spring poking her in the back.

Noticing that Kathlyn was still sitting up, she too sat up. "What's wrong?" She whispered.

"I don't know," Kathlyn answered honestly. "I just don't have a good feeling about this."

Despite feeling exhausted, Kelly now felt fully awake. Kathlyn had a six-sense for things and Kelly had learned to listen to her. "What do you want to do?" She whispered.

Kathlyn stood up and taking the top blanket off of her bed, she stuffed it under the door and then stuffed a chair under the handle to hopefully prevent someone from coming in.

Then she tiptoed over to the window and opened it. Nodding to Kelly, she indicated that they should leave, and Kelly nodded her consent.

Slipping out of the window, they waited a minute to see if anyone was around, and then they quietly making their way through the yard to the adjacent garden, where they took off running in the direction they had travelled.

Stopping to catch their breath, Kelly looked over at her sister. "Where should we go?"

Kathlyn shook her head, "I'm not sure. I just knew it didn't feel right back there."

Her sister nodded. She too hadn't felt comfortable but she had shrugged it off as just her nerves.

They had run for about forty minutes and they knew that they were still about a half hour away from the precinct. But neither seemed confident that the police station was the place they should go to.

Kelly had an idea, and grabbing her sister's hand, she pointed to a telephone booth. Running up to it, Kelly pulled out the phone book and started to search the one name that was running through her head. With her fingers mentally crossed, she hoped that she would find the number and address of the one person she felt sure they could trust.

Breathing a sigh of relief, she made a mental note of the address and then she stepped out of the telephone booth and hailed a taxi.

~

It was after two thirty in the morning by the time Jake got home. After searching the area around the safe house for possible clues, he had put out an APB on the women, in the hope that one of the beat cops would see them. Then he had headed home.

Opening his front door, he locked it behind him and stepped into his living room and poured himself a scotch. Downing it one swallow, he contemplated having another to drown out the guilty feelings he was having, when he heard a faint taping.

Reaching for his weapon, he turned his head, he tried to decide where the sound was coming from.

Hearing it again, he realised that it was coming from the kitchen. Quietly stepping into the hallway, he made his way to the kitchen. Looking inside, he couldn't see anything unusual, and then he heard the sound again. The tapping was coming from behind the kitchen door. Making his way to the door, he stood against the wall, and glanced out the backdoor window. At first, he couldn't see anything, and then he saw something towards the bottom. Reaching over, he turned on the outside light.

"Good God!"

Quickly opening the door, he found Kathlyn and Kelly huddled on the step outside his back door. Kelly had been tapping on the door with her knuckle.

As she looked up, he could see the relief on her face.

"Let's get you inside," he said to the ladies as he helped them stand up and then he locked the door, turned off outside light and then he pulled the blinds. "Stay here," he commanded them, and then he went about pulling all the blinds in his house and double checked the doors and windows to ensure they were all securely locked.

He returned in minutes to find the women sitting on the stools at his centre island. He had brought two blankets with him, and he opened one of them and placed it on Kathlyn's shoulders and then he repeated the action and put a blanket on Kelly's shoulders. Then he started the kettle to make the ladies something warm to drink.

"How did you get here?" He finally asked, once he was sure the women were warming up.

Kelly smiled at him. "We jogged most of the way, but grabbed a taxi when we figured out you lived out here in the boondocks."

Jake smiled at her. "I like the quiet," he replied by way of explanation for his out of the way location.

"But why did you leave?"

Kelly looked at her sister before answering him. For some reason, she felt like she could trust him, and that he wouldn't laugh at her. "Kathlyn got a feeling that we weren't safe there." Then she looked over at her sister again, "I felt it too. It just didn't feel right." She concluded.

Jake nodded. "You have a good six sense." He acknowledged.

"You mean we weren't safe?" Kathlyn spoke for the first time since they had entered Jake's house.

Jake shook his head. "But you are now," he said, not wanting to worry the women more than they already were.

Kelly could see the fatigue on her sister's face. "Would you mind if we crash here for the night?" She asked the kind detective.

"Of course. I've a couple of spare rooms, and they are all yours," he said with a nod.

Kelly stood up and put her arm around her sister and followed Jake to the two rooms, pointing out the bathroom on the way. "I'll grab some tee shirts and shorts for you to sleep in. I've two bathrobes you can use too."

He left the women for a moment while he grabbed the items he had mentioned, returning to find Kathlyn taking off her shoes. Putting the items on the bed, he nodded towards the bundle adding, "I found two new toothbrushes too. There are fresh towels in the bathroom if you want to take a shower either tonight or in the morning." Then he said goodnight and left the ladies to get situated.

Returning to the kitchen, he cleaned up the cups and was about to start the dishwasher when he heard a knock on the wall. Looking up, he found Kelly standing in the doorway. She was wearing his Van Halen tee shirt and one of his running shorts. "Is there something else I can get you?"

Kelly nodded. "A glass of scotch would be good," she whispered.

Jake nodded and motioned for her to follow him.

In the living room, he invited her to sit on his leather sofa while he poured two healthy glasses of scotch.

Handing her one of the glasses, he sat down next to her and took a sip of the whiskey. Kelly took a sip and then stared at the glass in her hands. "I hope we aren't inconveniencing you." She began, but Jake interrupted her.

"You'd never be an inconvenience." He heard himself saying.

"We didn't know where else to go," she said quietly.

"You came to the right place." He reassured her.

Kelly looked up at him. She was attracted to him, and right now, he looked like a knight in shining armour to her. But she knew better than to fall for that. She had been bitten before, and now she was cautious with her affections.

"Thank you," she said simply.

Jake knew that he would have to call his Captain, but he wasn't ready to leave this lovely lady alone as of yet. He had been attracted to her from the start, and seeing her sitting there, vulnerable, had him wanting to hold her and protect her.

Seeing her eyes droop a bit told him that exhaustion was starting to settle in.

"I think you'd better get some sleep."

Standing, he set his house alarm, and then taking the glass from her, helped her to her feet and taking her hand, walked her to the room next to the one her sister was sleeping in.

At the door, he turned to her. "I'll be right across the hall if you need anything." He offered. Nodding, she turned and entered the room, turning, she thanked him again and then he watched as she crawled into the bed and he quietly closed the door.

᷉

Jake stepped back in the living room and pulled his mobile phone out of his pocket and called his Captain.

"Weatherton," the Captain answered his phone with a voice groggy with sleep.

"Sorry to wake you sir." Jake began, knowing that would bring his Captain fully awake. "I thought I told you to take some time off."

Jake nodded into the phone. "You did sir, but there has been a development that I think you should hear."

"Go on." He was commanded.

As Jake explained that he had found the women at his house, his mind started to work on what the next step should be.

"Let's keep this on the quiet for now," Captain Weatherton said. "Right now, the women are safe because everyone thinks they are out there somewhere, or already found. Let's keep it that way."

Jake nodded. "We'll have to come up with a plan." He reminded his Captain.

"We will. In the meantime, we'll keep this quiet. I'll call you in the morning and we can make definite plans then."

Jake agreed to call the Captain at 8:30 and then he rang off.

Triple checking the windows and doors, and ensuring his alarm was fully activated, he walked back to his bedroom. He stopped briefly and listened in to the women's rooms. Hearing the faint sound of their breathing, told him that exhaustion had finally won and that they were both fast asleep.

Stepping into his room, he stripped out of his clothes and pulled on a pair of pyjama bottoms and then he cracked his door, to ensure he would hear the women if they needed him. Then he crawled into his bed and willed himself to sleep.

His alarm went off at 8:00 and he quickly turned it off, conscious that he didn't want to wake them. Taking a quick shower, he was dressed and in the kitchen by 8:25 making coffee. He had forgone having a shave as it would have taken too long. He could always shave later if he was required in the office.

Grabbing his phone, he dialled the Captain's phone number. It was answered on the second ring. "Weatherton."

"Captain. I have an idea," Jake said and then he launched into the plan he had come up with before he had drifted off to sleep.

It wasn't an orthodox plan, but he felt it would be the only way that he could ensure the women were safe until they put Prizrak safely behind bars.

Despite some reservations, the Captain agreed that the plan sounded like the best option.

Now the hard part would be convincing the ladies.

↲

180

Kelly woke to find Kathlyn sitting on her bed. It was obvious that she had taken a shower, as her hair was still wet, but she was now dressed in her own clothing and was drying her hair with the towel.

"How did you sleep?" Kelly asked her sister.

Kathlyn stopped what she was doing and looked at her sister, "As well as can be expected. You?"

"About the same, I suspect."

Sitting up, she slid her feet off the bed and stood up. "Well, let me jump in the shower and then let's see what the plan is."

Showered and dressed, the twins walked into the kitchen to find Jake making breakfast for them.

"Good morning, ladies, I hope you slept better than expected," he greeted them.

"Yes, thank you," the twins answered him in unison.

Jake smiled. "I have coffee made and I'm just about finished with breakfast if you want to have a seat at the table." He invited them.

"Is there anything we can do to help?" Kathlyn asked.

But Jake shook his head. "Thank you, but I've got this."

The ladies sat down as instructed and then Jake brought over the coffee pot and poured the coffee, pointing out the cream and sugar that he had already placed on the table.

Then he returned with two plates of food. He hadn't been sure what they would eat, so he had made his French toast with a side of scrambled eggs and bacon.

Kelly dug into the breakfast with gusto. She had always had a healthy appetite for breakfast and she moaned with delight at the delicious meal. "This is amazing."

Jake laughed. "You must be hungry," he answered her.

"Kelly's always hungry for breakfast." Kathlyn laughed. "But she's right. This is delicious Detective Summers."

Jake smiled. "It's Jake; and I'm glad you both like it."

After they had eaten, and Jake had cleared the plates, putting them into his dishwasher, he had sat down with the ladies.

"So, what's the plan Stan?" Kelly asked hesitantly.

Jake nodded. He knew he couldn't stall any longer. *Well, here goes nothing.* He thought to himself.

"I spoke with my Captain last night and let him know that you two were safe. We've agreed that we're going to keep your location a secret, as its best that everyone except a select few know of your location."

Kelly and Kathlyn nodded their agreement.

Then he continued. "To keep the number of people who know of your location to a minimum, the Captain has agreed to allow only two people to be your guardians."

"Our guardians?" Kelly frowned.

"Yes, for lack of a better word," Jake smiled. "We'll be taking each of you to a safe location, and will remain with you until it is safe to come out of hiding."

Hearing his phone, he glanced at the phone, and saw it was the other person he had called that morning. Standing up, he excused himself.

Jake returned within minutes and behind him was the fire investigator. "Ladies, you remember Kevin O'Brien, the fire investigator?"

Kelly nodded and Kathlyn seemed to blush. Of course, she remembered him. He was the man she already had a serious crush on, and they hadn't spoken but five words together.

"Hello Mr O'Brien, what brings you out to this neck of the woods?" Kelly asked him.

Kevin looked at Jake to explain.

Jake was about to explain when Kathlyn spoke up. "Is he one of the guardians?"

Jake nodded. "Who is the other one?" Kelly asked and Jake smiled. "I'll be taking on that responsibility."

"Okay, I understand your involvement, but how can Mr O'Brien help? Is he also a policeman? No offence," Kelly added.

Kevin smiled back at her, "None taken."

Jake spoke up. "Kevin has military experience and is well capable of protecting your sister."

"My sister?" Kelly frowned.

"Yes," Jake explained. "When I spoke with the Captain, we discussed various plans and first we agreed that the best way to insure both of your safeties, would be to split the two of you up."

Jake paused a moment before he continued, "If Prizrak discovers that there is a witness, and if he decides to act, then it will be doubly hard for him to locate either one of you." He paused again and waited for the sisters to respond.

Kelly and Kathlyn turned and smiled at each other. They couldn't help themselves. They both had a serious crush on of these men and it seemed like the perfect situation. Then taking each other's hands, they turned back towards the men, Kelly was the first to speak, "Okay. But we have some questions."

Jake nodded. "Will we be able to talk to each other, or see each other?"

Jake took a deep breath and then relayed the bad news. "Unfortunately, no. It would be safest if we kept communication at a minimum."

He saw Kathlyn squeeze her sister's hand. Continuing he added, "And while you might think that I may be the logical choice to guard your sister, the Captain feels it might be best to shift the focus off of her."

Kelly's frown made Jake hurry to continue. "Not that your safety isn't just as important, but as you've pointed out, your sister has military training and has experience with a firearm, so together she and Kevin would make a logical pairing."

Kathlyn was about to interrupt him, but Kelly stopped her. "You're right of course," she said as she looked over at her sister. Jake noticed that there seemed to be an unspoken conversation going on between the two and he wonder what it was about.

Kathlyn seemed to resign herself to keep quiet on whatever subject she was about to broach. When Kelly was satisfied that her sister wouldn't say anything, she turned to Kevin. "Do you have experience in this sort of thing?"

Kevin looked over towards Jake, unsure how to reply. There were things about his past that he wasn't sure he was at liberty discuss.

Jake spoke for him. "Yes, he has been tasked with protecting a witness in his past. He's not at liberty to discuss the details as it is still an ongoing investigation, but suffice to say that he is very capable or I wouldn't have called him in to help."

"You called him in?" Kathlyn spoke up. "I thought the Captain…" she trailed off, looking over at her sister.

Jake nodded, "Yes, the Captain suggested a number of men for the job but I suggested Kevin."

"Why?" Both the ladies asked at once.

Kevin spoke up. "To be frank, Jake is concerned about a leak in the department. So, the less the department knows, the safer you two will be."

"What's the cover story?" Kelly asked.

Jake smiled. He liked how quickly she got to the point. "It's quite simple. Since I allowed you ladies to walk into a trap, I'm taking some time off to reassess my position in the department."

"And Mr O'Brien?" Kathlyn asked, "What will be his excuse? I'm guessing that he's pretty busy as the fire investigator."

"It's Kevin;" Kevin smiled at her. "And yes, I am busy, but since my brother and sister-in-law have ties to Prizrak, I'm taking some time off to be there for them."

Kathlyn looked over at her sister and once again it appeared like they were having an unspoken conversation. Nodding her head, Kelly asked the last question they had. "When does this all kick off?"

Jake smiled, "Officially, it's already begun. Both Kevin and I are officially on temporary leave. As we speak, our respective departments are being told of our decisions."

"Officially, I'm here to drop off some camping gear that I borrowed," Kevin smiled.

"And when do we 'officially' part company?" Kathlyn asked hesitantly.

Jake nodded, "With in the next hour. In the meantime, we need to start your transformation."

"Our transformation?" The ladies said at once.

Jake smiled. "Yes, your transformation. We will need to change your physical appearance. I hate to say it, but since you are twins, we need to make you look less like yourselves and more…"

"Not identical," Kathlyn nodded her understanding.

Kelly laughed. "Leave that to us," she said, and Kathlyn laughed too. "Yeah, sorry guys, but there's no way we're going to let you decide our attire and what not."

Jake looked over at Kevin and the both looked a bit relieved.

"I bought a number of hair dyes and other stuff that my sister-in-law suggested." Kevin said as he handed Kathlyn a large bag of products.

Taking the bag, she nodded her head in the direction of the spare bathroom. "See you both in about an hour." She and Kelly turned to leave.

*

After they had closed the bathroom door, Kathlyn turned to Kelly, "What do you think?"

Kelly frowned. "I hate the idea of not knowing where you are, and not being about to contact you, but if it keeps you and me safe, then I guess we really don't have much of a choice."

Kathlyn nodded in agreement.

"As for the change in our appearance? Well, we both know that changing our hair colour isn't going to change how we look, so we'll have to take additional steps, but nothing we can't change back when this is all over," she added with a thin smile.

Kathlyn agreed and opened the bag that Kevin had brought with him. "Well, let's see what we have to work with."

An hour later, the twins were surveying their work. They had helped each other create their new personas. Since they were so close, they decided that it would be best to drastically change their appearances, and to swap their actual way of dressing.

Now Kathlyn was dressed a bit edgier, and Kelly was a bit more conservative. Although, with her piercings and tattoos, there was only so much they could do. They had covered a good portion of her tattoos with make-up, but the piercings couldn't be easily covered up, so they down played them with smaller earrings.

Whoever Kevin's sister-in-law was, she had some great taste in the products she had suggested.

Each twin had replaced her blond hair with a darker colour. Kathlyn had asked her sister to cut a good three inches off the length of her hair and had gone with an angled bob. Then she had dyed her hair a cherry black colour. The colour actually complemented her natural skin tone. Then she added dark make up, including black eye liner, dark purple lipstick and false eye lashes. Kelly had also talked her into letting her pierce her nose, something that she had learned to do when they were in high school.

Rutting through the cabinets, she found some rubbing alcohol and a needle. Then she had searched her purse for a spare nose ring. Finding one, she told her sister to brace herself and then she quickly pierced her nose and placed the nose ring in for her sister. Kathlyn had bit her lip to hold in the pain. "Remember to treat it with rubbing alcohol three times every day or it won't heal correctly." She reminded her sister.

Kathlyn nodded and then let out a small whimper, "Jesus that hurts."

Kelly smiled, "Whimp." But she knew that it had been painful. When she had gotten her nose pierced, they had first numbed the area. Kelly hadn't remembered to do that until it was too late.

Kathlyn frowned back at her sister, but knew that she was teasing. "Next time I'll pierced something on you then." Then she studied her sister's appearance and smiled. "You look nice, Kell."

Kelly had also cut some of the length off her hair, but hadn't gone as short as her sister, and they had angled her hair so that it framed her face. She had dyed her hair auburn and had added a few some darker streaks here and there to give it some dimension. Like her sister, the colour worked well with her skin tone, but she then added a dark self-tanning lotion over her body and now, as the colour was developing, she was looking more Mediterranean than Chicagoan. Like her sister, she added different make up, but had kept it lighter, adding brown mascara, brown eye liner and a light pink blush and lipstick.

Kevin had also brought a variety of clothes for the ladies to choose from, and they picked out two outfits each which matched their new looks and that could be mixed and matched to give them more options.

Standing now before the bathroom mirror, they giggled to themselves, wondering if the guys would have any clue who was who.

Glancing at her watch, Kathlyn noticed that their time was up, and then she slid her watch off her wrist and handed it to her sister. "Here, this is will definitely go better with your outfit," she said.

Kelly looked down at the classic watch. It had been a gift from their mother when Kathlyn had graduated from college. Kelly had received a similar one, but it had been broken during a fight with her ex. "Kat, are you sure?" She asked, knowing that the watch held a special place in her heart.

Kat smiled. "Yes, I'm sure." Then she added, "I want it back when all of this is over though."

Kelly hugged her sister. "Of course," she said, and the girls swallowed back the tears that threatened to fall.

Stepping back from the hug, Kelly started to fan Kathlyn's face. "No crying or you'll ruin your makeup," she smiled.

Linking arms, the girls left the bathroom and walked into the kitchen where they could hear the boys chatting.

Standing in the doorway, they waited for the guys to make their decision as to which twin was which.

Studying the ladies, Jake looked over at Kevin. "They did a good job," he said.

Kevin nodded. "They certainly did."

Neither twin wanted to speak, afraid they would spoil the surprise.

Jake walked towards them and studied them carefully. Then he turned to Kathlyn. "I'm going to guess that you're Kelly."

Kathlyn smiled slyly, "Why would you say that?"

"It's the earrings. I know that Kelly has her ears pierced several times, and that's something you can't easily hide, and…" He answered, pointing to her nose. "You have your nose pierced."

Kelly laughed, "Nice try, but no cigar."

"But the nose ring?" He questioned her.

"Yeah, that was the painful part," Kathlyn admitted.

Kevin winced and then said, "To be honest, I wouldn't have even guessed you were the same women. You did very well."

"We've always like dressing up for Halloween," Kathlyn explained.

Glancing at his watch, he saw that it was time to leave. "If you ladies are ready, we've got to get moving. If the house is being watched, they won't believe that Kevin is spending this much time talking to me."

Kathlyn was about to ask why but decided to let it slide. *Must be a guy thing,* she thought.

Hugging her sister, they both said, "See you later." And then they grabbed their bags and stepped towards the men who would be protecting them.

Kevin took out a large duffle bag and asked Kathlyn to step into it. "I'll put you in the back of the cab on the floor, and once we are out of the area, I'll get you out. Okay?"

Kathlyn nodded and stepped into the bag, got down on her side and waited for him to zip it up. She was amazed that the fit, but with her knees curled up to her chin, she fit surprisingly comfortably. Kevin picked up the bag and walked outside, carried it out to his car. Putting it in the back of the truck, he turned to Jake who had walked out with him, saying, "Thanks for this, Jake. I know Danny's been wanting to try your clubs out," he added a laugh for effect.

Closing the trunk, he turned and shook Jake's hand, and then got in his truck and headed out.

Kelly was still waiting in the kitchen, wondering what Jake had in mind for her.

Jake closed his garage door and then joined her in the kitchen. "We'll leave in about 15 minutes. Can I ask you to take these gloves and go around and make sure you wipe off anything you or Kathlyn could have touched? In case there is a leak in the department, I don't want any trace evidence that would prove that you were here. We've already taken care of the bedrooms and the rest of the house, so just concentration on the bathroom."

Kelly nodded, and went about wiping down all the surfaces, door handles and the like. Re-joining him in the kitchen, he took the wipes from her and tossed them in an open garbage bag and then threw it in the back of his truck.

Turning to Kelly, he said, "Okay, do you mind following the same example as your sister?"

Kelly wasn't as okay with enclosed environments and her breathing started to change. "I'm…I'm not really good with that kind of thing," She confessed.

Jake studied her a moment and then nodded. "No problem. Not sure I could do it myself," he said, trying to make her feel at ease. "Plan B," he smiled.

"What's Plan B?" Kelly asked.

"Can you sit on the floor in the front of the cab with some bags over you? They won't be heavy, but they will appear to be."

Kelly smiled. "I can even take the heavy ones."

"Perfect," Jake smiled back.

Walking out into the garage, he opened the front passenger door and waited for her to get in, and then he placed a dark blanket over her and added some newspapers, a banana peel and some of his luggage. "Will you be comfortable enough to sit like that for an hour or so?"

Hearing a faint, "I think so," he added a box of groceries on the seat and then said, "I'll be right back," he said as he closed the door.

Kelly waited in silence, listening to the sounds of him adding more things to the back of the truck and then she thought she heard the garage door opening.

A few minutes later, she heard the driver's door open and shut, then she heard the unmistakable sound of the seatbelt being locked into place and then she heard the engine start.

The news was on the radio and Jake verbally reacted to one of the news articles. "Come on, Sox, don't let me down."

Closing her eyes, she sat still and waited. She wasn't sure how long they would have to travel with her in this position, but she knew that it was necessary, and so she didn't complain.

Jake had commented on the news item only to let her know that he was in the truck. Being blind to what was going on around her, he wanted to reassure her that he was in control.

Thirty minutes later, Jake pulled off the highway and headed for a filling station. "I've got to get gas."

He whispered, "Stay down."

He had purposefully chosen a full-service gas station and as the attendant approached, he reached over and grabbed the banana peel and the newspaper.

Rolling down his window he greeted the attendee. "Hi, can you fill it up?"

"Sure," the young man replied. "Diesel or unleaded?"

"Diesel," Jake replied and then asked the man to throw away the banana peel and newspaper.

Five minutes later, Jake was back on the road. While the attendant had been filling up his car, Jake had taken the time to readjust the tailback, saying that he could hear things shifting around and it was doing his head in. He took the box of groceries out from the front seat and the suitcases and had placed them in the back of the truck, arranging the contents, and he even asked the attendant if he had a spare box to rearrange some of the items.

"Just another little bit," he whispered. Then he jumped back onto the highway and after a while when he was convinced that they weren't being followed, he pulled off and headed for a backroad picnic area that he knew of that even a helicopter couldn't follow them. Pulling over to the side of the road, he got out of the truck. Jogging around to the passenger side of the truck, he opened the door and told Kelly that she could come out now. Kelly moved the dark blanket and looked up at Jake. "Are you sure it's safe now?"

"Yes. I'm 100% sure."

Helping her out of her hiding place, he gave her a few minutes to stretch to get the circulation moving in her legs again.

Then he handed her a sandwich. "I got these at the filling station. If we get pulled over, I met you here, and we had a picnic. We've been dating for about a month."

Kelly smiled. "And do I have a name?"

"What's your middle name?" He asked her.

"Ann," she replied.

"Then it's Ann," he replied.

Feeling mischievous, she asked, "And have we kissed?"

Jake nearly choked on his sandwich. "What?"

Putting on an innocent look she replied, "I just want to get our story right. Have we kissed? How did we meet? Is this our third or fourth date."

Jake finished his bite and then studied her a moment. The twinkle in her eye confirmed his suspicion that she was toying with him, so he decided to play along. "It's our fourth date, we met on Tinder. The first date we met at the zoo, and on our second date we had dinner at Ed Debevic's. We seemed to hit it off, so on our third date I took you to Theo's. I wanted to impress you. You're a little shy and so we've only kissed, but you're definitely giving me signs that you'd like to take our relationship to the next level. This is our first weekend away. We're going to your friend's cabin, so we can have some privacy," he added with a wink.

He hadn't expected her to blush, but she did. Smiling, he finished his sandwich and then picked up her wrappers and put them back in the paper bag. "We better get going," he said and then he opened the passenger door for her.

Getting in, he started the engine, and looked over at her. "It'll take us another three hours to get to our destination. I'm not sure how much you slept last night, but if you want to take a nap, that's ok. Otherwise, you're in charge of the music. Anything but Beyoncé if you don't mind." Smiling, he added, "I'm not sure that on our fourth date you should be singing that I should have put a ring on it."

As he pulled away from the side of the road, he glanced over at Kelly and watched as she reached for the radio controls. He wondered what type of music she preferred and was pleasantly surprised when she turned on some old-time rock and roll. His kind of girl, he decided.

～

Kevin pulled the truck over at a drive through car wash half hour after they had begun. Pulling around the back of the filling station, he jumped out and pulled the bag with Kathlyn in it to the back of the bed and opened it. "We've got to hurry," he said, and then he turned and found his brother, David, sitting in the truck behind him. "This is my brother, David." He explained and then ushered her into David's SUV, and the brothers exchanged car keys.

"I've got everything you asked for," David said to him.

"Thanks," Kevin replied as David handed him the bag Kathlyn had brought with her from Jake's house.

David closed the back of the truck and as he got into the truck, he turned to his younger brother, "Be careful, and call me on the family phone if you need anything else."

Shaking his brother's hand, he got into the SUV, and backed out of the parking spot David had parked in and headed for the highway. He wondered briefly why David would suggest he call on the family phone.

The family phone was a number that only the O'Brien's knew existed. They had gotten it after Tara's house had been blown up by her ex-husband. The family had agreed that should there be an emergency, then they would call the family phone and David would act as point to alert the rest of the family. Danny joked that it was the Bat phone as it was an old Nokia that had seen better days, but still managed to work like a charm.

The vehicle Kevin was now driving was an SUV that David had bought second hand and it had come with tinted windows, so it was perfect for hiding Kathlyn. It was a relatively new purchase and David had yet to switch the registration, so it was also a bit safer in that if the plates were traced, it would lead to a family of four living in Missouri.

"How are you doing?" He asked as he glanced over at Kathlyn. "Sorry it took so long before I could get you out of that bag."

Kathlyn smiled over at him. "I understand. No problem. I practiced my yoga and then I took a cat nap." She admitted.

"Are you hungry or anything? David put some food in the cooler in the backseat and there should be some water as well."

Kathlyn reached into the back seat and found the cooler he had referred to. It was one of those that plugged into the cigarette lighter, and from the look of it, it was brand new. Opening the lid, she found that it had been well stocked with sandwiches, fruit, cheese slices and bottles of water and energy drinks. Grabbing a bottle of water, she asked Kevin if he'd like anything. "I'll take an energy drink," he replied.

Handing him the energy drink, she grabbed some grapes and then closed the lid. Sitting back in her seat, she opened the water and took a drink. It was ice cold and felt very refreshing. Popping a grape in her mouth, she held the bag out to him and he took a few in his hand. "Thanks."

David watched as Kevin drove off. He wasn't used to being secretive, but he knew that he had to be. The young FBI agent had given him a mission and he intended to follow it through to the end; and to do that meant that he couldn't tell anyone his plans.

~

David pulled into his driveway and walking into the hallway he pulled out his phone and hit his speed-dial.

"Are you ok?" He asked before the person on the other end of the phone had a chance to speak.

Jake smiled and nodded into the phone. "I am. Hope you are?"

"You punch like a sissy." David smiled as he rubbed the sore spot on his jaw. Jake laughed.

"I'll be taking a few weeks off work." David was saying. "I've been put on leave due to my behaviour."

"You too?" Jake admitted. "The Captain thinks I've gone off the deep end."

"Haven't you?" David smiled.

"Will you be going anywhere?" Jake asked cautiously.

"I may do some fishing," was David's answer. "I know a good place near Mittens that I might go up to. It's not too far, but it might be good to get away. I need to clear my head a bit."

Jake nodded in understanding. "Well, I won't keep you. Sorry again about the punch." Jake apologised.

"What punch?" David returned and then he hung up.

Jake looked down at Kelly. She had fallen asleep a half hour ago.

Mittens. Jake thought to himself. *Clever man.* Anyone who knew David, would think he was heading up to Wisconsin. Racine, Wisconsin to be exact. He had once dated a girl from up that way and he had always called her 'Mittens'. Jake wasn't exactly sure why he called her that, but the name had stuck.

But Jake knew that Mittens was also an inside joke that only the two of them shared, and it had nothing to do with Wisconsin.

~

David packed up Kevin's truck with his camping and fishing gear and changed the message on his answering machine to state that he had gone fishing. It was common practice for him to do so, always conscious that if someone needed to get a hold of him, then they would know where to find him. Today was an exception. He wouldn't be telling anyone where he was going, and for good reason. If there was a chance that he could save this girl, Sarah, then he was going to have to break all his rules to do so; and that included not telling his family where he was going.

Putting the last of his gear in the truck, he glanced down at his mobile phone and considered his options. Putting it back in the charger, he turned and left his house.

Pulling out of his drive way, he heading north on I94. It would take him about an hour and half to two hours depending on traffic to reach Racine. At 10:00 am, he figured the traffic would be fairly light so he expected that he'd get there in no time. From there, he would drive north towards Wind Point Lighthouse. There were several places to camp near there he would be able to launch his canoe and get some fishing done. This was the story he would tell anyone who asked.

Two hours later, he pulled up to the campsite about a mile from the lighthouse. Unpacking his gear, he made camp and then headed down to the lake. He had stopped on the way and picked up some bait and looking out at Lake Michigan he tried to decide which direction he should take. Then he pulled the canoe with the fishing gear onto the water and started to paddle north along the shoreline. About a mile out, he stopped paddling and threw out his first line, and then started casually paddling, trolling his fishing line behind him.

There was some fog on the lake, and David allowed his canoe to drift towards it. Within minutes, he was deep in the fog bank and then he pulled in his line and started paddling hard towards the Kate Kelly Shipwreck.

The Kate Kelly had been a 126-foot schooner that had sank in 1895 just two miles off the coast of the Wind Point Lighthouse. Laying at a depth of 55 feet, there wasn't anything to see, but it was the perfect rendezvous spot.

~

Pulling up to the rig, David called out, "Ahoy Captain."

Shane stuck his head out from the lower deck and nodded to his brother-in-law.

Shane and Tara had gotten married a couple months back and had recently announced that she was expecting their first child. They had bought the sail boat as a belated wedding gift to each other when they had moved back to Chicago a month ago. Tara had wanted to be closer to her family, and Shane was happy to have the extra help with the baby. Tara had wanted to return to her job as a fire fighter, but Shane had convinced her that the baby would need to have one of her parents out of harm's way. They had compromised and Tara had agreed to run the hoses and leave the firefighting to her husband.

Grabbing the rope that David threw to him, Shane helped him onto the sailboat and handed him a cup of coffee.

"What's up?" He asked. Shane had received a call from David's old phone number at 5:00 am, requesting a favour, and he had answered the call immediately.

"I can't say much," David admitted. "But let's just say I'm trying to help out an old friend."

Shane nodded his understanding. News had already travelled fast and he had already grasped part of the situation.

After reacquainting David with the workings of the boat, Shane slipped on his life jacket and climbed into the canoe. Waving goodbye to his brother-in-law, he called out, "Keep safe." and then he began paddling south towards the spot he had parked his car a few hours before.

David watched his brother-in-law disappear and then he started the inboard engine and started his journey towards Lake Huron and the big mitten.

~

Kevin and Kathlyn had been travelling in silence for a while, listening to the radio station that David had it turned to. Then Kevin glanced over at Kathlyn, and finding her still awake, he slowly turned down the radio. "You may have guessed that I'm not much of a talker," he said by way of an apology. Kathlyn smiled. "That's okay. I wasn't exactly being a chatty Kathy."

"What were you thinking about?" Kevin asked. He didn't want to pry, but he did want to know more about the woman sitting next to him.

Kathlyn took a deep breath. "I was thinking about how quickly life can change," she replied honestly. Then she chuckled. "If Kelly were here, she'd tell me to lighten up and to just embrace the adventure."

Kevin smiled. "That sounds like something Jake would say."

"How long have you known him?" Kathlyn asked, suddenly wanting to know everything she could about the man who was protecting her sister.

Kevin thought about the question a moment before answering. "I suppose it's been the better part of fifteen years. We met at one of the Sweeney's events."

"Sweeney's?" Kathlyn smiled.

"Sweeney is a retired firefighter. Back then he was still on active duty, but now, he hosts an annual Cops vs Fireman softball outing and barbeque. The softball game raises money for the Chicago Children's Hospital. They have a ward dedicated to children's cancer. Sweeney's daughter contracted it when she was three. Unfortunately, they didn't diagnose it early enough and she died from it before her tenth birthday."

"I'm sorry," Kathlyn replied.

Kevin nodded. "It shook Sweeney up quite a bit, but he and Louise, that's his wife, decided to dedicate their lives to ensuring that other parents wouldn't have to go through what they did."

Kevin continued. "It was my first C&F game, and as you can imagine, the competition is pretty fierce. Anyway, I was pitching and Jake nearly took my head off with his first at bat. He later claimed that he was trying to put manners on me, but between you and me, I think he just got lucky. Anyway, as tradition would have it, we bought each other a beer afterwards and that was how our friendship started."

"And David. He's your brother, right? Is he a fireman investigator as well?"

Kevin looked over at her, trying to gauge if she was just curious or if perhaps David had caught her attention. He was after all the most classically handsome of the O'Brien clan, taking the most after their father, who it had been said, looked like a young Sean Connery.

"David is a firefighter. I'm the only brother who branched off and got involved in the investigation of the fires."

Kathlyn smiled. "I've always admired people who broke from tradition." Then she added, "How many of your family are firemen?"

Kevin smiled. "All of us."

Kathlyn laughed. "Sounds like you come from a big family."

Kevin nodded. "There's four kids, and we are all in the fire department. Dad was also a fireman, but he died a couple of years ago."

"I'm sorry. Was it in a fire?" She couldn't help but ask.

"No. It was coronary disease. He was sixty-seven. He had retired a couple of years before that and had been told that he had to watch his diet. But I guess the doctors hadn't realised the extent of his blockage."

Kevin fell silent after that. Kathlyn reached over and squeezed the hand he had on the gear shift. "I'm very sorry, Kevin. I know it sounds like a cliché, but it does get easier."

Kevin turned his hand over and gave her hand a squeeze back. "Thank you, Kathlyn. How long ago did your father pass away?"

"We lost our parents seven years ago. They died in a car accident on their way home from church." She told him. "Kelly and I were away at the time."

Kevin gave her hand another squeeze. "That must have been very hard."

Kathlyn nodded. "It was. It was a seven-car pile-up on I90. We were told that they died instantly, so that was a blessing."

"Then it's just you and Kelly?"

Kathlyn nodded.

Her silence told him more than words ever would, so he squeezed her hand again to reassure her. "Jake will keep her safe," he said confidently. Then he added, "And I'll keep you safe. I promise."

Kathlyn continued to hold his hand, liking the feeling of her hand in his. She was feeling a bit down after having told him about their parent's death. He seemed be offering her comfort and she decided to take it.

Feeling that the mood had taken a downturn, she decided it was time to lighten things up a bit. "So, you have three brothers."

Kevin smiled. "Nope. Two brothers and a sister."

"Your sister is a fireman as well?"

Kevin nodded. "Well, at least for the time being. She's pregnant with her first and I'm not sure her husband will want her in the field again. He's a fireman as well."

"Does your mother work?" Kathlyn wondered if perhaps she too was a fireman.

Kevin smiled. "She's retired. She was a teacher, but retired when my dad did. Now she just wants grandkids in the picture for her to dote over."

Kathlyn remembered something he said before, "You said your sister-in-law was targeted by Prizrak, was that David's…"

"No," he interrupted her. "Danny, my youngest brother, it was his wife Shawnee who was targeted."

196

"And she is in the hospital?"

Kevin nodded, "Yes, she's expecting her first. It's a high-risk pregnancy, so she is in having some tests."

"First grandchildren. Your mom must be over the moon."

"She is. She's very protective. In fact, I'm surprised she isn't at the hospital with Shawnee."

Kathlyn smiled. "As every good grandmother should be."

They fell into silent then and Kathlyn was content to watch the countryside they were driving through.

An hour later, Kathlyn's curiosity started to get the best of her. "So, where are we going anyway?"

Kevin smiled. "Sorry about that, I should have said. We are heading to a secret hideout I have."

"A secret hideout?" Kathlyn asked.

"Yes. To be honest, you'll be the first person I've ever brought there. My family and Jake know I have a place I go to when the noise of the city gets too much, but they don't know where it is."

"Why not?" She couldn't help but ask.

Kevin glanced over at her. "When Shawnee was hiding from Prizrak, Danny took her to the family hunting shack. I would have taken you there, but as it's no longer a family secret, I thought it best to take you to my own little slice of quiet."

Kathlyn studied him a moment and waited for him to explain. "Go on." She prompted him.

"I always loved going to the shack on my own. It was quiet and no one but the family knew where it was. It was the perfect place to be away from things. So, when the incident with Shawnee happened, I realised that I needed to get my own place. I had some money saved up, and I finally pulled the trigger a couple of months ago. I will eventually tell my family about the place, but for now, it's my little secret."

Kathlyn smiled. She liked the idea of a place to go to where no one would be able to find her. Not because of her current situation, but because she too craved time away from the hustle and bustle of the city. "Well then, thank you for sharing it me. I look forward to seeing it."

Kevin laughed. "Well hopefully you won't find it too cramped."

Kathlyn laughed back. "After the half hour in that bag, I'm sure it will seem huge, no matter how small it is."

Turning off the main road, Kevin started driving down a series of dirt roads, explaining that he had the place way off the beaten track.

Kathlyn held on to the rollbar and watched as they drove through a series of forest lined roads.

"Out of curiosity," Kevin suddenly asked, "what is your middle name?"

Kathlyn frowned at the obscure question. "It's Marie. Why do you ask?"

Kevin didn't want to spoil the mood, but he knew they had to talk about a few things before they reached their destination. "Jake suggested that we call you by your middle name. It'll be safer that way." Kathlyn nodded.

Damn, she had almost managed to forget why she was travelling with this handsome man. "Makes sense. What else do I need to do?" She turned and asked him.

She thought she saw his cheeks redden, and wondered why he would be blushing. But his next statement told her why. "We also have to say that we're up here on a date," he said gruffly.

Kathlyn smiled. "Am I that bad?"

"No! I mean, what do you mean?" Kevin shot a look over her way.

"It's just that you don't seem too happy that we're on a date."

"I am!" Kevin was quick to correct her.

Kevin shook his head as he realised that he was blowing it.

Reaching for her hand again, he spoke from his heart. "To set the record straight, I would love to take you out on the date."

It was Kathlyn's turn to blush. "You do?"

Then Kevin brought her hand up to his lips and kissed it. "Yes. I do. I won't lie, I am attracted to you. I have been since I first saw you at the fire, but right now, I'm here to protect you, and that's what I'm going to do. After all of this is over, then I'd like to take you on a date, if that's ok with you."

Kathlyn blushed again. "I'd like that," she replied honestly.

"Besides, this isn't exactly how I would want our first day to be Kathlyn. I would prefer our first date to have been something more romantic."

"More romantic than saving me from a madman?" She smiled, "And it's Marie, remember?" She said, trying to steer the conversation on to safer grounds. She was attracted to him, but she knew that they would both have to keep their minds on the problem at hand if they were to keep safe.

Kevin smiled. "So, Marie, tell me more about yourself? When did you start dying your hair purple and when did you get your first tattoo?"

Kathlyn laughed. "Actually, I first dyed my hair pink. It was for a Breast Cancer charity event and my best friend and I decided we'd go pink. Unfortunately, or fortunately depending on your perspective, it was permanent hair dye and not temporary as we thought. We ended up having pink hair for about four months, and then we had to start working, so we had to get our hair dyed back to its natural colour."

"Did you like it?"

Kathlyn thought about that for a moment. "Yeah, I did. It was something different, and with my tan, it actually looked good. But the upkeep would be murder, so I opted not to keep it."

"And the tattoo?" Kevin asked mischievously.

Kathlyn gave him a seductive look. "That is something you'll have to see for yourself when we finally go on that date."

Kevin looked over at her to see if she was teasing but seeing the look in her eyes, told him that she was telling the truth, and he felt his jeans getting tighter. "I look forward to our date then." His voice sounded lower and Kathlyn smiled. He seemed to like the idea, and that was fine with her.

Turning his attention back to the road, he told himself to get a grip and that he should not get distracted, no matter how tempting this lovely lady was.

Turning down another narrow road, he concentrated again on the road ahead of him. Their destination was just ahead of them and he didn't want to miss the turn off. Seeing it up ahead, he glanced over at Kathlyn and wondered if she would like the place.

Taking the turn, he told her that they would be there in about ten minutes, and he could see her sitting up to take notice of their surroundings.

Through the trees, Kathlyn thought she could see something. It looked like a flag pole, and she smiled, wondering if perhaps he practiced sliding down the pole like she saw firemen do in the movies. But as they turned the corner, she couldn't help the sound of awe that escaped her lips, "Wow."

Before them, she saw a large sailboat. "This is your hideout?" She asked, to confirm.

Kevin nodded as he brought the truck to a stop and looked over at her. "I hope you like sailing."

"I love it," was her reply. Kevin smiled and stepped out of the truck.

Walking around to her side, he opened the door and offered his hand. "Then let's hit the water," he said to her.

Kathlyn laughed.

After gathering the items that were in the back of the SUV, Kevin pointed to an outhouse and suggest that if she needed the facilities that she should use it before they set sail, as it would take a bit of time to charge up the batteries, he would need to get the septic pump running. Nodding, she made her way to the outhouse and after taking an exploratory sniff, she found that it wasn't as smelly as she would have expected and she quickly closed the door and took care of her business.

Using the alcohol rub that he had provided to clean her hands; she stepped out of the outhouse and closed the latch.

Walking up to the boat, she called out to him, "Permission to come aboard, Captain?"

Kevin popped his head up from below and stepped up to offer his hand as he welcomed her aboard his boat.

"Welcome aboard the Stargazer," he said as he offered his hand to help her aboard.

Kathlyn took his hand and stepped up on deck. "She's beautiful." She admitted.

Kevin looked around. "She is. It's taken me four months getting her seaworthy, and now she's a beauty both inside and out."

"I'll show you below, and then let's shove off."

After Kevin gave her a quick tour of the galley, head and sleeping quarters, they worked together to unlatch the moorings and soon they were motoring across the lake.

"What lake is this?" Kathlyn asked as she watched him navigate through a series of tall weeds.

"It's Upper Michigan. We'll be heading to Lake Huron and then to Lake Superior. We can actually sail around for quite a few days before we have to repeat the trek."

Kathlyn smiled and looked out the stern of the boat. "I could live with that."

Kevin explained that the boat had both an inboard and an outboard motor, that they could use should the wind not cooperate. He preferred to sail, and had worked to design the riggings so he could sail the 45 ft boat on his own.

"I've sailed before, so I'm happy to help," Kathlyn said.

"Good. I'll take you up on that offer."

Kevin spent the next hour explaining the ins and outs of the boat. How to start the engines, and he even showed her how she could sail the boat on her own if she wanted. "I think I'll pass on that," she replied. "But it's nice to know," she added to thank him.

Kevin suggested that she sit back and enjoy the ride, and then he switched off the motor and pulled up the sails and set the boat cruising through the waves.

After they had been sailing for a couple of hours, Kevin, looked down at his map and asked Kathlyn which site she'd like to drop anchor at for the night.

Glancing at the map, she smiled. "What are my choices?"

Kevin pointed out two spots. "These are both nice. The one on the left will have a good sunset and the other will have the better sunrise. Which do you prefer?"

Kathlyn smiled. "Both? Let's go for the sunset tonight and then we can choose a sunrise location tomorrow night."

Kevin nodded. "Sounds good." Then he navigated to the spot on the map.

~

Jake slowed down as he pulled the truck off the main road and on to the dirt road that led to the cabin. It wasn't his. It belonged to an old army buddy.

Major Joe Kazcowski, Kaz for short, was currently serving a second tour in Afghanistan. He had told Jake that he was welcome to use the cabin anytime he wanted, on the provision that Jake restock the scotch and kept the place tidy.

Jake hadn't been up to the cabin for a number of months, and he had never mentioned it to any of his co-workers. Knowing the guys, they'd find a reason to 'need' it and then Jake would have to let them down.

He had served with Kaz when they were both stationed at Fort Walton when Kaz was learning to fly Huey helicopters and Jake was a MP. They had met under unusual circumstances but had become fast friends.

Kaz had been caught skinny dipping at the officer's club and Jake had been called in to get him out of the pool before the General found out.

What Jake hadn't known at the time, was that Kaz had just discovered his wife of two months in bed with another man, and it had prompted Kaz to go on a bender. Thus, the reason he thought it was a good idea to go swimming nude at three in the afternoon.

Jake had arrived and had tried at first to talk him out of the water. But the man had proceeded to explain that if his wife could fool around, then he could and that's why he was in the pool. "Best place to meet women." He declared. Jake had smiled and told him that while he agreed that ordinarily it was the best place to meet women, that usually it was best to meet them with clothing on, as then he could attract the shy ones as well. Kaz had thought about it, and then had agreed and had come out of the water in all his glory and had given Jake a big man hug.

Jake and his partner had decided that this was a usual circumstance and had each relinquished a part of their clothing to cover the man and had then proceeded in going bar hoping with the man, fully clothed, to help him drown his sorrows.

The next morning, Jake had woken with a massive hangover and had found Kaz passed out on his sofa.

After waking him, and throwing him in a shower, he had sat him down and got the rest of the story out of him.

Jake had offered the man a place to stay until he could finalise his divorce and they had been friends ever since.

Pulling up to the cabin, he glanced over at Kelly and found that she was still asleep. She had drifted off about a half hour after they had begun their journey, and he wondered if he should let her sleep, but then decided that she wouldn't be able to sleep tonight, and so he leaned over and gently shook her. "Kelly, we've arrived," he said softly, hoping that he wouldn't startle her.

Opening her eyes, Kelly blinked a few times and then realised that she wasn't dreaming. She was looking at a beautiful cabin in the middle of a forest.

"Sorry to wake you, but I thought it might be best to wake you, so you can sleep tonight," he apologised.

Kelly sat up and unbuckled her seatbelt. "It's a beautiful cabin, is it yours?"

Jake shook his head. "It belongs to a friend of mine. But if anyone asks, it's your ex-husbands."

Kelly frowned, but Jake could see a glint in her eye. "Does my ex know I'm bringing up my new boyfriend?"

Jake laughed. "Absolutely not! He'd never let you live it down." Then he opened the car door, "Come on, I'll give you the nickel tour."

After showing her the cabin, which consisted of two bedrooms, a bathroom and a large room that served as both the kitchen/dining room and the living room, Jake went out to the truck and started to cart in some supplies.

"Can I help?" Kelly offered.

"Sure, if you don't mind putting the groceries away, that would be great. I'll start bringing the cabin to life."

Kelly laughed. "Bringing the cabin to life?"

Jake smiled, "That's what Kaz calls it. Could you hand me that list there on the fridge?"

Kelly turned around and saw a piece of paper stuck to the refrigerator. Glancing at it, she saw it was a list of instructions. At the top of the list were the words, 'How to bring the beast back to life'.

Laughing, she handed the page to Jake and then she started putting the groceries away as he had requested.

Five minutes later, Jake had returned. Putting the instructions back, he covering it with a couple of the magnets that were scattered on the refrigerator. "Are you getting hungry?" He asked as he opened the fridge.

Kelly had just finished putting the last of the groceries away. Turning, she smiled. Her stomach had told her that the small sandwich she had eaten hadn't been enough and she had just been contemplating what she was hungry for. "Definitely," she replied. "What would you like?"

"I'll make you a deal," Jake winked, "if you make the lunches, I'll make the breakfast and dinners."

Kelly was surprised. "Really? What do you have against lunches?"

"I can never think of what to make," he answered her honestly.

Laughing, Kelly nodded her agreement. "Sounds good to me. Step aside rookie," she smiled and then pulled out some the cheese and the butter. "Go do something, I'll have lunch ready in a jiffy."

Jake thanked her and then grabbing their bags, took them back to the bedrooms. He would be giving her the 'master bedroom' which was in the back of the cabin, and he would be taking the front bedroom. While he would ordinarily prefer the master bedroom as it had a king size bed, he felt it would be safer if he took the first bedroom.

Putting the bag of her clothing on the bed, he looked around and made sure that everything was in order. Finding it so, he returned to the room he would be using and quickly unpacked his bag, putting his clothing in the drawers.

Walking back into the main room, he could smell something good. "Smells good. What are you making?"

Kelly looked up from what she was doing and smiled. "I'm making skillet BLTs."

"Sounds good. What's in them?" He asked as he stepped closer to the stove to see what she was doing.

"It's really simple." she explained. "It's like a regular BLT, but you build it in a skillet and instead of adding another slice of toast on the top, you add cheese and then you melt it in the oven."

"Well, it smells great," Jake complimented her.

"Thanks," she said and then concentrated on watching the cheese melt, making sure that it didn't burn.

Pulling it from the oven, she transferred the sandwiches to two plates and set them in front of him. "Eat up while it's hot."

"That didn't take long," he said as he took a bite.

"I cheated and nuked the bacon," she admitted as she took a bite of the hot sandwich.

"This is really good," he said after he had devoured half the sandwich.

"I'm glad you like it," she replied as she took another bite.

After they had finished eating, Jake suggested that they take a trip around the lake before it got too late. "We could even see if the fish are biting if you're up for a bit of fishing."

Kelly hadn't been fishing since she was a kid and told him so. "Then we'll definitely get the fishing rods," he decided.

~

They had been fishing for nearly three hours when Jake told her that they should start heading back.

They hadn't caught much, but he could tell that she had enjoyed herself.

Back at the cabin, Kelly excused herself, stating that she wanted to get cleaned up before dinner.

Stepping into the back bedroom, she closed the door behind her and leaned up against it. She had really enjoyed herself, and she had found Jake really easy to talk to. He had helped her bait her hook, and when she had started to reel in a catch, he gently instructed her, so that she wouldn't lose the fish. There had been no yelling, no criticising. It had been perfect. Shaking her head, she realised that she had been expecting him to act just as Stan would have.

But Kat had been right. He wasn't anything like Stan. Jake was one of the good guys. Smiling, she pushed away from the door and went into the on-suite bathroom and started to undress to get cleaned up.

Jake waited for Kelly to finish showering, and to come out of the bedroom before he stepped into the smaller bathroom to shower.

While they were fishing, Jake had laid out some ground rules, which surprisingly, Kelly had agreed to. One of those rules, was that if one of them were in getting dressed or showered that the other would wait. The reason for this is that at all times Jake wanted to make sure that one of them were in a position to alert the other of trouble.

He had also told her that under no circumstances was she to wander away from the cabin on her own. Again, she had agreed, obviously understanding that if she was on her own, she would be an easier target.

Lastly, he had taken his gun out of the holster and gave her some instructions as to how to use the weapon. He showed her how to take off the safety and how to squeeze the trigger slowly in order to steady her shot and ensure a more accurate mark.

Kelly had looked uncomfortable, and he wondering if perhaps she didn't like guns, but she seemed to understand the mechanics of the weapon easily enough, so he shrugged it off as just nervousness on her part.

He had decided that tomorrow they would have some target practice to get her use to firing the gun. If she needed to use it, he wanted her to be comfortable and confident to do so. If the need did arise, they couldn't afford for her to hesitate.

Hurrying through his shower, he was clean and dressed within ten minutes. Stepping into the main room, he found her going through the bookshelf looking for something to read.

"Sorry that there's no television," he apologised, "but there is a radio if you want to listen to something."

Kelly looked back and smiled at him but shook her head. "I like the quiet," she said.

Jake nodded, "So do it." He agreed.

Leaving her to search for a book, he stepped into the kitchen and started to pull out the ingredients to make his spaghetti bolognaise. The recipe was one he had once found on the internet and he had since made some creative adjustments to it. The sauce would take an hour and a half to cook, and they could freeze the leftovers for another night. Being a bachelor, he often made big batches of his meals for freezing, so he was well used to this.

Kelly had found a book and now she was sitting on the sofa reading. "Do you mind if I turn on a little music, or will it disturb your reading?" Jake enquired.

Kelly looked up from the book. "Not at all. Do you want me to help?"

"I've got this," he replied as he wiped off his hands on the tea towel. Turning on the radio, he turned the dial until he found the station he wanted. It was an oldies station that played artist like Frank Sinatra and Dean Martin.

Keeping the volume low as to not disturb her reading, he stepped back to the counter and continued chopping up the vegetables he would be adding to the sauce.

Twenty minutes later, he turned the heat down on the sauce and set the timer on his phone to remind him to start the pasta. He would be checking on the sauce over the next hour to make sure it wouldn't burn, but he knew from experience that it would reduce down to a thick sauce.

Looking out the window, he saw that the weather was starting to turn. Excusing himself, he stepped outside the cabin and ran down to the lake to pull the fishing boat up on to the shore. After taking the fishing equipment out of the boat, he turned the boat over, and then he grabbed the fishing poles and the tackle box and brought it back up to the cabin, putting it in the closet where he had found them.

Then he washed up and set the table. Pulling out a bottle of red wine, he put it on the table, deciding that he would allow her to open it if she wanted any. He would limit himself to one glass as he was still 'on duty'.

His phone beeped, telling him that the timer as up and he put a pot of water on the stove to start boiling, and then he grabbed the spaghetti from the cabinet. Grabbing the loaf of French bread, he cut several diagonal slices in the bread and then he took the garlic butter he had made earlier and spread it thickly between the slices. Then he cut the loaf in thirds and put two thirds of the loaf in tin foil and put them in the freezer for another night. The last third he put on a baking tray and slid it in the oven.

As the water began to boil, he added some salt and then he broke the spaghetti into the water. Giving it a stir, he made note of the time and then he checked the sauce again to see if he needed to turn down the heat under the pan. The sauce was thickening nicely, and he turned it down one degree and replaced the cover.

Filling two glasses with water, he placed them on the table and then walked over to Kelly.

Looking up from the book she was reading, he said, "Dinner will be ready in about seven minutes if you want to wash up."

Kelly smiled at him and then she grabbed the paper cover of the book and marked her place. "Thanks."

Standing, she stretched and then she walked into the kitchen, "It smells amazing," she said as she began to wash her hands as he had suggested.

"Let's hope you like how it tastes," was his reply.

"I'm sure I will," she answered him. "Is there anything I can do to help?"

"If you'd like some wine, you can open the bottle."

Kelly picked up the bottle and read the label. "Yellow Tail Shiraz. It's one of my favourites."

Then she opened the bottle to let it breath a bit before pouring it.

Turning, she saw Jake testing the spaghetti noodles and laughed as he threw a piece against the cabinet. He caught her watching him and he explained. "I've been told it's the best way to test spaghetti, so I always do it. I have to admit, tasting it probably just as accurate, but I think this is a fun way to do it."

Kelly laughed. "I imagine it is."

"Sit down there, and I'll serve you dinner."

Kelly smiled. "If you insist," she replied as she sat in the chair facing the windows. Outside it was now completely black and she could only see her own reflection staring back at her. Glancing at the image presented to her, she watched as Jake drained the noodles and then she watched as he began to dish up the spaghetti onto two large pasta bowls.

Then he reached into the oven and took out some toasted garlic bread, splitting the bread in two and putting the slices on the edge of the bowls.

Setting the bowls down on the table, he sat down. Lifting the glass of wine, she had poured for him, he saluted her. "Here's to you."

She touched her glass to his and replied, "Here's to us."

≈

The next morning, Jake woke early and after checking on Kelly, he started making a box of blueberry muffins for their breakfast.

When he had quietly opened the bedroom door to check on her, he had found her lying flat on her stomach sound asleep. She looked cute, he decided.

Now, as he put the muffins into the pre-heated oven, he could hear the sound of the shower and knew that she had woken up.

Starting the coffee to brew, he pulled out the plates and utensils that they would be using. She appeared a few minutes later and they ate their breakfast in silence.

As they finished their breakfast, Jake turned and looked outside. "The water's a bit rough today. I'm not sure we'll be able to take the boat out."

"That's ok," she replied.

"But we can take a walk in the woods, if you'd like," Jake said. "There's about ten miles of trails we can explore."

Kelly nodded, "That sounds nice, but I'm not sure I have the shoes for anything too rugged."

Jake looked down at the boots she was wearing. "I think you'll be ok. But we'll keep it light this first time out. If your feet don't hurt too bad tomorrow, then we can venture out further."

Smiling, she stood up, "I'll get my coat."

They had hiked for about an hour when Jake suggested they turn back. Kelly had been enjoying the hike and was about to suggest the continue on when he reminded her that he didn't want her to get any blisters. "I'd hate to wreck your feet." He reminded her, "Besides, I have something else I'd like us to do today, and I want to make sure we have plenty of light."

Kelly gave him a quizzical look. "What do you have in mind?"

Jake smiled secretively. "I'll tell you when we get back to the cabin."

Kelly laughed and followed him as he led the way back to the cabin.

It was after two when they arrived back at the cabin. While she made the lunch, he excused himself and stepped out of the cabin. He was back in a matter of minutes and after having a quick lunch, he finally told her his plan.

"I thought it might be good to practice your shooting, so I've set up some blocks so you can have some target practice."

Kelly smiled. "I'd like that," she confessed.

Jake spent the next two hours showing Kelly how to use a gun, telling her that she should always release her breath before slowly squeezing the trigger.

She seemed to catch on fairly quickly and he found her aim was very good.

"Are you sure you haven't shot a gun before?" He teased her.

She seemed to freeze and then said, "You had me shoot your gun yesterday."

Jake nodded. "That's right," he said, but he knew she wasn't telling him the whole story.

~

Later that evening, Kelly helped Jake make the dinner and after they had eaten, he had excused himself and stepped outside. Kelly had sat down to try and read the book she had found, but she couldn't keep her mind on it. Putting the book down, she looked out at the calming waters of the lake.

She had lied to him, and it wasn't sitting right with her. But it was a truth that wasn't just hers to share. She had made a promise, and she couldn't break her promise.

She thought about Kathlyn. She wondered where she was, and if she was alright. When they had gone into hiding before, their only concern had been for Stan not to find them. But they hadn't been as careful as they thought they had been.

Stan had found them, and only after a month of moving from house to house, trying to keep one step ahead of him.

When he had found them, she had been terrified. What transpired had changed her life forever. It had changed both hers and Kathlyn's.

Returning from putting the target practice items away, Jake glanced over at Kelly, and saw that she was staring out picture window at the lake, her book forgotten.

Walking over towards her, he sat down on the sofa next to her. He didn't say anything, but waited for her to acknowledge his presence. Glancing over at her, he could see that there were tears in her eyes. "She'll be fine," he said quietly, somehow knowing that she was worried about her sister.

Kelly bit her lip, trying to stop the tears she knew were threatening to spill. "How can you be so sure?"

Jake put his arm around her shoulders, "Because I know Kevin; and I know that he will do everything in his power to keep her safe."

Kelly leaned her head against his shoulder, welcoming the comfort he was offering. They sat there quietly looking out at the darkening night.

Jake felt her head growing heavier on his shoulder and realised that she had fallen asleep. Part of him knew that he should wake her and suggest that she go to bed, but he wasn't ready to do that.

He liked the feel of her in his arms, and as long as she was comfortable, he thought, *What's the harm?*

But he already knew the answer to that question.

He had always been guarded with the women he dated. Always keeping them at arm's length, emotionally. He guessed that was why he had been single for so long. At forty-two, most men he knew had already been married and divorced. He suspected that was why he didn't allow the women he dated to get too close. He knew that once he found the right woman, he would want it to be forever. He just hadn't found that woman yet.

Until now, he heard himself thinking.

Looking down at the woman in his arms he realised that he liked her. They had only spent a short period of time in each other's company, but he already knew that he could easily fall for her. She had a way of relaxing him, of making him laugh, and that was rare for him.

He knew that life with a detective wouldn't be easy, and he wondering if she was the type of woman who would be able to accept his life as it was? Kaz had once told him that his wife had left him because of the long hours, and the uncertainty that their plans wouldn't change at the last minute. Thus was the life of an army man. Thus was the life of a detective. He would never be able to guarantee that he would be available for dinner dates, much less for bigger events. Why would any woman put up with that life style?

But there were those who had. Milly Doyle, Officer John Doyle's wife had been able to make the adjustment. Hell, they had been married over fifteen years and they were still going strong. Milly had given birth to their daughter only a few months ago, which meant John had to be doing something right.

Shifting in his seat, he started to feel an argument coming forward. *Calm the fuck down,* he told himself.

"Are you alright?" He heard her ask.

Jake looked down at her. Her eyes were still shut, but he could sense that she was awake. "I'm sorry I woke you," he said briefly.

"That's alright," she yawned. "What's wrong?"

Jake frowned. "Nothing's wrong," he said defensively. What was she? Psychic?

Kelly tilted her head back. "Jake, you may be one hell of a detective, but you suck at lying. I can tell you're upset about something. What is it?"

"Would you marry a cop?" He asked bluntly.

Kelly sat back and looked him square in the face. "Yes, if I loved him."

Jake frowned. "Why?"

Kelly smiled. "Because what a person does for a living does not define who they are as a person. Love is about the person, not about the job. Being a cop is no different than being a doctor, or a teacher. The hours may not be as reliable as a teacher, but they can be equally as challenging as that of a doctor. If being a detective is something he wants to do, then who am I to take that away from him? If I love him, it shouldn't matter. All that should matter is that he loves me as much as I love him, and that he wants to spend his free time by my side and not next to another woman."

Jake studied her face and then he smiled back at her. "You are quite a woman," he whispered as he lowered his head and kissed her.

Kelly leaned into the kiss. She knew that they were probably complicating things but she somehow felt this was right. She had meant every word of what she had said. She didn't know why he had asked the question, nor what had been bothering him, but in her heart, she knew that she had been speaking the truth, just as she had known she had been thinking of him alone.

~

Kevin woke to the sound of singing in the galley. They had agreed to have an afternoon siesta before dinner, and he realised that she must have woken before him.

He smiled. Kathlyn was singing a song he recognised but didn't know the name of. She had a good voice he decided, and he slowly got up and threw on his shorts and a t-shirt.

Getting up, he slowly opened his cabin door and watched as Kathlyn did a bit of a slow dance with herself as she cooked their dinner.

"What's the name of that song?" He asked quietly.

Kathlyn turned her head and smiled with embarrassment. "It's 'You take my breath away' by Eva Cassidy," she admitted.

"That's right. I couldn't remember the name," He admitted.

"The dinner is nearly ready if you want to set the table," she said to change the subject.

Kevin smiled. "You don't like to sing in public?"

Kathlyn smiled back. "It's kind of like doing math in public." Then she added, "Actually, no, I don't mind singing in public, it's just that I feel a bit out of practice." She admitted.

"You're good," Kevin said. "And I'm not just saying that. I like your voice," he added. *And your dancing,* he thought to himself.

Kathlyn blushed.

As she handed him a plate of Chicken and Pasta with Pesto sauce, she asked, "Do you sing?"

Kevin smiled. "I'm Irish. Of course, I sing. But usually, I have a few on me when I do," He admitted. Kathlyn laughed.

They fell silent as they ate the meal she had prepared.

Kevin looked up from his plate and studied her. He could tell by the way she was playing with her meal that she was wrestling with something.

Reaching across the small table, he covered her hand with his. "Kat?" She looked up. "What's worrying you honey?" He gently asked her.

Kathlyn couldn't help but smile at the endearment. They had been sailing for three days and they had been enjoying each other's company. Every night after dinner they would spend the time playing cards or talking.

Last night they had started to talk about their pasts. Kevin had asked her about Kelly's ex and she had felt herself wanting to tell him about her past. But as he didn't ask, she thought that perhaps he wasn't interested.

But she did want to tell him about herself, and she wanted to get to know everything about him. It was then that she realised that she was falling for him.

"Kathlyn?" He prompted her, and she realised that she had been drawn into her own questions instead of answering him.

"Sorry about that," she replied and then she decided to take her courage in hand. "I was thinking that I'd like to get to know you better."

Kevin understood. He may not be the sensitive one in the family, but he thought he understood the lovely lady before him.

Smiling, he gave her hand a gentle squeeze. "I'd like that to," he replied. Then he decided to take the first step. "You already know that I come from a family of firemen, and I know that it's just you and Kelly now. I know that you've lost your parents, and you know that I've only my mom now. I know that you are loyal and caring, and I know that you were once in the army, and that you and Kelly now own your own business. I know that you are the technical genius at K&K."

Kathlyn laughed. "I wouldn't call myself a technical genius, but yes, I'm the one who in in-charge to the audio/visual effects."

Kevin stood up and pulled her to her feet as he continued. "I know that you are a good singer, and that I love how you dance. But what you don't know is that I've wanted to kiss you since I met you, and that I'm finding it hard to wait until all of this is behind us to start a relationship with you," he added as he slowly put his arms around her.

He held her lightly, wanting to give her the opportunity to back away if she wanted to. "And I know that whatever you tell me it won't change how I feel about you."

"How do you feel about me?" She asked in a quiet voice.

Kevin leaned his forehead onto hers. "I'm falling for you." he said simply.

Kathlyn looked up at him and stepped closer into his embrace and then she turned her face up to him and kissed him.

The kiss felt like a promise.

~

Kelly had been acting strangely since they had had their target practice, and Jake wondering if perhaps she wasn't comfortable with guns. But she had done very well. Exceptionally well in fact.

Perhaps it had been the kiss they had shared. They hadn't taken the kiss any further, but he had felt the pull on both their sides to move it up a notch or two. Instead, Jake had reined in his emotions, and had kept the intimacy limited to just a kiss and a snuggle. Perhaps she was feeling uncomfortable about that.

He had stepped out of the cabin to check the perimeter, and now, as he walked back into the cabin, he found Kelly sitting on the sofa reading the book she had found.

Sitting down in the chair across from her, he watched her for a moment and realised that she wasn't reading at all. She seemed to be staring off into space.

"Ok, what's up?" He asked her.

Kelly looked up from the book. "What are do you mean?"

"Kelly, I'm a detective. I can tell that something has been bothering you. What is it?"

Kelly put her book down and took a deep breath for courage. The kiss they had shared had changed things for her. She didn't want to keep secrets from him. No matter what the consequences.

Jake stood up and sat next to her on the sofa. Taking her hand in his, he tried to coax her to tell him. "No matter what it is, we'll figure it out." He told her. Feeling sure that whatever she was going to say wasn't going to be easy.

Kelly smiled down at his hand and decided that he was right. No matter what, she had to level with him.

"Don't be mad, ok?" She began. Jake smiled. She sounded like a little kid about to tell her parents that she broke the fine China.

"Go on," He encouraged her.

Kelly gave his hand a squeeze and then she began. "Do you remember when we were telling you about my ex?"

Nodding, Jake gently rubbed his thumb against her hand. Kelly smiled at the jester but she needed to draw on his strength, not his sympathy to tell her story.

"Stan was…"

"A piece of shit?" Jake offered.

Kelly nodded, "Yeah, he was that too," she said. "This is hard." She confessed.

"Take your time," Jake said, and Kelly nodded. "Stan was abusive." She finally said. "He wasn't always." She began to defend herself but she stopped. "Let me rephrase that. He didn't appear to be abusive at first. He would make comments that stung, but everyone used to say that I was just being too sensitive. When he started to get physical, then I knew that he wasn't a good man."

Reaching for her water, she took a drink before she continued. "We had lost our parents only a few months before things changed. I won't go into the details, but let's just say, it wasn't pretty. Kathlyn suggested that I leave him, and I did try, twice, but he would always find me. At first, I really didn't think he would become so…psycho, but he did. The second time he found me, I was at Kathlyn's."

"He wasn't happy, and he said that if she ever sheltered me again, that she would get the same treatment. So, we agreed that it would be best if we both moved. Kathlyn had already left the army and was between jobs, so it seemed

214

like it would be easy to just leave. Unfortunately, Stan got tipped off that we were going to leave, and he showed up at Kathlyn's house."

"That's where he was shot, right?"

Kelly looked up at him. "Yes."

"What happened?" Jake urged her to continue.

"We were packing up Kathlyn's stuff. There was a knock on the door and we thought it was the pizza guy. So, Kathlyn went to the door. She looked in the window and saw Stan's car and then she turned to warn me, but he kicked in the door and she got knocked down. I had been packing some of her things in her bedroom when I heard the noise and I knew that Stan had broken in."

Looking down she knew that now was the time to come clean.

"You did what you had to do sweetheart," Jake suddenly whispered.

Kelly looked up. "What?"

"Kelly, I know what happened. I know that it was you, not Kathlyn that shot your ex. I'm not really sure why you said it was Kathlyn, but I know that it was you."

"How?" She whispered.

Jake pulled her into a hug. "Your sister wouldn't have had time to get the gun and come back and shoot him if she was the one answering the door."

"How long have you known?" Kelly asked.

He looked down at her. "Since you first told me the story. Well, I suspected that what you were saying wasn't the whole story, so I did a little digging myself."

"I noticed some discrepancies in your accounts and in the evidence. I suspect that after the incident, that you and Kathlyn switched places and that she said she was you. I'm not really sure why, but I have my suspicions."

Kelly knew that she had to tell him the whole truth. "Kathlyn was afraid that I would be prosecuted because Stan was my ex-husband. Obviously, we weren't thinking straight."

She suddenly looked up at him. "It was self-defence," She declared.

Jake nodded, "I know sweetheart."

Kelly leaned into him, "Thank you."

"Continue," he prompted her.

"Anyway, since Stan and I had a history, Kathlyn and I were afraid the prosecution would just think I did it on purpose."

"So, you switched places," he confirmed.

Kelly nodded. "Will we get in trouble for this?"

Jake thought about it for a moment. He had learned quite a bit about her ex in his investigation and if the information he had gathered on Stan Abrams was all true, he had left behind a series of abuse allegations. In Jake's mind, it would have only been a matter of time before Abrams would have killed one of his targets.

Shaking his head, he finally answered her. "I don't think so. We will need to set the record straight, but with the history of abuse, and the fact that there was a restraining order in place, I think it should be ok."

Kelly leaned her head back on his shoulder. "Thank you, Jake."

"May I ask you another question?" Jake asked.

"Of course," was her reply.

"Why did you decide to tell me the truth?"

Kelly was silent for a moment. She was a little afraid to tell him the reason. She didn't want to ruin anything, but she did want to be completely honest with him.

Sitting up, away from his embrace, she faced him. "Because, I wanted there to be no secrets, no lies between us," she said simply.

"Because?" He urged her to continue.

Kelly knew that her courage was slipping, so she hurried to answer him, deciding to let the chips fall where they would.

"Because I'm falling for you," she admitted.

Jake smiled. Leaning into her, he kissed her. "That works," he said.

Kelly smiled, "What do you mean by that, Detective?"

Jake kissed her again. "It means, my dear Kelly Ann Flynn, that I'm falling for you too."

～

Heat

They had fallen asleep in each other's arms and Jake had carried Kelly to her bed, and after placing a gentle kiss on her forehead, he had stepped out her room and gently closed the door as to not wake her.

Walking into the kitchen, he poured himself a glass of water, then he heard his phone beep. Glancing down at the display, he saw that it as a message from his Captain, stating that there has been a development and that he should bring the ladies in.

Jake frowned. He knew that something is wrong. The Captain would never send a text like that to him. This could mean only one thing. It's a trap.

Rushing into the back bedroom, Jake woke Kelly, and told her to pack her things, that they had to move. "What happened?" She asked as she leapt out of the bed. "I'm not sure, but I do know that we need to move. Now," he added to ensure her compliance.

While she's packing, Jake carefully constructs his reply, "I don't know what the fuck you're on about. You and I both know Prizrak got the girls. Now leave me the fuck alone."

Then he took the sim out of his phone and destroyed it.

Turning around, he found Kelly waiting for him in the kitchen with her bag in hand. Jake could see the fear in her eyes.

"We're taking the boat," he told her as he ushered her from the cabin.

After locking up, they made their way down to the water and got into the speed boat.

Jake sat her down next to him and then handed a warmer jacket and a blanket. "Wrap this around you. It'll keep you warm." He promised and then he quietly backed the boat out of the slip.

Once they had reached open water, he hit the throttle and headed across the lake.

Kelly finally turned to Jake, "What happened?"

Jake slowed the throttle and reaching out, took her hand. "I'm not sure," he said honestly. "I got a text from the Captain saying I needed to bring you two in."

"But he knows Kat and I aren't together."

"Exactly," Jake said. "Someone was fishing for information."

Kelly thought about it for a moment, then she asked, "How did the Captain know how to reach you? I thought you were using an old phone."

Jake kissed her on the head. "You're bang on sweetheart. No one outside of three people have this number."

"Who are the three?" she asked. "The Captain, Kevin and my partner. The Captain and Kevin know the plan, and Caffrey hasn't been told anything about you and Kathlyn, so he wouldn't even know about any of this."

"Then who?" Kelly asked.

But Jake shook his head. "I've no idea, and that's what worries me." He told her honestly.

Pulling up to one of the resorts on the lake, Jake docked the boat in the slip, and after securing it, he grabbed Kelly's hand and they made their way up to the main cabin.

Jake peaked in the window and saw the kitchen was burning bright. Knocking on the door, he waited for the owner to come to the door.

"Jake Summers, what the hell brings you to my neck of the woods?" The elderly lady greeted him.

Jake smiled and stepped into the warm cabin. "Bernice, how have you been?"

Bernice Jones looked over at the woman next to Jake and smiled. "I'm good, Jakie. Now, what have you done to this poor girl? She looks frozen to the bone."

Taking Kelly by the shoulders, the elderly woman guided her to the kitchen and sat her down at the table. "Hot coffee to start and then something hot to eat I think," Bernice was saying.

Jake smiled at Kelly. "Bernice, this is Ann. Ann, this is Bernice."

"It's nice to meet you," Kelly replied. "I'm really sorry if we are intruding."

"Nonscience. Jakie knows that he is always welcome."

Jake smiled. "I took Ann camping up near Willow creek and well, let's just say that the tent wasn't as sturdy as expected."

"You poor thing," Bernice said as she put a cup of steaming hot coffee down in front of Kelly, along with a plate of homemade bread that was right out of the oven. "Don't be shy now, help yourself. I'll have some eggs cooked up in no

218

time."

"Thanks Bernice," Jake said and poured himself a cup of coffee.

After they had eaten, Jake took Bernice aside and told her that Ann had gotten freaked out about the sounds of the forest, and that was the reason they had shown up. "Any chance that I could borrow your truck to get her home? My car's still at the creek."

Bernice nodded. She knew that he was handing her a load of bull but she had known Jake for over twenty years, and she knew that if he was spinning her a line, it was for her own protection.

"It's yours," she replied. "I got a new Toyota last year, and I hardly ever drive the truck anymore so I won't be missing it."

"You're a star Bern." Jake gave her a hug and a kiss on the cheek.

Jake had meet Bernice when Kaz had first bought the cabin. Kaz had invited Jake up for some fishing and they had run into Bernice after she had gone a few rounds with her ex-husband. He had given her a black eye and some busted ribs before he had passed out. Jake had helped Bernice get a restraining order and had been there to protect her when her ex had tried to come after her. The man had since died of liver failure, and now Bernice was safe.

Thanking her again for the use of the truck, Jake waved goodbye and headed north.

They had been on the road for a half hour when Jake finally pulled over at a phone booth. Jumping out of the car, he called Kevin's answering machine.

"Hey Kev, sorry to bother you, but I don't seem to have Danny's current number, and I was just wondering how Danny got on with my clubs. I may be flying to California to do some golfing and I'm hoping to get my clubs off of him again. Could you give me a shout and let me know? I'll be back to my place by 6:30, so if you could call me after that. Thanks buddy." He ended the call.

Jake knew that Kevin was checking his messages every day and that he would understand the message. He just hoped that no one else would get to the message before him, and that no one would understand the meaning behind the message.

Then he called the only other person he could think of.

The phone was picked up on the second ring. "I need your help," he said to the person on the other end of the phone.

~

Kevin listened to the message again and tried to make heads or tails of it.

He had called his answering service every day since they had set sail, but today was the first time he had a message, and there were two.

The first had been from Jake. It had been in code, but he understood the message. He didn't want to worry Kathlyn, but it meant that they had to move.

The second message was the one he was having troubles understanding. It had been from the Commissioner, and he was demanding an update on Prizrak. It was the Commissioner's daughter, Kevin's sister-in-law Shawnee, who had been targeted by Prizrak. But the Commissioner would have known that Kevin wouldn't have any additional information, so why was he demanding an update?

Kevin listened to the message again and tried to hear what wasn't being said.

"O'Brien, this is the Commissioner. There's a worry that Prizrak is still out there. I want an update. Whoever this guy is, he's getting help, and I want to know my little fille is safe."

It finally sunk in.

"Kathlyn, I think it's time we changed direction." He called up to her. She had been taking the wheel more and more as her love for sailing became more evident as the days went by.

"Aye eye Captain," she teased him. "Where to?"

Kevin sat down next to her. "We've got to head back," he said gently.

"What's happened?" Kathlyn was concerned. "Is Kelly ok?"

Kevin put his arm around her. "I'm sure she is. I haven't heard anything different."

"Then what is it?"

"Jake left me a message that he needs his golf clubs back." Kevin began.

"What does that have to do with my sister?" Kathlyn asked hotly.

"It means that Jake and Kelly had to move, which means that somehow their location may have been compromised."

"How?" She asked, feeling the tears that already threatened to spill.

"I don't know sweetheart," Kevin gathered her in his arms.

"And why does this mean that we have to move?" Kathlyn asked.

"That's the part that I'm concerned about. I also got a message from the commissioner," Kevin told her.

"The commissioner? You mean your sister-in-law's father?" Kathlyn asked.

Kevin nodded. "If I understand his cryptic message, there's a worry that if Jake and Kelly have been found, then our location may also be compromised."

"But how?" Kathlyn whispered.

"There has to be a leak in the department. That's the only explanation."

"A leak?" Kathlyn asked.

Again, Kevin nodded. "Jake's been worried about it for a while. Too many things have happened, too many unanswered questions. If Jake's been found, then there is definitely a leak."

"Shit," Kathlyn let slip. "But if Jake's been found…" she felt the tears beginning to build.

Kevin shook his head. "Jake called me first, which tells me that he's already on the move, and he and your sister are safe."

Kathlyn took a deep breath. "Okay, so now what?"

Kevin smiled at her. "Now we go to plan C."

"Plan C?" Kathlyn asked, "what happened to Plan B?"

"If there's a leak, they may know about plan B, so we're going to improvise." Kevin answered her.

"OK," Kathlyn nodded, "what's Plan C?"

Kevin took the wheel. "I'll tell you when I think of it," was his answer.

Nine days later, Kevin pulled into Quebec Port. They had sailed from Lake Superior, through the Sault Ste. Marie, to Lake Huron, Georgian Bay, past Detroit to Lake Ontario, and then through the Saint Lawrence Seaway.

He hadn't heard any more word from Jake or the Commissioner, so he was hopeful that they had made the right move. Since no one knew Kevin had a boat, it felt fairly safe that they wouldn't be found out, but since Jake had alerted him, he had felt it best to move Kathlyn farther afield.

Besides, he knew someone who would be able to help them in Quebec. He just hoped Kathlyn wouldn't mind.

Over the past two weeks, despite his best efforts to keep their relationship friendly, it seemed that the fates had something else in mind.

While Kevin was a quiet man, he seemed to have no trouble talking to Kathlyn and it was this realisation that told him that he had fallen for the lovely lady.

Kathlyn too had let her guard down and despite the circumstances, she had allowed her heart to get involved.

While their relationship hadn't gotten physical, other than some harmless cuddling, she and Kevin had spent the time getting to know each other. They had shared their pasts, their wishes and dreams.

Jake was taking a chance that his plan would work. He had dropped Kelly off at Lafayette Airfield. He had called in a favour from an old army buddy, and now Kelly was on her way to safety. Of this, he was sure.

He realised that he had probably overstepped his jurisdiction, but he knew it had to be done. He now knew, beyond a shadow of a doubt that there was a leak in the department. Who it was, he had no idea, but he wasn't going to trust anyone?

Walking into the precinct, Jake made his way to Captain Weatherton's office.

Jake's partner Detective Allen Caffrey had returned from his medical leave and was sitting in the chair opposite of the Captain's and they were discussing one of the new cases.

Jake could see the surprise on both men's faces.

Caffrey was the first to speak. "The prodigal son returns."

Jake smiled thinly. Caffrey had always teased him that he was Weatherton's golden boy. Jake had always shrugged it off but now he couldn't help but wonder if there was something more behind it.

Captain Weatherton frowned. "I thought I told you to take some time off."

Jake nodded. "You did, sir." Jake thought he saw a frown cross Caffrey's face but he couldn't be sure.

As the atmosphere began to get hostile, Jake's partner stood up. "I'll check into these robberies," he said to his boss and then walked out, discretely closing the door behind him.

As Jake began to speak, he handed the Captain a note that said, "I did some digging and found another discrepancy in the FBI's records."

Weatherton frowned. They had been finding a number of 'discrepancies' as Jake put it, over the past few months.

Every time the FBI had been called in to assist with possible mob activities, they had sent an agent or agents there were under internal investigation; and while Weatherton knew that it couldn't be a coincidence, Jake and his team hadn't been able to find any concrete evidence that there was a conspiracy.

Weatherton concentrated on what Jake was saying, "Sir, I would like to step back from this investigation."

Weatherton looked back up at Jake. Jake fell silent, and his silence told his boss much more than words. Jake had long expressed the concern that there was a leak in the office and that quite possibly the whole CPD was under surveillance. Jake's silence told Weatherton that perhaps Jake finally had the proof.

Handing him back the note, he said, "I don't think so." Then he grabbed a scrap of paper and his pen and began to write something. As he wrote, he said, "You're a good man, Jake and I know that this investigation got out of our control, but you can't take that all on your shoulders. Now, as I told you before, I want you to take a long vacation. It hadn't been a suggestion. You need time to get your head straight, and to stop thinking about this case. So, get out of here. That's an order. Is that understood?" He added as he held out his hand to shake Jakes.

Jake nodded and as he withdrew his hand, he read the note that the Captain had handed to him, and he knew what to do next.

Walking out of the precinct, Jake headed for his favourite coffee shop. The note had suggested a meeting, and after ordering two coffees, he walked towards the park and sat down at a bench and waited. He wasn't sure if he would be met, but he knew that if no one showed that he had gambled wrong.

"What are the discrepancies?"

Jake turned to see his Captain approaching. Sitting down, Jake handed him the second cup of coffee he had bought and he started to explain himself.

After telling him about the text he had gotten, Weatherton shook his head, "Who the fuck are we dealing with? They always seem to be a step ahead of us."

Jake nodded. "Except this time," he said.

Weatherton nodded. "True. But that's only because we limited the exposure. We really need this guy to make a mistake."

"That's the way it's looking," Jake confirmed. "I've contacted a friend in the FBI, and he's doing his own investigation. So far, he's coming up short."

Weatherton looked over at Jake. "So, what's the next step?"

Jake glanced over at his Captain, "It's time to turn up the stakes."

"Meaning?" His Captain frowned.

"We need a hook. Something that will bring this guy out of the shadows," Jake continued. "I'd like to recommend that we go public with a story that we have an eye witness who can name the arsonist. We show our hand and let the chips fall."

"Gutsy move," Weatherton confirmed.

"Unless you have a better idea, it's the only thing I got going."

Captain Weatherton nodded. "I'd like to keep this between us. The few people in the know the better. There's definitely a leak in the department, and until we know for sure who we can trust, we can't trust anyone. Even those close to us."

Jake nodded. He knew his partner would be pissed off as soon he learned that he wasn't being trusted, but until they caught the culprit, they just couldn't take any chances.

~

Quebec is a lovely city, rich with history. Kevin had visited the city only once before, and on that occasion, he had been in much the same position as he found himself now.

It had been four years ago. Kevin had taken his vacation to the French city to relax before he started his studies to be a fire investigator.

He had stayed in a B&B owned by a French-Canadian family who, had offered their assistance in finding things to do to distract him for the week. As it transpired, they had needed his help more than his theirs.

Claire Tremblay opened the door and smiled. "Mon ami!" and then she gave Kevin a big hug and a lingering kiss.

Kathlyn frowned. Was this a girlfriend of Kevin's?

Kevin smiled down at the woman, "Bonjour mon ami, ça fait longtemps." *Hello my friend, it has been a long time.*

Then the lady looked around Kevin, suddenly noticing Kathlyn, "Oh, est-ce votre femme?"

Kevin smiled but shook his head. "Pas encore."

Claire suddenly realised that the young lady did not speak French. "Hello, apologies, but it has been a long time since I've seen my good friend. I am Claire Tremblay," she said as she held out her hand.

Kathlyn forced a smile on her lips. "I'm Kathlyn," she replied, taking the woman's hand.

"Kathlyn, that's my grandmama's name. You and I will be great friends." Claire said and then gave Kathlyn a big hug and two kisses.

Kathlyn's smile became genuine. "I'd like that," she replied, suddenly liking this lady.

"Kevin, are you and your lady friend here for pleasure or 'pleasure'?" She winked.

Kevin put his arm around Kathlyn. "A bit of both," he answered her.

After being shown to their room, Kevin put the bag he had packed on the bed, and then turned to find Kathlyn studying him. "What?"

"Is Claire your girlfriend, or former girlfriend?"

Kevin shook his head. He knew he would have to come clean about their relationship. "No. I helped her once."

"That was quite the kiss she gave you," she said, not convinced that he was telling her the truth.

"Claire is French," he replied as an explanation. Then he continued. "Jake told you that I once was asked to protect someone; Claire was that person. She was in a delicate situation and I helped her out," he said simply. He didn't feel that it was his place to tell Kathlyn all of Claire's business, so he hoped she would be happy with his answer.

Kathlyn studied him a moment. She could tell that he was holding back on something, but somehow, she knew that whatever it was, it was something that he didn't feel at liberty to discuss.

Then he said, "Hey, I've got to run an errand and I need you to stay in the room. I wouldn't be long, but I do need you to stay tight. Ok?"

Kathlyn agreed, but her heart fell. *He's probably meeting up with Claire.* She thought. Then she gave herself a shake. *He's not yours.* She reminded herself. They may have grown closer, but they hadn't made any promises.

Kathlyn hadn't always been a jealous person, but Matt, her ex, had taught her that she had to be cautious and that she should guard her heart.

Sitting down on the bed, she decided that she need to relax and so she started practicing her yoga. Anything that would take her mind off where she thought Kevin had gone and what he might be doing.

Hearing the door opening, she opened her eyes and blinked. She couldn't move.

"Hello Kat," she heard the familiar voice.

Then she moved.

Squealing she ran up and hugged her sister tightly. "Oh my God Kelly. I've missed you so much! Why are you here? When did you get here? How did you get here?" She asked the series of questions that were popping into her head.

Kelly laughed and hugged her sister back. Emotion was choking her.

Kathlyn looked up and saw Kevin walking in the room. "Thank you," she whispered to him.

As the ladies caught up, Kevin took his leave and went to speak with Claire.

Claire had met Kelly nine days earlier, when she had showed up at her door. Kelly had arrived with a message from Jake saying that Kelly needed to be hidden. Claire had jumped at the opportunity to help her old friend.

Kevin found Claire in the kitchen making some bread. "The ladies have met up?"

Kevin smiled. "Yes, they are talking now."

"They are sisters, no?" Marie asked as she continued to knead the dough.

Nodding, Kevin sat down at the table. "How have you been?" He asked her.

Claire paused in her ministry. "Bien. Jacques is in university. I think he's studying the girls more than the books, but he's young," she smiled.

"He's what, 19 now?" Kevin asked.

"Oui," then she laughed, "19 going on 30."

"I always thought it was the girls you said that about?" Kevin asked.

"Not with French boys. They rush to adulthood," she said.

Then Claire's curiosity got the best of her. "The ladies, they are in trouble, no?"

Kevin nodded his head. "They need our protection." He clarified.

Claire nodded. "Then we will keep them safe," She promised.

Kathlyn learned that Kelly was in the room next to hers, and Kevin had been given the room across the hall from them. Kelly had told her that when Claire had learned that Jake had sent her, that she had greeted her with open arms and that she had spent the last two days helping Claire run her business, which, it turned out was a bakery.

Since Kelly had always loved cooking, it was like a match made in heaven.

Kathlyn said she would love a shower, and Kelly agreed to meet her in half an hour, leaving her sister as she headed back down to the kitchen to help Claire.

After her shower, Kathlyn walked across the hall and knocked on Kevin's door. Opening the door, he invited Kathlyn in. After he had shut the door, Kathlyn turned to him and hugged him. "Thank you, Kevin."

Kevin breathed in her scent and smiled. He loved how she felt.

Leaning back, Kathlyn asked the question that had been burning in her mind. "What did she say before?"

"Who?" He frowned.

"Claire." She said, 'Est-ce votre femme?' "What does that mean?"

Kevin paused a moment and then said, "She asked if you were my friend."

Kathlyn smiled. She knew it had to be something more, because she knew that 'Pas encore' meant 'Not yet'. Giving him another hug, she decided that she would have to look up what the woman had actually said.

～

The news article ran on Thursday. It had first hit the evening news, and then the papers had it and it ran the next morning.

Series of fires linked to arsonist.

A series of fires have now been linked and a second eye witness has come forward who can identify the arsonist.

Police have confirmed that a previous eye witness has been missing for the last two weeks, and is presumed dead.

Jake read the headline and wondered if it would work, and if Prizrak would take the bait.

Prizrak

When Jake had learned that Prizrak was still alive, he had begun looking closer at the man who had gone after Shawnee. The man had been buried, but they had gathered forensics when he had been shot and killed at the cabin when he had gone after Shawnee.

Due to the circumstances surrounding his death, the forensics hadn't been as closely analysed as if the man had been caught red handed.

Now Jake and his team were looking at the evidence and it just didn't match. Whoever had gone after Shawnee didn't have any prints on file, and his image did not match any from the FBI database. But none of it made sense.

Jake reached for his phone as it started to ring. It was Officer John Doyle. "Jake, we have him," he was saying.

"What do you mean?" Jake asked, still concentrating on the file before him.

"The arsonist," he paused. "And the traitor. We have them, Jake."

Jake looked up, "Talk to me."

Doyle knocked on Jake's office door before walking in.

Handing the file to Jake, he began to explain. "After we confirmed that the prints for the Keegan file were falsely identified, I decided to run a comparison on the prints we got from the Rumours fire."

227

"And?" Jake prompted.

"They were a match."

"What?" Jake started to look at the file John had handed him.

"It gets better," John told him. "I decided to run the prints against a broader database."

Jake looked up, and John nodded. "The FBI also had the prints, on their files, but they didn't have a name to match it with. So, I went through the past few cases where we suspected Prizrak, and bingo. On three separate cases, I found the same prints. It has to be him."

Jake studied the evidence John had brought him. "Good work." He confirmed. Then he looked up at the officer.

"Who else have you shown this to?"

"No one sir." Smith confirmed. "I didn't want to chance it."

Jake frowned, "What do you mean?"

"I didn't want to chance it that the information would fall in to the wrong hands." Then he continued. "Sir, I know that you have suspected a leak in the department, and considering everything that's happened, I would agree with you. Besides, there's no way that Prizrak, or whoever that guy was, found the O'Brien's cabin. We've been trying to find that cabin for years without any luck, and we didn't have a real reason, other than curiosity to justify the search. And there's no way that he would have known the location of the Swan witness. So there has to be someone inside the precinct who is sharing the information. Someone who is close to the investigation." Then he paused.

He had his suspicions, but it was the kind of suspicions that got a guy put back on the beat. He trusted Jake, so he decided to take the chance. "There are only a handful of people who know all the details of this case, and despite all our efforts to keep the details secret, someone keeps leaking things."

He paused again, "I did a little digging and the only time we've ever caught a break in this case has been when we've been…" he searched for the right word.

"Understaffed." Looking down, he added, "I'm sorry sir, but there's only one person who it can be."

Jake studied the man whom he had known for the past 19 years. He trusted him. "You're right."

John relaxed. "Does the Captain know?"

"He knows of my suspicions," Jake answered him.

"Do you think Caffrey knows?" John asked.

Jake frowned. "I haven't spoken to him about it."

John studied the detective. "You've known him for 7 years."

Jake nodded. He couldn't quite explain it but there was something that had him holding back from bringing his partner in on the case.

Jake wasn't superstitious, but he did trust his instincts, and right now, they were telling him not to say a word to Caffrey.

Caffrey had been on sick leave for the past month, so he didn't see how he could be involved, but Jake still had a nagging feeling that he couldn't be trusted. Perhaps it was the jealousy that Caffrey seemed to have of his relationship with the Captain, or the fact that he was given the lead of the investigation. But whatever it was, he had decided not to bring him into his confidence.

"Let's just say that we're keeping the list of who knows small," he finally answered the officer.

Two days later the case finally broke.

They had been waiting for Prizrak to show himself, wondering when and how he would come out of hiding. Since they had announced that there was a second eye witness, they had been careful to keep the details of the witness a secret. But as with most secrets, they did allow bits and pieces to slip out, strategically setting the bait.

The story was that the man who had seen the arsonist running from the Swan had decided not to come forward since the girl already had. But when there wasn't anything on the news about an arrest, he had decided to come forward.

His location was still unknown to all but Jake, who, after losing the girl, had decided that he wasn't going to chance a second murder and wasn't telling a soul. He hadn't even brought the Captain into his confidence, much to his Captain's very vocal disapproval.

‏ؤ‎

Jake turned over in his sleep. He hadn't been sleeping well, thinking about Kelly and hoping that she was still safe. He had taken the chance that she wouldn't be found, and he had purposefully broken off all contact with her, in the hope that he wouldn't jeopardise her safety.

But he missed her. It had been over a week, and while he may have known her for only a short period of time, he felt that they had formed a bond far stronger than any he had ever had with another woman.

If he was honest with himself, he knew that he had finally found the woman he could see by his side until the end of time. *God, you sound like a harlequin romance,* he told himself. But he knew that no matter how sappy it sounded, even to himself, it was the truth. He had fallen in love, and there was a chance that he would never see her again.

He heard the squeak of the door and knew that he had a visitor.

Carefully reaching for the gun he had under his pillow, he waited.

The moonlight was coming in from his window, and it gave him a clear view of his bedroom door, but would shadow him from the intruder.

He saw the gun first, and he fought his instinct to shoot. He needed to get this guy, and he didn't want to chance a misfire.

As the intruder quietly made his way fully into Jake's room, he made his way toward Jake. Jake could see something in his other hand, and realised that it was a needle. *So, he plans on drugging me first.* He thought. But Jake wouldn't be giving him the chance.

"You're under arrest," he said, and when he saw the man lower his weapon, he acted. The gun he had pointed at the man tore through the man's left hand, taking the gun out of his hand, the second hit him in the knee, bringing him down.

Jake jumped out of bed and aimed his gun at the man, intent on stopping the man if he tried anything else.

"Hold it right there, Prizrak. You're under arrest."

Jake heard the glass behind him breaking a second before he felt the bullet graze his arm.

Ducking down, he manoeuvred his way to the wall and hazarded a glance outside. He couldn't see anything.

Glancing back at Prizrak he saw that he wasn't moving.

Making his way back to his suspect, he saw the reason why. He had a bullet in the centre of his forehead. The man was dead.

Jake reached under his bed and grabbed the walkie talkie he had hidden there and radioed in the incident; then he waited for the FBI to arrive.

∼

Sarah was tired, she hadn't been sleeping well since she had arrived at the cabin nearly two weeks ago.

When she had left Ann, she had driven west towards Michigan. She knew she had to keep going, no matter how tired she was.

At one point, she had nearly quit. It had taken her over a day of driving nonstop, but when she realised that she was nearly there, she had kept going. She had been driving for well over five hours and according to the sat nav, she should be getting close to her destination.

She remembered that it had been nearly seven thirty in the morning and despite having driven throughout the night, she had been surprised that she had remained alert most of the night.

She had been awed when she saw the sun rising over the countryside and had slowed down only a moment to take in the view. But she knew she couldn't dally, so she had continued on, telling herself that tomorrow she would get up early and watch the sunrise from the cabin she was told to drive to.

Hearing the sat nav start to give directions, she slowed down as it told her to take the next left, and to follow highway 75 north.

She had been travelling on 75N for about ten minutes when she saw a small grocery store up ahead. Pulling over, she decided that she should pick up some supplies so that she wouldn't have to run out again once she found the cabin. Lord only knew how far the place would be from the nearest store, so she thought it best to stock up now.

Twenty minutes later, the sat nav told her to slow down and to take the next right. Seeing what looked like a dirt road on her right, she took the turn and then continued driving.

The area around her was beautiful. Seeing a small sign, she slowed down again. Mill Creek State Historical Park. Well, that explained why she hadn't seen any houses, but where was she supposed to be staying? Where was this 'cabin on the hill'? On the note Ann had provided to her, she had written, 'The sat nav will take you to the cabin on the hill. The key is under the seventh rock next to the oak tree'.

Driving ahead, she waited for the sat nav to direct her again, praying that it would in fact take her to the cabin as Ann had said.

It took her another hour and then she saw it. It was indeed a cabin on the hill. Slowing to a stop. Sarah parked the bike and then looked around. There were several oak trees next to the house and she wondered which tree she was to look under as they all had decorative rocks around the base of them.

Stepping up to the one closest to the house, she saw that around this tree there were slightly less rocks than around the other trees. Taking a chance, she counted seven rocks from where she stepped off the warn path leading to the cabin. Lifting the rock, she smiled. Bingo. Lucky number seven came through.

The cabin door eventually opened, but only after she had finessed the key a bit. Stepping into the cabin, she called out to verify that she was alone. "Hello? Is anyone here?"

Only her echo came back in return and she decided that she was definitely quite alone. Walking around the cabin, she found a note stuck to the refrigerator door that gave directions as to how to start the water and electricity. Following the instructions, she soon saw the lights come on and then she heard the water running from the various taps.

As she went about shutting off the various lights and taps, she made a brief exploration of her new home. The cabin had three rooms. A bathroom, a bedroom and one large main room. The rooms were sparsely decorated and she wondered who the place belonged to. There weren't any photos that would have given her a clue to who the owner was, and she wondering if perhaps this was another of the FBI safe houses. But the fact that Ann had sent her there, after saying there had been a leak, made her think that perhaps this was Ann's cabin, or perhaps her family's cabin.

Then she went out to her bike and carefully manoeuvred it to the side of the cabin, out of view from the road. When she had stopped for the groceries, she had also filled the bike up with fuel. Now she positioned the bike so that she could leave quickly should she need to move in a hurry.

Grabbing her backpack and the bags of groceries she had bought, she walked back into the cabin and started to put things away. The groceries she had selected had been mainly canned and dry goods, but she had also picked up a few things that she could freeze. The milk, eggs and bread were things that she would have to resupply sooner than the other items.

Ann had given her two thousand dollars to survive on, and while she was confident that it would be more than enough, she wondering what she would do if she was left there for a long period of time. Her concerns about taking the bar were now replaced with concerns on how she was going to survive.

Despite feeling exhausted, Sarah decided that she should take stock into what supplies were already in the cabin, and then to make a budget to ensure she would be fine for a good long time. She wanted to be prepared no matter what happened.

An hour later, she was satisfied that she had a preliminary plan to work with, and after putting a few items back in her backpack on the contingency that she would need to leave in a hurry, she decided to explore her surroundings.

Despite it being only eleven in the morning, the temperature had started to rise, so she slipped into a pair of shorts she had found in the bedroom and stepped out onto the back porch.

The cabin, she soon discovered, was situated on a hill over-looking Lake Huron. From where she stood, she couldn't see any other houses, and she wondered if she wasn't in a Forest Ranger's cabin.

She remembered reading once that the Forestry service rented out the cabins to raise additional funds, perhaps they sold some off as well.

Eyeing an Adirondack chair on a spot over-looking the water, she made her way down to the chair and sat down.

She was tired. Bone tired, and she could feel her eyes already growing heavy at the thought of a nap.

Leaning back, Sarah closed her eyes and told herself to just listen to the sounds of the forest; knowing that it would soon lull her to sleep.

Sarah shifted in her seat. Opening her eyes, she saw that the sun was low in the sky, telling her that she had slept much longer than she had expected.

Sitting up, she stretched and then she looked out at the water below. It was so tranquil and she realised that it was the first time in five years that she had felt at peace.

Walking back into the cabin, she glanced at the clock on the wall and saw that it was nearly four o'clock. She had slept for five hours.

Taking out a few supplies, she decided that she would make some chili for dinner. She could freeze a good portion of it to eat later, and it would take care of a couple of the perishables that were in the refrigerator.

An hour and a half later, she sat down and ate a bowl of the chili while she glanced over a cookbook she had found on the shelf above the microwave.

After she had cleaned her dishes and bagged the rest of the chili into freezer proof bags, she stepped outside again.

The weather had started to dip, so she grabbed a sweatshirt she found handing by the door and slipped it on.

Walking down past the chair she had slept in earlier, she stood looking over the darkening skies.

To her left, in the far distance, she could see a light house, and she wondering if it was the Old Mackinac Light House, she had seen on the map. To her right, she could see the faint lights of a town, which she guessed was the town called Freedom. There were a smattering of other lights dotting the coast line, but other than a few clumps of civilisation, the terrain was dark.

It was a beautiful location she decided, and part of her thought she could live there the rest of her life. But then the reality of her situation seemed to come full circle as she thought about why she was there.

She remembered the desperation in Ann's voice when she told her to 'get the hell out of there'. Something was wrong, and that had forced Ann to take these drastic measures. Sarah was sure that her safety had been compromised, otherwise Ann would never have sent her off on her own.

That had been two days ago, and she still had no word.

Sarah closed her eyes and said a quick prayer that Ann was okay and that she would come to collect her, and that this whole mess would be over soon.

~

Jake knocked on the door to Captain Weatherton's office.

Captain Weatherton looked up and called him in. "Shut the door," he said and then motioned to the chair in front of his desk, continued, "I thought you'd still be on medical leave?" He asked, referring to the wound Jake had sustained when the bullet hit him. It had been obvious that the target hadn't been Jake, but the man who had been send to abduct him. But it had left him with a fractured arm.

Jake nodded. "I was sir," was all he said as he handed him an envelope and said, "but something has come up."

"Anything to do with the arson case?" He said and then as he began as he opened the envelope,

"Not exactly," was Jake's reply.

The Captain stopped, glancing down at the note in his hand, he saw that it was a note that simply said, "I have proof."

Frowning, the Captain looked up at his lead detective for an explanation. Jake handed the man another envelope. "I'd like to take an extended leave of absence."

"How extended? How much time are we talking here?" Weatherton asked, trying to get a handle on what Jake was trying to tell him. "I want you to take some time, but I do need you back here. We have a number of ongoing investigations that need your attention." He explained.

Jake nodded his head in understanding, but continued the façade. "After everything that's gone down lately, I think it would be good to just get away for a month or two. I've booked a flight to California leaving immediately. The doctor said that I should get this sling off with in a week or two, then I thought I'd get some golf in, visit some old army buddies. Considering everything, I think now is the best time to do it."

"A couple of months!" He shouted, playing his part. "I don't know if I can sanction that Summers."

Jake waited. He knew that if his hunch was true and the Captain's office, as well as his house, was being monitored, then his reply had to be perfectly timed. "I'm going sir, whether you sanction it or not," Jake replied quietly.

"God damn it!" Weatherton shouted. Then he too paused. Glancing down at his watch, he waited a minute before he replied, "You've really left me with no wiggle room haven't you. Go, get it out of your system. But I want you back here in a month, no longer," He concluded.

"Thank you, sir," Jake said and then he turned, and left.

~

After Jake left, Weatherton walked out of his office and as he passed Officer Doyle, he told him that he would be taking an early lunch, and then he headed home.

It was often his habit of going home for lunch when he was royally pissed off. There, he would grab his gym bag and leave, telling his wife that he was going to go play squash.

Captain Weatherton didn't play squash. What he did do was drink. He would go to his local and have two or three whiskeys and shoot some pool with the locals. He always told his wife he was playing squash because she disapproved strongly of drinking, and this was his way of sidestepping her look of disapproval.

Three hours later, and forty dollars poorer, he walked out of the bar and headed home. After kissing his wife, he said he wanted to take a shower and headed up to their room. Taking the bills out of his pocket, he found the note that had been slipped to him during one of the games.

'7 Shanty Café Riots'

Weatherton frowned. "Shit."

~

At 6:30 am, Weatherton slipped into the back door of the Shed Museum, and stepped into the security office and waited.

If he had understood the coded message correctly, '7 Shanty Café Riots' meant Caffery is rotten, and to meet him at the shed at 7. Looking back at the note, he shook his head. Jake and he had started this little coding game a long time ago, but he had never thought he'd see a message like this.

~

At 7 am, he was convinced that no one had followed him, and after thanking the man who had helped him, he walked into the employee coffee room.

Jake was there, sipping his second cup of coffee.

"This had better be good." Weatherton told his lead detective.

Jake nodded. Standing, he went to the counter and made his Captain a fresh cup of coffee. When the men were both seated at the table, Jake pulled out a thick envelope and put it on the table.

Weatherton took the envelope and open it. "What's this?"

Jake frowned. "It's the evidence we've been missing that shows that Caffery has been leaking information to an informant on the FBI and to Nemetskiy."

Weatherton looked up, "Are you sure?"

Jake nodded. "When I figured out that we must have a traitor in our presence, I pulled John Doyle into my confidence and he pulled all the evidence we have on Nemetskiy and Prizrak. Every bit of evidence has Caffery's name on it."

"We ran a check on his bank records and he has been receiving routine deposits of five grand from someone named Rita Turner."

"Who is she?" Weatherton asked.

"I'm getting to that," Jake said. He wanted to lay everything out clearly for the Captain so that there would be no misunderstandings.

"As I was saying, we pulled everything we could on Nemetskiy and Prizrak. If you remember, Caffery was running point on the initial investigation. He was the one who did the research and came up with the name Nemetskiy, claiming that it came from Interpol. Well, we've since conducted my own research and there's no such person. According to Interpol, they never even heard of Caffrey. He never contacted them. Oh, and when we mentioned the name Nemetskiy, the guy laughed. Did you know that Nemetskiy means German in Russian? The bastard has been paying us for fools."

Then he paused a moment before he dropped the second bomb. "It also proves that Prizrak never existed."

Weatherton leaned forward, "What do you mean he never existed?"

"There is no Prizrak," Jake confirmed. "That's why we've never been able to catch him. Prizrak is a fictional character dreamed up by Nemetskiy or Caffery. Either way, it looks like this guy Nemetskiy has had a number of people working for him all along, and all the while we're chasing our tails looking for one man. One fictional man. I looked it up, Prizrak means Ghost in Russian."

Weatherton frowned, and opening the packet of information, he started to read the evidence Jake had gathered.

"What about the finger prints we've gathered?" Weatherton needed those explained.

"From what I've been able to gather, Caffery created fake fingerprints from a number of John Does."

Weatherton shook his head. "Continue."

Jake took a sip of his coffee and then continued. "From what I've been able to pull together, the finger prints, or part of the prints match at least four John Does on our database."

"So, what went wrong?" Captain Weatherton had to ask. "Why kill four FBI agent if the girl can't even ID anyone?"

Jake frowned, "I suspect that she said something that told them that she knows more than even she realises."

Jake pointed to one of the pages in the pack as he continued, "Remember when she said the man had an accent?"

Weatherton nodded, "The linguist."

"Mathew Travers," Jake confirmed, "Travers said that accent is German. From the Bavarian region. I did a little more digging into whoever this Nemetskiy could be, and what I discovered was very enlightening."

Jake took a sip of his coffee before continuing. "I sent the description and MO over to Interpol and they were able to confirm a few things for me. Nemetskiy resembles a man named Hicke, Josef Hicke."

Weatherton frowned. "You're not saying…"

Jake nodded. "Josef Hicke is Joseph Hickok."

"He's in prison," Weatherton tried to debunk the theory, but Jake continued.

"I've checked, and Caffrey makes regular visits to the man. I've also looked more closely into August Productions. Caffrey has property that sits on land appropriated by August Productions."

"And the finger prints of Scott Turner?" Jake continued. "Turner, I've discovered, is not only Hicke's top man, but he's actually his son. He was born in Germany to Rita Turner, Hicke's mistress. She gave him an American name and got an American passport for him so that he wouldn't be directly tied to Hicke. Daddy's been grooming his son to take over for years."

"So, it must have been Turner who killed the good doctor." Weatherton hypothesised. Jake nodded. "And once we find Turner, we find the murder weapon."

"But why were his finger prints on the fire extinguisher?" The Captain asked. "He's managed to escape detection up until now? I can't believe he would slip up."

"I'm not sure he did," was Jake's reply. "I don't know, maybe Caffrey thought Turner was looking to get rid of him, or maybe he was trying to break out from under Hicke's hold. Whatever the case, it looks like the finger prints were planted. I had forensics reinvestigate the extinguisher, and Caffrey's prints were also found. Now, while he could say that they were there only after the initial investigation was completed, I don't believe it."

Looking down at the evidence that Jake had gathered, he asked the obvious question. "Do we have enough to convict?"

Jake finished his coffee and got up and washed the cup and put it in the dishwasher. "We've got all the evidence we need, but we need one more piece to hit the final nail in the coffin."

"Sarah Coffey." Weatherton answered for him. "Then that's it." He frowned. Jake shook his head.

"She's probably dead, Jake." He tried to reason with his lead detective. "I'm guessing they took her and then made sure she hadn't and wouldn't speak to anyone else."

Jake shook his head again.

"Explain yourself, Summers." Weatherton was losing his patience.

"You're not going to like this, sir."

~

David had been sailing for nearly a week, and despite stopping to sleep, he was tired. But he knew that he needed to get to the girl as soon as he could. By his calculations, he would have to sail a little over 127 nautical miles to get to his destination, and it was taking longer than expected. He had to conserve his fuel, and so he had to rely on wind power, and the gods hadn't been kind. Based on his calculations, if he could manage 7 knots, he would cover 100 nm in a little over fourteen hours, instead he had found himself having to wait out a sudden storm that had lasted two days and now he was rushing to get to the girl before someone else did.

Consulting his maps, he figured that he would get there sometime in the afternoon. That was if the wind kept up, and if he could find the cabin. He knew he had very little to go by, but he hoped that what the dying agent had whispered to him had told him just enough.

Three hours later, he pulled down the sails and started the outboard motor to control the speed of his ship. She had told him, "South of the lighthouse. Look for the dip in the trees. The lone cabin on the hill. Before Freedom."

Now, as he once again consulted his map, he found himself sailing past the old lighthouse and then he started looking for the dip in the trees, hoping he would see the cabin on the hill.

~

Sarah yawned, she had been reading the Lord of the Rings novel that she had found in the cabin for the past few hours and her eyes were getting tired.

Funny how when you have nothing to do but wait, that you get so tired of doing nothing. If she had been able to bring her books, she would have been spending her time studying, but that was not a possibility. She was glad when she found the novel. It was one of her favourite movies, but she had never made the time to read the book, so now it was her goal to get it read before she left the cabin. She had limited her reading to the evenings, and had tried to stretch the novel. But despite her efforts, she was nearly finished with the book.

Glancing at the clock, she saw that it was after ten in the evening. Thumbing through the remaining pages, she found that she only had a couple of more pages and decide she would finish it and then turn in for the night. Tomorrow, she'd have to find a new distraction.

Closing the book, she smiled. She was glad she had finally read the book. Turning out the lights, she rechecked the doors and windows and then she crawled into bed.

She was asleep in minutes.

~

David checked his watch and saw that it was just after eleven. He wondered briefly if it was too late to approach her, but he figured that the sooner the better, so he knocked on the door.

He hadn't quite figured out how he was going to convince her that he was there to help her, but he figured he would wing it. Worst case scenario, he would throw her over his shoulder and just make her come with him.

Sarah opened her eyes. Something had woken her and she wondered what it was. Then she heard a knock on the door and froze. *Oh my god, they've found me.* She panicked, but then she realised that they wouldn't knock. They would just bust down the door and come in.

It had to be Ann! Jumping out of the bed, she quickly threw on the sweatshirt she had been wearing and ran to the door, turning on all the lights in the cabin as she made her way to the door.

"Ann! I knew you'd come!" She yelled as she threw the door open.

David looked down at the woman standing before him. His first thought was that he had the wrong cabin. This woman looked nothing like the photo Jake had shown him. But then he registered what she had said and he knew he had found Sarah Coffey.

The shock on her face at seeing him was evident, and he rushed to calm her before she closed the door or ran. "Ann sent me," he said, "I'm David O'Brien. Jake Summers is a friend of mine and they asked me to come get you," he said gently.

Sarah took a step back, "Ann sent you? Why didn't she come herself?"

"Do you mind if I come in? I'll explain everything then." He promised.

Sarah frowned. She wasn't sure if she should let him in. But then again, he was about a foot taller than she was and he could easily push his way in if he wanted to.

Stepping back another step, she motioned for him to come in, and then she took several steps back to stand away from him.

David stepped into the cabin and quietly closed the door behind him. Looking around the cabin he saw that it was a small cabin but looked very comfortable. "Could I ask you for a cup of coffee? I've been travelling quite a long way."

Sarah took in his appearance and noticed that he had quite a few days' beard growth on his face and realised that he also looked exhausted. "Of course," she said and then stepped into the kitchen and started the coffee maker.

When the coffee was ready, she placed it on the centre island and then waited for him to take a couple of drinks of the hot liquid. "This is very good. Thank you."

"You said your name is David O'Brien?" She prompted.

David nodded. "Yes, I believe you met my brother? Kevin O'Brien? He is the fire investigator working with Detective Jake Summers?"

Sarah nodded. She remembered meeting the man briefly. She wondered if this man was a police officer as well. "Where's Ann?"

David set his coffee mug down and faced her. "I'm sorry," he began, and then he saw the tears start to fall.

"She, she didn't make it, did she?" Sarah asked.

David shook his head and then he walked around the counter and gathered her up in his arms to comfort her. He knew that he would have to tell her the whole story, but there was time for that later. Right now, he didn't want to send her into shock.

"She sounded so, so frantic. I could tell something was wrong. She, she said that there had been a leak. I think she knew that it wasn't safe for me, so she put me on the bike and told me to go. She gave me the address to this place and told me to go," she cried. "She said she'd come get me."

"I'm sorry," David tried to comfort her.

As her tears began to cease, David pulled back and looked in her eyes. "I'm sorry that she couldn't be here. But she told me where to find you, and I promise I'll do everything in my power to keep you safe."

Sarah rubbed her tears away with the back of her hand and nodded. Taking a shaky breath, she asked, "Are you with the FBI or the police?"

David smiled. "Neither. I'm with the fire department."

Sarah stepped back out of his embrace, "The fire department, but why?" She began, but he nodded.

"I know, not the first person you'd think of for a rescue party, but Jake asked me to help." Frowning, he continued, "Ann was right. There is a leak, and until Jake knows for sure where it's coming from, he's not trusting anyone. Not the FBI, or the guys in his precinct; and since he wasn't sure who to trust, he went outside his jurisdiction and asked me to help."

Sarah rubbed her face and tried to make sense out of it all. "None of this makes sense." She admitted.

David agreed. "It is a bit messed up. But all I know is that Jake said that you have to keep safe, and I'm here to ensure just that."

Sarah looked at the tall man in front of her. "How?"

Smiling, he said, "By doing the unexpected." Sarah gave him a quizzical look. "Unexpected as in?"

David flashed her a smile. "I'm going to need you to trust me on this one."

Sarah suddenly felt exhaustion creeping in on her. "Do we need to do anything tonight?"

"It would be best," David admitted. "But if you want to catch some shut eye, I can get the ball rolling and wake you when it's time to leave."

Sarah tried to stifle a yawn as she asked, "What kinds of things?"

"We need to make it look like you were never here," He admitted.

Sarah reached for her sleeve and started to push it up. "Okay, tell me what to do," she said with a slight smile.

An hour later, they had washed down every surface that she might had touched. They had also bagged up all the food she had bought and she had packed her belongings back in her backpack. She also had packed the Lord of the Rings novel and the few pieces of clothing she had been wearing over the last two days as there wouldn't be time to wash them.

The bed clothes she had put in the washing machine when they had started packing things up and then had transferred them the dryer. They would be dry enough before they shut off the power, and would be ready for the next occupants.

Running out to the Adirondack chair, she washed that as well, to make sure that nothing was left to chance.

Satisfied that they had turned off all the switches she had turned on when she had first arrived, they locked up the cabin and after washing the key, slid it back into the spot she had first found it.

Washing down the rock, they walked to the back of the house and got onto the motorcycle.

David had hiked up from where he had left the boat and it had taken him two hours to do so. Now, with the motorcycle, it took them only thirty minutes to reach the boat.

"Wow! Is that yours?" She said as she saw the sail boat.

"I wish. It's actually my brother-in-law's boat. He's just let me borrow it." He explained.

"What do we do with the bike?" Sarah asked.

"I'm sorry to say this, but we're going to have to destroy it," he admitted. "We can't take a chance that it's found."

Sarah nodded and after they had transferred all the goods to the boat, David pushed the bike back up the hill they had just came down and then, she watched as he lifted it over his head and threw it into the water.

Strong man, she thought to herself. She couldn't even pick up the bike from a fallen position, and here he was lifting over his head.

Running back down the hill, he jumped onto the boat, and then starting the outboard engine, David turned to her, "If you'd like to get some rest, you can take the berth at the front of the boat. It hasn't been used." He directed her and then he concentrated on navigating the boat back towards Lake Michigan.

Burning

Chicago, IL

Jake hadn't heard from David in over a week, nor had he gotten any updates on the whereabouts of his lead witnesses.

With no other leads, he concentrated on building is case against his partner. When Officer Doyle had shown him the evidence, he hadn't believed it. He had known Allen Caffery nearly as long as he had been on the force and had been his partner for nearly a decade.

He had always thought he could count on him, and that he was a straight as they come. But he had doubled check the evidence and it all pointed to the same conclusion. Caffrey was crooked.

Jake wondered if perhaps Hicke had something on him. Something that persuaded Caffrey to work in collaboration with him. But the evidence wasn't looking that way. If he was coerced to work with him, he would not be benefiting financially, as the evidence was showing.

Picking up the report before him, he began working again on how they were going to snag him.

"Summers, do you have the August Productions financial report there?" Agent Pete Monroe asked Jake.

Agent Monroe and Jake had been working together on various assignments for a number of years, and he knew he could be trusted. It had been Agent Monroe who had first brought the evidence against Agents Sanders and Thomas to Jake's attention.

Monroe had been furious at his superior's callous approach to the witness protection and had gone above his head.

Now, Agent Anderson too was under investigation. Pete had been brought on board to collaborate with the internal revenue team's investigation into Anderson and the other rogue FBI agents, and assist in the investigations with Jake's team into Caffrey's connections with Hicke.

So far, the evidence they had gathered showed that Anderson had been the ring leader, assigning only those agents he could trust to guard key witnesses. In total, fourteen witnesses had either decided not to testify, or more than likely, had been persuaded not to testify. Three witnesses had gone missing and one had died of a heart attack under their watch.

They had requested the exhumation of the man who had the heart attack. His family claimed that he didn't have a history of heart issues and they questioned the cause of death.

The evidence against Caffrey was also mounting. Jake had pulled additional CCTV evidence from the courthouse where Scott Chamberlain had been murdered. While it was not conclusive, there was an image of Caffrey walking into the security office that held the CCTV tapes just moments after Scott had been murdered. While it didn't prove that Caffrey had murdered the man, it did raise suspicions that he had aided and abetted who ever had killed him.

Jake's research had also unearthed evidence that pointed to Scott's business relationship with Hicke. After a conversation with Chamberlain's attorney, Jake had learned that his client was indeed ready to make a plea for a lighter sentencing in exchange for evidence implicating Hicke. It was that plea bargain that had cost him his life.

Handing Agent Monroe the file he requested, Jake frowned. "Do you have something?"

Pete Monroe studied the document in front of him and smiled. Looking up, he nodded. "I think we have them."

~

Chicago, IL

Jake knew that while the evidence was compelling, that they needed to get Caffery and Anderson with their hands in the cookie jar.

While Agent Monroe set up a sting for Anderson, it was up to him to catch Caffery; and while it wasn't his policy to put witnesses in harm's way, he knew that only one witness could put him at the scene of Dr Wilson's murder. Sarah would be needed to testify. Now that they had Turner in custody, Sarah would need to be the one who pointed the finger at both men.

Picking up his phone, he called Kevin's answering machine and left another message. This one however was not for Kevin.

"Hi Kev, It's Jake. Listen, I've been trying to get a hold of David, but he must be out of cell rang. I wanted to get my rescue club off of him. Can you ask him to call me? Thanks."

After leaving the message, he looked over at Pete. "Let's hope this works," he said.

Walking into the precinct, with Agent Monroe, Jake approached his Captain who was talking with Allen Caffrey. "Sir, we have a situation."

Jake thought he saw a frown cross Caffrey's face but he couldn't be sure.

Captain Weatherton nodded and the four men walked into the interrogation room that Officer Doyle had prepared the night before.

Closing the door behind them, Jake looked over at Pete Monroe and then began.

"Sir, as you know, I've suspected for some time that there is a leak in the team. I mean, there has to be. Too many things have gone wrong, there have been too many coincidences that it's the only explanation."

"A leak?" Caffrey tried to sound surprised.

Jake solemnly nodded. "I'm afraid so."

"Agent Monroe and I have been looking into some of the evidence and, well sir, we think we have our man."

"Well don't leave me in suspect, Summer. Who the hell is the traitor?" Weatherton said with fervour.

Jake looked over at Caffrey wondering how he would react. "It's John," he said.

"John? John Doyle?" Caffrey laughed. "You can't be serious."

"Officer Doyle?" The Captain asked just as incredulously.

"Doyle, the mastermind behind the scenes?" Caffrey continued. "You can't be serious."

Jake knew he had taken the bait. He had always been conceited. He would find it an insult to have someone else named as the architect behind the operation. Now it was time to reel him in.

"I'm afraid so. Agent Monroe has found links between Officer Doyle and FBI Agent Anderson, who right now is being arrested on suspicion of coerced and murder."

Jake could see his mind working. He was trying to make the link himself. Had he missed something? Was Anderson trying to double-cross him? Jake wondered if his arrogance would have him confessing.

Captain Weatherton leaned forward. "Well, bring him in."

Jake looked over at Agent Monroe who spoke up. "We can't just yet, sir."

"And why the hell not?" The Captain demanded.

"There's still the matter of the witness," Monroe replied.

"What about her?" Weatherton prompted.

"I thought she was dead," Caffrey asked.

Monroe shook his head. "We've had her in hiding, but…"

"But?" Weatherton looked like he was going to blow a blood vessel.

"But she's having second thoughts," Jake admitted.

"Second thoughts?" Caffrey asked.

Jake nodded. "It seems that she wasn't entirely forthcoming with some of the evidence. And now…well I guess now, she's realising that if she testifies against Turner, that the other accomplish she saw will come after her."

"What other accomplish?" Caffrey asked.

Jake looked over at Agent Monroe. They had rehearsed this so much that it almost felt natural.

"She now claims that she saw the other man who was with Turner. She said that she's seen him before, but didn't say anything because he was a cop."

Jake could see the vein in Caffrey's temple moving. He was definitely concerned.

"Where is this girl?" Caffrey asked.

Agent Monroe shook his head.

"Come on, we've got to bring her in and ensure that she testifies," Caffrey was saying.

Captain Weatherton nodded. "I have to agree with Caffrey. Now that we know it's Doyle, we can keep her safe."

Jake looked over at Agent Monroe. "He has a point."

Agent Monroe seemed to consider his options. "Alright. We can bring her in. But on one condition," he added, "no one outside of this room can know where she is. We need to ensure her safety and we can't afford another incident like at the safe house."

Captain Weatherton nodded.

"We'll wait until tonight. Doyle might be watching us, and I don't think it would be particularly safe to waltz up to her hotel room in broad daylight."

"She's been staying at a hotel?" Caffrey quizzed.

Monroe nodded. "Yeah, we moved her there a couple of weeks ago. Agent Cane had suspected that Thomas was on the take and had instructed the girl to go there and wait for her. I was informed of her location and we decided to keep it quiet. We've had an agent visiting her every night to make sure she's alright. So far, we've managed to keep it under wraps. This is why I must insist on 100% compliance. No one, not even your mother, needs to know this information."

The men nodded. "So, when do we spring her?" Caffrey asked again.

Looking up at the clock, Monroe noted the time, "Well, it's two o'clock now. I'd say we wait until tonight, say, eight o'clock?" Was his answer. "That's the time the agent makes his nightly visits."

"Okay, will we meet here, or there?" Caffrey was asking.

Captain Weatherton seemed to take up the next part of the script. "We'll meet there. It will draw less attention if we all arrive separately. Jake, I think you should sit this one out. Doyle is smart. He's probably been watching your every move." Jake frowned, and was about to disagree, but what the Captain had said made sense.

Turning to Monroe, the Captain continued. "Tell your agent that we'll be there at five minutes after eight. That way he can alert the witness that we'll be coming. I'd hate for her to get spooked and run."

Jake nodded. "Then let's meet at eight o'clock in the lobby. We can take the elevator up together."

"What's the room number?" Captain Weatherton asked.

"234" was Monroe's reply.

"Okay. Eight o'clock it is. Now remember everyone. Mums the word."

As they started to leave, Caffrey asked the final question. "What hotel is it?"

Monroe shook his head. "Yeah, kind of the vital part. It's the Renaissance on Wacker Drive."

Caffrey nodded. "Ok, see you there."

࠸

After their meeting, Jake said he wanted to check in with the lab to check on a few other details he was working on to convict Doyle. After he left the precinct, he had instead, headed to the Renaissance hotel. He doubted that Caffrey would wait until that evening to make his move and he wanted to get the scene prepare.

At 3:00 pm, Officer Amy Klockner was ready. The Captain had briefed her on what was to be expected, but to expect the unexpected. She knew the risks.

She had been given a theatrical makeover, so that she now looked more like the witness as she had when she first was interviewed. She had been given a bullet proof vest and a photo of the man they expected would come.

She had turned on the radio to a classical music station and she had several law books spread out on the bed as if she was studying.

In the same room, the two FBI agents who were there to protect her, were hiding in various places in the large hotel room. Despite this, Officer Klockner found herself pacing around the room, trying to kill some of the nervous energy she felt rising up inside her.

At 3:20, she heard the elevator announce the arrival of the car and she waited. She heard one of the FBI agents check in. The man they expected had arrived.

Sitting back on the bed, she took a deep breath and tried to control her breathing. Picking up one of the law books, she began reading the text.

Hearing a knock on the door, she asked, "Who is it?"

"Room service," she heard the man say.

Then he added, "I know I'm a bit early, but Detective Summers asked me to check in on you," he said by way of explanation.

Taking a peek through the small peephole in the door, she saw the man whose photo had been shared with her.

"Miss Coffey?" He asked again.

Stepping back from the door, she slowly unlocked the door and stepped back.

"Thanks," he said, as he walked in the door, and closed it behind him. She noticed that he had gloves on.

"You said that Detective Summers asked you to check on me?" She prompted him.

"Yes. We need to move you tonight," he said as he took another step towards her.

Officer Klockner heard a faint whisper in her ear. "It's him."

Looking up at the man, she frowned. "I, I know you," she said on cue.

"Yes, we met when you first came to the precinct," he replied. But she shook her head. "No. I, I saw you," she whispered as directed.

He took another step towards her. "I was afraid you were going to say that." Then he pushed her on the bed and grabbed her by the neck.

The FBI agents rushed in, and pulled the man from the officer. Captain Weatherton and Agent Monroe walked in the door with Jake behind them.

Walking past them, Jake stepped up to his former partner and punched Caffrey in the face, breaking his nose. "Get this piece of shit out of my sight."

In the room next door, Sarah cried into David's arms.

～

Kathlyn and Kelly were sitting at the breakfast table when the doorbell rang.

"Are you expecting anyone?" Kevin asked Claire.

"Non. Pas que je sache." *No. not that I know of.* But she laughed at him, "It's probably just a delivery."

As Claire excused herself to answer the door, Kevin stood and stepped behind the door.

Kathlyn and Kelly looked at each other, and wondered what they should be doing. Kathlyn was about to ask him if they should be worried when he put his hand to his lips telling her to be quiet.

Listening carefully, he tried to hear what Marie was saying to the visitor.

Hearing the door close, he waited.

Marie walked in the door and he could see a smile on her face as she carried a bouquet of flowers. Stepping out from behind the door, Kevin looked behind the woman and stopped.

"What the hell are you doing here?"

Kathlyn and Kelly stood, ready to run, when Claire put her hands out. "Non, it is our friend," she said as she stepped aside.

Kelly was the first to move. Taking a step forward, she couldn't believe her eyes.

There stood Jake, his arm was in a sling, but he was there. In the flesh. Unable to control herself, she ran up to him and threw her arms around him.

Jake pulled her closer and buried his face in her neck. "I missed you," he whispered.

"I missed you too," she whispered back.

Kathlyn had made her way around the table and took Kevin's hand. Looking up at him, she had to ask. "Did you know?"

Kevin shook his head no, and then the two were silent as they watched as Kelly and Jake embrace. Each knowing that there was more there than just friendship.

Jake looked over and saw Kevin and Kathlyn holding hands. One look at Kevin's face as he looked down at Kathlyn told him everything he needed to know.

Stepping back from Kelly's embraced, he smiled down at her. "Why don't you and Kathlyn get your jackets. I need to talk to Kevin for a moment, and then we'll take you ladies out to see a bit of Quebec."

Kathlyn and Kelly smiled at each other. "So, it's safe?" Kathlyn asked. Jake nodded. "It is now." The ladies hugged each other. Their nightmare was finally over. Linking their arms, they went to their rooms to get ready.

Claire had been watching the foursome and she turned to the men. "So, when will be the wedding? I fully expect to be invited."

~

It had taken four months, but the prosecution was finally ready with their evidence.

Between Jake and Kevin, they had gathered all the pertinent evidence and had already delivered it to the DA's office. Now all they had to do was wait for the court date.

Kevin was reviewing the final evidence, in the hope of finding more when he heard his office phone ringing. "O'Brien," he said into the phone. "Hi Kevin, I've been trying to reach you on your cell." It was his brother Danny.

"Sorry, I turned it off," Kevin replied absently, before something registered in the back of his mind. Making a quick note as to the location he had last examined, he sat back from his work. "Danny, what's wrong? Is everything ok with Shawnee?"

"She's beautiful! And so are the boys."

Frowning, Kevin asked, "Boys? What do mean you by that?"

"Well, you know Shawnee, she can't do anything easy, so instead of giving me one healthy baby, she decided to make it twins."

"Twins! Oh my God! Congratulations! When did it happen?" Kevin couldn't help but yell into the phone.

"Oh, about eight months ago," Danny chuckled.

"Shut up! Seriously, how are they all doing?"

"Great, really. Shawnee screamed like a banshee. Ouch! Just kidding honey!" Kevin could hear Shawnee berating him in the background.

"Hey, let me talk to her," Kevin commanded.

"Hi Kevin," He heard her voice on the other end.

"Congratulations Shawnee. I am so happy for you!"

"Thanks Kevin," he could hear her smiling into the phone.

"So, what did you name them?"

"Mac and Connor. We named them after our grandfathers," she replied.

"I like it," he smiled into the phone.

"Listen, I know you must be busy." She apologised, "But we had to call and tell you the news."

"Hey, no problem, I'm glad you did." he answered back, "Listen, I've got to get this project done, but I'll stop by a little later this evening if that's ok."

"That would be great. See you then."

As he hung up, he sat back on his chair and shook his head. "Twins."

Picking up his phone again, he called Kathlyn and told her the good news. She had been delighted. He had offered to collect her, but she and Kelly were busy working at a wedding trade show. "Besides, it might be nice for you to meet your new nephews on you own. There will be plenty of time for us to get to know them later. But please give them a big kiss for me." She had added.

∻

When Kevin was finally able to go to the hospital, it was nearly seven in the evening, and he wasn't sure if he would be allowed in to see the new mother. Luckily, he saw his older brother David at the nurses' station and together they walked into Shawnee's room.

They found Danny and Shawnee standing beside two baby cots, holding hands and looking down at their new-borns.

"Hey Mom and Dad, how are the kids?" David was the first to break the silence. Turning, the new parents beamed.

"They're amazing," Shawnee said with tears in her eyes.

David walked up to her and gave her a big hug before turning to his youngest brother and pulling him into a bear hug. "Congratulations you two!"

Kevin waited his turn and hugged Shawnee and gave Danny a hardy handshake. "I'm proud of you two," he smiled back at them.

Then the two brothers looked down at their nephews.

The twins were small, only five pounds each, but they were healthy. They had been placed in incubators to ensure that they kept warm, but the doctor had confirmed that all of their major organs had fully developed.

One of the baby's was covered with a yellow blanket with bumble bees embroidered all over it, and had the words, 'Bee quiet, I'm sleeping'. The other twin had a similar blanket over him that was mint green with yellow and green butterflies sewn all over it. The wording on this blanket said, 'Butterfly kisses for our little one'.

"They are so tiny," Kevin remarked. "When will you be able to hold them?"

"You can hold them now if you'd like," Shawnee smiled at him. "You just need to grab one of the yellow gowns at the nurse's desk and you are good to go."

Kevin smiled and turned to go out to get the garment when he saw the nurse handing them yellow gowns.

Once they were in the gowns, they washed their hands in the bathroom, and then they were ready.

"Here, one of you sit down in that chair and the other one of you can sit on my bed. Danny and I will hand you the boys." Shawnee instructed them.

Kevin peered down at the small baby in his hands. The baby had been introduced to him as Mac, and he couldn't help but smile down at the beautiful child. Mac had been born with a full head of black hair, and Kevin could instantly see Shawnee's features on his small face.

Glancing over at David, he saw that he too had been handed a baby and was now cooing over Conner, who also had a full head of black hair. Looking back down at Mac, he couldn't help but laugh.

Danny smiled at him, "What's so funny?"

"You had to make them identical didn't you," he replied with a smile.

Danny put his arm around his beautiful wife. "Who says you can't duplicate perfection?"

Shawnee laughed. "Don't say that too loudly, the boys might hear you and make a liar out of you."

"So, when do you get to take the boys home?" David asked.

Shawnee smiled. "We hope to take them home by the weekend. They're doing remarkably well, and the doctor said that as long as nothing changes over the few days, then we should be good to go." Then she laughed. "My mom keeps telling me to keep them in as long as the hospital allows me to so I can get as much rest as possible before the real chaos starts."

Kevin laughed. "Probably good advice." After handing the babies back to their parents, Kevin took a step towards the door. "I'm sure you two want some time on your own, so I won't keep you. Let me know if there's anything I can do."

"Want to babysit?" Danny chuckled.

"Ask me in a few weeks. By then, you'll know if the twins have settled into some kind of schedule," was his reply.

"When did you get so knowledgeable about baby's schedules?" Danny laughed.

"When you told me Shawnee was expecting," was Kevin's reply as he headed out the door.

After saying goodbye to David, Kevin headed to his car. The truth was, he had been terrified when they had announced that she was pregnant. He knew little to nothing about babies and he didn't want to be a hands-off uncle. So, he had went to the library and took out every book he could find about new babies and the like and had spent the past seven months doing his research. Of course, it was all theoretical at this stage of the game. He hadn't actually changed a baby, much less fed one; and from what he read, there could be any number of problems that could arise just from performing these seemingly simple tasks.

The twins were the first babies to grace the O'Brien clan and he was not going to be the uncle they never saw. He would definitely babysit for them, and he wanted them to feel at ease when he did. Nothing would be worse than to give them the night off, only to have them worrying that he was failing in his duties as a babysitter the entire time.

He realised that they would be nervous the first time. That would only be natural. But he wanted to make sure that their nerves were unfounded.

Getting into his car, he started the engine and then he headed off to his fiancée's house to tell her the good news about the babies.

Decay

The courtroom was packed to the hilt. The press had been prevented from attending due to the high sensitivity of the case.

But the evidence was clear.

As the judge read out the list of crimes being brought against the defendant, it was clear to all, that the prosecutor had been through in their investigations.

"It is the finding of this court that, the defendant, Allen Caffrey, will be made to answer to the following crimes. On the charge of first-degree murder of Federal Agent Ann Cane, the defendant has been found guilty as charged."

"On the charge of first-degree murder of Jimmy Strausmann, aka, James Prizrak, the defendant has been found guilty as charged."

"On the charge of assessor to the murder of Scott Chamberlain, the defendant has been found guilty as charged."

"On the charge of coercion, intimidation of witnesses and in the aiding and abetting known criminals, the defendant has been found guilty as charged."

The judge went on for a total of seventeen counts against Caffery.

He ended his dissertation by adding, "Mr Caffrey, I find your total disregard for the privilege bestowed upon you as a detective in the Chicago police department appalling. It is, therefore, the finding of this court that you spend the rest of your life in the maximum state prison, without possibly of parole. It is also the recommendation of this court that due to the charge of first-degree murder of Federal Agent Ann Cane, that the matter be brought before the federal government, where I will recommend that you be given the death penalty."

~

Jake was putting the case away, and he shook his head. All of this for some property.

It turned out, that in addition to the property at Area 14 that Hicke had tried to get from the Commissioner, that he had orchestrated the arson attacks at the Swan and the Rumours because of their locations. He had been trying to 'encourage' the tenants to leave for months, and when they refused, he had torched the places, forcing them to move. Then he would sweep in like the vulture he was to get the property.

As for the murder of Dr Wilson, Turner had confessed that he had been seeing the doctor for psychological treatments. Dr Wilson had agreed at first, but when he had learned Turner's background, he had sought to break the relationship, which had led to his death. Caffrey had gone with Turner to the doctor's office to try and convince him to continue the treatment, when Turner had killed the doctor.

The meth lab had been Caffrey's idea. He knew that Turner had a key policy of not associating with his properties, so he had little doubt that he'd be found out.

When word of the meth lab's existence had surfaced, Turner admitted that he had started his own investigation and had learned that it had been Caffrey who was running the lab.

When he asked his father about it, Hicke had told him not to act. Stating that, "He'll be getting his soon enough."

Jake had learned about the conversation when they had reviewed a recorded conversation between father and son shortly before Turner's arrest. Because Hicke was a known mobster, the judge had mandated that all visits be monitored, on the pretence that it was for his safety. These visits were also recorded.

Jake had once again called upon the linguist, Mathew Travers to review the tape. Travers was an expert lip reader, having learned the skill from his parents who were both deaf.

Travers confirmed that in subsequent recordings, that Hicke had met with Agent Anderson, and had provided evidence to several conversations regarding the location of the witnesses and confirming that Anderson had been Hicke's key contact in the FBI.

Jake wondered how Hicke knew that they were about to arrest Caffrey, but he suspected that it had been Anderson. Hicke would have known that Caffrey would be sent to the same prison as he was in, and then once inside, Hicke would be able to deal with him as he saw fit.

With this in mind, Jake had approached the judge and made the recommendation that he have him incarcerated in a different prison. But the judge had taken it one step further and recommended that his case be escalated to the federal courts.

Jake put the lid on the case box and marked it 'Closed'. Then he picked up his keys and headed home for the day. He had a date he had to get ready for. He had booked Theo's and he wanted to pick up some flowers for Kelly.

~

Time

Three a half years later.

It was a sunny day in St Lucia.

Tara smoothed her hand over her stomach and smiled. Grabbing her husband's hand, she pushed his hand to her growing belly. "Your son wants to dance," she whispered to him. Shane smiled down at her as he felt the kick from the baby, she had growing inside her.

"Mommy, can I feel?" Maddie, their oldest child ran up and put her hand on her mother's belly. "Oh, I felt it!" She giggled in delight.

Picking his daughter up, he reminded her that she had to keep her voice down and then handed her off to the wedding organiser.

As the ceremony was about to begin, they heard the starting notes of 'Canon in D' by Pachabel and they all turned.

Around them they could hear the sounds of the ocean and the giggle of the children.

Taking her mother's hand, Tara gave it a squeeze. Smiling over at Shawnee, she saw the tears of happiness as she watched her sons Connor and Mac walking down the aisle as the ring bearers. By her side were her parents, who had also made the trip.

Then came Maddie, throwing pedals in the air and giggling all the way down the aisle.

Shane corralled the kids in and after depositing them with their respective parents, he joined his wife.

As the music continued to play, they watched as Danny and David walked down the aisle and took their places on either side of the celebrant. Danny winked at his wife and threw a kiss to his sons. David looked up and saw the woman he had been dating smiling from behind Tara. Sarah looked beautiful. She had gone back to her natural hair colour, a vibrant red, which he loved. When he had first introduced her to his family, he hadn't been sure what to call her. He knew that Sarah was the name she had been going by but it wasn't her real name. But thanks to Jake's help, they had managed to make her name change official while keeping her true identity from becoming public. Soon she would be going by a different name again. David had asked her to marry him, and she had said yes. They hadn't told the family yet, not wanting to upstage Kevin and Jake. But he suspected that Tara already knew as she kept winking at him.

Kevin and Jake then walked up the aisle and joined their groomsmen.

Kevin had asked his younger brother Danny, to be his best man and Jake had asked the eldest O'Brien, Danny, to be his best man.

Then as the music changed to 'A Thousand Years'.by Christina Perri, they all stood and watched as Kathlyn and Kelly walked hand in hand down the aisle.

The ceremony was beautiful, and after they had said their 'I dos', there had been fireworks lit over the water.

The fireworks continued to explode overhead, as if to signify the beginning of a new life.

~

Martha O'Brien watched as her children danced the night away. She liked the people whom each had brought into the family. They had found love despite rough beginnings.

Watching as her eldest danced with his fiancée, she was reminded of her own beginnings. Quite like her children, her life had been heading in a different path until fate stepped in and brought her to where she was today.

She thought about her husband John and of the man who she had left behind, and she wondered briefly what her life would have been like if she hadn't taken the trip that had changed the course of her life.

The trip that had forced her to run from her betrothed and into the arms of another man.

Looking up, she caught Jake looking at her. He smiled and nodded. There was a look in his eyes that seemed to say that he knew her secret; and she wondered if perhaps he did.

The End